AIRSHIPS *and* RAY

Barry Hannah was born in Clinton, Mississippi. He was awarded the William Faulkner Prize for his first novel, *Geronimo Rex*. A second novel, *Nightwatchmen*, was followed by *Airships*, a collection of stories, which won the Arnold Gingrich Short Fiction Award. His achievement in fiction was honoured by the American Academy of Arts and Letters.

Airships and *Ray* are published in Vintage as an original paperback.

AIRSHIPS

'Talents as broad as this thrive in novels but rarely take to the more constricted form of the short story. *Airships* proves Barry Hannah an exception ... artfully rounded-off vignettes jumping with humor and menace ... The stories bounce off and echo one another giving the book an impact greater than the sum of its parts ... Most young Southern writers resent being compared to such giants as Faulkner and Flannery O'Connor. In embracing the gothic mode, Hannah has planted himself firmly on their turf. On the evidence of this book, their shadows are not stunting his growth.'

Time

'These stories are wonderful in the ways Mark Twain, Faulkner and Flannery O'Connor are wonderful when they are working the great vein of fierce and pitiless Southern comedy. The war stories in particular – joining, as they do for me, the clownish misery and colossal overkill of Vietnam to the American Civil War – are masterpieces of their kind. Hannah is more than just a new voice – he is half a dozen brilliant new voices.'

Philip Roth

'The best young writer to appear in the South since Flannery O'Connor.'

Larry McMurtry

RAY

'Ray is the funniest, weirdest, soul-happiest work of fiction by a genuinely young American author that I've read in a long while. You need a fresh lingo to do justice to this much magic, mystery and hilarity.'

New York Times Book Review

'The lust and violence in this little book isn't a schoolteacher's gratuitous high-jinks, but the brutish, menacing, driven stuff of life. Barry Hannah is the real thing, a young writer as true and original as any writing fiction anywhere.'

Philip Roth

'A shorthand epic of extraordinary power, a novel of brilliant particulars, dizzying juxtapositions.'

Newsweek

Barry Hannah

AIRSHIPS *and* RAY

VINTAGE

VINTAGE
20 Vauxhall Bridge Road, London SW1V 2SA

London Melbourne Sydney Auckland Johannesburg
and agencies throughout the world

The author wishes to express his gratitude to the
Research Grant Committee of the University of Alabama for financial assistance given in the course of this
writing.

Photypeset by Input Typesetting Ltd, London
Printed and bound in Great Britain by
Cox & Wyman Ltd, Reading

ISBN 0 09 974870 3

AIRSHIPS

This book is for
PATRICIA b.,
blue-eyed Nebraska lady

This book honors the memory of Arnold Gingrich. Its publication was in part provided for by the men and women who were his colleagues at *Esquire*, the magazine he founded and edited with distinction.

CONTENTS

WATER LIARS

WHEN I AM run down and flocked around by the world, I go down to Farte Cove off the Yazoo River and take my beer to the end of the pier where the old liars are still snapping and wheezing at one another. The line-up is always different, because they're always dying out or succumbing to constipation, etc., whereupon they go back to the cabins and wait for a good day when they can come out and lie again, leaning on the rail with coats full of bran cookies. The son of the man the cove was named for is often out there. He pronounces his name Far*tay*, with a great French stress on the last syllable. Otherwise you might laugh at his history or ignore it in favor of the name as it's spelled on the sign.

I'm glad it's not my name.

This poor dignified man has had to explain his nobility to the semiliterate of half of America before he could even begin a decent conversation with them. On the other hand, Farte, Jr., is a great liar himself. He tells about seeing ghost people around the lake and tells big loose ones about the size of the fish those ghosts took out of Farte Cove in years past.

Last year I turned thirty-three years old and, raised a Baptist, I had a sense of being Jesus and coming to something decided in my life – because we all know Jesus was crucified at thirty-three. It had all seemed especially important, what you do in this year, and holy with meaning.

On the morning after my birthday party, during which I

1

and my wife almost drowned in vodka cocktails, we both woke up to the making of a truth session about the lovers we'd had before we met each other. I had a mildly exciting and usual history, and she had about the same, which surprised me. For ten years she'd sworn I was the first. I could not believe her history was exactly equal with mine. It hurt me to think that in the era when there were supposed to be virgins she had allowed anyone but *me*, and so on.

I was dazed and exhilarated by this information for several weeks. Finally, it drove me crazy, and I came out to Farte Cove to rest, under the pretense of a fishing week with my chum Wyatt.

I'm still figuring out why I couldn't handle it.

My sense of the past is vivid and slow. I hear every sign and see every shadow. The movement of every limb in every passionate event occupies my mind. I have a prurience on the grand scale. It makes no sense that I should be angry about happenings before she and I ever saw each other. Yet I feel an impotent homicidal urge in the matter of her lovers. She has excused my episodes as the course of things, though she has a vivid memory too. But there is a blurred nostalgia women have that men don't.

You could not believe how handsome and delicate my wife is naked.

I was driven wild by the bodies that had trespassed her twelve and thirteen years ago.

My vacation at Farte Cove wasn't like that easy little bit you get as a rich New Yorker. My finances weren't in great shape; to be true, they were about in ruin, and I left the house knowing my wife would have to answer the phone to hold off, for instance, the phone company itself. Everybody wanted money and I didn't have any.

I was going to take the next week in the house while she went away, watch our three kids and all the rest. When you

2

both teach part-time in the high schools, the income can be slow in summer.

No poor-mouthing here. I don't want anybody's pity. I just want to explain. I've got good hopes of a job over at Alabama next year. Then I'll get myself among higher-paid liars, that's all.

Sidney Farte was out there prevaricating away at the end of the pier when Wyatt and I got there Friday evening. The old faces I recognized; a few new harkening idlers I didn't.

'Now, Doctor Mooney, he not only saw the ghost of Lily, he says he had intercourse with her. Said it was involuntary. Before he knew what he was doing, he was on her making cadence and all their clothes blown away off in the trees around the shore. She turned into a wax candle right under him.'

'Intercourse,' said an old-timer, breathing heavy. He sat up on the rail. It was a word of high danger to his old mind. He said it with a long disgust, glad, I guess, he was not involved.

'MacIntire, a Presbyterian preacher, I seen him come out here with his son-and-law, anchor near the bridge, and pull up fifty or more white perch big as small pumpkins. You know what they was using for bait?'

'What?' asked another geezer.

'*Nuthin.* Caught on the bare hook. It was Gawd made them fish bite,' said Sidney Farte, going at it good.

'Naw. There be a season they bite a bare hook. Gawd didn't have to've done that,' said another old guy, with a fringe of red hair and a racy Florida shirt.

'Nother night,' said Sidney Farte, 'I saw the ghost of Yazoo hisself with my pa, who's dead. A Indian king with four deer around him.'

The old boys seemed to be used to this one. Nobody said anything. They ignored Sidney.

'Tell you what,' said a well-built small old boy. 'That was somethin when we come down here and had to chase

3

that whole high-school party off the end of this pier, them drunken children. They was smokin dope and two-thirds a them nekid swimmin in the water. Good hunnerd of em. From your so-called *good* high school. What you think's happnin at the bad ones?'

I dropped my beer and grew suddenly sick. Wyatt asked me what was wrong. I could see my wife in 1960 in the group of high-schoolers she must have had. My jealousy went out into the stars of the night above me. I could not bear the roving carelessness of teen-agers, their judgeless tangling of wanting and bodies. But I was the worst back then. In the mad days back then, I dragged the panties off girls I hated and talked badly about them once the sun came up.

'Worst time in my life,' said a new, younger man, maybe sixty but with the face of a man who had surrendered, 'me and Woody was fishing. Had a lantern. It was about eleven. We was catching a few fish but rowed on into that little cove over there near town. We heard all these sounds, like they was ghosts. We was scared. We thought it might be the Yazoo hisself. We known of some fellows the Yazoo had killed to death just from fright. It was the over the sounds of what was normal human sighin and amoanin. It was big unhuman sounds. We just stood still in the boat. Ain't nuthin else us to do. For thirty minutes.'

'An what was it?' said the old geezer, letting himself off the rail.

'We had a big flashlight. There came up this rustlin in the brush and I beamed it over there. The two of em makin the sounds get up with half they clothes on. It was my own daughter Charlotte and an older guy I didn't even know with a mustache. My *own* daughter, and them sounds over the water scarin us like ghosts.'

'My Gawd, that's awful,' said the old geezer by the rail. 'Is that the truth? I wouldn't've told that. That's terrible.'

Sidney Farte was really upset.

4

'This ain't the place!' he said. 'Tell your kind of story somewhere else.'

The old man who'd told his story was calm and fixed to his place. He'd told the truth. The crowd on the pier was outraged and discomfited. He wasn't one of them. But he stood his place. He had a distressed pride. You could see he had never recovered from the thing he'd told about.

I told Wyatt to bring the old man back to the cabin. He was out here away from his wife the same as me and Wyatt. Just an older guy with a big hurting bosom. He wore a suit and the only way you'd know he was on vacation was he'd removed his tie. He didn't know where the bait house was. He didn't know what to do on vacation at all. But he got drunk with us and I can tell you he and I went out the next morning with our poles, Wyatt driving the motorboat, fishing for white perch in the cove near the town. And we were kindred.

We were both crucified by the truth.

Love Too Long

MY HEAD'S BURNING off and I got a heart about to burst out of my ribs. All I can do is move from chair to chair with my cigarette. I wear shades. I can't read a magazine. Some days I take my binoculars and look out in the air. They laid me off. I can't find work. My wife's got a job and she takes flying lessons. When she comes over the house in her airplane, I'm afraid she'll screw up and crash.

I got to get back to work and get dulled out again. I got to be a man again. You can't walk around the house drinking coffee and beer all day, thinking about her taking her brassiere off. We been married and divorced twice. Sometimes I wish I had a sport. I bought a croquet set on credit at Penney's. First day I got so tired of it I knocked the balls off in the weeds and they're out there rotting, mildew all over them, I bet, but I don't want to see.

Some afternoons she'll come right over the roof of the house and turn the plane upside down. Or maybe it's her teacher. I don't know how far she's got along. I'm afraid to ask, on the every third night or so she comes in the house. I want to rip her arm off. I want to sleep in her uterus with my foot hanging out. Some nights she lets me lick her ears and knees. I can't talk about it. It's driving me into a sorry person. Maybe Hobe Lewis would let me pump gas and sell bait at his service station. My mind's around to where I'd do nigger work now.

I'd do Jew work, Swiss, Spanish. Anything.

She never took anything. She just left. She can be a lot of things – she got a college degree. She always had her own bank account. She wanted a better house than this house, but she was patient. She'd eat any food with a sweet smile. She moved through the house with a happy pace, like it meant something.

I think women are closer to God than we are. They walk right out there like they know what they're doing. She moved around the house, reading a book. I never saw her sitting down much, unless she's drinking. She can drink you under the table. Then she'll get up on the spot of eight and fix you an omelet with sardines and peppers. She taught me to like this, a little hot ketchup on the edge of the plate.

When she walks through the house, she has a roll from side to side. I've looked at her face too many times when she falls asleep. The omelet tastes like her. I go crazy.

There're things to be done in this world, she said. This love affair went on too long. It's going to make us both worthless, she said. Our love is not such a love as to swell the heart. So she said. She was never unfaithful to me that I know. And if I knew it, I wouldn't care because I know she's sworn to me.

I am her always and she is my always and that's the whole trouble.

For two years I tried to make her pregnant. It didn't work. The doctor said she was too nervous to hold a baby, first time she ever had an examination. She was a nurse at the hospital and brought home all the papers that she forged whenever I needed a report. For example, when I first got on as a fly in elevated construction. A fly can crawl and balance where nobody else can. I was always working at the thing I feared the most. I tell you true. But it was high pay out there at the beam joints. Here's the laugh. I was light and nimble, but the sun always made me sick up there under its nose. I got a permanent suntan. Some people think I'm Arab. I was good.

*

7

When I was in the Navy, I finished two years at Bakersfield Junior College in California. Which is to say, I can read and feel fine things and count. Those women who cash your check don't cause any distress to me, all their steel, accents and computers. I'll tell you what I liked that we studied at Bakersfield. It was old James Joyce and his book *The Canterbury Tales*. You wouldn't have thought anybody would write 'A fart that well nigh blinded Absalom' in ancient days. All those people hopping and humping at night, framming around, just like last year at Ollie's party that she and I left when they got into threesomes and Polaroids. Because we loved each other too much. She said it was something you'd be sorry about the next morning.

Her name is Jane.

Once I cheated on her. I was drunk in Pittsburgh. They bragged on me for being a fly in the South. This girl and I were left together in a fancy apartment of the Oakland section. The girl did everything. I was homesick during the whole time for Jane. When you get down to it, there isn't much to do. It's just arms and legs. It's not worth a damn.

The first thing Jane did was go out on that houseboat trip with that movie star who was using this town we were in in South Carolina to make his comeback film. I can't tell his name, but he's short and his face is old and piglike now instead of the way it was in the days he was piling up the money. He used to be a star and now he was trying to return as a main partner in a movie about hatred and backstabbing in Dixie. Everybody on board made crude passes at her. I wasn't invited. She'd been chosen as an extra for the movie. The guy who chose her made animalistic comments to her. This was during our first divorce. She jumped off the boat and swam home. But that's how good-looking she is. There was a cameraman on the houseboat who saw her swimming and filmed her. It was in the movie. I sat there and watched her when they showed it local.

The next thing she did was take up with an architect who

had a mustache. He was designing her dream house for free and she was putting money in the bank waiting on it. She claimed he never touched her. He just wore his mustache and a gold medallion around his neck and ate yogurt and drew houses all day. She worked for him as a secretary and landscape consultant. Jane was always good about trees, bushes, flowers and so on. She's led many a Spare That Tree campaign almost on her own. She'll write a letter to the editor in a minute.

Only two buildings I ever worked on pleased her. She said the rest looked like death standing up.

The architect made her wear his ring on her finger. I saw her wearing it on the street in Biloxi, Mississippi, one afternoon, coming out of a store. There she was with a new hairdo and a narrow halter and by God I was glad I saw. I was in a bus on the way to the Palms House hotel we were putting up after the hurricane. I almost puked out my kidneys with the grief.

Maybe I need to go to church, I said to myself. I can't stand this alone. I wished I was Jesus. Somebody who never drank or wanted nooky. Or knew Jane.

She and the architect were having some fancy drinks together at a beach lounge when his ex-wife from New Hampshire showed up naked with a single-shotgun gun that was used in the Franco-Prussian War – it was a quaint piece hanging on the wall in their house when he was at Dartmouth – and screaming. The whole bar cleared out, including Jane. The ex-wife tried to get the architect with the bayonet. She took off the whole wall mural behind him and he was rolling around under tables. Then she tried to cock the gun. The policeman who'd come in got scared and left. The architect got out and threw himself into the arms of Jane, who was out on the patio thinking she was safe. He wanted to die holding his love. Jane didn't want to die in any fashion. Here comes the nude woman, screaming with the cocked gun.

'Hey, hey,' says Jane. 'Honey, you don't need a gun. You

9

got a hell of a body. I don't see how Lawrence could've left that.'

The woman lowered the gun. She was dripping with sweat and pale as an egg out there in the bright sun over the sea. Her hair was nearabout down to her ass and her face was crazy.

'Look at her, Lawrence,' said Jane.

The guy turned around and looked at his ex-wife. He whispered: 'She was lovely. But her personality was a disease. She was killing me. It was slow murder.'

When I got there, the naked woman was on Lawrence's lap. Jane and a lot of people were standing around looking at them. They'd fallen back in love. Lawrence was sucking her breast. She wasn't a bad-looking sight. The long gun lay off in the sand. No law was needed. I was just humiliated. I tried to get away before Jane saw me, but I'd been drinking and smoking a lot the night before and I gave out this ninety-nine-year-old cough. Everybody on the patio except Lawrence and his woman looked around.

But in Mobile we got it going together again. She taught art in a private school where they admitted high-type Negroes only. And I was a fly on the city's first high-rise parking garage. We had so much money we ate out even for breakfast. She thought she was pregnant for a while and I was happy as hell. I wanted a heavenly blessing – as the pastors say – with Jane. I thought it would form the living chain between us that would never be broken. It would be beyond biology and into magic. But it was only eighteen months in Mobile and we left on a rainy day in the winter without her pregnant. She was just lean and her eyes were brown diamonds like always, and she had begun having headaches.

Let me tell you about Jane drinking punch at one of the parties at the University of Florida where she had a job. Some hippie had put LSD in it and there was nothing but teacher types in the house, leaning around, commenting on the azaleas and the evil of the administration. I never took any punch because I brought my own dynamite in the car. Here I was, complimenting myself on holding my own with these profs. One of the profs looked at Jane in her long gown, not knowing she was with me. He said to another: 'She's pleasant to look at, as far as *that* goes.' I said to him that I'd heard she was smart too, and had taken the all-Missouri swimming meet when she was just a junior in high school. Another guy spoke up. The LSD had hit. I didn't know.

'I'd like to stick her brain. I'll bet her brain would be better than her crack. I'd like to have her hair falling around my honker. I'd love to pull on those ears with silver loops hanging around, at, on, above – what is it? – *them*.'

This guy was the chairman of the whole department.

'If I was an earthquake, I'd take care of her,' said a fellow with a goatee and an ivory filter for his cigarette.

'Beauty is fleeting,' said his ugly wife. 'What stays is your basic endurance of pettiness and ennui. And perhaps, most of all, your ability to hide farts.'

'Oh, Sandra!' says her husband. 'I thought I'd taught you better. You went to Vassar, you bitch, so you wouldn't say things like that.'

'I went to Vassar so I'd meet a dashing man with a fortune and a huge cucumber. Then I came back home, to assholing Florida and you,' she said. 'Washing socks, underwear, arguing with some idiot at Sears.'

I met Jane at the punch bowl. She was socking it down and chatting with the librarian who was her boss. He was a Scotsman with a mountain of book titles for his mind. Jane said he'd never read a book in thirty years, but he knew the hell out of their names. Jane truly liked to talk to fat and old guys best of all. She didn't ever converse much with young men. Her ideal of a conversation was when sex was nowhere near it at all. She hated all her speech with her admirers because every word was shaded with lust implications. One of her strange little dreams was to be sort of a cloud with eyes, ears, mouth. I walked up on them without their seeing

11

and heard her say: 'I love you. I'd like to pet you to death.' She put her hand on his poochy stomach.

So then I was hitting the librarian in the throat and chest. He was a huge person, looked something like a statue of some notable gentleman in ancient history. I couldn't do anything to bring him down. He took all my blows without batting an eye.

'You great bastard!' I yelled up there. 'I believed in You on and off all my life! There better be something up there like Jane or I'll humiliate You! I'll swine myself all over this town. I'll appear in public places and embarrass the shit out of You, screaming that I'm a Christian!'

We divorced the second time right after that.

Now we're in Richmond, Virginia. They laid me off. Inflation or recession or whatever rubbed me out. Oh, it was nobody's fault, says the boss. I got to sell my third car off myself, says he. At my house we don't eat near the meat we used to, says he.

So I'm in this house with my binoculars, moving from chair to chair with my cigarettes. She flies over my house upside down every afternoon. Is she saying she wants me so much she'd pay for a plane to my yard? Or is she saying: Look at this, I never gave a damn for anything but fun in the air?

Nothing in the world matters but you and your woman. Friendship and politics go to hell. My friend Dan three doors down, who's also unemployed, comes over when he can make the price of a six-pack.

It's not the same.

I'm going to die from love.

TESTIMONY OF PILOT

WHEN I WAS ten, eleven and twelve, I did a good bit of my play in the backyard of a three-story wooden house my father had bought and rented out, his first venture into real estate. We lived right across the street from it, but over here was the place to do your real play. Here there was a harrowed but overgrown garden, a vine-swallowed fence at the back end, and beyond the fence a cornfield which belonged to someone else. This was not the country. This was the town, Clinton, Mississippi, between Jackson on the east and Vicksburg on the west. On this lot stood a few water oaks, a few plum bushes, and much overgrowth of honeysuckle vine. At the very back end, at the fence, stood three strong nude chinaberry trees.

In Mississippi it is difficult to achieve a vista. But my friends and I had one here at the back corner of the garden. We could see across the cornfield, see the one lone tin-roofed house this side of the railroad tracks, then on across the tracks many other bleaker houses with rustier tin roofs, smoke coming out of the chimneys in the late fall. This was niggertown. We had binoculars and could see the colored children hustling about and perhaps a hopeless sow or two with her brood enclosed in a tiny boarded-up area. Through the binoculars one afternoon in October we watched some men corner and beat a large hog on the brain. They used an ax and the thing kept running around, head leaning toward the ground, for several minutes before it lay down. I thought

I saw the men laughing when it finally did. One of them was staggering, plainly drunk to my sight from three hundred yards away. He had the long knife. Because of that scene I considered Negroes savage cowards for a good five more years of my life. Our maid brought some sausage to my mother and when it was put in the pan to fry, I made a point of running out of the house.

I went directly across the street and to the back end of the garden behind the apartment house we owned, without my breakfast. That was Saturday. Eventually, Radcleve saw me. His parents had him mowing the yard that ran alongside my dad's property. He clicked off the power mower and I went over to his fence, which was storm wire. His mother maintained handsome flowery grounds at all costs; she had a leaf-mold bin and St. Augustine grass as solid as a rug.

Radcleve himself was a violent experimental chemist. When Radcleve was eight, he threw a whole package of .22 shells against the sidewalk in front of his house until one of them went off, driving lead fragments into his calf, most of them still deep in there where the surgeons never dared tamper. Radcleve knew about the sulfur, potassium nitrate and charcoal mixture for gunpowder when he was ten. He bought things through the mail when he ran out of ingredients in his chemistry sets. When he was an infant, his father, a quiet man who owned the Chevrolet agency in town, bought an entire bankrupt sporting-goods store, and in the middle of their backyard he built a house, plain-painted and neat, one room and a heater, where Radcleve's redundant toys forevermore were kept – all the possible toys he would need for boyhood. There were things in there that Radcleve and I were not mature enough for and did not know the real use of. When we were eleven, we uncrated the new Dunlop golf balls and went on up a shelf for the tennis rackets, went out in the middle of his yard, and served new golf ball after new golf ball with blasts of the rackets over into the cornfield, out of sight. When the strings busted we just went in and got another racket. We were absorbed by how a good smack would set the heavy little pills on an endless flight. Then Radcleve's father came down. He simply dismissed me. He took Radcleve into the house and covered his whole body with a belt. But within the week Radcleve had invented the mortar. It was a steel pipe into which a flashlight battery fit perfectly, like a bullet into a muzzle. He had drilled a hole for the fuse of an M-80 firecracker at the base, for the charge. It was a grand cannon, set up on a stack of bricks at the back of my dad's property, which was the free place to play. When it shot, it would back up violently with thick smoke and you could hear the flashlight battery whistling off. So that morning when I ran out of the house protesting the hog sausage, I told Radcleve to bring over the mortar. His ma and dad were in Jackson for the day, and he came right over with the pipe, the batteries and the M-80 explosives. He had two gross of them.

Before, we'd shot off toward the woods to the right of niggertown. I turned the bricks to the left; I made us a very fine cannon carriage pointing toward niggertown. When Radcleve appeared, he had two pairs of binoculars around his neck, one pair a newly plundered German unit as big as a brace of whiskey bottles. I told him I wanted to shoot for that house where we saw them killing the pig. Radcleve loved the idea. We singled out the house with heavy use of the binoculars.

There were children in the yard. Then they all went in. Two men came out of the back door. I thought I recognized the drunkard from the other afternoon. I helped Radcleve fix the direction of the cannon. We estimated the altitude we needed to get down there. Radcleve put the M-80 in the breech with its fuse standing out of the hole. I dropped the flashlight battery in. I lit the fuse. We backed off. The M-80 blasted off deafeningly, smoke rose, but my concentration was on that particular house over there. I brought the binoculars up. We waited six or seven seconds. I heard a great joyful wallop on tin. 'We've hit him on the first try, the first try!' I yelled. Radcleve was ecstatic. 'Right on his roof!' We bolstered up the brick carriage. Radcleve remembered the correct height of the cannon exactly. So we fixed it, loaded it, lit it and backed off. The battery landed on the roof, blat, again, louder. I looked to see if there wasn't a great dent or hole in the roof. I could not understand why niggers weren't pouring out distraught from that house. We shot the mortar again and again, and always our battery hit the tin roof. Sometimes there was only a dull thud, but other times there was a wild distress of tin. I was still looking through the binoculars, amazed that the niggers wouldn't even come out of their house to see what was hitting their roof. Radcleve was on to it better than me. I looked over at him and he had the huge German binocs much lower than I did. He was looking straight through the cornfield, which was all bare and open, with nothing left but rotten stalks. 'What we've been hitting is the roof of that house just this side of the tracks. White people live in there,' he said.

I took up my binoculars again. I looked around the yard of that white wooden house on this side of the tracks, almost next to the railroad. When I found the tin roof, I saw four significant dents in it. I saw one of our batteries lying in the middle of a sort of crater. I took the binoculars down into the yard and saw a blond middle-aged woman looking our way.

'Somebody's coming up toward us. He's from that house and he's got, I think, some sort of fancy gun with him. It might be an automatic weapon.'

I ran my binoculars all over the cornfield. Then, in a line with the house, I saw him. He was coming our way but having some trouble with the rows and dead stalks of the cornfield.

'That is just a boy like us. All he's got is a saxophone with him,' I told Radcleve. I had recently got in the school band, playing drums, and had seen all the weird horns that made up a band.

I watched this boy with the saxophone through the binoculars until he was ten feet from us. This was Quadberry. His

16

name was Ard, short for Arden. His shoes were foot-square wads of mud from the cornfield. When he saw us across the fence and above him, he stuck out his arm in my direction.

'My dad says stop it!'

'We weren't doing anything,' says Radcleve.

'Mother saw the smoke puff up from here. Dad has a hangover.'

'A what?'

'It's a headache from indiscretion. You're lucky he does. He's picked up the poker to rap on you, but he can't move further the way his head is.'

'What's your name? You're not in the band,' I said, focusing on the saxophone.

'It's Ard Quadberry. Why do you keep looking at me through the binoculars?'

It was because he was odd, with his hair and its white ends, and his Arab nose, and now his name. Add to that the saxophone.

'My dad's a doctor at the college. Mother's a musician. You better quit what you're doing . . . I was out practicing in the garage. I saw one of those flashlight batteries roll off the roof. Could I see what you shoot 'em with?'

'No,' said Radcleve. Then he said: 'If you'll play that horn.'

Quadberry stood out there ten feet below us in the field, skinny, feet and pants booted with black mud, and at his chest the slung-on, very complex, radiant horn.

Quadberry began sucking and licking the reed. I didn't care much for this act, and there was too much desperate oralness in his face when he began playing. That was why I chose the drums. One had to engage himself like suck's revenge with a horn. But what Quadberry was playing was pleasant and intricate. I was sure it was advanced, and there was no squawking, as from the other eleven-year-olds on sax in the band room. He made the end with a clean upward riff, holding the final note high, pure and unwavering.

'Good!' I called to him.

Quadberry was trying to move out of the sunken row toward us, but his heavy shoes were impeding him.

'Sounded like a duck. Sounded like a girl duck,' said Radcleve, who was kneeling down and packing a mudball around one of the M-80s. I saw and I was an accomplice, because I did nothing. Radcleve lit the fuse and heaved the mudball over the fence. An M-80 is a very serious firecracker; it is like the charge they use to shoot up those sprays six hundred feet on July Fourth at country clubs. It went off, this one, even bigger than most M-80s.

When we looked over the fence, we saw Quadberry all muck specks and fragments of stalks. He was covering the mouthpiece of his horn with both hands. Then I saw there was blood pouring out of, it seemed, his right eye. I thought he was bleeding directly out of his eye.

'Quadberry?' I called.

He turned around and never said a word to me until I was eighteen. He walked back holding his eye and staggering through the cornstalks. Radcleve had him in the binoculars. Radcleve was trembling . . . but intrigued.

'His mother just screamed. She's running out in the field to get him.'

I thought we'd blinded him, but we hadn't. I thought the Quadberrys would get the police or call my father, but they didn't. The upshot of this is that Quadberry had a permanent white space next to his right eye, a spot that looked like a tiny upset crown.

I went from sixth through half of twelfth grade ignoring him and that wound. I was coming on as a drummer and a lover, but if Quadberry happened to appear within fifty feet of me and my most tender, intimate sweetheart, I would duck out. Quadberry grew up just like the rest of us. His father was still a doctor – professor of history – at the town college; his mother was still blond, and a musician. She was organist at an Episcopalian church in Jackson, the big capital city ten miles east of us.

18

As for Radcleve, he still had no ear for music, but he was there, my buddy. He was repentant about Quadberry, although not so much as I. He'd thrown the mud grenade over the fence only to see what would happen. He had not really wanted to maim. Quadberry had played his tune on the sax, Radcleve had played his tune on the mud grenade. It was just a shame they happened to cross talents.

Radcleve went into a long period of nearly nothing after he gave up violent explosives. Then he trained himself to copy the comic strips, *Steve Canyon* to *Major Hoople*, until he became quite a versatile cartoonist with some very provocative new faces and bodies that were gesturing intriguingly. He could never fill in the speech balloons with the smart words they needed. Sometimes he would pencil in 'Err' or 'What?' in the empty speech places. I saw him a great deal. Radcleve was not spooked by Quadberry. He even once asked Quadberry what his opinion was of his future as a cartoonist. Quadberry told Radcleve that if he took all his cartoons and stuffed himself with them, he would make an interesting dead man. After that, Radcleve was shy of him too.

When I was a senior we had an extraordinary band. Word was we had outplayed all the big A.A.A. division bands last April in the state contest. Then came news that a new blazing saxophone player was coming into the band as first chair. This person had spent summers in Vermont in music camps, and he was coming in with us for the concert season. Our director, a lovable aesthete named Richard Prender, announced to us in a proud silent moment that the boy was joining us tomorrow night. The effect was that everybody should push over a seat or two and make room for this boy and his talent. I was annoyed. Here I'd been with the band and had kept hold of the taste among the whole percussion section. I could play rock and jazz drum and didn't even really need to be here. I could be in Vermont too, give me a piano and a bass. I looked at the kid on first sax, who was going to be supplanted tomorrow. For two years he had

19

thought he was the star, then suddenly enters this boy who's three times better.

The new boy was Quadberry. He came in, but he was meek, and when he turned up he put his head almost on the floor, bending over trying to be inconspicuous. The girls in the band had wanted him to be handsome, but Quadberry refused and kept himself in such hiding among the sax section that he was neither handsome, ugly, cute or anything. What he was was pretty near invisible, except for the bell of his horn, the all-but-closed eyes, the Arabian nose, the brown hair with its halo of white ends, the desperate oralness, the giant reed punched into his face, and hazy Quadberry, loving the wound in a private dignified ecstasy.

I say dignified because of what came out of the end of his horn. He was more than what Prender had told us he would be. Because of Quadberry, we could take the band arrangement of Ravel's *Bolero* with us to the state contest. Quadberry would do the saxophone solo. He would switch to alto sax, he would do the sly Moorish ride. When he played, I heard the sweetness, I heard the horn which finally brought human *talk* into the realm of music. It could sound like the mutterings of a field nigger, and then it could get up into inhumanly careless beauty, it could get among mutinous helium bursts around Saturn. I already loved *Bolero* for the constant drum part. The percussion was always there, driving along with the subtly increasing triplets, insistent, insistent, at last outraged and trying to steal the whole show from the horns and the others. I knew a large boy with dirty blond hair, name of Wyatt, who played viola in the Jackson Symphony and sousaphone in our band – one of the rare closet transmutations of my time – who was forever claiming to have discovered the central *Bolero* one Sunday afternoon over FM radio as he had seven distinct sexual moments with a certain B., girl flutist with black bangs and skin like mayonnaise, while the drums of Ravel carried them on and on in a ceremony of Spanish sex. It was agreed by all the canny in the band that *Bolero* was exactly the piece to make

20

the band soar – now especially as we had Quadberry, who made his walk into the piece like an actual lean Spanish bandit. This boy could blow his horn. He was, as I had suspected, a genius. His solo was not quite the same as the New York Phil's saxophonist's, but it was better. It came in and was with us. It entered my spine and, I am sure, went up the skirts of the girls. I had almost deafened myself playing drums in the most famous rock and jazz band in the state, but I could hear the voice that went through and out that horn. It sounded like a very troubled forty-year-old man, a man who had had his brow in his hands a long time.

The next time I saw Quadberry up close, in fact the first time I had seen him up close since we were eleven and he was bleeding in the cornfield, was in late February. I had only three classes this last semester, and went up to the band room often, to loaf and complain and keep up my touch on the drums. Prender let me keep my set in one of the instrument rooms, with a tarpaulin thrown over it, and I would drag it out to the practice room and whale away. Sometimes a group of sophomores would come up and I would make them marvel, whaling away as if not only deaf but blind to them, although I wasn't at all. If I saw a sophomore girl with exceptional body or face, I would do miracles of technique I never knew were in me. I would amaze myself. I would be threatening Buddy Rich and Sam Morello. But this time when I went into the instrument room, there was Quadberry on one side, and, back in a dark corner, a small ninth-grade euphonium player whose face was all red. The little boy was weeping and grinning at the same time.

'Queerberry,' the boy said softly.

Quadberry flew upon him like a demon. He grabbed the boy's collar, slapped his face, and yanked his arm behind him in a merciless wrestler's grip, the one that made them bawl on TV. Then the boy broke it and slugged Quadberry in the lips and ran across to my side of the room. He said. 'Queerberry' softly again and jumped for the door. Quadberry plunged across the room and tackled him on the threshold. Now that the boy was under him, Quadberry pounded the top of his head with his fist made like a mallet. The boy kept calling him 'Queerberry' throughout this. He had not learned his lesson. The boy seemed to be going into concussion, so I stepped over and touched Quadberry, telling him to quit. Quadberry obeyed and stood up off the boy, who crawled on out into the band room. But once more the boy looked back with a bruised grin, saying 'Queerberry.' Quadberry made a move toward him, but I blocked it.

'Why are you beating up on this little guy?' I said. Quadberry was sweating and his eyes were wild with hate; he was a big fellow now, though lean. He was, at six feet tall, bigger than me.

'He kept calling me Queerberry.'

'What do you care?' I asked.

'I care,' Quadberry said, and left me standing there.

We were to play at Millsaps College Auditorium for the concert. It was April. We got on the buses, a few took their cars, and were a big tense crowd getting over there. To Jackson was only a twenty-minute trip. The director, Prender, followed the bus in his Volkswagen. There was a thick fog. A flashing ambulance, snaking the lanes, piled into him head on. Prender, who I would imagine was thinking of *Bolero* and hearing the young horn voices in his band – perhaps he was dwelling on Quadberry's spectacular gypsy entrance, or perhaps he was meditating on the percussion section, of which I was the king – passed into the airs of band-director heaven. We were told by the student director as we set up on the stage. The student director was a senior from the town college, very much afflicted, almost to the point of drooling, by a love and respect for Dick Prender, and now afflicted by a heartbreaking esteem for his ghost. As were we all.

I loved the tough and tender director awesomely and never knew it until I found myself bawling along with all the rest of the boys of the percussion. I told them to keep setting up, keep tuning, keep screwing the stands together, keep hauling in the kettledrums. To just quit and bawl seemed a betrayal to Prender. I caught some girl clarinetists trying to flee the stage and go have their cry. I told them to get the hell back to their section. They obeyed me. Then I found the student director. I had to have my say.

'Look. I say we just play *Bolero* and junk the rest. That's our horse. We can't play *Brighton Beach* and *Neptune's Daughter*. We'll never make it through them. And they're too happy.'

'We aren't going to play anything,' he said. 'Man, to play is filthy. Did you ever hear Prender play piano? Do you know what a cool man he was in all things?'

'We play. He got us ready, and we play.'

'Man, you can't play any more than I can direct. You're bawling your face off. Look out there at the rest of them. Man, it's a herd, it's a weeping herd.'

'What's wrong? Why aren't you pulling this crowd together?' This was Quadberry, who had come up urgently. 'I got those little brats in my section sitting down, but we've got people abandoning the stage, tearful little finks throwing their horns on the floor.'

'I'm not directing,' said the mustached college man.

'Then get out of here. You're weak, weak!'

'Man, we've got teen-agers in ruin here, we got sorrowville. Nobody can—'

'Go ahead. Do your number. Weak out on us.'

'Man, I—'

Quadberry was already up on the podium, shaking his arms.

'We're right here! The band is right here! Tell your friends to get back in their seats. We're doing *Bolero*. Just put *Bolero* up and start tuning. *I'm* directing. I'll be right here in front of you. You look at *me*! Don't you dare quit on Prender. Don't you dare quit on me. You've got to be heard. *I've* got to be heard. Prender wanted me to be heard. I am the star, and I say we sit down and blow.'

And so we did. We all tuned and were burning low for

23

the advent into *Bolero*, though we couldn't believe that Quadberry was going to remain with his saxophone strapped to him and conduct us as well as play his solo. The judges, who apparently hadn't heard about Prender's death, walked down to their balcony desks.

One of them called out 'Ready' and Quadberry's hand was instantly up in the air, his fingers hard as if around the stem of something like a torch. This was not Prender's way, but it had to do. We went into the number cleanly and Quadberry one-armed it in the conducting. He kept his face, this look of hostility, at the reeds and the trumpets. I was glad he did not look toward me and the percussion boys like that. But he must have known we would be constant and tasteful because I was the king there. As for the others, the soloists especially, he was scaring them into excellence. Prender had never got quite this from them. Boys became men and girls became women as Quadberry directed us through *Bolero*. I even became a bit better of a man myself, though Quadberry did not look my way. When he turned around toward the people in the auditorium to enter on his solo, I knew it was my baby. I and the drums were the metronome. That was no trouble. It was talent to keep the metronome ticking amidst any given chaos of sound.

But this keeps one's mind occupied and I have no idea what Quadberry sounded like on his sax ride. All I know is that he looked grief-stricken and pale, and small. Sweat had popped out on his forehead. He bent over extremely. He was wearing the red brass-button jacket and black pants, black bow tie at the throat, just like the rest of us. In this outfit he bent over his horn almost out of sight. For a moment, before I caught the glint of his horn through the music stands, I thought he had pitched forward off the stage. He went down so far to do his deep oral thing, his conducting arm had disappeared so quickly, I didn't know but what he was having a seizure.

When *Bolero* was over, the audience stood up and made meat out of their hands applauding. The judges themselves

24

applauded. The band stood up, bawling again, for Prender and because we had done so well. The student director rushed out crying to embrace Quadberry, who eluded him with his dipping shoulders. The crowd was still clapping insanely. I wanted to see Quadberry myself. I waded through the red backs, through the bow ties, over the white bucks. Here was the first-chair clarinetist, who had done his bit like an angel; he sat close to the podium and could hear Quadberry.

'Was Quadberry good?' I asked him.

'Are you kidding? These tears in my eyes, they're for how good he was. He was too good. I'll never touch my clarinet again.' The clarinetist slung the pieces of his horn into their case like underwear and a toothbrush.

I found Quadberry fitting the sections of his alto in the velvet holds of his case.

'Hooray,' I said. 'Hip damn hooray for you.'

Arden was smiling too, showing a lot of teeth I had never seen. His smile was sly. He knew he had pulled off a monster unlikelihood.

'Hip hip hooray for me,' he said. 'Look at her. I had the bell of the horn almost smack in her face.'

There was a woman of about thirty sitting in the front row of the auditorium. She wore a sundress with a drastic cleavage up front; looked like something that hung around New Orleans and kneaded your heart to death with her feet. She was still mesmerized by Quadberry. She bore on him with a stare and there was moisture in her cleavage.

'You played well.'

'Well? Play well? Yes.'

He was trying to look at her directly. Look at *me*, I beckoned to her with full face: I was the *drums*. She arose and left.

'I was walking downhill in a valley, is all I was doing.' said Quadberry. 'Another man, a wizard, was playing my horn.' He locked his sax case. 'I feel nasty for not being able to cry like the rest of them. Look at them. Look at them crying.'

25

True, the children of the band were still weeping, standing around the stage. Several moms and dads had come up among them, and they were misty-eyed too. The mixture of grief and superb music had been unbearable.

A girl in tears appeared next to Quadberry. She was a majorette in football season and played third-chair sax during the concert season. Not even her violent sorrow could take the beauty out of the face of this girl. I had watched her for a number of years – her alertness to her own beauty, the pride of legs in the majorette outfit – and had taken out her younger sister, a second-rate version of her and a wayward overcompensating nymphomaniac whom several of us made a hobby out of pitying. Well, here was Lilian herself crying in Quadberry's face. She told him that she'd run off the stage when she heard about Prender, dropped her horn and everything, and had thrown herself into a tavern across the street and drunk two beers quickly for some kind of relief. But she had come back through the front doors of the auditorium and sat down, dizzy with beer, and seen Quadberry, the miraculous way he had gone on with *Bolero*. And now she was eaten up by feelings of guilt, weakness, cowardice.

'We didn't miss you,' said Quadberry.

'Please forgive me. Tell me to do something to make up for it.'

'Don't breathe my way, then. You've got beer all over your breath.'

'I want to talk to you.'

'Take my horn case and go out, get in my car, and wait for me. It's the ugly Plymouth in front of the school bus.'

'I know,' she said.

Lilian Field, this lovely teary thing, with the rather pious grace of her carriage, with the voice full of imminent swoon, picked up Quadberry's horn case and her own and walked off the stage.

I told the percussion boys to wrap up the packing. Into my suitcase I put my own gear and also managed to steal drum keys, two pairs of brushes, a twenty-inch Turkish cymbal, a Gretsch snare drum that I desired for my collection, a wood block, kettledrum mallets, a tuning harp and a score sheet of *Bolero* full of marginal notes I'd written down straight from the mouth of Dick Prender, thinking I might want to look at the score sheet sometime in the future when I was having a fit of nostalgia such as I am having right now as I write this. I had never done any serious stealing before, and I was stealing for my art. Prender was dead, the band had done its last thing of the year, I was a senior. Things were finished at the high school. I was just looting a sinking ship. I could hardly lift the suitcase. As I was pushing it across the stage, Quadberry was there again.

'You can ride back with me if you want to.'

'But you've got Lilian.'

'Please ride back with me . . . us. Please.'

'Why?'

'To help me get rid of her. Her breath is full of beer. My father always had that breath. Every time he was friendly, he had that breath. And she looks a great deal like my mother.' We were interrupted by the Tupelo band director. He put his baton against Quadberry's arm.

'You were big with *Bolero*, son, but that doesn't mean you own the stage.'

Quadberry caught the end of the suitcase and helped me with it out to the steps behind the auditorium. The buses were gone. There sat his ugly ocher Plymouth; it was a failed, gay, experimental shade from the Chrysler people. Lilian was sitting in the front seat wearing her shirt and bow tie, her coat off.

'Are you going to ride back with me?' Quadberry said to me.

'I think I would spoil something. You never saw her when she was a majorette. She's not stupid, either. She likes to show off a little, but she's not stupid. She's in the History Club.'

'My father has a doctorate in history. She smells of beer.'

27

I said, 'She drank two cans of beer when she heard about Prender.'

'There are a lot of other things to do when you hear about death. What I did, for example. She ran away. She fell to pieces.'

'She's waiting for us,' I said.

'One damned thing I am never going to do is drink.'

'I've never seen your mother up close, but Lilian doesn't look like your mother. She doesn't look like anybody's mother.'

I rode with them silently to Clinton. Lilian made no bones about being disappointed I was in the car, though she said nothing. I knew it would be like this and I hated it. Other girls in town would not be so unhappy that I was in the car with them. I looked for flaws in Lilian's face and neck and hair, but there weren't any. Couldn't there be a mole, an enlarged pore, too much gum on a tooth, a single awkward hair around the ear? No. Memory, the whole lying opera of it, is killing me now. Lilian was faultless beauty, even sweating, even and especially in the white man's shirt and the bow tie clamping together her collar, when one knew her uncomfortable bosoms, her poor nipples. . . .

'Don't take me back to the band room. Turn off here and let me off at my house,' I said to Quadberry. He didn't turn off.

'Don't tell Arden what to do. He can do what he wants to,' said Lilian, ignoring me and speaking to me at the same time. I couldn't bear her hatred. I asked Quadberry to please just stop the car and let me out here, wherever he was: this front yard of the mobile home would do. I was so earnest that he stopped the car. He handed back the keys and I dragged my suitcase out of the trunk, then flung the keys back at him and kicked the car to get it going again.

My band came together in the summer. We were the Bop Fiends . . . that was our name. Two of them were from Ole Miss, our bass player was from Memphis State, but when we got together this time, I didn't call the tenor sax, who went to Mississippi Southern, because Quadberry wanted to play with us. During the school year the college boys and I fell into minor groups to pick up twenty dollars on a weekend, playing dances for the Moose Lodge, medical-student fraternities in Jackson, teen-age recreation centers in Greenwood, and such as that. But come summer we were the Bop Fiends again, and the price for us went up to $1,200 a gig. Where they wanted the best rock and bop and they had some bread, we were called. The summer after I was a senior, we played in Alabama, Louisiana and Arkansas. Our fame was getting out there on the interstate route.

This was the summer that I made myself deaf.

Years ago Prender had invited down an old friend from a high school in Michigan. He asked me over to meet the friend, who had been a drummer with Stan Kenton at one time and was now a band director just like Prender. This fellow was almost totally deaf and he warned me very sincerely about deafening myself. He said there would come a point when you had to lean over and concentrate all your hearing on what the band was doing and that was the time to quit for a while, because if you didn't you would be irrevocably deaf like him in a month or two. I listened to him but could not take him seriously. Here was an oldish man who had his problems. My ears had ages of hearing left. Not so. I played the drums so loud the summer after I graduated from high school that I made myself, eventually, stone deaf.

We were at, say, the National Guard Armory in Lake Village, Arkansas, Quadberry out in front of us on the stage they'd built. Down on the floor were hundreds of sweaty teen-agers. Four girls in sundresses, showing what they could, were leaning on the stage with broad ignorant lust on their minds. I'd play so loud for one particular chick, I'd get absolutely out of control. The guitar boys would have to turn the volume up full blast to compensate. Thus I went deaf. Anyhow, the dramatic idea was to release Quadberry on a very soft sweet ballad right in the middle of a long ear-piercing run of rock-and-roll tunes. I'd get out the brushes and we would astonish the crowd with our tenderness. By August, I was so deaf I had to watch Quadberry's fingers changing notes on the saxophone, had to use my eyes to keep time. The other members of the Bop Fiends told me I was hitting out of time. I pretended I was trying to do experimental things with rhythm when the truth was I simply could no longer hear. I was no longer a tasteful drummer, either. I had become deaf through lack of taste.

Which was − taste − exactly the quality that made Quadberry wicked on the saxophone. During the howling, during the churning, Quadberry had taste. The noise did not affect his personality; he was solid as a brick. He could blend. Oh, he could hoot through his horn when the right time came, but he could do supporting roles for an hour. Then, when we brought him out front for his solo on something like 'Take Five,' he would play with such light blissful technique that he even eclipsed Paul Desmond. The girls around the stage did not cause him to enter into excessive loudness or vibrato.

Quadberry had his own girl friend now, Lilian back at Clinton, who put all the sundressed things around the stage in the shade. In my mind I had congratulated him for getting up next to this beauty, but in June and July, when I was still hearing things a little, he never said a word about her. It was one night in August, when I could hear nothing and was driving him to his house, that he asked me to turn on the inside light and spoke in a retarded deliberate way. He knew I was deaf and counted on my being able to read lips.

'Don't . . . make . . . fun . . . of her . . . or me. . . . We . . . think . . . she . . . is . . . in trouble.'

I wagged my head. Never would I make fun of him or her. She detested me because I had taken out her helpless little sister for a few weeks, but I would never think there was anything funny about Lilian, for all her haughtiness. I only thought of this event as monumentally curious.

'No one except you knows,' he said.

'Why did you tell me?'

'Because I'm going away and you have to take care of her. I wouldn't trust her with anybody but you.'

'She hates the sight of my face. Where are you going?'

'Annapolis.'

'You aren't going to any damned Annapolis.'

'That was the only school that wanted me.'

'You're going to play your saxophone on a boat?'

'I don't know what I'm going to do.'

'How . . . how can you just leave her?'

'She wants me to. She's very excited about me at Annapolis. William [this is my name], there is no girl I could imagine who has more inner sweetness than Lilian.'

I entered the town college, as did Lilian. She was in the same chemistry class I was. But she was rows away. It was difficult to learn anything, being deaf. The professor wasn't a pantomimer – but finally he went to the blackboard with the formulas and the algebra of problems, to my happiness. I hung in and made a B. At the end of the semester I was swaggering around the grade sheet he'd posted. I happened to see Lilian's grade. She'd only made a C. Beautiful Lilian got only a C while I, with my handicap, had made a B.

It had been a very difficult chemistry class. I had watched Lilian's stomach the whole way through. It was not growing. I wanted to see her look like a watermelon, make herself an amazing mother shape.

When I made the B and Lilian made the C, I got up my courage and finally went by to see her. She answered the door. Her parents weren't home. I'd never wanted this office of watching over her as Quadberry wanted me to, and this is what I told her. She asked me into the house. The rooms smelled of nail polish and pipe smoke. I was hoping her little sister wasn't in the house, and my wish came true. We were alone.

'You can quit watching over me.'

31

'Are you pregnant?'

'No.' Then she started crying. 'I wanted to be. But I'm not.'

'What do you hear from Quadberry?'

She said something, but she had her back to me. She looked to me for an answer, but I had nothing to say. I knew she'd said something, but I hadn't heard it.

'He doesn't play the saxophone anymore,' she said.

This made me angry.

'Why not?'

'Too much math and science and navigation. He wants to fly. That's what his dream is now. He wants to get into an F-something jet.'

I asked her to say this over and she did. Lilian really was full of inner sweetness, as Quadberry had said. She understood that I was deaf. Perhaps Quadberry had told her.

The rest of the time in her house I simply witnessed her beauty and her mouth moving.

I went through college. To me it is interesting that I kept a B average and did it all deaf, though I know this isn't interesting to people who aren't deaf. I loved music, and never heard it. I loved poetry, and never heard a word that came out of the mouths of the visiting poets who read at the campus. I loved my mother and dad, but never heard a sound they made. One Christmas Eve, Radcleve was back from Ole Miss and threw an M-80 out in the street for old times' sake. I saw it explode, but there was only a pressure in my ears. I was at parties when lusts were raging and I went home with two girls (I am medium handsome) who lived in apartments of the old two-story 1920 vintage, and I took my shirt off and made love to them. But I have no real idea what their reaction was. They were stunned and all smiles when I got up, but I have no idea whether I gave them the last pleasure or not. I hope I did. I've always been partial to women and have always wanted to see them satisfied till their eyes popped out.

*

Through Lilian I got the word that Quadberry was out of Annapolis and now flying jets off the *Bonhomme Richard*, an aircraft carrier headed for Vietnam. He telegrammed her that he would set down at the Jackson airport at ten o'clock one night. So Lilian and I were out there waiting. It was a familiar place to her. She was a stewardess and her loops were mainly in the South. She wore a beige raincoat, had red sandals on her feet; I was in a black turtleneck and corduroy jacket, feeling significant, so significant I could barely stand it. I'd already made myself the lead writer at Gordon-Marx Advertising in Jackson. I hadn't seen Lilian in a year. Her eyes were strained, no longer the bright blue things they were when she was a pious beauty. We drank coffee together. I loved her. As far as I knew, she'd been faithful to Quadberry.

He came down in an F-something Navy jet right on the dot of ten. She ran out on the airport pavement to meet him. I saw her crawl up the ladder. Quadberry never got out of the plane. I could see him in his blue helmet. Lilian backed down the ladder. Then Quadberry had the cockpit cover him again. He turned the plane around so its flaming red end was at us. He took it down the runway. We saw him leap out into the night at the middle of the runway going west, toward San Diego and the *Bonhomme Richard*. Lilian was crying.

'What did he say?' I asked.

'He said, "I am a dragon. America the beautiful, like you will never know." He wanted to give you a message. He was glad you were here.'

'What was the message?'

'The same thing. "I am a dragon. America the beautiful, like you will never know." '

'Did he say anything else?'

'Not a thing.'

'Did he express any love toward you?'

'He wasn't Ard. He was somebody with a sneer in a helmet.'

'He's going to war, Lilian.'

33

'I asked him to kiss me and he told me to get off the plane, he was firing up and it was dangerous.'

'Arden is going to war. He's just on his way to Vietnam and he wanted us to know that. It wasn't just him he wanted us to see. It was him in the jet he wanted us to see. He *is* that black jet. You can't kiss an airplane.'

'And what are we supposed to do?' cried sweet Lilian.

'We've just got to hang around. He didn't have to lift off and disappear straight up like that. That was to tell us how he isn't with us anymore.'

Lilian asked me what she was supposed to do now. I told her she was supposed to come with me to my apartment in the old 1920 Clinton place where I was. I was supposed to take care of her. Quadberry had said so. His six-year-old directive was still working.

She slept on the fold-out bed of the sofa for a while. This was the only bed in my place. I stood in the dark in the kitchen and drank a quarter bottle of gin on ice. I would not turn on the light and spoil her sleep. The prospect of Lilian asleep in my apartment made me feel like a chaplain on a visit to the Holy Land; I stood there getting drunk, biting my tongue when dreams of lust burst on me. That black jet Quadberry wanted us to see him in, its flaming rear end, his blasting straight up into the night at mid-runway – what precisely was he wanting to say in this stunt? Was he saying remember him forever or forget him forever? But I had my own life and was neither going to mother-hen it over his memory nor his old sweetheart. What did he mean, *America the beautiful, like you will never know*? I, William Howly, knew a goddamn good bit about America the beautiful, even as a deaf man. Being deaf had brought me up closer to people. There were only about five I knew, but I knew their mouth movements, the perspiration under their noses, their tongues moving over the crowns of their teeth, their fingers on their lips. Quadberry, I said, you don't have to get up next to the stars in your black jet to see America the beautiful.

I was deciding to lie down on the kitchen floor and sleep

the night, when Lilian turned on the light and appeared in her panties and bra. Her body was perfect except for a tiny bit of fat on her upper thighs. She'd sunbathed herself so her limbs were brown, and her stomach, and the instinct was to rip off the white underwear and lick, suck, say something terrific into the flesh that you discovered.

She was moving her mouth.

'Say it again slowly.'

'I'm lonely. When he took off in his jet, I think it meant he wasn't ever going to see me again. I think it meant he was laughing at both of us. He's an astronaut and he spits on us.'

'You want me on the bed with you?' I asked.

'I know you're an intellectual. We could keep on the lights so you'd know what I said.'

'You want to say things? This isn't going to be just sex?'

'It could never be just sex.'

'I agree. Go to sleep. Let me make up my mind whether to come in there. Turn out the lights.'

Again the dark, and I thought I would cheat not only Quadberry but the entire Quadberry family if I did what was natural.

I fell asleep.

Quadberry escorted B-52s on bombing missions into North Vietnam. He was catapulted off the *Bonhomme Richard* in his suit at 100 degrees temperature, often at night, and put the F-8 on all it could get – the tiny cockpit, the immense long two-million-dollar fuselage, wings, tail and jet engine. Quadberry, the genius master of his dragon, going up to twenty thousand feet to be cool. He'd meet with the big B-52 turtle of the air and get in a position, his cockpit glowing with green and orange lights, and turn on his transistor radio. There was only one really good band, never mind the old American rock-and-roll from Cambodia, and that was Red Chinese opera. Quadberry loved it. He loved the nasal horde in the finale, when the peasants won over the old fat dilettante mayor. Then he'd turn the jet around when he saw the

35

squatty abrupt little fires way down there after the B-52s had dropped their diet. It was a seven-hour trip. Sometimes he slept, but his body knew when to wake up. Another thirty minutes and there was his ship waiting for him out in the waves.

All his trips weren't this easy. He'd have to blast out in daytime and get with the B-52s, and a SAM missile would come up among them. Two of his mates were taken down by these missiles. But Quadberry, as on saxophone, had endless learned technique. He'd put his jet perpendicular in the air and make the SAMs look silly. He even shot down two of them. Then, one day in daylight, a MIG came floating up level with him and his squadron. Quadberry couldn't believe it. Others in the squadron were shy, but Quadberry knew where and how the MIG could shoot. He flew below the cannons and then came in behind it. He knew the MIG wanted one of the B-52s and not mainly him. The MIG was so concentrated on the fat B-52 that he forgot about Quadberry. It was really an amateur suicide pilot in the MIG. Quadberry got on top of him and let down a missile, rising out of the way of it. The missile blew off the tail of the MIG. But then Quadberry wanted to see if the man got out of the cockpit. He thought it would be pleasant if the fellow got out with his parachute working. Then Quadberry saw that the fellow wanted to collide his wreckage with the B-52, so Quadberry turned himself over and cannoned, evaporated the pilot and cockpit. It was the first man he'd killed.

The next trip out, Quadberry was hit by a ground missile. But his jet kept flying. He flew it a hundred miles and got to the sea. There was the *Bonhomme Richard*, so he ejected. His back was snapped but, by God, he landed right on the deck. His mates caught him in their arms and cut the parachute off him. His back hurt for weeks, but he was all right. He rested and recuperated in Hawaii for a month.

Then he went off the front of the ship. Just like that, his F-6 plopped in the ocean and sank like a rock. Quadberry saw the ship go over him. He knew he shouldn't eject just yet. If he ejected now he'd knock his head on the bottom and get chewed up in the motor blades. So Quadberry waited. His plane was sinking in the green and he could see the hull of the aircraft carrier getting smaller, but he had oxygen through his mask and it didn't seem that urgent a decision. Just let the big ship get over. Down what later proved to be sixty feet, he pushed the ejection button. It fired him away, bless it, and he woke up ten feet under the surface swimming against an almost overwhelming body of underwater parachute. But two of his mates were in a helicopter, one of them on the ladder to lift him out.

Now Quadberry's back was really hurt. He was out of this war and all wars for good.

Lilian, the stewardess, was killed in a crash. Her jet exploded with a hijacker's bomb, an inept bomb which wasn't supposed to go off, fifteen miles out of Havana; the poor pilot, the poor passengers, the poor stewardesses were all splattered like flesh sparklers over the water just out of Cuba. A fisherman found one seat of the airplane. Castro expressed regrets.

Quadberry came back to Clinton two weeks after Lilian and the others bound for Tampa were dead. He hadn't heard about her. So I told him Lilian was dead when I met him at the airport. Quadberry was thin and rather meek in his civvies — a gray suit and an out-of-style tie. The white ends of his hair were not there — the halo had disappeared — because his hair was cut short. The Arab nose seemed a pitiable defect in an ash-whiskered face that was beyond anemic now. He looked shorter, stooped. The truth was he was sick, his back was killing him. His breath was heavy-laden with airplane martinis and in his limp right hand he held a wet cigar. I told him about Lilian. He mumbled something sideways that I could not possibly make out.

'You've got to speak right at me, remember? Remember me, Quadberry?'

'Mom and Dad of course aren't here.'

'No. Why aren't they?'

37

'He wrote me a letter after we bombed Hué. Said he hadn't sent me to Annapolis to bomb the architecture of Hué. He had been there once and had some important experience – French-kissed the queen of Hué or the like. Anyway, he said I'd have to do a hell of a lot of repentance for that. But he and Mom are separate people. Why isn't *she* here?'

'I don't know.'

'I'm not asking you the question. The question is to God.'

He shook his head. Then he sat down on the floor of the terminal. People had to walk around. I asked him to get up.

'No. How is old Clinton?'

'Horrible. Aluminum subdivisions, cigar boxes with four thin columns in front, thick as a hive. We got a turquoise water tank; got a shopping center, a monster Jitney Jungle, fifth-rate teenyboppers covering the place like ants.' Why was I being so frank just now, as Quadberry sat on the floor downcast, drooped over like a long weak candle? 'It's not our town anymore, Ard. It's going to hurt to drive back into it. Hurts me every day. Please get up.'

'And Lilian's not even over there now.'

'No. She's a cloud over the Gulf of Mexico. You flew out of Pensacola once. You know what beauty those pink and blue clouds are. That's how I think of her.'

'Was there a funeral?'

'Oh, yes. Her Methodist preacher and a big crowd over at Wright Ferguson funeral home. Your mother and father were there. Your father shouldn't have come. He could barely walk. Please get up.'

'Why? What am I going to do, where am I going?'

'You've got your saxophone.'

'Was there a coffin? Did you all go by and see the pink or blue cloud in it?' He was sneering now as he had done when he was eleven and fourteen and seventeen.

'Yes, they had a very ornate coffin.'

'Lilian was the Unknown Stewardess. I'm not getting up.'

'I said you still have your saxophone.'

'No, I don't. I tried to play it on the ship after the last

38

time I hurt my back. No go. I can't bend my neck or spine to play it. The pain kills me.'

'Well, *don't* get up, then. Why am I asking you to get up? I'm just a deaf drummer, too vain to buy a hearing aid. Can't stand to write the ad copy I do. Wasn't I a good drummer?'

'Superb.'

'But we can't be in this condition forever. The police are going to come and make you get up if we do it much longer.'

The police didn't come. It was Quadberry's mother who came. She looked me in the face and grabbed my shoulders before she saw Ard on the floor. When she saw him she yanked him off the floor, hugging him passionately. She was shaking with sobs. Quadberry was gathered to her as if he were a rope she was trying to wrap around herself. Her mouth was all over him. Quadberry's mother was a good-looking woman of fifty. I simply held her purse. He cried out that his back was hurting. At last she let him go.

'So now we walk,' I said.

'Dad's in the car trying to quit crying,' said his mother.

'This is nice,' Quadberry said. 'I thought everything and everybody was dead around here.' He put his arms around his mother. 'Let's all go off and kill some time together.' His mother's hair was on his lips. 'You?' he asked me.

'Murder the devil out of it,' I said.

I pretended to follow their car back to their house in Clinton. But when we were going through Jackson, I took the North 55 exit and disappeared from them, exhibiting a great amount of taste, I thought. I would get in their way in this reunion. I had an unimprovable apartment on Old Canton Road in a huge plaster house, Spanish style, with a terrace and ferns and yucca plants, and a green door where I went in. When I woke up I didn't have to make my coffee or fry my egg. The girl who slept in my bed did that. She was Lilian's little sister, Esther Field. Esther was pretty in a minor way and I was proud how I had tamed her to clean and cook around the place. The Field family would appreciate how I lived with her. I showed her the broom and the

39

skillet, and she loved them. She also learned to speak very slowly when she had to say something.

Esther answered the phone when Quadberry called me seven months later. She gave me his message. He wanted to know my opinion on a decision he had to make. There was this Dr. Gordon, a surgeon at Emory Hospital in Atlanta, who said he could cure Quadberry's back problem. Quadberry's back was killing him. He was in torture even holding up the phone to say this. The surgeon said there was a seventy-five/twenty-five chance. Seventy-five that it would be successful, twenty-five that it would be fatal. Esther waited for my opinion. I told her to tell Quadberry to go over to Emory. He'd got through with luck in Vietnam, and now he should ride it out in this petty back operation.

Esther delivered the message and hung up.

'He said the surgeon's just his age; he's some genius from Johns Hopkins Hospital. He said this Gordon guy has published a lot of articles on spinal operations,' said Esther.

'Fine and good. All is happy. Come to bed.'

I felt her mouth and her voice on my ears, but I could hear only a sort of loud pulse from the girl. All I could do was move toward moisture and nipples and hair.

Quadberry lost his gamble at Emory Hospital in Atlanta. The brilliant surgeon his age lost him. Quadberry died. He died with his Arabian nose up in the air.

That is why I told this story and will never tell another.

COMING CLOSE TO DONNA

FISTFIGHT ON THE old cemetery. Both of them want Donna, square off, and Donna and I watch from the Lincoln convertible.

I'm neutral. I wear sharp clothes and everybody thinks I'm a fag, though it's not true. The truth is, I'm not all that crazy about Donna, that's all, and I tend to be sissy of voice. Never had a chance otherwise — raised by a dreadfully vocal old aunt after my parents were killed by vicious homosexuals in Panama City. Further, I am fat. I've got fat ankles going into my suede boots.

I ask her, 'Say, what you think about that, Donna? Are you going to be whoever wins's girl friend?'

'Why not? They're both cute,' she says.

Her big lips are moist. She starts taking her sweater off. When it comes off, I see she's got great humpers in her bra. There's a nice brown valley of hair between them.

'I can't lose,' she says.

Then she takes off her shoes and her skirt. There is extra hair on her thighs near her pantie rim. Out in the cemetery, the guys are knocking the spunk out of each other's cheeks. Bare, Donna's feet are red and not handsome around the toes. She has some serious bunions from her weird shoes, even at eighteen.

My age is twenty. I tried to go to college but couldn't sit in the seats long enough to learn anything. Plus, I hated English composition, where you had to correct your phrases.

They cast me out like so much wastepaper. The junior college system in California is tough. So I just went back home. I like to wear smart clothes and walk up and down Sunset Strip. That will show them.

By now, Donna is naked. The boys, Hank and Ken, are still battering each other out in the cemetery. I look away from the brutal fight and from Donna's nakedness. If I were a father, I couldn't conceive of this from my daughter.

'Warm me up, Vince. Do me. Or are you really a fag like they say?'

'Not that much,' I say.

I lost my virginity. It was like swimming in a warm, oily room – rather pleasant – but I couldn't finish. I thought about the creases in my outfit.

'Come in me, you fag,' says she. 'Don't hurt my feelings. I want a fag to come in me.'

'Oh, you pornographic witch, I can't,' says I.

She stands up, nude as an oyster. We look over at the fight in the cemetery. When she had clothes on, she wasn't much to look at. But naked, she is a vision. She has an urgent body that makes you forget the crooked nose. Her hair is dyed pink, but her organ hair isn't.'

We watch Hank and Ken slugging each other. They are her age and both of them are on the swimming team.

Something is wrong. They are too serious. They keep pounding each other in the face past what a human could take.

Donna falls on her knees in the green tufted grass.

She faints. Her body is the color of an egg. She fainted supine, titties and hair upward.

The boys are hitting to kill. They are not fooling around. I go ahead in my smart bell-bottom cuffed trousers. By the time I reach them, they are both on the ground. Their scalps are cold.

They are both dead.

'This is awful. They're *dead*,' I tell Donna, whose eyes are closed.

'What?' says she.

'They killed each other,' says I.

'Touch me,' she says. 'Make me know I'm here.'

I thrust my hand to her organ.

'What do we do?' says I.

She goes to the two bodies, and is absorbed in a tender unnatural act over the blue jeans of Hank and Ken. In former days, these boys had sung a pretty fine duet in their rock band.

'I can't make anybody come! I'm no good!' she says.

'Don't be silly,' I say. 'They're dead. Let's get out of here.'

'I can't just get out of here! They were my sweethearts!' she screams. 'Do me right now, Vince! It's the only thing that makes sense.'

Well, I flung in and tried.

A half year later, I saw her in Hooper's, the pizza parlor. I asked her how it was going. She was gone on heroin. The drug had made her prettier for a while. Her eyes were wise and wide, all black, but she knew nothing except desperation.

'Vince,' she said, 'if you'd come lay your joint in me, I wouldn't be lost anymore. You're the only one of the old crowd. Screw me and I could get back to my old neighborhood.'

I took her into my overcoat, and when I joined her in the street in back of a huge garbage can, she kept asking: 'Tell me where it is, the cemetery!'

At the moment, I was high on cocaine from a rich woman's party.

But I drove her – that is, took a taxi – to the cemetery where her lovers were dead. She knelt at the stones for a while. Then I noted she was stripping off. Pretty soon she was naked again.

'Climb me, mount me, fight for me, fuck me!' she screamed.

I picked up a neighboring tombstone with a great effort. It was an old thing, perhaps going back to the nineteenth

43

century. I crushed her head with it. Then I fled right out of there.

Some of us are made to live for a long time. Others for a short time. Donna wanted what she wanted.

I gave it to her.

DRAGGED FIGHTING FROM
HIS TOMB

IT WAS A rout.

We hit them, but they were ready this time.

His great idea was to erupt in the middle of the loungers. Stuart was a profound laugher. His banjo-nigger was with him almost all the time, a man who could make a ballad instantly after an ambush. We had very funny songs about the wide-eyed loungers and pickets, the people of negligent spine leisuring around the depots and warehouses, straightening their cuffs and holding their guns as if they were fishing poles. Jeb loved to break out of cover in the clearing in front of these guards. He offered them first shot if they were ready, but they never were. It was us and the dirty gray, sabers out, and a bunch of fleeing boys in blue.

Except the last time, at Two Roads Junction in Pennsylvania.

These boys had repeaters and they were waiting for us. Maybe they had better scouts than the others. We'd surprised a couple of their pickets and shot them down. But I suppose there were others who got back. This was my fault. My talent was supposed to be circling behind the pickets and slaying every one of them. So I blame myself for the rout, though there are always uncertainties in an ambush. This time it was us that were routed.

We rode in. They were ready with the repeating rifles, and we were blown apart. I myself took a bullet through the throat. It didn't take me off my mount, but I rode about a hundred yards out under a big shade tree and readied myself to die. I offered my prayers.

'Christ, I am dead. Comfort me in the valley of the shadow. Take me through it with honor. Don't let me make the banshee noises I've heard so many times in the field. You and I know I am worth more than that.'

I heard the repeating rifles behind me and the shrieks, but my head was a calm green church. I was prepared to accept the big shadow. But I didn't seem to be dying. I felt my neck. I thrust my forefinger in the hole. It was to the right of my windpipe and there was blood on the rear of my neck. The thing had passed clean through the muscle of my right neck. In truth, it didn't even hurt.

I had been thinking: Death does not especially hurt. Then I was merely asleep on the neck of the horse, a red-haired genius for me and a steady one. I'd named him Mount Auburn. We took him from a big farm outside Gettysburg. He wanted me as I wanted him. He was mine. He was the Confederacy.

As I slept on him, he was curious but stable as a rock. The great beast felt my need to lie against his neck and suffered me. He lay the neck out there for my comfort and stood his front heels.

A very old cavalryman in blue woke me up. He was touching me with a flagstaff. He didn't even have a weapon out.

'Eh, boy, you're a pretty dead one, ain't you? Got your hoss's head all bloody. Did you think Jeb was gonna surprise us forever?'

We were alone.

He was amazed when I stood up in the saddle. I could see beyond him through the hanging limbs. A few men in blue were picking things up. It was very quiet. Without a thought, I already had my pistol on his thin chest. I could not see him for a moment for the snout of my pistol.

He went to quivering, of course, the old fool. I saw he had a bardlike face.

What I began was half sport and half earnest.

'Say wise things to me or die, patriot,' I said.

'But but but but but but,' he said.

'Shhh!' I said. 'Let nobody else hear. Only me. Tell the most exquisite truths you know.'

He paled and squirmed.

'What's wrong?' I asked.

A stream of water came out the cuff of his pants.

I don't laugh. I've seen pretty much all of it. Nothing a body does disgusts me. After you've seen them burst in the field in two days of sun, you are not surprised by much that the mortal torso can do.

'I've soiled myself, you gray motherfucker,' said the old guy.

'Get on with it. No profanity necessary,' I said.

'I believe in Jehovah, the Lord; in Jesus Christ, his son; and in the Holy Ghost. I believe in the Trinity of God's bride, the church. To be honest. To be square with you neighbor. To be American and free,' he said.

'I asked for the truths, not beliefs,' I said.

'But I don't understand what you mean,' said the shivering home guard. 'Give me an example.'

'You're thrice as old as I. You should give *me* the examples. For instance: Where is the angry machine of all of us? Why is God such a blurred magician? Why are you begging for your life if you believe those things? Prove to me that you're better than the rabbits we ate last night.'

'I'm better because I know I'm better,' he said.

I said, 'I've read Darwin and floundered in him. You give me aid, old man. Find your way out of this forest. Earn your life back for your trouble.'

'Don't shoot me. They'll hear the shot down there and come blow you over. All the boys got Winchester repeaters,' he said.

By this time he'd dropped the regiment flag into a steaming pile of turd from his horse. I noticed that his mount was scared too. The layman does not know how the currents of

47

the rider affect that dumb beast he bestrides. *I've seen a thoroughbred horse refuse to move at all under a man well known as an idiot with a plume. It happened in the early days in the streets of Richmond with Wailing Ott, a colonel too quick if I've ever seen one. His horse just wouldn't move when Ott's boys paraded out to Manassas. He screamed and there were guffaws. He even cut the beast with his saber. The horse sat right down on the ground like a deaf beggar of a darky. Later, in fact during the battle of Manassas, Colonel Ott, loaded with pistols, sabers and even a Prussian dagger, used a rotten outhouse and fell through the aperture (or split it by his outlandish weight in iron) and drowned head down in night soil. I saw his horse roaming. It took to me. I loved it and its name (I christened it afresh) was Black Answer, because a mare had just died under me and here this other beast ran into my arms. It ran for me. I had to rein Black Answer to keep him behind General Smith himself. (Though Jeb was just another colonel then.) I am saying that a good animal knows his man. I was riding Black Answer on a bluff over the York when a puff went out of a little boat we were harassing with Pelhams's cannon from the shore. I said to Black Answer, 'Look at McClellan's little sailors playing war down there, boy.' The horse gave a sporty little snort in appreciation. He knew what I was saying.*

It wasn't a full fifteen minutes before a cannon ball took him right out from under me. I was standing on the ground and really not even stunned, my boots solid in the dust. But over to my right Black Answer was rolling up in the vines, broken in two. That moment is what raised my anger about the war. I recalled it as I held the pistol on the old makeshift soldier. I pulled back the hammer. I recalled the eyes of the horse were still bright when I went to comfort it. I picked up the great head of Black Answer and it came away from the body very easily. What a deliberate and pure expression Black Answer retained, even in death.

What a bog and labyrinth the human essence is, in comparison. We are all overbrained and overemotioned. No wonder my professor at the University of Virginia pointed out to us the horses of that great fantast Jonathan Swift and his Gulliver book. Compared with horses, we are all a dizzy and smelly farce. An old man cannot tell you the truth. An old man, even inspired by death, simply foams and is addled like a crab.

'Tell me,' I said, 'do you hate me because I hold niggers in bondage? Because I do not hold niggers in bondage. I can't afford it. You know what I'm fighting for? I asked you a question.'

'What're you fighting for?'

'For the North to keep off.'

'But you're here in Pennsylvania, boy. You attacked *us*. This time we were ready. I'm sorry it made you mad. I'm grievous sorry about your neck, son.'

'You never told me any truths. Not one. Look at that head. Look at all those gray hairs spilling out of your cap. Say something wise. I'm about to kill you,' I said.

'I have daughters and sons who look up to me,' he said.

'Say I am one of your sons. Why do I look up to you?' I said.

'Because I've tried to know the world and have tried to pass it on to the others.' He jumped off the horse right into the droppings. He looked as if he were venturing to run. 'We're not simple animals. There's a god in every one of us, if we find him,' he said.

'Don't try to run. I'd kill you before I even thought,' I said.

His horse ran away. It didn't like him.

On the ground, below my big horse Mount Auburn, the old man was a little earthling in an overbig uniform. He kept chattering.

'I want a single important truth from you,' I said.

'My mouth can't do it,' he said. 'But there's something here!' He struck his chest at the heart place. Then he started running back to the depot, slapping hanging limbs out of his way. I turned Mount Auburn and rode after. We hit the clearing and Mount Auburn was in an easy prance. The old

49

man was about ten yards ahead, too breathless to warn the troops.

In an idle way I watched their progress too. Captain Swain had been killed during our ambush. I saw the blueboys had put his body up on a pole with a rope around his neck, a target in dirty gray. His body was turning around as they tried out the repeaters on him. But ahead of me the old man bounced like a snowtail in front of Mount Auburn. We were in a harrowed field. The next time I looked up, a stand of repeaters was under my left hand three strides ahead. I was into their camp. Mount Auburn stopped for me as I picked up a handful of the rifles by the muzzles.

The old man finally let out something.

'It's a secesh!' he shouted.

Only a couple looked back. I noticed a crock of whiskey on a stool where the brave ones were reloading to shoot at Captain Swain again. I jumped off Mount Auburn and went in the back door of the staff house. I kicked the old man through the half-open door and pulled Mount Auburn into the room with me, got his big sweaty withers inside. When I looked around I saw their captain standing up and trying to get out his horse pistol. He was about my age, maybe twenty-five, and he had spectacles. My piece was already cocked and I shot him square in the chest. He backed up and died in another little off-room behind his desk. A woman ran out of the room. She threw open the front door and bullets smacked into the space all around her. She shut the door. A couple of bullets broke wood.

'Lay down,' I said.

She had a little Derringer double-shot pistol hanging in her hand. The old man was lying flat on the floor behind the desk with me.

The woman was a painted type, lips like blood. 'Get down,' I told her. She was ugly, just lips, tan hair, and a huge bottom under a petticoat. I wondered what she was going to try with the little pistol. She lay down flat on the floor. I asked her to throw me the pistol. She wouldn't. Then she wormed it across to us behind the big desk. She looked me over, her face grimy from the floor. She had no underwear and her petticoat was hiked up around her middle. The old man and I were looking at her organ.

'Wha? War again?' she said. 'I thought we already won.'

The woman and the old man laid themselves out like a carpet. I knew the blueboys thought they had me down and were about ready to come in. I was in that position at Chancellorsville. There should be about six fools, I thought. I made it to the open window. Then I moved into the window. With the repeater, I killed four, and the other two limped off. Some histrionic plumehead was raising his saber up and down on the top of a pyramid of crossties. I shot him just for fun. Then I brought up another repeater and sprayed the yard.

This brought on a silence. Nothing was moving. Nobody was shooting. I knew what they were about to do. I had five minutes to live, until they brought the cannon up. It would be canister or the straight big ball. Then the firing started again. The bullets were nicking the wall in the back of me. I saw Mount Auburn behind the desk. He was just standing there, my friend, my legs. Christ, how could I have forgotten him? 'Roll down, Auburn!' I shouted. He lay down quick. He lay down behind the thick oak desk alongside the slut and the old man.

Then what do you think? With nothing to do but have patience until they got the cannon up, somebody's hero came in the back door with a flambeau and a pistol, his eyes closed, shooting everywhere. Mount Auburn winnied. The moron had shot Auburn. This man I overmurdered. I hit him four times in the face, and his torch flew out the back door with one of the bullets.

I was looking at the hole in Auburn when the roof of the house disappeared. It was a canister blast. The sound was deafening. Auburn was hurting but he was keeping it in. His breaths were deeper, the huge bold eyes waiting on me. I had done a lead-out once before on a corporal who was shot in

51

the buttocks. He screamed the whole time, but he lives now, with a trifling scar on his arse, now the war is over. You put your stiletto very hard to one side of the hole until you feel metal – the bullet – and then you twist. The bullet comes out of the hole by this coiling motion and may even jump up in your hand.

So it was with the lead in Auburn's flank. It hopped right out. The thing to do then is get a sanitary piece of paper and stuff it into the wound. I took a leaf from the middle of the pile of stationery on the captain's table, spun it, and rammed it down.

Auburn never made a complaint. It was I who was mad. I mean, angry beyond myself.

When I went out the front door with the two repeaters, firing and levering, through a dream of revenge – fire from my right hand and fire from my left – the cannoneers did not expect it. I knocked down five of them. Then I knelt and started shooting to kill. I let the maimed go by. But I saw the little team of blue screeching and trying to shoot me, and I killed four of them. Then they all ran off.

There was nothing to shoot at.

I turned around and walked back toward the shack I'd been in. The roof was blown off. The roof was in the backyard lying on the toilet. A Yank with a broken leg had squirmed out from under it.

'Don't kill me,' he said.

'Lay still and leave me alone,' I said. 'I won't kill you.'

Mount Auburn had got out of the house and was standing with no expression in the bare dirt. I saw the paper sticking out of his wound. He made an alarmed sound. I turned. The Yank with a broken leg had found that slut's double-barreled Derringer. I suppose she threw it up in the air about the time the roof was blown over.

He shot at me with both barrels. One shot hit my boot and the other hit me right in the chin, but did nothing. It had been misloaded or maybe it wasn't ever a good pistol to begin with. The bullet hit me and just fell off.

'Leave me alone,' I said. 'Come here, Auburn,' I called to the big horse. 'Hurt him.'

I went back in the house while Mount Auburn ran back and forth over the Yank. I cast aside some of the rafters and paper in search of the old man and the slut. They were unscathed. They were under the big desk in a carnal act. I was out of ammunition or I would have slaughtered them too. I went out to the yard and called Mount Auburn off the Yank, who was hollering and running on one leg.

By the time the old man and the slut got through, I had reloaded. They came out the back slot that used to be the door.

'Tell me something. Tell me something wise!' I screamed.

He was a much braver man than I'd seen when I'd seen him in the shade of the tree.

'Tell me *something*. Tell me *something wise*!' I screamed.

'There is no wisdom, Johnny Reb,' the old man said. 'There's only tomorrow if you're lucky. Don't kill us. Let us have tomorrow.'

I spared them. They wandered out through the corpses into the plowed rows. I couldn't see them very far because of the dirty moon. I was petting Mount Auburn when Jeb and fifteen others of the cavalry rode up. Jeb has the great beard to hide his weak chin and his basic ugliness. He's shy. I'm standing here and we've got this whole depot to plunder and burn. So he starts being chums with me. Damned if I don't think he was jealous.

'You stayed and won it, Howard, all on your own?' he says.

'Yes, sir. I did.'

'There's lots of dead Christians on the ground,' he said. 'You've got blood all over your shirt. You're a stout fellow, aren't you?'

'You remember what you said to me when you came back

and I was holding Black Answer's head in my hands when he'd been shot out from under me?'

'I recall the time but not what I said,' said Jeb Stuart.

'You said, "Use your weeping on people, not on animals," ' I said.

'I think I'd hold by that,' said Stuart.

'You shit! What are we doing killing people in Pennsylvania?' I screamed.

'Showing them that we can, Captain Howard!'

They arrested me and I was taken back (by the nightways) to a detention room in North Carolina. But that was easy to break out of.

I rode my horse, another steed that knew me, named Vermont Nose.

I made it across the Mason-Dixon.

Then I went down with Grant when he had them at Cold Harbor and in the Wilderness. My uniform was blue.

I did not care if it was violet.

I knew how Stuart moved. We were equal Virginia boys. All I needed was twenty cavalry.

I saw him on the road, still dashing around and stroking his beard.

'Stuarrrrrrrrt!' I yelled.

He trotted over on his big gray horse.

'Don't I know this voice?' he said.

'It's Howard,' I said.

'But I sent you away. What uniform are you wearing?'

'Of your enemy,' I said.

They had furnished me with a shotgun. But I preferred the old Colt. I shot him right in the brow, so that not another thought would pass about me or about himself or about the South, before death. I knew I was killing a man with wife and children.

I never looked at what the body did on its big horse.

Then Booth shot Lincoln, issuing in the graft of the Grant administration.

*

54

I am dying from emphysema in a Miami hotel, from a twenty-five-year routine of cigars and whiskey. I can't raise my arm without gasping.

I know I am not going to make it through 1901. I am the old guy in a blue uniform. I want a woman to lie down for me. I am still functional. I believe we must eradicate all the old soldiers and all their assemblies. My lusts surpass my frame. I don't dare show my pale ribs on the beach. I hire a woman who breast-feeds me and lets me moil over her body. I've got twenty thousand left in the till from the Feds.

The only friends of the human sort I have are the ghosts that I killed. They speak when I am really drunk.

'Welcome,' they say. Then I enter a large gray hall, and Stuart comes up.

'Awwww!' he groans. 'Treason.'

'That's right,' I say.

In 1900 they had a convention of Confederate veterans at the hotel, this lonely tall thing on the barbarous waves. I was well into my third stewed mango, wearing my grays merely to be decorous. I heard a group of old coots of about my age hissing at a nearby table. It became clear that I was the object of distaste.

I stood up.

'What is it?' I asked them.

I was answered by a bearded high-mannered coot struck half dead by Parkinson's disease. He was nodding like a reed in wind. He rose in his colonel's cape. Beside him his cane clattered to the floor.

'I say I saw you in the road, dog. I'm a Virginian, and I saw it by these good eyes. You killed Jeb Stuart. *You*! Your presence is a mockery to us of the Old Cause.'

'Leave me alone, you old toy,' I said.

I raised my freckled fists. His companions brought him down.

When the convention left, I dressed in my grays again and walked to the beach. Presently Charlie came out of the little corral over the dune, walking Mount Auburn's grandchild. If President Grant lied to me, I don't want to know. I have proof positive that it came from a Pennsylvania farm in the region where we foraged and ambushed.

It was an exquisitely shouldered red horse, the good look in its eye.

Charlie let me have the rein and I led the animal down to the hard sand next to the water. It took me some time to mount. My overcoat fell over his withers.

'You need any help, Captain Howard?' Charlie asked.

'I don't need a goddamned thing except privacy,' I said.

There was nothing on the beach, only the waves, the hard sand, and the spray. The beauty I sat on ran to the verge of his heartburst. I had never given the horse a name. I suppose I was waiting for him to say what he wanted, to talk.

But Christ is his name, this muscle and heart striding under me.

QUO VADIS, SMUT?

THE OTHER DAY we cornered a man, a lout named Reggy John. It was in a barn near the Kansas and Missouri border. The weather was freezing and moist. John was unarmed and covered with cow manure. We had shotguns, but I saw this creature under the straw and took pity on him. I told the guys to lay their guns down. In a stall was his supposed sweetheart, tied underneath a bull with rope, all naked. One of the boys had blown off the latch of the stall so the bull was wandering about among us with the woman under him. The bull seemed to be tranquil, having had his last desire with the woman.

Sheriff Folger lost his reason and grabbed the pitchfork from the wall and stuck it in the bull's eyes. We forgot the criminal and kept to the sides of the barn, watching the bull with gore spewing from its sockets. The woman underneath him was awakened by the jumping. The bull twisted so in its death that the ropes were loosened and the beast could kick her in the head. He did it in his throes, kicked her out of bondage entirely. We couldn't stand any more. Sergeant Leet shot the thing in the brain with his shotgun. It was at peace.

We were all hungry after the big hunt. Under Leet's direction, three of the privates skinned the bull, three others started the fire. One made coffee, two brought in potatoes and the kettle, and a corporal brought in a sack full of onions and cabbages from the farmer's house, to boil with the

57

potatoes. The farmer came along. We sent him back for salt and pepper. We hadn't eaten anything substantial in five days. The farmer was smiling. He wanted to introduce us to his wife and children. The barn was getting warmer and warmer. When the farmer opened the door, I saw the snow was coming down in big tumbling flakes. The degree was zero.

Leet directed three of the privates to knock out a hole in the roof so the smoke could get out of the barn, and it was done.

They had slabbed the meat and were turning it on the coals with their own little implements or such as they could pick up in the barn. Leet and I watched the men eat. The sheriff was using the pitchfork he'd used on the bull. Somebody had thrown a horse blanket over the woman, who by report was named Elizabeth (Betsy) Allen, from New Albany, Mississippi. The kettle was bubbling with potatoes, cabbages and onions. Coffee was boiling high. The aromas were thick. I pulled my last cigarette from my jacket. The filter was broken off but I lit the shredded end. I thought: This is delicious. The smoke went down in my lungs and touched all the big hollow parts of me. I was hungry and began feeling somewhat lecherous. But I had been so long without food, I did not want food; and I had been so long without a woman, I did not want a woman.

Farmer Lutz brought out his wife and children. His wife was blond and ugly, but his children were beautiful like elves. The wife looked straight at me with astonishment. I'm tall and lean and rather young for a colonel.

Lutz wanted to know what we were going to do with John and his sweetheart. The woman was sitting up, holding the blanket over her chest. Her face was bruised so much. You could tell she was a dyed blonde from her secret hair. The odor of bull discharge was strong on her. She was, however, being treated well by the corporal, Wooten, who had her sipping coffee. He was treating her tenderly, but for my money it was the wrong drug. Coffee would make her wake up and talk. I didn't want to hear what she would say.

'We're going to do them justice,' I told Lutz.

Sergeant Leet gave him five hundred cash for the use and damage of his barn.

'Keep it,' said farmer Lutz. 'It was worth the thrill.'

But the wife snatched the money. She was looking straight at me. Something both of anger and of desire was in her stare.

'Can you turn your jet around and take off in that big meadow again?' farmer Lutz asked me.

'Yes. I fly it. Taking off's nothing. We already did the hard part. We'll be out of here before you wake up.'

'How many women did he kill before you got to him?'

'Read the newspaper a couple days from now. That's where the number will be.' When he was turning away, I said, 'Thanks for your telephone call.'

'We all got to help one another,' farmer Lutz said.

Then I hit the steaks, the potatoes, the onions, the cabbage, the coffee, everything.

'I can't stand it here,' Reggy John said. 'There ain't no radio, no music.'

He went on talking. Christ.

'I written poems. Beauty and death is the same thing. Death is nothing. I love it so much I got to look at it. I written songs.' He began crooning something demented.

I kicked him in the stomach. When he passed out, he was still crooning.

The men got up and went back to the coffee. The privates sang a song they had made up just for me. Rawr rawr rawr! for Colonel Feather!/Rawr rawr rawr! (pause, then with gusto) *forever*!

I was in a paradise of affinity. I blushed. I saluted.

'I want to die, Colonel Feather,' Reggy John said. 'Would you give me some of them steak leftovers?' This was all spoken very wheezingly. I was sorry. He looked like a philosopher. I hated him with a certain tender feeling. I despise this sort of confusion.

Then the woman, Betsy, came up. She was ashamed and stood with her organ showing. The corporal was behind her. Her head was wrapped up in bandages.

'Don't hurt Reggy,' she said. 'He don't mean to do nothing.'

Reggy John was right at my shoulder. What a breath.

'Death isn't nothing,' he said, trying to chew.

'All right, philosopher,' I said.

'I want to adopt her. This ravished child, this babe of the starving South,' the corporal said. He was extraordinarily ugly with his big nose and thick-lensed glasses.

He continued, the corporal did.

'This poor thing never finished even junior high. Her home was a ruined trailer. Three of her brothers were retarded. The other three had no interest in the higher things of life. This here woman touched something new in my heart, sir,' he said.

I told them let's get out of here. We straightened the barn and walked to the jet. It was good hearing it crank. I backed up and was looking at the sun through the snowflakes. I raised the jet on the elevators and leaned it back. We got out of there.

In the air, making for Atlanta, Reggy John came into the cockpit.

'Death is nothing,' he said. 'This is fun. First time I've been in a jet.'

The sky had blued up in south Tennessee and we had a rainbow to the left.

'I always thought death was *something*,' said Leet. 'Generally it means the end of what good you can do your fellow man.'

'There ain't no fellow man but me,' said John. His breath was devastating. 'I'm thirsty. You got a drink?'

Leet fixed him the drink. It came in a martini glass. The taste is exquisite but there are flakes of glass in the gin. They burn constantly but do not kill. Elimination can become a problem. John, who was thirty, would last many years with it. The drink creates a slavish thirst for the next drink. It calms the need for six hours. Then the great thirst comes again. He drank it. The man thinks he is an alcoholic but the need is much worse than that.

He will come crawling back to us forever and we will give him the drink and kick him out.

He was surprised there were no cops in Atlanta. He told me, as he walked off in the airport, that he was really surprised.

'Live a long time, like the rest of us,' I said.

The corporal took away the woman dressed in his own fatigues. The fool.

I am so rich. I am so important.

My wife knows this. She is ready. I am exactly on time. She is drenched in perfume and is in the veil. Her secret hair is trimmed and shaped. On her feet are silver sandals. Her rear is raised. She has her face on a cushion of velvet. The child is asleep upstairs. A few logs are burning in the fireplace. I shower and enrobe myself. She is still on the floor, knees on the rug, rear high and overcomingly sweet with perfume. She says darling darling darling.

This is my fifth wife. Lucky for me at last I got the right one.

RETURN TO RETURN

THEY USED TO call French Edward the happiest man on the court, and the prettiest. The crowds hated to see him beaten. Women anguished to conceive of his departure from a tournament. Once, when Edward lost a dreadfully long match at Forest Hills, an old man in the audience roared with sobs, then female voices joined in. It was like seeing the death of Mercutio or Hamlet going down with a resigned smile.

Dr. Levaster drove the Lincoln. It was rusty and the valves stuck. On the rear floorboard two rain pools sloshed, disturbing the mosquitoes that rode the beer cans. The other day Dr. Levaster became forty. His hair was thin, his eyes swollen beneath the sunglasses, his ears small and red. Yet he was not monstrous. He seemed, though, to have just retreated from conflict. The man with him was two years younger, curly passionate hair, face dashed with sun. His name was French Edward, the tennis pro.

A mosquito flew from one of the beer cans and bit French Edward before it was taken out by the draft. Edward became remarkably angry, slapping his neck, turning around in the seat, rising and peering down on the cans in the back, reaching over and smacking at them. Then he fell over the seat head-down into the puddles and clawed in the water. Dr. Levaster slowed the Lincoln and drove into the grass off the highway.

'Here now, here now! Moan, moan!' Dr. Levaster had

given up profanity when he turned forty, formerly having been known as the filthiest-mouthed citizen of Louisiana or Mississippi. He opened the back door and dragged Edward out into the sedge. 'You mule.' He slapped Edward over-vigorously, continuing beyond the therapeutic moment.

'He got me again . . . I thought. He. Doctor Word,' said Edward.

'A bug. Mule, who do you think would be riding in the back of my car? How much do you have left, anything?'

'It's clear. A bug. It felt just like what he was doing.'

'He's dead. Drowned.'

'They never found him.'

'He can't walk on water.'

'I did.'

'You just think you did.' Dr. Levaster looked in the back seat. 'One of your rackets is in the water, got wet. The strings are ruined.'

'I'm all right,' French Edward said.

'You'd better be. I'm not taking you one mile more if we don't get some clarity. Where are we?'

'Outside New York City.'

'Where, more exactly?'

'New Jersey. The Garden State.'

At his three-room place over the spaghetti store on Eighty-ninth, Baby Levaster, M.D., discovered teen-agers living. He knew two of them. They had broken in the door but had otherwise respected his quarters, washed the dishes, swept, even revived his house plants. They were diligent little street people. They claimed they knew by intuition he was coming back to the city and wanted to clean up for him. Two of them thought they might have gonorrhea. Dr. Levaster got his bag and jabbed ten million units of penicillin in them. Then French Edward came up the stairs with the baggage and rackets and went to the back.

'Dear God! He's, oh. Oh, he looks like *love*!' said Carina. She wore steep-heeled sandals and clocked about nineteen on the age scale. The others hung back, her friends. Levaster knew her well. She had shared his sheets, and, in nightmares of remorse, he had shared her body, waking with drastic regret, feeling as soiled and soilsome as the city itself.

'Are you still the mind, him the body?' Carina asked.

'Now more than ever. I'd say he now has about an eighth of the head he was given,' Levaster said.

'What happened?'

'He drowned. And then he lived,' Levaster said.

'Well, he looks happy.'

'I am happy,' said French Edward, coming back to the room. 'Whose thing is this? You children break in Baby's apartment and, not only that, you carry firearms. I don't like any kind of gun. Who are those hoodlums you're talking to, Baby?' Edward was carrying a double-barreled .410 shotgun/pistol; the handle was of cherrywood and silver vines embossed the length of the barrels.

'I'll take that,' said Dr. Levaster, since it was his. It was his Central Park nighttime gun. The shells that went with it were loaded with popcorn. He ran the teen-agers out of his apartment, and when he returned, Edward was asleep on the couch, the sweet peace of the athlete beaming through his twisted curls.

'I've never slept like that,' Lester said to Carina, who had remained. 'Nor will I ever.'

'I saw him on TV once. It was a match in Boston, I think. I didn't care a rat's prick about tennis. But when I saw him, that face and in his shorts, wow. I told everybody to come here and watch this man.'

'He won that one,' Dr. Levaster said.

Levaster and Carina took a cab to Central Park. It was raining, which gave a congruous fashion to Levaster's raincoat, wherein, at the left breast pocket, the shotgun/pistol hung in a cunning leather holster. Levaster swooned in the close nostalgia of the city. Everything was so exquisitely true and forthright. Not only was the vicious city there, but he, a meddlesome worthless loud failure from Vicksburg, was jammed amok in the viciousness himself, a willing lout in a nightmare. He stroked Carina's thigh, rather enjoying her distaste.

They entered the park under a light broken by vandals. She came close to him near the dark hedges. What with the inconsequential introversion of his youth, in which he had not honed any skill but only squatted in derision of every-thing in Vicksburg, Levaster had missed the Southern hunting experience. This was more sporting, bait for muggers. They might have their own pistols, etc. He signaled Carina to lie on the grass and make with her act.

'Oh, I'm coming, I'm coming! And I'm so rich, rich, rich! Only money could make me come like this!'

The rain had stopped and a moon was pouring through the leaves. Two stout bums, one with a beer can opened in his hand, circled out of the bush and edged in on Carina. The armed bum made a threatening jab. In a small tenor voice. Levaster protested.

'Please! We're only visitors here. Don't take our money! Don't tell my wife!' They came toward Levaster, who was speaking. 'Do you fellows know Jesus? The Prince of Peace?' When they were six feet away, he shot them both in the thigh, whimpering, 'Glory be! Sorry! Goodness. Oh, wasn't that *loud*!'

After the accosters had stumbled away, astounded at being alive, Levaster sank into the usual fit of contrition. He removed his sunglasses. He seemed racked by the advantage of new vision. It was the first natural light he had seen since leaving French Edward's house in Covington, across the bridge from New Orleans.

They took a cab back and passed by French Edward, asleep again. He had taken off his trousers and shirt, appeared to have shucked them off in the wild impatience of his sleep, like an infant, and the lithe clusters of his muscles rose and fell with his breathing. Carina sat on the bed with Levaster.

He removed his raincoat and everything else. Over his spread-collar shirt was printed a sort of Confederate flag as drawn by a three-year-old with a sludge brush. Levaster wore it to Elaine's to provoke fights but was ignored and never even got to buy a writer or actor a drink. Undressed, it was seen how oversized his head was and how foolishly outsized his sex, hanging large and purple, a slain ogre. Undressed, Levaster seemed more like a mutinous gland than a whole male figure. He jumped up and down on his bed, using it for a trampoline. Carina was appalled.

'I'm the worst, the awfulest!' he said. Carina gathered her bag and edged to the door. She said she was leaving. As he bounced on the bed, he saw her kneeling next to the couch with her hand on Edward's wrist. 'Hands off!' Levaster screamed. 'No body without the mind! Besides, he's married. A New Orleans woman wears his ring!' Jump, jump! 'She makes you look like a chimney sweep. You chimney sweep!' Levaster bounced as Carina left.

He fell on the bed and moiled two minutes before going into black sleep. He dreamed. He dreamed about his own estranged wife, a crazy in Arizona who sent him photographs of herself with her hair cut shorter in every picture. She had a crew cut and was riding a horse out front of a cactus field in the last one. She thought hair interfered with rationality. Now she was happy, having become ugly as a rock. Levaster did not dream about himself and French Edward, although the dream lay on him like the bricks of an hysterical mansion.

In high school, Baby Levaster was the best tennis player. He was small but devious and could run and get the ball like a terrier. Dr. Word coached the college team. Dr. Word was a professor of botany and was suspected as the town queer. Word drew up close to the boys, holding them to show them the full backhand and forehand of tennis, snuggled up to their bodies and worked them like puppets as large as he was. Rumorers said Dr. Word got a thrill from the rear closeness to his players. But his team won the regional championship.

Dr. Word tried to coach Baby Levaster, but Levaster resisted being touched and handled like a big puppet and had heard Word was a queer. What he had heard was true — until a few months before French Edward came onto the courts.

Dr. Word first saw French Edward in a junior-high football game; the boy moved like a genius, finding all the openings, sprinting away from all the other boys on the field. French was the quarterback. He ran for a touchdown nearly every time the ball was centered to him, whenever the play was busted. The only thing that held him back was passing and handing off. Otherwise, he scored, or almost did. An absurd clutter of bodies would be gnashing behind him on the field. It was then that Dr. Word saw French's mother, Olive, sitting in the bleachers, looking calm, auburn-haired and handsome. From then on Dr. Word was queer no more. Mrs. Edward was a secretary for the P.E. department, and Dr. Word was baldheaded and virile, suave with the grace of his Ph.D. from Michigan State, obtained years ago but still appropriating him some charm as an exotic scholar. Three weeks of tender words and French's mother was his, in any shadow of Word's choosing.

Curious and flaming like a pubescent, he caressed her on back roads and in the darkened basement of the gym, their trysts protected by his repute as a queer or, at the outside, an oyster. Her husband — a man turned lopsided and cyclop-tic by sports mania — never discovered them. It was her son, French Edward, who did, walking into his own home wearing sneakers and thus unheard — and unwitting — to discover them coiled infamously. Mr. Edward was away as an unin-vited delegate to a rules-review board meeting of the South-eastern Conference in Mobile. French was not seen. He crawled under the bed of his room and slept so as to gather the episode into a dream that would vanish when he awoke. What he dreamed was exactly what he had just seen, with the addition that he was present in her room, practicing his strokes with ball and racket, using a great mirror as a backboard, while on the bed his mother and this man groaned in approval, a monstrous twin-headed nude spectator.

Because by that time Word had taken French Edward over and made him quite a tennis player. French could beat Baby Levaster and all the college aces. At eighteen, he was a large angel-bodied tyrant of the court, who drove tennis balls through, outside, beyond and over the reach of any challenger Dr. Word could dig up. The only one who could give French Edward a match was Word himself, who was sixty and could run and knew the few faults French had, such as disbelieving Dr. Word could keep racing after the balls and knocking them back, French then knocking the odd ball ten feet out of court in an expression of sheer wonder. Furthermore, French had a tendency to soft-serve players he disliked, perhaps an unthinking gesture of derision or perhaps a self-inflicted handicap, to punish himself for ill will. For French's love of the game was so intense he did not want it fouled by personal uglinesses. He had never liked Dr. Word, even as he learned from him. He had never liked Word's closeness, nor his manufactured British or Boston accent, nor the zeal of his interest in him, which French supposed surpassed that of mere coach. For instance, Dr Word would every now and then give French Edward a *pinch*, a hard, affectionate little nip of the fingers.

And now French Edward was swollen with hatred of the man, the degree of which had no name. It was expelled on the second day of August, hottest day of the year. He called up Word for a match. Not practice, French said. A match. Dr. Word would have played with him in the rain. At the net, he pinched French as they took the balls out of the can. French knocked his hand away and lost games deliberately to keep the match going. Word glowed with a perilous self-congratulation for staying in there; French had fooled Word into thinking he was playing even with him. French pretended to fail in the heat, knocking slow balls from corner to corner, easing over a drop shot to watch the old man ramble up for it. French himself was tiring in the disguise of his ruse when the old devil keeled over, falling out in the alley with his racket clattering away. Dr. Word did not move, though the concrete must have been burning him. French had hoped for a heart attack. Word mumbled that he was cold and couldn't see anything. He asked French to get help.

'No. Buck up. Run it out. Nothing wrong with you,' said French.

'Is that you, French, my son?'

'I ain't your son. You might treat my mother like I was, but I ain't. I saw you.'

'A doctor. Out of the cold. I need medical help,' Dr. Word said.

'I got another idea. Why don't you kick the bucket?'

'Help.'

'Go on. Die. It's easy.'

When French got home, he discovered his mother escaping the heat in a tub of cold water. Their house was an unprosperous and unlevel connection of boxes. No door of any room shut properly. He heard her sloshing the water on herself. His father was up at Dick Lee's grocery watching the Cardinals on the television. French walked in on her. Her body lay under water up to her neck.'

'Your romance has been terminated,' he said.

'French?' She grabbed a towel off the rack and pulled it in the water over her.

'He's blind. He can't even find his way to the house anymore.'

'This was a sin, you to look at me!' Mrs. Edward cried.

'Maybe so,' French said, 'but I've looked before, when you had company.'

French left home for Baton Rouge, on the bounty of the scholarship Dr. Word had hustled for him through the athletic department at Louisiana State. French swore never to return. His father was a fool, his mother a lewd traitor, his mentor a snake from the blind side, the river a brown ditch of bile, his town a hill range of ashes and gloomy souvenirs of the Great Moment in Vicksburg. His days at college were numbered. Like that of most natural athletes, half French Edward's mind was taken over by a sort of tidal barbarous desert where men ran and struggled, grappling, hitting, cursing as some fell into the sands of defeat. The only professor he liked was one who spoke of 'muscular thought.' The professor said he was sick and tired of thought that sat on its ass and vapored around the room for the benefit of limp-wrists and their whiskey.

As for Dr. Word, he stumbled from clinic to clinic, guided by his brother Wilbur, veteran of Korea and colossal military boredoms all over the globe, before resettling in Vicksburg on the avant-garde of ennui.

Baby Levaster saw the pair in Charity Hospital when he was a med student at Tulane. Word's arm was still curled up with stroke and he had only a sort of quarter vision in one eye. His voice was frightful, like that of a man in a cave of wasps. Levaster was stunned by seeing Dr. Word in New Orleans. He hid in a closet, but Word had already recognized him. Brother Wilbur flung the door open, illuminating Levaster demurring under a bale of puke sheets.

'Our boy won the Southern!' shouted Word. 'He's the real thing, more than I ever thought!'

'Who are you talking about?' said Baby Levaster. The volume of the man had blown Levaster's eyebrows out of order.

'Well, French! French Edward! He won the Southern tournament in Mobile!'

Levaster looked to Wilbur for some mediator in this loudness. Wilbur cut away to the water fountain. He acted deaf.

'And the Davis Cup!' Word screamed. 'He held up America in the Davis Cup! Don't you read the papers? Then he went to Wimbledon!'

'French went to Wimbledon?'

'Yes! Made the quarterfinals!'

A nurse and a man in white came up to crush the noise from Word. Levaster went back into the closet and shut the door. Then he peeped out, seeing Word and his brother small in the corridor, Word limping slightly to the left, proceeding with a roll and capitulation. The stroke had wrecked him from brain to ankles, had fouled the centers that prevent screaming. Levaster heard Word bleating a quarter mile down the corridor.

Baby Levaster read in the *Times-Picayune* that French was resident pro at the Metairie Club, that French was representing the club in a tournament. Levaster hated med school. He hated the sight of pain and blood, and by this time he had become a thin, weak, balding drunkard of a very disagreeable order, even to himself. He dragged himself from one peak of cowardice to the next and began wearing sunglasses, and when he saw French Edward fend off Aussie, Wop, Frog, Brit and Hun in defending the pride of the Metairie Club, Levaster's body left him and was gathered into the body of French. He had never seen anything so handsome as French Edward. He had never before witnessed a man as happy and winsome in his occupation. Edward moved as if certain animal secrets were known to him. He originated a new, dangerous tennis, taking the ball into his racket with a muscular patience; then one heard the sweet crack, heard the singing ball, and hung cold with a little terror at the speed and the smart violent arc it made into the green. French was by then wearing spectacles. His coiled hair, the color of a kind of charred gold, blazed with sweat. On his lips was the charmed smile of the seraphim. Something of the priest and the brute mingled, perhaps warred, in his expression. Baby Levaster, who had no culture, could not place the line of beauty that French Edward descended from, but finally remembered a photograph of the David statue he'd seen in an old encyclopedia. French Edward looked like that.

When French Edward won, Levaster heard a louder, bale-

71

ful, unclublike bravo from the gallery. It was Dr. Word. Levaster watched Word fight through the crowd toward French. The man was crazed with partisanship. Levaster, wanting to get close to the person of French himself, three-quarters drunk on gin he'd poured into the iced Cokes from the stand, saw Word reach for French's buttock and give it a pinch. French turned, hate in his eyes. He said something quick and corrosive to Word. All the smiles around them turned to straight mouths of concern. Dr Word looked harmless, a tanned old fellow wearing a beige beret.

'You ought to be dead,' said French.

'As graceful, powerful an exhibition of the grandest game as your old coach would ever hope to see! I saw some of the old tricks I taught you! Oh, son, son!' Dr. Word screamed.

Everyone knew he was ill then.

'Go home,' said French, looking very soon sorry as he said it.

'You come home and see us!' Word bellowed, and left.

French's woman, Cecilia Emile, put her head on his chest. She was short, bosomy and pregnant, a Franco-Italian blessed with a fine large nose, the arrogance of which few men forgot. Next came her hair, a black field of delight. French had found her at LSU. They married almost on the spot. Her father was Fat Tim Emile, a low-key monopolist in pinball and wrestling concessions in New Orleans – filthy rich. Levaster did not know this. He stared at the strained hot eyes of French, having surrendered his body to the man, and French saw him.

'Baby Levaster? Is it you? From Vicksburg? You look terrible.'

'But you, you . . .' Levaster tripped on a tape and fell into the green clay around Edward's sneakers '. . . are beauty . . . my youth memory elegant, forever!'

The Edwards took Levaster home to Covington, across the bridge. The Edwards lived in a great glassy house with a pool in back and tall pines hanging over.

French was sad. He said, 'She still carries it on with him.

They meet out in the Civil War park at night and go to it in those marble houses. One of my old high-school sweethearts saw them and wrote me about it. She wrote it to hurt me, and it did hurt me.'

'That old fart Word? Impossible. He's too goddamn loud to carry on any secret rendezvous, for one thing. You could hear the bastard sigh from a half mile off.'

'My mother accepts him for what he is.'

'That man is destroyed by stroke.'

'I know. I gave it to him. She doesn't care. She takes the limping and the bad arm and the hollering. He got under her skin.'

'I remember her,' Baby Levaster said. 'Some handsome woman, auburn hair with a few gray ends. Forgive me, but I had teen-age dreams about her myself. I always thought she was waiting for a romance, living on the hope of something out there, something. . .'

'Don't leave me, Baby. I need your mind with me. Somebody from the hometown. Somebody who knows.'

'I used to whip your little ass at tennis,' Levaster said.

'Yes.' French smiled. 'You barely moved and I was running all over the court. You just stood there and knocked them everywhere like I was hitting into a fan.'

They became fast friends. Baby Levaster became an intern. He arrived sober at the funeral of the Edwards' newborn son and saw the tiny black grave its coffin went into behind the Catholic chapel. He looked over to mourners at the fringe. There were Dr. Word and his brother Wilbur under a mimosa, lingering off fifty feet from the rest. Word held his beret to his heart. Levaster was very glad that French never saw Word. They all heard a loud voice, but Word was on the other side of the hill by then, bellowing his sympathetic distress to Wilbur, and the Edwards could not see him.

'Whose voice was that?' asked French.

'Just a voice,' said Levaster.

'Whose? Don't I know it? It makes me sick.' French turned

back to Cecilia, covered with a black veil, her handkerchief pressed to lips. Her child had been born with dysfunction of the involuntary muscles. Her eyes rose toward the hot null blue of the sky. French supported her. His gaze was angrier. It penetrated the careless heart of nature, right in there to its sullen root.

On the other side of the cemetery, Dr. Word closed the door of the car. Wilbur drove. Loyal to his brother to the end, almost deaf from the pitch of his voice, Wilbur wheeled the car with veteran patience. Dr. Word wiped his head and held the beret to his chest.

'Ah, Wilbur! They were so unlucky! Nowhere could there be a handsomer couple! They had every right to expect a little Odysseus! Ah, to see doubt and sorrow cloud the faces of those young lovers! Bereft of hope, philosophy!'

Wilbur reached under the seat for the pint of philosophy he had developed since his tour of Korea. It was cognac. The brotherly high music came, tasting of burnt plums, revealing the faces of old officer friends to him.

'James,' he said. 'I think after this . . . that this is the moment, now, to break it off with Olive – forever. Unless you want to see more doubt and sorrow cloud the face of your young friend.'

Word's reply was curiously quiet.

'We cannot do what we cannot do. If she will not end it – and she will not – I cannot. Too deep a sense of joy, Wilbur. The whole quality of my life determined by it.'

'Ah, Jimmy,' Wilbur said, 'you were just too long a queer. The first piece you found had to be permanent. She ain't Cleopatra. If you'd just've started early, nailing the odd twat like the rest of us . . .'

'I don't want old soldier's reason! No reason! I will not suffer that contamination! Though I love you!'

Dr. Word was hollering again. Wilbur drove them back to Vicksburg.

Cecilia was too frightened to have another child after she

lost the first one. Her body would not carry one longer than a month. She was constantly pregnant for a while, and then she stopped conceiving. She began doing watercolors, the faintest violets and greens. French Edward took up the clarinet. Baby Levaster saw it: they were attempting to become art people. Cecilia was pitiful. French went beyond that into dreadfulness, ruesome honks poured from his horn. How wrong and unfortunate that they should have taken their grief into art, thought Levaster. It made them fools who were cut from glory's cloth, who were charmed darlings of the sun.

'What do you think?' asked French, after he'd hacked a little ditty from Mozart into a hundred froggish leavings.

'Yes,' Dr. Levaster said. 'I think I'll look through some of Cissy's pictures now.'

'You didn't like it,' French said, downcast, even angry.

'When are you going to get into another tournament? Why sit around here revealing your scabs to me and the neighbors? You need to get out and hit the ball.'

French left, walked out, smoldering and spiteful. Baby Levaster remained there. He knocked on Cecilia's door. She was at her spattered art desk working over a watercolor, her bare back to Levaster, her hair lying thick to the small of it, and below, her naked heels. Her efforts were thumb-tacked around from ceiling to molding, arresting one with their meek, awkward redundancies, things so demure they resisted making an image against the retina. They were not even clouds; rather, the pale ghosts of clouds: the advent of stains, hardly noticeable against paper.

'I can't turn around, but hello,' said Cecilia.

'What are all these about?'

'What do you think?'

'I don't know . . . smudges? The vagueness of all things?'

'They aren't things. They're emotions.'

'You mean hate, fear, desire, envy?'

'Yes. And triumph and despair.' She pointed.

'This is subtle. They look the same,' Levaster said.

75

'I know. I'm a nihilist.'

'You aren't any such thing.'

'Oh? Why not?'

'Because you've combed your hair. You wanted me to come in here and discover that you're a nihilist,' Levaster said.

'Nihilists can comb their hair.' She bit her lip, pouting.

'I'd like to see your chest. That's art.'

'You toilet. Leave us alone.'

'Maybe if you *are* art, Cissy, you shouldn't try to *do* art.'

'You want me to be just a decoration?'

'Yes,' Levaster said. 'A decoration of the air. Decoration is more important than art.'

'Is that what you learned in med school? That's dumb.' She turned around. 'A boob is a boob is a boob.'

Dr. Levaster fainted.

At the River Oaks Club in Houston, French played again. The old happiness came back to him, a delight that seemed to feed off his grace. The sunburned Levaster held French's towel for him, rosined French's racket handles, and coached him on the weaknesses of the opponents, which is unsportsmanly, untennislike, and all but illegal. A Spaniard Edward was creaming complained, and they threw Levaster off the court and back to the stands. He watched French work the court, roving back and forth, touching the ball with a deft chip, knocking the cooties off it, serving as if firing a curved musket across the net, the Spaniard falling distraught. And throughout, French's smile, widening and widening until it was just this side of loony. Here was a man truly at play, thought Levaster, at one with the pleasant rectangle of the court, at home, in his own field, something *peaceful* in the violent sweep of his racket. A certain slow anomalous serenity invested French Edward's motion. The thought of this parched Levaster.

'Christ, for a drink!' he said out loud.

'Here, son. Cold brandy.' The man Levaster sat next to

brought out a pint from the ice in a Styrofoam box. Levaster chugged it – exquisite! – then almost spat up the boon as he noticed the fellow on the far side of the brandy man. It was Dr. Word. The man beside Levaster was Wilbur. Word's noble cranium glinted under the sun. His voice had modulated.

'Ah, ah, my boy! An arc of genius,' Word whispered as they saw French lay a disguised lob thirty feet from the Spaniard. 'He's learned the lob, Wilbur! Our boy has it all now!' Word's voice went on in soft screaming. He seemed to be seeing keenly out of the left eye. The right was covered by eyelid, the muscles there having finally surrendered. So, Levaster thought, this is what the stroke finally left him.

'How's Vicksburg?' Levaster asked Wilbur.

'Nothing explosive, Doctor. Kudzu and the usual erosion.'

'What say you try to keep Professor Word away from French until he does his bit in the tournament. A lot depends on his making the finals here.'

'I'm afraid the professor's carrying a letter on him from Olive to French. That's why he's not hollering. He's got the letter. It's supposed to say everything.'

'But don't let French see him till it's over. And could I hit the brandy again?' Levaster said.

'Of course,' said Wilbur. 'One man can't drink the amount I brought over. Tennis bores the shit out of me.'

In the finals, Edward met Whitney Humble, a tall man from South Africa whose image and manner refuted the usual notion of the tennis star. He was pale, spindly, hairy, with the posture of a derelict. He spat phlegm on the court and picked his nose between serves. Humble appeared to be splitting the contest between one against his opponent and another against the excrescence of his own person. Some in the gallery suspected he served a wet ball. Playing as if with exasperated distaste for the next movement this game had dragged him to, Humble was nevertheless there when the ball came and knocked everything back with either speed or a snarling spin. The voice of Dr Word came cheering, bellowing for French. Humble identified the bald head in the audience that had hurrahed his error at the net. He served a line drive into the gallery that hit Word square in his good eye.

'Fault!' cried the judge. The crowd was horrified.

Humble placed his high-crawling second serve to French.

Levaster saw little of the remaining match. Under the bleachers, where they had dragged Word, Levaster and Wilbur attended to the great black peach that was growing around Word's good eye. With ice and a handkerchief, they abated the swelling, and then all three men returned to their seats. Dr Word could see out of a black slit of his optic cavity, see French win in a sequel of preposterous dives at the net. Levaster's body fled away from his bones and gathered on the muscles of French Edward. The crowd was screaming over the victory. Nowhere, nowhere, would they ever see again such a clear win of beauty over smut.

Fat Tim, Cecilia's father, would be happy and put five thousand in French's bank if French won this tournament, and Fat Tim would pay Levaster one thousand, as promised, for getting French back on the track of fame. Fat Tim Emile, thumbing those greasy accounts of his concessions, saw French as the family knight, a jouster among grandees, a champion in the whitest sport of all, a game Fat Tim viewed as a species of cunning highbrowism under glass. So he paid French simply for being himself, for wearing white, for symbolizing the pedigree Fat Tim was without, being himself a sweaty dago, a tubby with smudged shirt cuffs and phlebitis. 'Get our boy back winning. I want to read his name in the paper,' said Fat Tim. 'I will,' said Levaster.

So I did, thought Levaster. French won.

Dr. Levaster saw Dr. Word crowding up, getting swarmed out to the side by all the little club bitches and fuzzchins with programs for autographing in hand. Word fought back in, however, approaching French from the back. Levaster saw Word pinch French and heard Word bellow something hearty. By the time Levaster reached the court, the altercation had spread through the crowd. A letter lay in the clay dust, and Word, holding up his hand to ameliorate, was backing out of sight, his good eye but a glint in a cracked bruise, the lid falling gruesome.

'Baby! Baby!' called French, the voice baffled. Levaster reached him. 'He pinched me!' French screamed. 'He got me right there, really hard!'

Levaster picked up the letter and collected the rackets, then led French straight to the car. No shower, no street clothes.

My dearest French,

This is your mother Olive writing in case you had forgotten what my handwriting looks like. You have lost your baby son and I have thought of you these months. Now I ask you to think of me. I lost my grown son years ago. You know when, and you know the sin which is old history. I do not want to lose you, my darling. You are such a strange hand-somely made boy I would forget you were mine until I remem-bered you fed at my breast and I changed your diapers. When I saw you wearing new glasses at your wedding if I looked funny it was because I wanted to touch your eyes under them they changed you even more. But I knew you didn't want me anywhere near you. Your bride Cissy was charming as well as stunning and I'm deeply glad her father is well-off and you don't have to work for a living if you don't want to. Your father tried to play for a living or get near where there was athletics but it didn't work as smoothly for him. It drove him crazy, to be truthful. He was lost for a week in February until James Word, the bearer of this letter, found him at the college baseball field throwing an old wet football at home plate. He had been sleeping in the dugout and eating nothing but these dextrose and salt tablets. I didn't write you this before because you were being an expectant father and then the loss of your child. Maybe you get all your sports drive from your father. But you see how awfully difficult it was to live with him? Certain other things have happened before, I never told you about. He refereed a high-school football game between Nat-chez and Vicksburg and when it was tight at the end he threw a block on a Natchez player. We love him, French, but he has been away from us a long time.

So I fell in love with James Word. Don't worry, your father still knows nothing. That is sort of proof where his mind is, in a way. Your father has not even wanted 'relations' with me in years. He said he was saving himself up. He was in a poker game with some coaches at the college but they threw him out for cheating. James tried to arrange a tennis doubles game with me and your father against another couple, but your father tried to hit it so hard when it came to him that he knocked them over into the service station and etc. so we had no more balls.

The reason I sent this by James is because I thought if it was right from his hand you would see that it was not just a nasty slipping-around thing between us but a thing of the heart. His stroke has left him blind in one eye and without sure control of his voice. But he loves you. And he loves me. I believe God is with us too. Please take us all together and let's smile again. I am crying as I write this. But maybe that's not fair to mention that. James has mentioned taking us all, your father included, on a vacation to Padre Island in Texas, him paying all the expenses. Can't you please say yes and make everything happy?

Love, Mother

'It was his fingers pinching me,' whined French. 'He pinched me all the time when he was coaching me.'

Levaster said, 'And if he hadn't coached you, you wouldn't be anything at all, would you? You'd be selling storm fencing in Vicksburg, wouldn't you? You'd never have pumped that snatch or had the swimming pool.'

Back at his clinic, Levaster slept on a plastic couch in the waiting room. The nurse woke him up. He was so lonely and horny that he proposed to her, though he'd never had a clear picture of her face. Months ago he'd called her into his office. He'd had an erection for four days without rest.

'Can you make anything of this, Louise? Get the *Merck Manual*. Severe hardship even to walk.' She had been charming. But when he moved to her leg, clasping on it like a spaniel on the hot, she denied him, and he had since considered her a woman of principle.

She accepted his proposal. They married. Her parents, strong Methodists living somewhere out in New Mexico, appeared at the wedding. They stood in a corner, leaning inward like a pair of sculling oars. Levaster's mother came too, talking about the weather and her new shoes. Someone mistook her for nothing in one of the chairs and sat on her lap. French was best man. Cecilia was there, a dress of lime sherbet and titties, black hair laid back with gemlike roses at the temples. She made Levaster's bride look like something dumped out of a ship, a swathed burial at sea. Cecilia's beauty was unfair to all women. Furthermore, Levaster himself, compared to French (nugget-cheeked in a tux), was no beau of the ball. He was balding, waxen, all sweat, a small man with bad posture to boot.

Levaster expected to lean on the tough inner goodness of his bride, Louise. He wanted his life bathed and rectified. They resumed their life as doctor and nurse at the alley clinic, where Levaster undercharged the bums, winos, hustlers, hookers, artists and the occasional wayward debutante, becoming something of an expert on pneumonia, herpes, potassium famine and other diseases of the street. He leaned on the tough inner goodness of Louise, leaning and leaning, prone, supine, baby-opossum position. Levaster played tennis, he swam in the Edwards' pool, he stuck to beer and wine. In the last whole surge of his life, he won a set from French at the Metairie Club. This act caused Dr. Levaster a hernia and a frightful depletion of something untold in his cells, the rare *it* of life, the balm that washes and assures the brain happiness is around the corner. Levaster lost this sense for three months. He became a creature of the barbarous moment; he had lost patience. Now he cursed his patients and treated them as malingering clutter. He drank straight from a flask of rye laced with cocaine, swearing to the sick about the abominations they had wreaked on themselves. At

81

nights Levaster wore an oversized black sombrero and forced Louise into awkward and nameless desecrations. And when they were over, he called her an idiot, a puppet. Then one morning the hopeful clarity of the mind returned to him. He believed again in sun and grass and the affable complicity of the human race. But where was his wife? He wanted to lean on her inner goodness some more. Her plain face, her fine muscular pale legs, where were they? Louise was gone. She had typed a note. 'One more week of this and you'd have taken us to the bottom of hell. I used to be a weak but good person. Now I am strong and evil. I hope you're satisfied. Good-bye.'

At the clinic, his patients were afraid of him. The freeloaders and gutter cowboys shuddered. What will it be, Doc? 'French. It was French Edward who . . . took it away from me. It cost me. I suppose I wanted to defeat beauty, the outrage of the natural, the glibness of the God-favored. All in that one set of tennis. Ladies and gentlemen, the physician has been sick and he apologizes.' He coughed, dry in the throat. 'It cost me my wife, but I am open for business.' They swarmed him with the astounded love of sinners for a fallen angel. Levaster was nursed by whores. A rummy with a crutch fetched him coffee. Something, someone, in a sputum-colored blanket, functioned as receptionist.

At last he was home. He lived in a room of the clinic. On his thirty-fourth birthday, they almost killed him with a party and congratulations. The Edwards came. Early in the morning French found Levaster gasping over his fifth Cuban cigar on the roof of the clinic. The sky over New Orleans was a glorious blank pink.

'We're getting older, Baby.'

'You're still all right, French. You had all the moves at Forest Hills. Some bad luck, three bad calls. But still the crowd's darling. You could've beat Jesus at Wimbledon.'

'I always liked to play better than to win,' said French.

'I always liked to win better than to play,' said Levaster.

'But, Baby, I never played. First it was my father, then

Word. I don't know what kind of player I would be like if I truly *played* when I play.'

'But you smile when you play.'

'I love the game, on theory. And I admire myself.'

'You fool a lot of people. We thought you were happy.'

'I am. I feel like I'm doing something nearly as well as it could ever be done. But it's not play. It's slavery.'

'A slave to your talent.'

'And to the idea of tennis. But, Baby, when I die I don't want my last thought to be a tennis court. You've got people you've cured of disease to think about. They're down there giving you a party. Here I am, thirty-two.'

'I'm thirty-four. So what?'

'I want you to tell me, give me something to think about. You've done it before, but I want something big.' French pointed to the sky.

'I won't do that. Don't you understand that the main reason you're a star is the perfect mental desert you're able to maintain between your ears for hours and hours? You memorize the court and the memory sinks straight to your muscles, because there is nothing else in there to cloud the vision.'

'Are you calling me stupid?'

'No. But a wild psychic desert. I'm sure it works for artists as well as jocks.'

'You mean,' said French, 'I can't have a thought?'

'You could have one, but it wouldn't live for very long. Like most athletes, you'll go straight from glory to senility with no interlude of thought. I love you.' Levaster said.

French said, 'I love you, Baby.'

Dr. Levaster could no longer bear the flood of respect and affection spilling from the growing horde at the clinic. The *Times-Picayune* had an article about his work among the down-and-out. It was as if Levaster had to eat a tremendous barge of candy every day. The affection and esteem bore hard on a man convinced he was worthless. He had a hundred thousand in the bank. No longer could he resist. He bought a Lincoln demonstrator, shut the clinic, and drove to New York, carrying the double-barreled .410 shotgun/pistol with cherrywood handle paid to him in lieu of fee. He sifted into Elaine's, drunk, Southern and insulting, but was ignored. By the time Levaster had been directed to a sullen playwright, some target frailer than he, on whom he could pour the black beaker of his hatred of art, the movement of the crowd would change and Levaster would be swept away to a group of new enemies. Idlers, armchairers, martini wags, curators of the great empty museums (themselves), he called them. Not one of them could hold a candle to Willum Faulkner, Levaster shouted, having never read a page of the man. He drove his Lincoln everywhere, reveling in the hate and avarice of the city, disappearing into it with a shout of ecstasy.

Then Dr. Levaster met V.T., the Yugoslav sensation, drinking a beer at Elaine's with a noted sportswriter. Forest Hills was to begin the next day. Levaster approved of V.T. Heroic bitterness informed V.T.'s face and he dressed in bad taste, a suit with padded shoulders, narrow tie, pointy shoes.

'Who did you draw first round?' asked Levaster.

'Freench Edwaird,' V.T. said.

'Edward won't get around your serve if you're hitting it,' said the sportswriter. V.T.'s serve had been clocked at 170 mph at Wimbledon.

'Ees always who find the beeg rhythm. You find the beeg rhythm or you play on luck.'

'If you beat Edward tomorrow,' Levaster said, 'I will eat your suit.'

But the two men had turned away and never heard.

He took the Lincoln out to the West Side Tennis Club and tore his sweater clambering over a fence. He slept in a blanket he had brought with him, out of the dew, under the bleachers. When morning came, Levaster found the right court. The grass was sparkling. It was a heavy minor classic in the realm of tennis. The crowd loved French Edward and V.T., the both of them. When Edward hit one from behind the back for a winner off an unseen overhead smash from V.T., the crowd screamed. V.T. was in his rhythm and knocking his serve in at 160 mph. The crowd adored this too. French, who had always had a big, very adequate serve, took up the velocity of it to match the great bullet of V.T. At the end, they were men fielding nothing but white blurs against each other. Edward won.

For a half second the crowd was quiet. They had never imagined the ball could be kept in play at such stupendous speed. Then they roared. French Edward leaped over the net. Levaster swooned. His head sailed and joined the head of French Edward, rolled and tossed in the ale-colored curls. Then Levaster saw Dr. Word run out onto the grass, his bellowing lost in the crowd's bellowing. The old man, whose beret had fallen off on the churned service court, put his hand on French's back. Word looked frail, liver spots on his forearms, his scalp speckled and lined. Levaster saw French turn in anger. Then the both of them were overrun by a whirlpool of well-groomed tennis children and mothers and men who rode trains to work, half of their mental life revolving around improvement of the backhand. Levaster wished for his elegant pistol. He left, picking fights with those who looked askance at his blanket.

A few years passed and Levaster was almost forty. He opened the clinic in New Orleans again. Then he closed it and returned to New York. Now Levaster admitted that he languished when French Edward was out of his vision. A hollow inconsequence filled his acts, good or evil, whenever Edward was not near. He flew with Edward to France, to Madrid, to Prague. He lay angry and mordant with hangover on hotel beds as French Edward worked out on the terrible physical schedule Levaster had prescribed – miles of running, sit-ups, swimming, shadow-boxing.

Edward was hardly ever beaten in an early round, but he was fading in the third and fourth day of tournaments now.

He had become a spoiler against high seeds in early rounds, though never a winner. His style was greatly admired. A Portuguese writer called him 'the New Orleans ace who will not surrender his youth.' The Prague paper advocated him as 'the dangerous happy cavalier'; Madrid said, 'He fights windmills, but, viewing his style, we are convinced his contests matter. 'Yes, thought Levaster, this style must run its full lustrous route. It cannot throw in the towel until there is the last humiliation, something neither one of us can take.

Then it occurred to Levaster. French had never been humiliated in a match. He had lost, but he had never been humiliated. Not in a single match, not a single game. The handsome head had never bowed, the rusting gold of French Edward's curls stayed high in the sun. He remained the sage and brute that he was when he was nineteen. There was still the occasional winner off his racket that could never have been predicted by the scholars of the game. Levaster felt his soul rise in the applause for this. In Mexico City, there was a standing ovation for the most uncanny movement ever seen on the court. El Niño de Merida smacked down an overhead that bounced high and out of play over the backstop. But Edward had climbed the fence to field it, legs and one arm in the wire, racket hand free for the half second it took to strike the ball back, underhanded. The ball took a boomerang arc to the other side and notched the corner of the ad court. My Christ, thought Levaster, as the Mexicans screamed, he climbed the fence and never lost style.

When they returned from this trip, Levaster read in the paper about an open tournament at Vicksburg. Whitney Humble had already been signed up. The prize money was two thousand dollars, singles winner take all. They called it the Delta Open.

'I know Word has something to do with this. Nobody in Vicksburg ever gave a damn about tennis but him, you Baby, and me,' French Edward said.

'You should let the home folks finally see you. Your image would do wonders for the place,' said Levaster. 'They've read

86

about you. Now they want to see you. Why not? I've been wanting to go back and put a head-marker on my mother's grave, though it would be false to what she was. I've got all this money hanging around. I get sentimental, guilty. Don't you ever?'

'Yes,' French Edward said.

They went back to Vicksburg. On the second day of the tournament, they got a call at the Holiday Inn. Fat Tim Emile had died. Nobody had known he was dying but him. He had written a short letter full of pride and appreciation to Cecilia and French, thanking French for his association with the family and for valiant contests in the tennis world. Fat Tim left them two hundred thousand and insisted on nobody giving any ceremony. He wanted his remaining body to go straight to the Tulane med school. 'This body,' he wrote, 'it was fat maybe, but I was proud of it. Those young doctors-to-be, like Baby Levaster, might find something new in me. I was scared all my life and stayed honest. I never hurt another man or woman, that I know of. When I made money, I started eating well. Baby Levaster warned me. I guess I've died of success.'

'My poor Cecilia,' said French.

'Cissy is fine,' said Levaster. 'She said for you to finish the tournament.'

So he did.

Levaster looked on in a delirium of sober nostalgia. Through the trees, in a slit of the bluffs, he could see the river. French's mother and father sat together and watched their son. Dr. Word, near eighty, was a linesman. They are old people, thought Levaster, looking at the Edwards. And him, Word, he's a goddamned *relic*. A spry relic. Younger brother Wilbur was not there because he was dead.

Whitney Humble and French Edward met in the finals. Humble had aged gruesomely too, Levaster saw, and knew it was from fighting it out in small tournaments for almost two decades, earning bus fare and tiny fame in newspapers from Alabama to Idaho. But Humble still wanted to play. The color of a dead perch, thinner in the calf, Humble smoked cigarettes between ad games. All his equipment was gray and dirty, even his racket. He could not run much anymore. Some teeth were busted out.

A wild crowd of Vicksburg people, greasers and their pregnant brides from the mobile homes included, met to cheer French. Humble did not have a fan. He was hacking up phlegm and coughing out lengths of it, catching it on his shirt, a tort even those for the underdog could not abide. The greasers felt lifted to some estate of taste by Humble.

It was a long and sparkling match. Humble won.

Humble took the check and the sterling platter, hurled the platter outside the fence and into the trees, then slumped off.

The image of tennis was ruined for years in Vicksburg.

Dr. Word and the Edwards met French on the court. Levaster saw Word lift an old crabby arm to French's shoulder, saw French wince. Mr. Edward said he had to hurry to his job. He wore a comical uniform and cap. His job was checking vegetable produce at the bridge house of the river so that boll weevils would not enter Mississippi from Louisiana. Levaster looked into the eyes of Mrs. Edward. Yes, he decided, she still loves Word; her eyes touch him like fingers, and perhaps he still cuts it, and perhaps they rendezvous out in the Civil War cemetery so he won't have far to fall when he explodes with fornication, the old infantryman of lust.

'Mother,' said French, 'let's all meet at the bridge house.'

Levaster saw the desperate light in French's eye.

'Don't you, don't you!' said Levaster afterward, driving the Lincoln.

'I've got to. It'll clear the trash. I can't live in the world if Word's still in it.'

'He's nothing but bones,' said Levaster. 'He's done for.'

'She still loves him,' said French.

They all gathered at the bridge house, and French told his

father that his wife had been cheating on him for twenty years, and brought up his hands, and began crying, and pointed to Word. Mr. Edward looked at Word, then back to his son. He was terribly concerned. He asked Word to leave the little hut for a second, apologizing to Word. He asked Olive to come stand by him, and put his arm over his wife's shoulders.

'Son,' he whispered, 'Jimmy Word, friend to us and steady as a brick to us, is a homosexual. Look out there, what you've done to him. He's running.'

Then they were all strung out on the walkway of the bridge, Levaster marveling at how swift old Word was, for Word was out there nearing the middle of the bridge, Mrs. Edward next, fifty yards behind, French passing his mother, gaining on Word. Levaster was running too. He, too, passed Olive, who had given out and was leaning on the rail. Levaster saw Word mount the rail and balance on it like a gymnast. He put on a burst of speed and caught up with French, who had stopped running and was walking toward Word cautiously, his hand on the rail.

'Just close your eyes, son, I'll be gone,' Word said, looking negligible as a spirit in his smart tennis jacket and beret. He trembled on the rail. Below Word was the sheen of the river, the evening sun lying over it down there, low reds flashing on the brow water.

That's a hundred feet down there, Levaster thought. When he looked up, French had gotten up on the rail and was balancing himself, moving step by step toward Word.

'Don't,' said Levaster and Word together.

French, the natural, was walking on the rail with the ease of an avenue hustler. He had found his purchase: this sport was nothing.

'Son! No closer!' bawled Word.

'I'm not your son. I'm bringing you back, old bastard.'

They met. French seemed to be trying to pick up Word in an infant position, arm under legs. Word's beret fell off and floated, puffed out, into the deep hole over the river. French had him, had him wrestled into the shape of a fetus. Then Word gave a kick and Olive screamed, and the two men fell backward into the red air and down. Levaster watched them coil together in the drop.

There was a great deal of time until they hit. At the end, Edward flung the old suicide off and hit the river in a nice straight-legged jump. Word hit the water flat as a board. Levaster thought he heard the sound of Word's back breaking.

The river was shallow here, with strong devious currents. Nothing came up. By the time the patrol got out, there was no hope. Then Levaster, standing in a boat, spotted French, sitting under a willow a half mile downriver from the bridge. French had drowned and broken one leg, but had crawled out of the river by instinct. His brain was already choked.

French Edward stared at the rescue boat as if it were a turtle with vermin gesturing toward him, Levaster and Olive making their cries of discovery.

Carina, Levaster's teen-ager, woke him up. She handed him a cold beer and a Dexedrine. At first Levaster did not understand. Then he knew that the sun had come up again, seeing the grainy abominable light on the alley through the window. This was New York. Who was this child? Why was he naked on the sheets?

Ah, Carina.

'Will you marry me, Carina?' Levaster said.

'Before I saw your friend, I might have,' she said.

French Edward came into the room, fully dressed, hair wet from a shower.

'Where do I run, Baby?' he said.

Levaster told him to run around the block fifty times.

'He does everything you tell him?' said Carina.

'Of course he does. Fry me some eggs, you dumb twat.'

As the eggs and bacon were sizzling, Levaster came into the kitchen in his Taiwan bathrobe, the huge black sombrero on his head. He had oiled and loaded the .410 shotgun/pistol.

90

'Put two more eggs on for French. He's really hungry after he runs.'

Carina broke two more eggs.

'He's so magnificent,' she said. 'How much of his brain does he really have left?'

'Enough,' Levaster said.

Levaster drove them to New Hampshire, to Bretton Woods. He saw Laver and Ashe approach French Edward in the lobby of the inn. They wanted to shake hands with French, but he did not recognize them. French stood there with hands down, looking ahead into the wall.

The next day Levaster took French out on the court for his first match. He put the Japanese Huta into his hand. It was a funny manganese and fiberglass racket with a split throat. The Huta firm had paid French ten thousand to use it on the circuit just before he drowned in the river. French had never hit with it before.

French was looking dull. Levaster struck him a hard blow against the heart. French started and gave a sudden happy regard to the court.

'I'm here,' said French.

'You're damned right. Don't let us down.'

Edward played better than he had in years. He was going against an Indian twenty years his junior. The boy had a serve and a wicked deceptive blast off his backhand. The crowd loved the Indian. The boy was polite and beautiful. But then French Edward had him at match point on his serve.

Edward threw the ball up.

'Hit it, *hit*. My life, hit it,' whispered Levaster.

91

GREEN GETS IT

UNABLE TO SWIM, he had maneuvered to fall off an old-timers' party yacht in the Hudson River. His departure was not remarked by the revelers. They motored on toward the Atlantic and he bobbed around in the wash. He couldn't swim. But he did. He learned how. Before he knew it, he was making time and nearing the dock where a small Italian liner sat dead still, white, three stories high. Nobody was around when he pulled up on a stray rope on the wharf and walked erect to the street, where cars were flashing. Day after tomorrow was his seventieth birthday. What a past, he said. I've *survived*. Further, I'm horny and vindictive. Does the fire never stop?

Out of his wet billfold he withdrew the sodden money and his government card, yellow, with his name on it: Quarles Green. His parents wanted to compensate for the last name with a fancy front one, poor dogs of Alabama, 1900. Hell of a year for dumb fornication, though, said Quarles aloud. Like all years.

He had never had a satisfactory carnal experience in his life.

What about the letters I wrote? he said as he walked to the concrete and traffic. Can I bear the humiliation of surviving after them, especially the one to Jill Jones? Won't she see it as the last feather on the ton of boredom, my appearing, hello, I'm not dead, let's do it again? Walk around in the nude doing house duties, cleaning, sweeping, cooking, me trailing in the wheelchair behind, taking her fathom like crazy. I've seen better bodies, but hers is earnest and scandalous enough. Pretending to be a crip so my lust would not disgust her from the room. Developed a real crush on her. At forty a week per Wednesday, I ought to be allowed it. Apologized for the crude sniffing episode unfortunately when I rolled in behind her as she was using the vacuum cleaner. Inadvertence of the wheel here, dear. She never heard the snorts for her vacuum.

I burn to see her, but she lives in Yonkers. Dye my hair, appear at her window with a cello.

He paid the cab with his wet money.

'What'd you do, fall in the river?' said the guy.

But Quarles didn't answer. Quarles was busy whispering:

My beloved Daughter,

Thanks to you for being one of the few who never blamed me for your petty, cheerless and malign personality. But perhaps you were too busy being awful to ever think of the cause. I hear you take self-defense classes now. Don't you understand nobody could take anything from you without leaving you richer? If I thought rape would change you, I'd hire a randy cad myself. I leave a few dollars to your husband. Bother him about them and suffer the curse of this old pair of eyes spying blind at the minnows in the Hudson.

Your Dad, Crabfood

At the Y he found his suitcase and left for La Guardia on bicycle. Once out into the real mainway traffic, he heard the outraged automobiles blowing at him. Let no policeman interfere, he pleaded. This is New York's last chance at me. He passed the toll at the bridge without even looking their way. There was a shout. Kill me, kill me, he shouted, answering. Then up into the wind of the Triborough Bridge. Shit, I've overpedaled; where's La Guardia, anyway? he cursed himself. Then he remembered and turned around mid-bridge. He made it back and passed the tollkeepers, shouting imprecations.

His bike came in near thirty miles an hour over the last hump of the bridge, and there wasn't much traffic now. He extinguished the lights.

Why didn't I ever drink or smoke? he asked. I killed two men who did when I was intercepting hooch. I never had any bad habits. My body keeps on. I think I'm getting stronger. I've gotten a third wind. He turned back toward La Guardia.

This is such small tooling. I rode the first mass-produced motorcycle in America. Because of my lust habit, I can't afford even a city Honda. Hundred sixty a month to trail Jill around in my phony wheelchair. Rental of the wheelchair fifty per. If I get back to Memphis I can afford something, if I've got to live.

My car was full of prime confiscated booze. It was summer in the Ozarks. I got her drunk and possessed her on the pine needles. She went hysterical and wouldn't put her clothes back on without promise of marriage. After I married her, she seldom took them off again. Some nights she slept in overalls and a belted cold-weather coat. I stared at ceilings all over America and practiced self-abuse, thinking there was a government camera in the wall and hurling myself under the sacred bed of my snoring matrimony, afraid of God. Then that morning I crawled out over the towel of her latest shampoo, full of flint-colored hair. I gazed in my palms with terror, thinking the hair of the old stories was true.

Later in the day she cooked three hot meals, wildly neutral as to taste. She told me she thought a blessed event was coming to us. How? When? I wondered. I was dismayed by the holiness of my marriage. I got a glimpse of her ankle and climbed up on the roof, weeping. When I came down I didn't care anymore. I wore the purple smoking jacket I'd bought for our honeymoon and stored away when she said it was snaky. When she said something, I said (I had lime-scented oil in my hair):

'So you don't even have natural needs?' pouring myself a near beer. 'All you care about is moving chairs and pictures, from room to room. Between me and a bucket of paint to freshen up the front porch, you'd choose the paint and we both know it. Me and God hate you.'

She fell in a spasm. She cried out how she could be a full wife.

'Let's go all the way,' says I.

'Anything to please you and the Lord,' says she.

Soon afterward I had to blast a stiller who locked himself in a hooch shack, but he was underground and we didn't know it when we set it afire. I heard the voice calling me. He knew me. It was just outside Mobile in my home grounds and they knew I was with the Volstead people. Calling me, Quarles? Quarles? I ran up to the door and there was Weeber Batson's oldest son standing at the window with his clothes on fire and a double-barrel eight-gauge in his hands right on me, cocking it.

I had to blast him. I hit him right in the hair.

The guys kept calling him just a stiller, but I knew better and I was sick at heart. Oh, she really got interested in me when I was sick. That's when she comes alive, going around with cold towels and that cold mud porridge she got off the recipe of her aunt who was even a colder warp than her, or more honest: the aunt never married. When I got well, we were in Arizona holding down the corn beer production on the Apache reservation. It suited me. I didn't want to be near Mobile again. And on the reservation there was a drunk Indian I shot, about seventy years old. He claimed he'd been under old Geronimo, who died in aught-twelve or so. Nobody had a gun when the old guy run up all corned to the eyes, five of us agents sitting around a fire lying about strange vegetation and nooky we'd been among. For fifteen minutes we heard him yell he was going to kill us with his bow and arrow he had on him. We tried to kid it off him, but he kept stamping around and aiming it. I wasn't scared, but the senior was, and he told me to get the heater out of the car. It was a Tommy gun. When I got back, the old Indian was stamping on their feet and spitting on them,

95

making sounds like *otta, otta*! over and over. He took their hats off them and threw them in the fire.

When he saw me come up with the gun, he smiled like a coon. For an old guy he had surprising white teeth even though all the rest of him was filthy. Then he took the arrow back and shot me square in the solar plexus with it, the crazy idiot. This filthy arrow was in me, it felt like right in my heart, and I looked over and all the agents were so juiced on corn beer they still thought it was a fun house when I needed help. So I shot about a quarter of the Tommy into him and he backed up ten yards and fell flat. I didn't want to die alone. It sobered them up, quick, before I fainted. Luckily I had a big chest when I was young and the point was hanging in there a half inch from the fatals, said the doctor. The old Indian never bothered my sleep much. I think he wanted it bad.

Like me now, said Quarles on his bike. He saw the lights of La Guardia. I'm going to make it. Again, dammit.

I ride this bicycle in honor of the other one I got, he thought. The drive-in barbecue in Mobile when I chanced to go down again.

My wife had left to join Billy Graham's World Crusade, in the choir. I never even knew she could sing before Graham came to Chicago. Graham came to town and she did a voice audition for the choir. They put her in the first rank of sopranos. Tokyo, Stockholm, The Hague, Glasgow, Dallas, and even New York. I saw her in my telescope at Shea Stadium, weighs about two hundred, but a mouth like a harp-shaped cunt. Thank Ol' Massa I don't have to run those rapids anymore, said Quarles Green. I used to play my little pieces on the cello to heat her up. She'd fall asleep and break her Christian wind.

If only I'd married a good pagan woman who never tired of the pleasures of the flesh, said Green in the wind of the entrance to La Guardia.

Don't lie, he said louder. You would have done the same. You would have killed the same two. Perish clean at least.

I was in the new FBI of America. I had my card. Three of us were in the drive-in barbecue lot in Mobile. Somebody recognized me as the killer of Weeber Batson's son. They started calling out at me when I was eating my ribs, which was a large part of why I took another Mobile assignment, the ribs at Boudreaux's Pit. Some of the waiters used bicycles. I didn't know they paid the Negro to come over and say these things to me.

'Pardon me. Is yo name Toid?'

'What?' I said.

'Erruh, yo name Mister Terrid?'

'He's saying *turd*,' said one of the agents.

'It certainly is,' I said to the boy on the bicycle. 'I'm Mister Turd. How did you find me?' He was a pretty mulatto boy and looked very wise.

'I just find you, Mister Terrid,' said he. He pedaled back to the rear of the blockhouse where the cooking was.

I put the silencer attachment on my pistol. It was the first mass-produced silencer to come out. I told them we had to follow that boy home. He knew things about me.

It was easy. He left at one in the morning on his bicycle and struck out toward the west end, heart of niggertown. We trolled behind as if looking at the bay. His bike was lit up front and back and you could see him like a new dime on black cloth. We got into niggertown and stopped at a vacant lot where an old house had been pulled over. Somebody came out of the boards in man's clothes but you could tell it was a girl. She hugged him while he was standing astraddle the bike. We went by like an idle lost car and I saw the girl was white. She was a plain white girl, no beauty about her. But she was passionate. She was all over him.

The next time we passed, I got out of the car.

'Hi. I'm Mister Turd. Remember?'

'Yes suh.'

'What're you doing, boy, begging on your hands and knees

97

for bad news? Don't you know anything about Mobile's miscegenation law?'

'Its what?'

'No black on white.'

'But you with the federals. You kill Weeber Batson's boy.'

'You know everything. Is that why you're sweet on him, 'cause he knows everything?' I said. But the girl never uttered a word.

One of the agents told me to get back in the car. I told them shut up, I wasn't any hothead. The thing was, I was mortified, confused and jealous.

'Wouldn't nobody else have you at your high school?' I said to her.

Standing astraddle his bike, the boy chopped me right in the jaw. I had the gun and he saw it and he still chopped me. I was seeing through a hot orange mist. At least I had the presence of mind not to kill him. I only shot him in the thigh. You could hear the rush of a whisper from the silencer. I was immediately repentant.

'Let's get you to the hospital, son,' says I. He was still astride the bike.

'I ain't going to no hospiter you takes me to,' he said. 'Miss Edith, you come sit behind and pedal for my bad leg. I'll do the other one with the good one.'

She sat on the rear fender and they went off in the damned most bizarre juxtaposition you ever saw. Similar to a circus tandem but not for fun. This was loyalty and romance, brothers. I know he was leaving blood up the road, though you couldn't see it at night. The bike was wobbling all over the place, but they were going ahead.

And since then I have been a worm.

I left the south for ten years, then got my quarters in Memphis. That was some man, that boy. I wouldn't touch Mobile again with a three-hundred-mile pole.

Quarles Green made La Guardia and waited a cold six hours

for the plane to Memphis. He was a miracle of patience. He read nothing, hardly changed position, smoked nothing, watched no pay TV, wet his underwear imperceptibly.

Reynolds will be the only one in Memphis who might be alive that would remember me from the old days, he thought. Reynolds who's had thirty names in his time, on three continents. I did my bit in the Second. Cornered the Nazi czar of Fort Worth and his fifteen rifles.

When the plane was in the air he asked for headphones.

The stewardess passed him. She was a big leggy blond girl, a superlative quite at ease in the jumbo jet. She was desire trebled out. Quarles Green felt the last big pang. He wanted to take up habitation in her, such as a baby kangaroo.

A terrific fist bashed him directly on the heart.

He smiled at her with his headphones on, snapping his fingers.

'Catchy,' he said, pointing at the phones. 'Groovy, for your generation.'

She winked and passed by. He sat there awhile and died. The stewardess wanted to know the tune the old white-haired boy was grooving on. She lifted up her own pair in her dressing room. Nothing was coming over them. There was only a howling, like waves in a storm of particles.

When she was out of the room, she saw Dana and asked her.

'The whole system's screwed up by lightning or something. None of the headphone FMs are any good,' said Dana.

The stewardess walked back to look at Quarles Green. He had a tight smug smile on him, his eyes closed, like every dead man who finally hears his tune.

MIDNIGHT AND
I'M NOT FAMOUS YET

I WAS WALKING around Gon one night, and this C-man —
I saw him open the window, and there was a girl in back of
him, so I thought it was all right — peeled down on me and
shot the back heel off my boot. Nearest I came to getting
mailed home when I was there. A jeep came by almost
instantly with a thirty cal mounted, couple of allies in it. I
pointed over to the window. They shot out about a box and
a half on the apartment, just about burned out the dark slot
up there. As if the dude was hanging around digging the
weather after he shot at me. There were shrieks in the night,
etc.. But then a man opened the bottom door and started
running in the street. This ARVN fellow knocked the shit
out of his buddy's head turning the gun to zap the running
man. Then I saw something as the dude hit a light: he was
fat. I never saw a fat Cong. So I screamed out in Vietnamese.
He didn't shoot. I took out my machine pistol and ran after
the man, who was up the street by now, and I was hobbling
without a heel on my left boot.

Some kind of warm nerve sparklers were getting all over
me. I believe in magic, because, million-to-one odds, it was
Ike 'Tubby' Wooten, from Redwood, a town just north of
Vicksburg. He was leaning on a rail, couldn't run anymore.
He was wearing the uniform of our Army with a patch on
it I didn't even know what was. Old Tubby would remember
me. I was the joker at our school. I once pissed in a Dixie
cup and eased three drops of it on the library radiator. But

100

Tubby was so serious, reading some photo magazine. He peeped up and saw me do it, then looked down quickly. When the smell came over the place, he asked me, Why? What do you want? What profit is there in that? I guess I just giggled. Sometimes around midnight I'd wake up and think of his questions, and it disturbed me that there was no answer. I giggled my whole youth away. Then I joined the Army. So I thought it was fitting I'd play a Nelda on him now. A Nelda was invented by a corporal when they massacred a patrol up north on a mountain and he was the only one left. The NVA ran all around him and he had his empty rifle hanging on him. They spared him.

'I'm a virgin! Spare me!'

'You, holding the gun? Did you say you were a virgin?' said poor Tubby, trying to get air.

'I am a virgin,' I said, which was true, but hoping to get a laugh, anyway.

'And a Southern virgin. A captain. Please to God, don't shoot me,' that fat boy said. 'I was cheating on my wife for the first time. The penalty shouldn't be death.'

'Why'd you run from the house, Tubby?'

'You know me.' Up the street they had searchlights moved up all over the apartment house. They shot about fifty rounds into the house. They were shooting tracers now. It must've lit up my face; then a spotlight went by us.

'Bobby Smith,' said Tubby. 'My God, I thought you were God.'

'I'm not. But it seems holy. Here we are looking at each other.'

'Aw, Bobby, they were three beautiful girls. I'd never have done the thing with one, but there were *three*.' He was a man with a small pretty face laid around by three layers of jowl and chin. 'I heard the machine gun and the guilt struck me. I had to get out. So I just ran.'

'Why're you in Nam, anyway?'

'I joined. I wasn't getting anything done but being in love with my wife. That wasn't doing America any good.'

'What's that patch on you?'

'Photography.' He lifted his hands to hold an imaginary camera. 'I'm with the Big Red. I've done a few things out of helicopters.'

'You want to see a ground unit? With me. Or does Big Red own you?'

'I have no idea. There hasn't been much to shoot. Some smoking villages. A fire in a bamboo forest. I'd like to see a face.'

'You got any pictures of Vicksburg?'

'Oh, well, a few I brought over.'

The next day I found out he was doing idlework and Big Red didn't care where he was, so I got him over in my unit. I worried about his weight, etc., and the fact he might be killed. But the boys liked a movie-cameraist being along and I wanted to see the pictures from Vicksburg. It was nice to have Tubby alongside. He was hometown, such as he was. Before we flew out north, he showed me what he had. There was a fine touch in his pictures. There was a cute little Negro on roller skates, and an old woman on a porch, a little boy sleeping in a speedboat with the river in the background. Then there was a blurred picture of his wife naked, just moving through the kitchen, nothing sexy. The last picture was the best. It was John Whitelaw about to crack a golf ball. Tubby had taken it at Augusta, at the Masters. I used to live about five houses away from the Whitelaws. John had his mouth open and his arms, the forearm muscles, were bulked up plain as wires.

John was ten years older than me, but I knew about him. John Whitelaw was our only celebrity since the Civil War. In the picture he wore spectacles. It struck me as something deep, brave, mighty and, well, modern; he had to have the eyeglasses on him to see the mighty thing he was about to do. Maybe I sympathized too much, since I have to wear glasses too, but I thought this picture was worthy of a statue. Tubby had taken it in a striking gray-and-white grain. John seemed to be hitting under a heroic deficiency. You could see

the sweat droplets on his neck. His eyes were in an agony.
But the thing that got me was that John Whitelaw *cared* so
much about what he was doing. It made me love America to
know he was in it, and I hadn't loved anything for nigh three
years then. Tubby was talking about all this 'our country'
eagle and stars mooky and had seen all the war movies
coming over on the boat. I never saw a higher case of fresh
and crazy in my life.

But the picture of John at Augusta, it moved me. It was a
man at work and play at the same time, doing his damnedest.
And Whitelaw was a beautiful man. They pass that term
'beautiful' around like pennies nowadays, but I saw him in
the flesh once. It was fall in Baton Rouge, around the campus
of LSU. He was getting out of a car with a gypsyish girl on
his hand. I was ten, I guess, and he was twenty. We were
down for a ball game, Mississippi vs. Louisiana, a classic
that makes you goo-goo eyed when you're a full-grown man
if your heart's in Dixie, etc. At ten, it's Ozville. So in the
middle of it, this feeling, I saw Whitelaw and his woman.
My dad stopped the car.

'Wasn't that Johnny Whitelaw?' he asked my grandfather.

'You mean that little peacock who left football for golf?
He ought to be quarterbacking. Ole Miss right now. It
wouldn't be no contest,' said my grandfather.

I got my whole idea of what a woman should look like
that day . . . and what a man should be. The way John
Whitelaw looked, it sort of rebuked yourself ever hoping to
call yourself a man. The girl he was with woke up my clammy
little dreams about, not even sex, but the perfect thing – it
was something like her. As for Whitelaw, his face was curled
around by that wild hair the color of beer; his chest was
deep, just about to bust out of that collar and bow tie.

'That girl he had, she had a drink in her hand. You could
hardly see her for her hair,' said my grandfather.

'Johnny got him something Cajun,' said my father.

Then my grandfather turned around, looking at me like I
was a crab who could say a couple of words. 'You look like

103

your mother, but you got gray eyes. What's wrong? You have to take a leak?'

Nothing was wrong with me. I'd just seen John Whitelaw and his girl, that was all.

Tubby had jumped a half-dozen times at Fort Bragg, but he had that heavy box harnessed on him now and I knew he was going down fast and better know how to hit. I explained to him. I went off the plane four behind him, cupping a joint. I didn't want Tubby seeing me smoking grass, but it's just about the only way to get down. If the Cong saw the plane, you'd fall into a barbecue. They've killed a whole unit before, using shotguns and flame bullets, just like your ducks floating in. You hear a lot of noise going in with a whole unit in the air like this. We start shooting about a hundred feet from ground. If you ever hear one bullet pass you, you get sick thinking there might be a lot of them. All you can do is point your gun down and shoot it all out. You can't reload. You never hit anything. There's a sharpshooter, McIntire, who killed a C shooting from his chute, but that's unlikely. They've got you like a gallery of rabbits if they're down there.

I saw Tubby sinking fast over the wrong part of the field. I had two chutes out, so I cut one off and dropped over toward him, pulling on the left lines so hard I almost didn't have a chute at all for a while. I got level with him and he looked over, pointing down. He was doing his arm up and down. Could have been farmers or just curious rubbernecks down in the field, but there were about ten of them grouped up together, holding things. They weren't shooting, though. I was carrying an experimental gun, me and about ten of my boys. It was a big, light thing; really, it was just a launcher. There were five shells in it, bigger than shotgun shells. If you shot one of them, it was supposed to explode on impact and burn out everything in a twenty-five-yard radius. It was a mean little mother of phosphorus, is what it was. I saw the boys shooting them down into the other side of the field.

104

This stuff would take down a whole tree and you'd chute into a quiet smoking bare area.

I don't know. I don't like a group waiting on me when I jump out of a plane. I almost zapped them, but they weren't throwing anything up. Me and Tubby hit the ground about the same time. They were farmers. I talked to them. They said there were three Cong with them until we were about a hundred feet over. The Cong knew we had the phosphorus shotgun and showed ass, loping out to the woods fifty yards to the north when me and Tubby were coming in.

Tubby took some film of the farmers. All of them had thin chin beards and soft hands because their wives did most of the work. They essentially just lay around and were hung with philosophy, and actually were pretty happy. Nothing had happened around here till we jumped in. These were fresh people. I told them to get everybody out of the huts because we were going to have a thing in the field. It was a crisis point. A huge army of NVA was coming down and they just couldn't avoid us if they wanted to have any run of the valley five miles south. We were there to harass the front point of the army, whatever it was like.

'We're here to check their advance,' Tubby told the farmers.

Then we all collected in the woods, five hundred and fifty souls, scared out of mind. What we had going was we knew the NVA general bringing them down was not too bright. He went to the Sorbonne and we had this report from his professor: 'Li Dap speaks French very well and had studied Napoleon before he got to me. He knows Robert Lee and the strategy of Jeb Stuart, whose daring circles around an immense army captured his mind. Li Dap wants to be Jeb Stuart. I cannot imagine him in command of more than five hundred troops.'

And what we knew stood up. Li Dap had tried to circle left with twenty thousand and got the hell kicked out of him by idle Navy guns sitting outside Gon. He just wasn't very bright. He had half his army climbing around these bluffs, no artillery or air force with them, and it was New Year's Eve for our side.

'So we're here just to kill the edge of their army?' said Tubby.

'That's what I'm here for, why I'm elected. We kill more C's than anybody else in the Army.'

'But what if they take a big run at you, all of them?' said Tubby.

'There'll be lots of cooking.'

We went out in the edge of the woods and I glassed the field. It was almost night. I saw two tanks come out of the other side of our pickets running back. Pock, pock, pock from the tanks. Then you saw this white glare on one tank where somebody on our team had laid on with one of the phosphorus shotguns. It got white and throbbing, like a little star, and the gun wilted off of it. The other tank ran off a gully into a hell of a cow pond. You wouldn't have known it was that deep. It went underwater over the gun, and they let off the cannon when they went under, raising the water in a spray. It was the silliest-looking thing. Some of them got out and a sergeant yelled for me to come up. It was about a quarter mile out there. Tubby got his camera, and we went out with about fifteen troops.

At the edge of the pond, looking into flashlights, two tankmen sat, one tiny, the other about my size. They were wet, and the big guy was mad. Lot of the troops were chortling, etc. It was awfully damned funny, if you didn't happen to be one of the C-men in the tank.

'Of all the fuck-ups. This is truly saddening.' The big guy was saying something like that. I took a flashlight and looked him over. Then I didn't believe it. I told Tubby to get a shot of the big cursing one. Then they brought them on back. I told the boys to tie up the big one and carry him in.

I sat on the ground, talking to Tubby.

'It's so quiet. You'd think they'd be shelling us,' he said.

'We're spread out too good. They don't have much ammo now. They really galloped down here. That's the way Li Dap

106

does it. Their side's got big trouble now. And, Tubby, me and you are famous.'

'Me, what?'

'You took his picture. You can get some more, more arty angles on him tomorrow.'

'Him?'

'It's Li Dap himself. He was in the tank in the pond.'

'No. Their general?'

'You want me to go prove it?'

We walked over. They had him tied around a tree. His hands were above his head and he was sitting down. I smelled some hash in the air. The guy who was blowing it was a boy from Detroit I really liked, and I hated to come down on him, but I really beat him up. He never got a lick in. I kicked his rump when he was crawling away and some friends picked him up. You can't have lighting up that shit at night on the ground. Li Dap was watching the fight, still cursing.

'Asshole of the mountains.' He was saying something like that. 'Fortune's ninny.'

'Hi, General. My French isn't too good. You speak English. Honor us.'

He wouldn't say anything.

'You have a lot of courage, running out front with the tanks.' There were some snickers in the bush, but I cut them out quick. We had a real romantic here and I didn't want him laughed at. He wasn't hearing much, though. About that time two of their rockets flashed into the woods. They went off in the treetops and scattered.

'It was worthy of Patton,' I said. 'You had some bad luck. But we're glad you made it alive.'

'Kiss my ass.'

'You want your hands free? Oliver, get his ropes off the tree.' The guy I beat up cut him off the tree.

'You scared us very deeply. How many tanks do you have over there?'

'Nonsense,' he said.

'What do you have except for a few rockets?'

'I had no credence in the phosphorus gun.'

'Your men saw us use them when we landed.'

'I had no credence.'

'So you just came out to see.'

'I say to them never to fear the machine when the cause is just. To throw oneself past the technology tricks of the monsters and into his soft soul.'

'And there you will win, huh?'

'Of course. It is our country.' He smiled at me. 'It's relative to your war in the nineteenth century. The South had slavery. The North must purge it so that it is a healthy region of our country.'

'You were out in the tank as an example to your men?'

'Yes!'

All this hero needed was a plumed hat.

'Sleep well,' I said, and told Oliver to get him a blanket and feed him, and feed the tiny gunner with him.

When we got back to my dump, I walked away for a while, not wanting to talk with Tubby. I started crying. It started with these hard sobs coming up like rocks in my throat. I started looking out at forever, across the field. They shot up three more rockets from the woods below the hill. I waited for the things to land on us. They fell on the tops of trees, nothing near me, but there was some howling off to the right. Somebody had got some shrapnel.

I'd killed so many gooks. I'd killed them with machine guns, mortars, howitzers, knives, wire, me and my boys. My boys loved me. They were lying all around me, laying this great cloud of trust on me. The picture of John Whitelaw about to hit the ball at Augusta was jammed in my head. There was such care in his eyes, and it was only a golf ball, a goddamned piece of nothing. But it was wonderful and peaceful. Nobody was being killed. Whitelaw had the right. He had the beloved American right to the pursuit of happiness. The tears were out of my jaws then. Here we shot each other up. All we had going was the pursuit of horror. It seemed to me my life had gone straight from teen-age giggling to horror. I had never had time to be but two things, a giggler and a killer.

Christ, I was crying for myself. I had nothing for the other side, understand that. North Vietnam was a land full of lousy little Commie robots, as far as I knew. A place of the worst propaganda and hypocrisy. You should have read some of their agitprop around Gon, talking about freedom and throwing off the yoke, etc. The gooks went for Communism because they were so ignorant and had nothing to lose. The South Vietnamese, too. I couldn't believe we had them as allies. They were such a pretty and uniformly indecent people. I once saw a little taxi boy, a kid is all, walk into a Medevac with one arm and a hand blown off by a mine he'd picked up. These housewives were walking behind him in the street, right in the middle of Gon. Know what they were doing? They were laughing. They thought it was the most hysterical misadventure they'd ever seen. These people were on our side. These were our friends and lovers. That happened early when I got there. I was a virgin when I got to Nam and stayed a virgin, through a horde of B-girls, the most base and luscious-lipped hustlers. Because I did not want to mingle with this race.

In an ARVN hospital tent you see the hurt officers lined up in front of a private who's holding in his guts with his hands. They'll treat the officer with a bad pimple before they treat the dying private. We're supposed to be shaking hands with these people. Why can't we be fighting for some place like England? When you train yourself to blow gooks away, like I did, something happens, some kind of popping returning dream of murder-with-a-smile.

I needed away. I was sick. In another three months I'd be zapping orphanages.

'Bobby, are you all right?' said Tubby, waddling out to the tree I was hanging on.

'I shouldn't ever've seen that picture of John Whitelaw. I shouldn't've.'

109

'Do you really think we'll be famous?' Tubby got an enchanted look on him, sort of a dumb angel look in that small pretty face amid the fat rolls. It was about midnight. There was a fine Southern moon lighting up the field. You could see every piece of straw out there. Tubby, by my ass, had the high daze on him. He'd stepped out here in the boonies and put down his foot in Ozville.

'This'll get me Major, anyhow. Sure. Fame. Both of us,' I said.

Tubby said: 'I tried to get nice touches in with the light coming over his face. These pictures could turn out awfully interesting. I was thinking about the cover of *Time* or *Newsweek*.'

'It'll change your whole life, Tubby,' I said.

Tubby was just about to die for love of fate. He was shivering.

I started enjoying the field again. This time the straws were waving. It was covered with rushing little triangles, these sort of toiling dots. Our side opened up. All the boys came up to join within a minute and it was a sheet of lightning rolling back and forth along the outside of the woods. I could see it all while I was walking back to the radio. I mean humping low. Tubby must've been walking straight up. He took something big right in the square of his back. It rolled him up twenty feet in front of me. He was dead and smoking when I made it to him.

'C'mon, I've got to get the pictures,' he said.

I think he was already dead.

I got my phosphorus shotgun. Couldn't think of anything but the radio and getting it over how we were being hit, so we could get dragons – helicopters with fifty cals – in quick. The dragons are nice. They've got searchlights, and you put two of them over a field like we were looking at, they'd clean it out in half an hour. So I made it to the radio and the boys had already called the dragons in, everything was fine. Only we had to hold them for an hour and a half until the dragons

110

got there. I humped up front. Every now and then you'd see somebody use one of the experimental guns. The bad thing was that it lit up the gunner too much at night, too much shine out of the muzzle. I took note of that to tell them when we got back. But the gun really smacked the gook assault. It was good for about seventy-five yards and hit with a huge circle burn about the way they said it would. The gooks' first force was knocked off. You could see men who were still burning running back through the straw, hear them screaming.

I don't remember too well. I was just loitering near the radio, a few fires out in the field, everything mainly quiet. Copters on the way. I decided to go take a look at Li Dap. I thought it was our boys around him, though I didn't know why. They were wearing green and standing up plain as day. There was Oliver, smoking a joint. His rifle was on the ground. The NVA were all around him and he hadn't even noticed. There were so many of them – twenty or so – they were clanking rifles against each other. One of them was going up behind Oliver with a bayonet, just about on him. If I'd had a carbine like usual, I could've taken the bayoneteer off and at least five of the others. Oliver and Li Dap might've ducked and survived.

But I couldn't pick and choose. I hardly even thought. The barrel of the shotgun was up and I pulled on the trigger, aiming at the bayoneteer.

I burned them all up.

Nobody even made a squeak.

There was a flare and they were gone.

Some of my boys rushed over with guns. All they were good for was stomping out the little fires on the edges.

When we got back, I handed over Tubby's pictures. The old man was beside himself over my killing a general, a captured general. He couldn't understand what kind of laxity I'd allowed to let twenty gooks come up on us like that. They thought I might have a court-martial, and I was under arrest

111

for a week. The story got out to UPI and they were saying things like 'atrocity,' with my name spelled all over the column.

But it was dropped and I was pulled out and went home a lieutenant.

That's all right. I've got four hundred and two boys out there — the ones that got back — who love me and know the truth, who love me *because* they know the truth.

It's Tubby's lost fame I dream about.

The Army confiscated the roll and all his pictures. I wrote the Pentagon a letter asking for a print and waited two years here in Vicksburg without even a statement they received the note. I see his wife, who's remarried and is fat herself now, at the discount drugstore every now and then. She has the look of a kind of hopeless cheer. I got a print from the Pentagon when the war was over and it didn't matter. Li Dap looked wonderful — strained, abused, and wild, his hair flying over his eyes while he's making a statement full of conviction.

It made me start thinking of faces again.

Since I've been home I've crawled in bed with almost anything that would have me. I've slept with high-school teachers, Negroes and, the other night, my own aunt. It made her smile. All those years of keeping her body in trim came to something, the big naughty surprise that the other women look for in religion, God showing up and killing their neighbors, sparing them. But she knows a lot about things and I think I'll be in love with her.

We were at the John Whitelaw vs. Whitney Maxwell play-off together. It was a piece of wonder. I felt thankful to the wind or God or whoever who brought that fine contest near enough by. When they hit the ball, the sound traveled like a rifle snap out over the bluffs. When it was impossible to hit the ball, that is exactly when they hit it.

My aunt grabbed hold of my fingers when the tension was

112

almost up to a roar. The last two holes. Ah, John lost. I looked over the despondency of the home crowd.

Fools! Fools! I thought. Love it! Love the loss as well as the gain. Go home and dig it. Nobody was killed. We saw victory and defeat, and they were both wonderful.

OUR SECRET HOME

I THREW A party, wore a very sharp suit. My wife had out all sorts of hors d'oeuvres, some ordered from long off – little briny peppery seafoods you wouldn't have thought of as something to eat. We waited for the guests. Some of the food went bad. Hardly anybody came. It was the night of the lunar eclipse, I think. Underwood, the pianist, showed up and maybe twelve other people. Three I never invited were there. We'd planned on sixty-five.

I guess this was the signal we weren't liked anymore in town.

Well, this had happened before.

Several we invited were lushes who normally wouldn't pass up cocktails at the home of Hitler. Also, there were two nymphomaniacs you could trust to come over in their high-fashion halters so as to disappear around one in the morning with some new innocent lecher. We furthermore invited a few good dull souls who got on an occasional list because they were *good* and furnished a balance to the doubtful others. There was a passionate drudge in landscaping horticulture, for example.

But none of them came.

It was a hot evening and my air-conditioner broke down an hour before the party started.

An overall wretched event was in the stars.

Underwood came only for the piano. I own a huge in-time

114

Yamaha he cannot separate himself from. Late in the evening I like to join him on my electric bass.

Underwood never held much for electric instruments. He's forty-two, a traveler from the old beatnik and Charlie Parker tribe. I believe he thinks electric instruments are cowardly and unmanly. He does not like the basic idea of men joining talents with a wall socket. In the old days it was just hands, head and lungs, he says. The boys in the fifties were better all-around men, and the women were proud of being after-set quim.

Underwood liked to play with this particular drummer, about his age. But that night the drummer didn't show up, either. This, to my mind, was the most significant absentee at our party. That drummer had always come before. I thought he was addicted to playing with Underwood. So when Underwood had loosened up on a few numbers and the twelve of us had clapped and he came over for a drink, I asked him, 'Why isn't Fred Poor here?'

'I don't know. Fred's got a big family now,' said Underwood.

'He's always come before. Last month. What's wrong with tonight? Something is wrong with tonight,' I said.

'The food's good. I can remember twenty friends in the old days around Detroit who'd be grooving up on this table. You'd thank em for taking your food. That's how solid they were,' said Underwood, drinking vodka straight off the ice and smelling at one of the fish hors d'oeuvres.

I saw my wife go into the bathroom. I eased back with a greeting to the sweated-up young priest who had the reputation of a terrific sex counselor. He was out there with the great lyrical lie that made everybody feel good. Is that why he showed up and the others not? His message was that modern man had invented psychology, mental illness, the whole arrogant malaise, to replace the soul. Sex he called God's rule to keep us simple and merry, as we were meant to be, lest we forget we are creatures and figure ourselves

totally mental. One night I asked him what of Christ and
Mary and the cult of celibacy. 'Reason is, Mr. Lee, believe
or disbelieve and let be,' he answered. 'I'm only a goddamned
priest. I don't have to be smart or be a star in forensics.'

He headed out for more bourbon, and I trucked on after
my wife.

I whispered in the bathroom keyhole and she let me in.
She was rebuckling her sandal with a foot on the commode.

'Why didn't anybody come tonight? What do you think's
wrong?' I asked her.

'I only know about why five aren't here. Talked to Jill.'
She paused. One of Carolyn's habits is making you pose a
question.

'Why?' I asked.

'The people Jill knew about said there was something
about our life they didn't like. It made them feel edgy and
depressed.'

'*What?*'

'Jill wouldn't ever say. She left right after she told me.'

When I went out, there weren't as many as before. Underwood was playing the piano and the priest was leaning on
the table talking to one of the uninvited, a fat off-duty cop
from about four houses up the row I'd wave to in the mornings when he was going out in his patrol car. Sitting down
fanning herself was a slight old friend of my wife's who had
never showed up at our other parties. She was some sort of
monument to alert age in the neighborhood – about eighty,
open mind, colorful anecdotes, crepy skin, a dress over-
formal and thick stockings.

'Hi, Mrs. Craft,' I said.

'Isn't this a dreadful party? Poor Carolyn, all this food and
drink. Which one's her husband?' the old lady said.

I realized maybe she'd never got a good look at me, or
had poor eyes.

'I really don't know which one's her husband. What would

116

you say was wrong with them, the Lees? Why have people stayed away from their party?' I said.

'I saw it happen to another couple once,' she said. 'Everyone suddenly quit them.'

'Whose fault was it?'

'Oh, definitely theirs. Or rather *his*. She was congenial, similar to Carolyn. And everybody wanted a party. Oh, those gay sultry evenings!' She gave a delicate cough. 'We invented gin and tonic, you know.'

'What was wrong with her husband?' I asked.

'He suddenly changed. He went bad. A handsome devil too. But we couldn't stand him after the change.'

'What sort of change?' I offered her the hearts of palm and the herring, which, I smelled, was getting gamy in the heat. She ate for a while. Then she looked ill.

'A change . . . I've got to leave. This heat is destroying me.'

She rose and went out the kitchen, opening the door herself and leaving for good.

Then I went back to the bathroom mirror. The same hopeful man with the sardonic grin was there, the same religious eyes and sensual mouth, sweetened up by the sharp suit and soft violet collar. I could see no diminution of my previous good graces. This was Washington and my vocation was interesting and perhaps even important. I generally tolerated everybody – no worms sought vent from my heart that I knew of. My wife and other women had said I had an unsettling charm.

I got out the electric bass and played along with Underwood. But I noticed a baleful look from him, something he'd never revealed before. So I quit and turned off the amplifier. I took a hard drink of Scotch in a cup and opened a closet in my study, got in, shut the door, and sat down on all my old school papers and newspaper notices in the cardboard boxes in the corner.

Here was me and the pitch dark, the odor of old paper and some of my outdoor clothes.

How have I offended? I asked. How do I cause depression and edginess? How have I perhaps changed for the bad, as old Mrs. Craft hinted?

By my cigarette lighter I read a few of the newspaper notices on me and my work. I looked at my tough moral face, the spectacles that put me at a sort of intellectual remove, the sensual mouth to balance it, abetted by the curls of my auburn hair. In fact, no man I knew looked nearly anything like me. My wife told me that when we first met at Vanderbilt my looks pure and simple were what attracted her to me. Yet I was not vain. She was a brown-haired comely girl, in looks like many other brown-haired comely girls, and I loved her for her strong cheerful averageness. Salt of the earth. A few minor talents. Sturdy womb for our two children.

It was not her. It was me!

What have I done? I asked myself.

Then I heard heels on the stairs of my study. A pair was coming down, man and woman. They walked into the study and were silent for a while. Then I heard the sucking and the groans. For three or four minutes they must have kissed. Then:

'It's not any good *here*.'

'I know. I feel it. Even sex wouldn't be any good *here*.'

'You notice how all this good liquor tastes like iodine?'

They moaned and smacked a few more minutes. Then the man said, 'Let's get out of here.'

When they went away, I let myself out of the closet. Underwood was standing at my desk. He looked at me crawling out of the closet. I had nothing to say. Neither did he for a while.

Then he said, 'I guess I better not come over anymore.'

'What's wrong?' I said.

'The crazy . . . or *off* chick that lives upstairs that always comes down and leans on the piano about midnight every

118

night? She's good-looking, but she sets me off. I get the creeps.'

'Did she come down again? I guess it's the piano. You ought to be flattered. Most of the time she sits up there in her chair reading.'

'Somebody said it was your sister. I don't know. She *looks* like you. Got the same curly auburn hair. It's like you with tits, if you think about it.'

'Well, of course it *is* my sister. For a while we had a reason for not telling that around. Trust me.'

'I trust you. But she makes my hair cold.'

'You loved all types back in the time of the beatniks. I always thought of you as a large-hearted person.'

'Something goes cold when she talks. I can't get with the thing she's after. For a while I thought she was far-out, some kind of philosopheress. But nothing hangs *in* in what she says.'

'She can have her moments. Don't you think she has a certain charm?'

'No doubt on that, with her lungs dripping over her gown. But when she talks, well . . .' He closed his eyes in an unsatisfactory dreaming sort of trance.

'Can't you see it? Can't you see the charm?' I demanded.

'Whatever, it don't sweeten me,' he said, setting down his glass.

He went out the study door.

There, leaning on the piano, in her perfect cobalt gown, was Patricia. She was waiting for Underwood. Near her, as I have intimated, I sometimes have no sense of my own petty mobility from one place to another. I appear, I hover, I turn. Her lush curls burned slowly round and round in the fire of the candle of the mantel. A blaze of silver came from her throatpiece, a lash of gemmy light bounced from her earrings.

Not a soul was in the room with her.

'Underwood's left,' I said.

'Music gone?' she said, holding out her hand and clutching her fingers.

'It would be cooler upstairs with your little window unit. You could read. What were you reading tonight?'

'*Heidi*. Such a sugar,' she said.

'Oh, yes. Much sugar. The old uncle.'

'Mountain,' she said.

By this time only the priest was left. He was having an almost rabidly sympathetic conversation with my wife. The man was flushed out and well drunk, a ship's captain crying his *full speed ahead* in the stern house of a boat rotting to pieces.

I looked over the long table of uneaten fish tasties. The heat had worked on them a couple more hours now and had brought them up to a really unacceptable sort of presence.

'Well. Ho ho. Look at all the stuff. All the cost,' I said.

'Just garbage God knows who, namely me, has to haul off and bury,' said my wife.

'Ah, no madam. I'll see to all. Trust me. I'm made for it,' swore the priest.

With that he began circling the table, grabbing up the fish dainties and cramming them in his pockets, coat and pants, wadding them into his hat. He spun by me with a high tilt of adieu. But then he bumped into Patricia, who had come in, and spilled some of the muck in his hat on the front of her gown. She didn't move. Then she looked downward into her bosom to the grease and fish flesh that smeared her gown.

'Fishies,' she said.

'What a *blight* I am! On this one, on this innocent belle! Strike me down!'

The priest wanted to touch her and clean her off, but could not. His hands trembled before the oil and flakes of fish on her stomach. He uttered a groan and ran from the house.

After he'd gone, the three of us stood there, offering no movement or special expression.

*

120

'You ought to go up and clean yourself,' Carolyn said to Patricia.

Patricia put her foot on the first stair and looked at me with an appeal. But then she went rapidly up and we could hear her air-conditioner going when she opened her door and then nothing when she closed it.

We straightened up awhile, but not very thoroughly. Then we got in bed.

'You've ruined my life,' said my wife. 'This party showed it.'

'What's *wrong*? What do you mean?'

'Stop it. What's to pretend? Your twin goddamned sister. Your wonderful spiritual feeble-minded sister.'

'Not! Not! It's just not our language she speaks! Don't say that!'

'*You* taught her all the goddamned English she knows. Oh, when you explained, when she first came, that she was just silent, different! We went through all that. Then we've had her out of pity. . . .'

'She doesn't need anybody's pity! Shut your mouth!'

There was a long hot silence. Above us we heard rocking sounds.

My wife hissed: 'She's never even cleaned herself up.'

'I'll see.'

'Oh, yes, you'll *see*! Don't bother to wake me when you come back.'

Carolyn had drunk a lot. I went to brush my teeth and when I came back out she was snoring.

I rose on the stairs.

The cool in Patricia's room had surpassed what is comfortable. It was almost frigid, and the unit was still heaving more cold into the room. She sat in the rocking chair reading her book. The soiled gown was still on her. She raised her hand as I passed her to turn down the air-conditioning, and I held her hand, coming back to stare over her shoulder.

There was a picture of Heidi and her goat upside down.

121

'Let's get you in your little tub,' I said.

I stripped the gown from her. Then I picked her up and put her in the tub, turning on the water very slow as I lathered her all over.

I gave her a shampoo. Pulling an arm up, I saw what was needed, ran the razor gently over her pits, then saw to the slight stubble on her legs. This is when she always sang. A high but almost inaudible melody of the weirdest and most dreamlike temptation, it would never come from another person in this world.

I began sobbing and she detected it.

'I love you with everything that lives me,' she said. 'You love me the identical?'

'Everything. Yes.'

'Mickey,' she said. She clutched one breast and with the other hand she raised the red curls and lips of her virgin sex. 'Are you like me?'

I looked away and was getting a towel.

'Yes. I'm exactly like you. We're twins. We're just alike,' I said.

'That's why we can love each other everything,' she said.

'Exactly. Just the same.'

'Show me you.'

'We can't. I can't because of the rules.'

'Oh, yeah, darling, the rules!'

She'd always shown a peculiar happiness about the rules.

When I got her in bed, I wound up downstairs, no memory of having traveled anywhere.

I was breathless. My heart was big. Sometimes like this I thought it would just burst and spray its nerves into the dark that would not care, into the friends that would not care.

In bed again I found Carolyn was not asleep at all. She was sitting up.

'Did you finish with her?'

'Yes.'

'Don't tell me what went on. I don't want to know. I love

you too much to do anything about it. But look what you've dragged me into.'

'I know.'

'You can't sleep with me tonight. Get out of here.'

'I know,' I said.

I got the flashlight and got in the closet again, pulling the door to. I went through all the newspaper notices and the college term papers and picked up the love letters. They were on lined paper, grammar-school paper. It was the summer after I'd taught her to write.

Mickey I love you. There isn't anything but love of you for me. I see the way you walk and your shoes are nice. I desire to thank you with my tongue and my legs too. The tongue and legs are good places. But the most is under my chest where it beats.

Sincerely yours, Patricia

I held all the others, her letters, as the handwriting improved, and saw the last ones with their graceful script, even prettier than I could write on a good day. My essence yearned and rose from the closet and my roots tore from me, standing up like a tangled tree in dark heaven. My mother gave Patricia to me before she threw herself into what she called her patriotic suicide – that is, she used Kentucky whiskey and tobacco and overate fried foods in a long faithful ritual before she joined my old man in the soil near Lexington.

I thought heavily and decided I'd go back down South.

I was tired of Washington, D.C.

I was tired of my vocation.

I was tired of me.

Somewhere near the sea we'd go. Carolyn and Patricia both loved the sea. I'd find a town that would appreciate me for my little gifts and we'd move there. Have new friends, more privacy. I might turn back into a Democrat.

Changes like that never bothered my heart.

123

EATING WIFE AND FRIENDS

WE WERE VERY fond of Mrs. Neap's place – even though it was near the railroad. It was a rambling inn of the old days, with its five bathrooms and balcony over the dining room. We had been harboring there for a couple of weeks and thought we were getting on well enough. But then she comes downstairs one morning holding a swab, and she tells me, looking at the rest of them asleep on the couches and rug: 'This is enough. Get out by this afternoon.'

'Last night you said we were your adorable vagabonds.'

'In the light of day you look more like trash. I had too much of that potato liquor you brought,' says Mrs. Neap.

I say, 'Give us another chance. It might be your hangover talking. Let's have another conference, say two o'clock. Invite down all the tenants. We'll talk it out.'

She says, 'It's my decision. I own the place. Property is nine-tenths the law,' forearm muscles standing out as she kneads the cleaning rag, one of the lenses of her spectacles cracked.

I say, 'But we're the tenth that gives existence quality, the quantum of hope and dream, of laughter, of music. Further, please, Miz Neap, we'll clean, keep this place in shape, paint it up.'

'Where paint? What paint? It's ten dollars a quart if you can even find it. You can't find more than four quarts in all South and North Carolina.'

'We make our own liquor. We can find a way to make

124

paint too. Gardiner there is close to being a bona-fide chemist.'

She says, 'None of you is any good. You never brought any food into the house. Oh, that sack of onions that fell off a truck and a few blackbirds.'

I say, 'How can you forget the turkey we brought when we came?'

'Sure,' says she, 'that's what you got in with, the turkey. But what since, besides potato liquor? Then you ate all the magnolias,' says she.

'*One* foolish evening. Your other tenants ate some too,' say I.

'You broke the handle on the faucet.'

'Nobody ever proved it was one of us.'

'There was no fleas before you came, no cockroaches.'

'Unproven. Besides, seeing as how there's no more turkey . . .'

The house begins the shiver it does when a train is entering the curve. The train is always, beyond other concerns, an amazement. Mrs. Neap and I walk out to the warped porch to watch. The train is coming in, all right, rolling its fifteen miles an hour, and you can see the people, hundreds and hundreds, standing and sitting on the wooden platforms the company built over the cars, those pipes and chicken wire boxing in about ninety 'air-riders' per car top.

Even an air-riding ticket is exorbitant, but that fifteen-mile-an-hour breeze must be nice.

The train passes three times a week. This one must've been carrying about five thousand in all if you were to count the between-car riders and the maintenance-ladder riders.

Resettlers.

When the bad times really came, they brought families back together, and mainly everybody started coming South. Everybody would travel back to the most prosperous member of his family, taking his own light fortune along to pool it. It healed a lot of divorces and feuds. The best thing you could have was a relative with land. You showed up at his place offering your prodigal soul and those of your family as guards of the land, pulling out your soft hands to garden up the soil and watch over it.

There are no idle murders to speak of anymore. Almost all of them are deliberate and have to do with food, water, seeds or such as a ticket on the train. For example, if I tried to jump that train Mrs. Neap and I are looking at, a man in street clothes (you'd never know which one but usually a fellow mixing with the air-riders) would shoot me in the head. The worst to come of that would be some mother would see her child see the cloud of blood flying out of my face, and she'd have to cover its mouth before it could yell because you don't want a child making noise in a public area. Be seen and not heard applies to them, and better not even to be seen very much.

The little ones are considered emblems of felony.

When bad times first settled into reality, the radio announcers told us what conversationalists and musicians Americans were proving to be and that our natural fine wit was going to be retreasured. People began working on their communication. Tales were told. Every other guy had a harmonica, a tonette or at least was honking on two blades of grass. But that was before they started *eating* grass in New York and then buying up the rest of the nation's.

On the National Radio two years ago, we heard the Surgeon General report on the studies done on survivors of lost expeditions, polar and mountaintop sorties. The thing of it was that you could stay alive a phenomenal length of time on almost nothing if you *did* almost nothing, counting talking and singing. Which sent communication and melody back into the crapper.

The Surgeon General said you had to be sure whatever food you were after surpassed in calories the effort getting it would burn up. Don't run after a clump of celery, for example. *Chewing* celery takes more calories than eating it gives you. But cockroaches, moths and butterflies will come *to* you

126

and can be caught and ingested with a *bonus* of calories and protein. Wash the cockroaches if possible, the Surgeon General said.

We were chewing on our rutabagas and radishes when this came out and we considered it all laughable, radical over-science for the ghettos above the Mason-Dixon.

That was in the days of cheese.

Then all the blacks started returning to the South, walking. Five thousand of them came through Maryland, *eating* three or four swamps around Chesapeake Bay, stripping every leaf, boiling and salting all the greenery in huge iron cauldrons they pulled along on carts.

Those blacks hit Virginia and ate a senator's cotton plantation. People started shooting at them, and some of the nigs had guns themselves.

It was a bloodbath.

There were rumors that the blacks cooked their own dead and that you could see that's where their strength was coming from.

When the walking poor of Chicago went through the fields of southern Illinois, over to Kansas, down through Missouri, this sort of thing was avoided. All of America knew about the Virginia horror, and steps were apparently taken among leaders to prevent its recurrence. The radio announcers urged all the walkers to spread out, don't go in large groups. The vegetation of America would feed everybody if all the Resettlers would spread out.

This was good advice, unless you spread out on somebody's acres.

The South was filling up with railroad people from the big defunct hives in the North. Theoretically, everybody could have his own hundred-foot-square place. But too many came back to the South. There were five million Resettlers in Atlanta, they say. Atlanta is very sorry that it prospered as a railhead. The mayor, a Puerto Rican with his Chinese wife, abdicated, leaving everything to the wardens and the stateside CIA.

Everybody is quiet. No more music or talking or needless exertion.

Crowds everywhere are immense and docile.

We hear it on the radio.

'They all look at this place covetously, those air-riders,' says Mrs. Neap. 'Poor souls.'

You also had the right to kill anybody who jumped *off* the train *into* your yard. An old coroner might come by on his bicycle and stare at the body for a while, letting off a few platitudes about the old days. Like as not, a town officer, usually a nig or Vietnamese, appears and digs a hole three feet deep and prods the body over into it. This is slow going because the man will eat every worm, every grub, every spider and juicy root he upturns with his spade.

Even Mrs. Neap's run-down house probably looks as if it has gunners at it. But it had no protection at all before we got here. I carry a knife.

The direly thin guy six and half feet tall who melted into the dawn fog with his bow and arrow before anybody got up and returned at evening with almost all his arrows lost and not a goddamn ounce of meat to show — to be fair, four blackbirds and a rabbit smaller than the hunting arrow — wanted you to think he was Slinking Invisible itself on the borders of our landhold, when the truth was he was miles away missing ten-foot shots on trifling birds and sticking his homemade arrows into high limbs where he couldn't retrieve them.

He calls himself JIM, I mean loud and significantly, like that.

Says he knows the game world. When we walked up on that big wild turkey just before we found Mrs. Neap's house, I watched that sucker fire off three different arrows at it. The turkey stood there just like the rest of us, unbelieving. At this point I sicked soft-spoken Vince on the turkey. Vince is so patient and soft-spoken, he could talk a snake into leaving

128

his poison behind and pulling up a chair for stud or Go Fish, whatever you wanted to play.

Vince talked the turkey right into his arms.

Then came the last arrow from JIM.

It went through Vince's hand and into the heart of the turkey.

We didn't need this. You can't get medical help. There's nothing left but home remedies.

We started despising JIM right then and there.

But Vince's hand healed and is merely unusable instead of gangrenous.

'My God, one of them jumped off,' says Mrs. Neap.

I saw. It was an Oriental.

He is wobbling on the gravel in front of the yard. I pull my knife. This close in to a town you have to perform the law.

But one of the wardens in the air-rider cages shoots at him – then the next one, who has a shotgun, really blasts the gook.

The guy lies down.

I couldn't tell whether he went to the dirt before or after the gun blast.

Mrs. Neap kneels down with delicate attention to the dead man. With her cracked lens, she seems a benevolent patient scholar.

Mrs. Neap says, 'He's a handsome little man. We don't need to call the coroner about him. Look at the muscles. He was well fed. I wonder why he come running toward the house. I guess he wanted to end up here. He chose,' says Mrs. Neap.

'I'll get the bike and tell the coroner,' I say.

'I said *not* get the coroner. This is my property. Look. His head is across my legal property line,' says Mrs. Neap.

Say I, 'Let's push him back a few feet. Then he's the city's. There's no reason for you to take the responsibility or cost of burying him.'

The old lady is intent. She'd been through the minor Depression in the thirties. She'd seen some things, I guess.

'Have you never?' says Mrs. Neap.

Her spectacles are flaming with the rising sun.

Say I, 'Have I never what?' slipping my knife back into my hip scabbard.

'Eaten it?'

'*It*?'

'Human being.'

'Human *being*?'

'Neither have I,' says Mrs. Neap. 'But I'm so starving, and Orientals are so *clean*. I used to know Chinese in the Mississippi delta. They were squeaky clean and good-smelling. They didn't eat much but vegetables. Help me drag him back,' she says.

She didn't need help.

She has the man under the arms and drags him at top speed over the scrub weeds and onto her lawn. Every now and then she gives me a ferocious look. There is a huge broken-down barbecue pit behind the house. I can see that is her destination.

I go up the front steps and wake up our 'family.' Vince is already awake, his hand hanging red and limp. He has watched the whole process since the gook jumped off the train.

JIM is not there. He is our invisible in the woods, taking dramatic inept shots at mountains.

(To complete his history, when we move on, after the end of this, JIM kills a dog and is dressing him out when a land-owner comes up on him and shoots him several times with a .22 automatic. JIM strangles the land-owner and the two of them die in an epic of trespass.)

My wife wakes up. Then Gardiner, the chemist who keeps us in booze, wakes up.

Vince has grown even softer since the loss of his right hand. Larry (you don't need to know any more about him) and his girl never wake up.

'Mrs. Neap wants to cook the man,' I say.

'What strength. She did a miracle,' says soft Vince.

When we get to the rotisserie, Mrs. Neap has the man all cleaned. Her Doberman is eating and chasing the intestines around the backyard.

My family goes into a huddle, pow-wowing over whether to eat the Doberman.

We don't know what she did with the man's head.

By this time she is cutting off steaks and has the fire going good.

Two more tenants come out on the patio, rubbing their eyes, waked up by the smell of that meal broiling on the grill.

Mrs. Neap is slathering on the tomato sauce and pepper.

The rest of the tenants come down.

Meat!

They pick it off the grill and bite away.

Vince has taken the main part of the skeleton back to the garage, faithful to his deep emotion for good taste.

When it is all over, Mrs. Neap appears in the living room, where we are all lying around. Her face is smeary with grease and tomato sauce. She is sponging off her hideous cheeks with a rag even as she speaks.

She says, 'I accepted you for a while, you romantic nomads. Oh, you came and sang and improved the conversation. Thanks to JIM for protecting my place and my dried-out garden, wherever he is. But you have to get out by this afternoon. Leave by three o'clock,' says she.

'*Why?*' say I.

'Because, for all your music and merriment, you make too many of us. I don't think you'll bring in anything,' she says.

'But we *will*,' says soft Vince. 'We'll pick big luscious weeds. We'll drag honeysuckles back to the hearth.'

She looks around at all of us severely.

She says, 'I hate to get this down to tacks, but I hear noises in the house since you're here.' This old amazing woman was whispering. 'You know what goes in America. You know all the announcements about food value. You, one of you, had *old dangerous relations* with Clarisse, the tenant next to my room. I heard. You may be romantic, but you are trash.'

She places herself with her glasses so as to fix herself in the image of an unanswerable beacon.

She says, 'We all know the *Survival News*. Once I was a prude and resisted. But if we're going to win through for America, I go along. *Only* oral relations are allowed. We must not waste the food from each other, the rich minerals, the raw protein. We are our own gardens,' Mrs. Neap says, trembling over her poetry.

It costs her a lot to be so frank, I can see.

'But you cooked a human being and ate him,' say I.

'I couldn't help it,' says she. 'I remember the cattle steaks of the old days, the juicy pork, the dripping joints of lamb, the venison.'

'The *what*?' say we.

'Get out of here. I give you to four o'clock,' says she.

So the four of us hit the road that afternoon.

We head to the shady green by the compass in my head.

I am the leader and my wife is on my arm.

There are plenty of leaves.

I think we are getting over into Georgia.

My wife whispers in my ear: 'Did you go up there with Clarisse?'

I grab off a plump leaf from a yearling ash. In my time I've eaten poison ivy and oak too. The rash erupts around your scrotum, but it raises your head and gives you hope when the poison's in your brain.

I confess. 'Yes.'

She whispers on. 'I wanted JIM. He tried. But he couldn't find my place. He never could find my place.'

'JIM?' say I. 'He just can't hit any target, now can he?'

'I saw Clarisse eating her own eyelashes,' she whispers, from the weakness, I suppose.

132

'It's okay,' say I, wanting to comfort her with an arm over to her shoulder. But with that arm I am too busy taking up good leaves off a stout little palmetto. And ahead of us is a real find, rims of fungus standing off a grandfather oak.

I've never let the family down. Something in my head tells me where the green places are. What a pleasure to me it is to see soft Vince, when his useless floppy red hand, looking happy as he sucks the delicious fungus off the big oak.

My wife throws herself into the feast. Near the oak are two terrapins. She munches the fungus and holds them up. They are huge turtles, probably mates. They'd been eating the fungus themselves.

'Meat!' says the wife.

'We won't!' say I. 'I won't eat a hungry animal. I just want to hold and pet one.'

The hunting arrow from JIM gets me right in the navel when I take the cuter of the turtles into my arms.

The wife can't cook.

JIM's feeling too awful to pitch in.

So it'll be up to soft Vince to do me up the best he can with his only one good hand.

ALL THE OLD HARKENING
FACES AT THE RAIL

A FEW OF the old liars were cranking it up around the pier when Oliver brought his one-man boat out. He was holding the boat in one hand and the motor in the other. Oliver probably went about fifty-seven or eight. He had stringy hair that used to be romantic-looking in the old days. But he still had his muscles, for a short guy.

'What you got there?' said Smokey.

'Are you blind, you muttering old dog? It's a one-man boat,' said Oliver.

Oliver didn't want to be troubled.

'I seen one of them in the Sears book, didn't I? How much that put you back?'

'I don't recall ever studying your checkbook,' said Oliver.

'This man's feisty this afternoon, ain't he?' said a relative newcomer named Ulrich. He was sitting on the rail next to the steps where Oliver wanted to get his boat down them and to the water. For a moment this Ulrich didn't move out of Oliver's way. 'You buy it on credit?'

Oliver never answered. He stared at Ulrich until the old man moved, then went down the steps with his little boat to the water and eased the thing in. It was fiberglass of a factory hue that is no real color. Then Oliver went back up the steps where he'd left the motor. It was brand new. He pondered for a moment. Then he pulled the back of the boat up and screwed on the boat clamps of the motor. It was nifty. You had something ready to go in five minutes.

All the old liars were peering over the edge at his operation.

'Don't you need fuel and a battery?' said Smokey, lifting up his sunglasses. One of his eyes was taped over from cataract surgery.

'A man that buys on credit is whipped from the start,' said Ulrich.

When Oliver looked up the pier on all the old harkening faces at the rail, he felt young in an ancient way. He had talked with this crew many an evening into the night. There was a month there when he thought he was one of them, with his hernia and his sciatica, his lies, and his workman's compensation, out here with his cheap roachy lake house on the reservoir that formed out of the big Yazoo. Here Oliver was with his hopeful poverty, his low-rent resort, his wife who never had a bad habit in her life having died of an unfair kidney condition. All it's unfair, he'd often thought. But he never took it to heart until Warneeta passed over to the other side.

There was a gallery of pecking old faces scrutinizing him from the rail. Some of them were widowers too, and some were leaking away toward the great surrender very fast. Their common denominator was that none of them was honest.

They perhaps had become liars by way of joining the evening pier crowd. One old man spoke of the last manly war, America against Spain. Another gummed away about his thirty pints and fifteen women one night in Mexico. Oliver had lied too. He had told them that he loved his wife and that he had a number of prosperous children.

Well, he had respected his wife, and when the respect wore off, he had twenty years of habit with her. One thing was he was never unfaithful.

And he had one son who was the drum major of the band for Lamar Tech in Beaumont, and who had graduated last year utterly astonished that his beautiful hair and outgoing teeth wouldn't get him employment.

But now I'm in love, thought Oliver. God help me, it's unfair to Warneeta in the cold ground, but I'm in love. I'm so warm in love I don't even care what these old birds got to say.

'Have you ever drove one of them power boats before, son?' This was asked by Sergeant Fish, who had had some education and was a caring sort of fellow with emphysema.

Oliver walked through them and back across the planks of the pier to his car that was parked in the lot at the end. He opened the trunk of his car and lifted out the battery and the gas can. He managed to hold the marine oil under his armpit. He said something into the car, and then all the men at the end of the pier saw the woman get out of Oliver's Dodge and walk to him and pull the marine oil can from under his arm to relieve the load. She was about thirty-five, lean, and looked like one of those kind of women over at the Rolling Fork Country Club who might play tennis, drink Cokes and sit around spraddle-legged with their nooks humped out aimless.

Jaws were dropped on the end of the pier.

Smokey couldn't see that far and was agitated by the groans around him.

Sergeant Fish said: 'My Gawd. It's Pearl Harbor, summer of forty-one!'

When she and Oliver got near enough the liars, they saw her face and it was cute – pinkish big mouth, a jot pinched, but cute, though maybe a little scarred by acne.

Oliver rigged up the gas line and mixed the oil into the tank. He attached the battery cables. The woman sat two steps above him while he did this alone in the back of the boat. There was one seat in the boat, about a yard wide. Oliver floated off a good bit while he was readying the boat. The woman had a scarf on her hair. She sat there and watched him float off thirty feet away as he was getting everything set. Then he pulled the crank on the motor. It took right up and Oliver was thrown back because the motor was in gear. The boat went out very fast about two hundred yards in the water. Then he got control and circled around and puttered back in.

The woman got in the boat. She sat in Oliver's lap. He turned the handle, and they scooted away so fast they were almost out of sight by the time one of the liars got his tongue going.

'It was Pearl Harbor, summer of forty-one, until you saw her complexion,' said Sergeant Fish.

'I'll bet they was some women in Hawawyer back then,' said the tall proud man with freckles. He waved his cane.

'Rainbow days,' lied Fish. 'The women were so pretty they slept right in the bed with me and the wife. She forgave me everything. It was just like stroking puppies, all of them the color of a goldfish.'

'Can that boat *hold* the two of 'em?' said Smokey.

'As long as it keeps goin' it can,' said Ulrich, who featured himself a scientist.

'Oliver got him a babe,' said another liar.

'I guess we're all old enough to see fools run their course,' said old Dan. Dan was a liar who bored even the pier crowd. He lied about having met great men and what they said. He claimed he had met Winston Churchill. He claimed he was on friendly terms with George Wallace.

'You'd give your right one to have a chance with Oliver's woman, indifferent of face as she is,' said Sergeant Fish.

'When the motor ever gives out, the whole thing will sink,' said Ulrich.

They watched awhile. Then they all went home and slept.

137

KNOWING HE WAS NOT
MY KIND YET I FOLLOWED

IT MAKES ME sick when we kill them or ride horses over them. My gun is blazing just like the rest of them, but I hate it.

One day I rode up on a fellow in blue and we were both out of ammunition. He was trying to draw his saber and I was so outraged I slapped him right off his horse. The horseman behind me cheered. He said I'd broken the man's neck. I was horrified. Oh, life, life – you kill what you love. I have seen such handsome faces with their mouths open, their necks open to the Pennsylvania sun. I love stealing for forage and food, but I hate this murdering business that goes along with it.

Some nights I amble in near the fire to take a cup with the boys, but they chase me away. I don't scold, but in my mind there are the words: All right, have your way in this twinkling mortal world.

Our Jeb Stuart is never tired. You could wake him with a message any time of night and he's awake on the instant. He's such a bull. They call him 'Beauty' at West Point. We're fighting and killing all his old classmates and even his father-in-law, General Philip St. George Cooke. Jeb wrote about this man once when he failed to join the Confederacy: 'He will regret it but once, and that will be continuously.'

Gee, he can use the word, Jeb can. I was with him through the ostrich feathers in his hat and the early harassments, when we had nothing but shotguns and pretty horses. He was always a fool at running around his enemy. I was with him when we rode down a lane around a confused Yank picket, risking the Miniés. But he's a good family man too, they say.

I was with him when he first went around McClellan and scouted Porter's wing. That's when I fell in love with burning and looting. We threw ourselves on railroad cars and wagons, we collected carbines, uniforms and cow steaks that we roasted on sticks over the embers of the rails. Jeb passed right by when I was chewing my beef and dipping water out of the great tank. He had his banjo man and his dancing nigger with him. Jeb has terrific body odor along with his mud-spattered boots, but it rather draws than repels, like the musk of a woman.

When we were celebrating in Richmond, even I was escorted by a woman out into the shadows and this is why I say this. She surrendered to me, her hoop skirt was around her eyebrows, her white nakedness lying under me if I wanted it, and I suppose I did, because I went laboring at her, head full of smoke and unreason. I left her with her dress over her face like a tent and have no clear notion of what her face was like, though my acquaintance Ruppert Longstreet told me in daylight she was a troll.

That was when young Pelham set fire to the Yank boat in the James with his one Napoleon cannon. We whipped a warship from the shore. Pelham was a genius about artillery. I loved that too.

It's killing close up that bothers me. Once a blue-suited man on the ground was holding his hands out after his horse fell over. This was at Manassas. He seemed to be unclear about whether this was an actual event; he seemed to be asking for directions back to his place in a stunned friendly way. My horse, Pardon Me, was rearing way high and I couldn't put the muzzle of my shotgun at him. Then Jeb rode in, plumes shivering. He slashed the man deep in the shoulder with his saber. The man knelt down, closing his eyes as if to

pray. Jeb rode next to me. What a body odor he had. On
his horse, he said:

'Finish that poor Christian off, soldier.'

My horse settled down and I blew the man over. Pardon
Me reared at the shot and tore away in his own race down
a vacant meadow – fortunate for me, since I never had to
look at the carnage but only thought of holding on.

After McClellan placed himself back on the York, we slipped
through Maryland and here we are in Pennsylvania. We go
spying and cavorting and looting. I'm wearing out. Pardon
Me, I think, feels the lunacy even in this smooth countryside.
We're too far from home. We are not defending our beloved
Dixie anymore. We're just bandits and maniacal. The gleam
in the men's eyes tells this. Everyone is getting crazier on the
craziness of being simply too far from home for decent return.
It is like Ruth in the alien corn, or a troop of men given
wings over the terrain they cherished and taken by the wind
to trees they do not know.

Jeb leads us. Some days he has the sneer of Satan himself.

Nothing but bad news comes up from home, when it
comes.

Lee is valiant but always too few.

All the great bullies I used to see out front are dead or
wounded past use.

The truth is, not a one of us except Jeb Stuart believes in
anything any longer. The man himself the exception. There
is nobody who does not believe in Jeb Stuart. Oh, the zany
purposeful eyes, the haggard gleam, the feet of his lean horse
high in the air, his rotting flannel shirt under the old soiled
grays, and his heroic body odor! He makes one want to be
a Christian. I wish I could be one. I'm afraid the only things
I count on are chance and safety.

The other night I got my nerve up and asked for him in
his tent. When I went in, he had his head on the field desk,
dead asleep. The quill was still in hand. I took up the letter.
It was to his wife, Flora. A daguerreotype of her lay next to

the paper. It was still wet from Jeb's tears. At the beginning of the letter there was small talk about finding her the black silk she'd always wanted near Gettysburg. Then it continued: 'After the shameful defeat at Gettysburg,' etc.

I was shocked. I always thought we won at Gettysburg. All the fellows I knew thought we had won. Further, he said:

'The only thing that keeps me going on my mission is the sacred inalienable right of the Confederacy, Christ Our Lord, and the memory of your hot hairy jumping nexus when I return.'

I placed the letter back on the table. This motion woke him.

I was incredulous that he knew my first name. He looked as if he had not slept a second.

The stories were true.

'Corporal Deed Ainsworth,' he said.

'Sorry to wake you, General.'

'Your grievance?' he said.

'No one is my friend,' I mumbled.

'Because the Creator made you strange, my man. I never met a chap more loyal in the saddle than you. God made us different and we should love His differences as well as His likenesses.'

'I'd like to kiss you, General,' I said.

'Oh, no. He made me abhor that. Take to your good sleep, my man. We surprise the railroad tomorrow.'

'Our raids still entertain you?' I asked.

'Not so much. But I believe our course has been written. We'll kill ten and lose two. Our old Bobbie Lee will smile when we send the nigger back to him with the message. I'll do hell for Lee's smile.'

The nigger came in the tent about then. He was highfalutin, never hardly glanced at me. They had a magnificent bay waiting for the letters. Two soldiers came in and took an armload of missives from General Stuart's trunk, passing them into the saddlebags. The nigger, in civilian clothes, finally looked at me.

141

'Who dis?' he said.

'Corporal Deed Ainsworth; shake hands,' said General Stuart.

I have a glass shop in Biloxi. I never shook hands with any nigger. Yet the moment constrained me to. He was Jeb's best minstrel. He played the guitar better than anything one might want to hear, and the banjo. His voice singing 'All Hail the Power' was the only feeling I ever had to fall on my knees and pray. But now he was going back down South as a rider with the messages.

'Ain't shaking hands with no nancy,' said the nigger. 'They say he lay down with a Choctaw chief in Mississip, say he lick a heathen all over his feathers.'

'You're getting opinions for a nigger, George,' said Jeb, standing. 'I don't believe Our Lord has room for another nigger's thoughts. You are tiring God when you use your mouth, George.'

'Yessuh,' said George.

'Do you want to apologize to Corporal Ainsworth?'

'I real sorry. I don't know what I say,' the nigger said to me. 'General Jeb taught me how to talk and sometimes I justs go on talking to try it out.'

'Ah, my brother George,' Jeb suddenly erupted.

He rushed the nigger and threw his arms around him. His eyes were full of tears. He embraced the black man in the manner of my dreams of how he might embrace me.

'My chap, my chum. Don't get yourself killed,' said Jeb to George. 'Try to look ignorant when you get near the road pickets, same as when I found you and saved you from drink.'

'I loves you too, General Jeb. I ain't touched nothing since you saved me. Promise. I gon look ignorant like you say, tills I get to Richmond. Then I might have me a beer.'

'Even Christ wouldn't deny you that. Ah, my George, there's a heaven where we'll all prosper together. Even this sissy, Corporal Ainsworth.'

They both looked at me benevolently. I felt below the nigger.

George got on the horse and took off South.

At five the next morning we came out of a stand of birches and all of us flew high over the railroad, shooting down the men. I had two stolen repeaters on my hip in the middle of the rout and let myself off Pardon Me. A poor torn Yank, driven out of the attack, with no arm but a kitchen fork, straggled up to me. We'd burned and killed almost everything else.

Stuart rode by me screaming in his rich bass to mount. The blue cavalry was coming across the fire towards us. The wounded man was stabbing me in the chest with his fork. Jeb took his saber out in the old grand style to cleave the man from me. I drew the pistol on my right hip and put it almost against Jeb's nose when he leaned to me.

'You kill him, I kill you, General,' I said.

There was no time for a puzzled look, but he boomed out: 'Are you happy, Corporal Ainsworth? Are you satisfied, my good man Deed?'

I nodded.

'Go with your nature and remember our Savior!' he shouted, last in the retreat.

I have seen it many times, but there is no glory like Jeb Stuart putting spurs in his sorrel and escaping the Minié balls.

They captured me and sent me to Albany prison, where I write this.

I am well fed and wretched.

A gleeful little floorwipe came in the other day to say they'd killed Jeb in Virginia. I don't think there's much reservoir of self left to me now.

This earth will never see his kind again.

THAT'S TRUE

I'LL NEVER FORGET the summer old Lardner went up to New York with forged credits as a psychiatrist. He'd been studying in med school with designs of becoming a psychiatrist. Then he got into the modern psychiatric scene, had enough of it, and having no other employment for the summer, he went up to New York all fit out with thick glasses and a mustache and an ailing gnarled hand, which he was of course putting on too. He said people in therapy got close to a shrink with an outstanding defect. He had a few contacts, and before you knew it, he was all set up in his office, five phony pieces of paper on the wall.

Old Lardner, I never knew what his real voice was, he had so many, though I knew he came from Louisiana like me. He loved Northerners – Jew, Navajo and nigger alike. He was a broad soul with no spleen in his back pocket for anybody. Except whiners who knew better. You ought to hear some of the tapes he brought back. He never taped anybody without their knowledge of it.

All of them *liked* to be taped, Lardner said.

It was their creativity.

They went like this:

Patient: I feel ugly all the time. I can't quit cigarettes. The two Great Danes I bought won't mate. I'm starting to cry over sentimental things, songs on the radio. Is it basically wrong for a man to like macramé? I never feel intimate with

144

anybody until we talk about Nixon, how awful he was. My kid looks away when I give him an order. I mean a gentle order. Let me take a breath.

Lardner: Jesus Damn Christ! What an *interesting* case! Your story takes the ticket. This is beyond trouble, Mr. ——, this is *art*!

Patient: What? My story *art*?

Lardner: Yes. You *are* ugly. But so very important.

Patient: You think so?

And so on.

The next one might go:

Patient: I'm angry, angry, Doctor Lardner.

Lardner: Why?

Patient: Because I'm a woman. I've taken such evil crap over the years.

Lardner: Why?

Patient: I thought you'd want to know *what*.

Lardner: You got the wrong doctor. Down on Fifth Avenue, about a dozen doors away, there's a good *what* doctor. A little more expensive.

Patient: I'm so angry at men everywhere. Nothing will ever cure me of this hatred.

Lardner: You're wasting money on me. I'm a man.

Patient: But with time, you and I might produce a cure for me.

Lardner: Well, we can start with your basic remedy and work out from there. How about a glass of pure gin on the rocks and a hard dick? (*Sounds of fistfight between Lardner and patient.*) You hit my gnarled hand!

Patient: Oh, I'm so sorry! Christ! I didn't want to.

Lardner: I think you did.

Patient: I . . . yes! I did! We've produced a cure together. You work so fast. (*Sounds of slipped-off panties.*) Have me, have! Let me make up for the hand!

And the only other one I recall:

Patient: It's the end of the world. It's the Big Fight. I read the *Times* on the subway, and think about my people, the Jews. I think of my good job and prosperity. The oil issue is going to wipe Israel out in ten years. There won't be an Israel. My people will be raped and burned over. And I want to fight. I want to leave Westchester County and fight. I want to bear arms and defend Israel. How can I stand walking around the streets of this town, this loud confusing city, when there are issues so clear-cut?

Lardner: Shit, I don't know. Why don't you fly out tomorrow morning?

When Lardner came back home to the South, he invited me over for a drink in his backyard at Baton Rouge. There'd been a storm in the afternoon and it had made June seem like October all of a sudden when it left. Here he was asking me whether he should go on and finish med school or not, and then he played me the tape recordings.

'The only thing we're sure about anymore is how much money we need,' said I. 'That's about as profound as I ever get. I've got a wife and two kids. Me and the wife drink a great deal in the evenings of Baton Rouge. We're happy. The great questions seemed to have passed us by. I'm a radiologist. All day long I look for shadows. We've got two Chinese elm trees in our backyard and a fat calico named Sidney. Our children are beautiful and I've got stock in Shell.'

'You're right,' said Lardner.

'Every man can be a king if he wants to,' I said. 'That's what my father said. He had harder times than me or you.'

'That's true,' Lardner said.

The last thing I heard about Lardner, he was on a boat out of New Orleans headed for Rio. From there he took ship to Spain.

I don't know another thing about him.

ESCAPE TO NEWARK

CARLOS, PLEASE PUT me on the Significant Persons list, she said. We didn't know you had any faith. You never acted like a Catholic. You swore and whored and were petty like the rest of us. Please, please let me and Robinson on your ship. Robinson is *always* religious when he has a hangover. I myself had a suspicion there were some old verities. We used to go down to the pond and throw bread at the ducks. They always reminded me of the old verities, so white and natural. Robinson even at his worst claimed he was wandering toward the ancient basics, but he was scared numb that he might have found them already. The point is, we always meant well, Carlos.

We loved kikes and niggers, she continued softly.

Perhaps we just had too much confidence, she sighed. The rest was almost inaudible.

We were a handsome couple and knew it, besides – she gasped – talented.

She had thick blond hair and soft-set eyes and had once been a female polo player of some note on the greenest and wealthiest fields of the Carolinas and New York State. Furthermore, she had a style of being stylish that was the envy of thousands of the envious. Carlos was one of those who had coveted her in years past. He quivered in his garage that she was here at last.

Tell me the story of your life, Carlos said sternly.

At heart he was jealous and nosy, and he bit himself

147

inwardly for his poor motives. In her automobile's windshield he caught a reflection of himself in shorts, bald head, hairy Catholic titties.

Carlos and this woman were the same age, had gone to the same prep school in Boston, both rubes together there. He was from Santa Fe and she was from Alaska. But she got rid of Alaska very early, homed in Florida for seven years, was fourteen and bored in Pennsylvania; over to Boston, thence to college and New York, where she found Robinson among the hundreds of New Yorkers who managed to make a great amount of money for doing almost nothing at all but was pretty as a god and possessed of a voice like a French horn, so that at crucial parties he could say practically nothing and leave the impression among the more musically eared that profundity of the eternal sort had passed near. She was caught.

Her dad was filthy rich from a corrupt deal on the Alaskan pipeline. Everything was guaranteed for a blast of manna and romance. So they married. Robinson was a very clean man and shocked by the filth of the assault she made on him. He developed hobbies to escape her. But when he got ready and had grown to her needs and pressed her, she turned into a sort of brilliant nag who deserted him and had developed her own expensive hobbies. So that one day a helicopter landed on the roof of the club and took her off to the Caribbean. He went to the bar and, among the kind, garrulous blacks in their livery, he became a dreamer on alcohol.

She was faithful to him except for one night with drugs in her, given to her by a friend she trusted in Rio. Oh, Rio, Rio, Rio. Women are patient and men are not. Women are softer and carouse like feathers against each other. She allowed herself to be taken by the featherly Vera and, as she recalled, reciprocated somewhat. Some days she blamed it on the drug and some days she blamed her past, other days she blamed her glands, and on horrible bright days she blamed herself entire.

While in the meantime Robinson drove a lonely, horny

and faithful course around the main cities of the nation, sometimes visiting a library or an observatory, making money hand over fist. He did it with the only talent he had never cultivated, his honesty. They bought snowmobiles from his company in Kentucky, because by that time the weather had turned very weird. All the upper South was white and frigid.

She did not tell Carlos much of this. Her story was full of modest lies that proved she had not had an interesting life at all. The taste of Vera came into her mouth as she thinned her tale. She censored one after another the scenes of bliss that she had passed, sometimes in the company of Robinson and sometimes when not, feeling like a lone released atom of rapture in Key West, in Charleston, in New York, in the sky over Ontario in Winston's glider: oh, the quiet, oh, the blue, Winston at the stick, handsome but not a lover, just the best *friend* she ever had. Oh, the thick green forest, the fierce rocks below, the eagle who sailed tandem six feet from their window and turned to look directly at her face, as much as saying he was their friend; she had never imagined birds smiled when they flew.

Say, she said, if I'm going on with this, could I see the ship in the silo? Wouldn't you let me?

Tell about your intimate life with Robinson, said Carlos, leading her around the garage.

The silo was about a hundred and fifty feet tall, about sixty feet around, bricks bright red from the rain and sleet, and there was something venerable about the thing even though it had been thrown up hastily around the ship only six months ago.

Perhaps because I want inside so much, she told herself. But there are limits to that too. Some things are worth perishing with as secrets.

I mean, the way you *are* together, this Carlos said, your spoiled little definition of love. It's all been frightfully easy for you, hasn't it? You copied my exam answers in prep school. I let you. You traded your beauty so openly I could kick myself, as if every one of your smiles were worth a dollar and a great deal of trouble. You used me as fodder for the ongoing of your beauty. But now we're both forty-two, aren't we?

Yes, Carlos. Would you let me see the ship?

Nobody can see the ship except the pilot and me. That is, of course, until we all get in it Saturday. But go on with your story. I'm amused by the trifling episodes you consider important. About your relationship with Robinson?

Wait. I'm not going to empty out myself for anybody about Robinson. That's our secret, she said. If you want me to lower myself so I can get on the ship this way, I'm not going to. I'll stay here and die with Robinson. Maybe we'll screw each other to death on our bed. It has a brass bedstead and there's a . . . the whole ceiling's a mirror, Carlos. It's like looking at your own happiness. There's nothing sick about it. Robinson always said the only sure thing the gods gave us was each other, all our faces and armpits and little skin rashes, she said.

Carlos winced. He wanted something gravely miserable. He had once married a girl from Grand Forks. They were both fat. She had hair on her back and her toes were black with fur. In fact, she was almost a man, seemed to have missed it by one flick of agitation of a gene. She dressed in cowboy fashion, jeans, boots, thirty-dollar hat now that she'd married a guy in the money. Carlos was a Presbyterian then, trying to be a preacher in Tucson, where Navajos started a fistfight during Carlos's sermons and the women simply fell dead asleep, this being their only period of rest in the week. His wife ate near five pounds of food a day. She was a wonderful cook, but mainly for herself. She ate directly out of the big iron pots while the food was still steaming, using a big ladle. There was just enough left for him, time it got to the table. Sunday afternoons she would come in, no regard for his weariness after his sermon and the meal. Food gave her an insufferable burst of energy, as if she'd swallowed a pound of drugs. Carlos would be thinking about God, about what a wretched nasty trip it was in this world of clumsy sorrow, about the holiness of the Law, about converting to Catholicism because of its stubborn travel throughout history. She, who was dead now by heart attack in the act of fornication, would roll and swagger into his bedroom. 'Get them trousers down, you little dude. Old Nancy needs some fun.' She outweighed him by fifty pounds. As she swelled to hard flab, her desires and etiquette became a miracle of irritation to him. She made him despise his own flesh, and drove him further into his meditations in the desert. Once he prayed the Lord to shorten his member and turn his testicles to ash. He viewed her as a sort of rabid hippopotamus cornering him in one bad dream after another. And she smoked five packs a day, often as not an ember between her lips as she rutted above him, spitting out fire all over him on the arrival of her moment. The last horror was when she thought she needed a child. She wanted to call it Buck or Francine, depending. She got melancholy and cried huge tears because nothing 'took.' She had her heart attack trying again. Not only did she die on the spot, but he thought she was asleep, and suffered her weight until he smelled something odd.

When he knew she was dead, Carlos smiled. Then he walked out of the house in a rampage over the idiocy of this earthly toil.

Then he became a priest.

He got fatter and went without a shirt, proud of his fat because it proved how vile the flesh was. And in five years he became very important. The dead spirit of his wife entered him, and he was conscious of two souls in his single bosom. At strange moments he would smile and find himself in love with the memory of his old Nancy. I have been through so much, the very limit, Carlos told himself.

They had let him put five Significant Persons on the ship's roster. His hand had formed their names with his fountain pen. But two of them had killed themselves last Saturday night. There were two more places abroad, though she did not know it.

151

Please let me see the ship, she said.

I'm sorry, said Carlos. He hated her because she reminded him of the old world of small desires and petty nostalgia. He hated her also because she knew that he chased women, made gossip and was a sorry priest. In fact, she could ruin him if she wanted to.

We want to *live*, Carlos, she said. How can you kill us? I was your friend. It's murder.

There *is* one place, Carlos said. *One* place. But not two. Robinson can't go . . . For auld lang syne, I can get you on. Provided.

Yes, all right. Robinson says he'll live or die by the seasons.

Look at the seasons, said Carlos. In August it's a hundred fifty degrees. In December it's minus twenty-five and three feet of snow in Mississippi. In April the big trees explode.

We know all that. Listen: why didn't you put us on the list? she said. We weren't bad.

I thought you lacked a basic seriousness about life.

But I've always been very serious.

You always gave me the sense that you were winking at everything. Nothing seemed deep to you.

What do I do? she said.

Lick me with your tongue all over my body. Suck the hair curls on my ankles, said Carlos.

She knelt down and pulled her hair back. She closed her eyes and her tongue appeared, red as a flame. Carlos saw the sweetly ordered blond hair, given a natural part by nature. She was beginning on his kneecap.

Are you serious? demanded Carlos.

She halted and picked a hair from her strawberry lips.

Oh, Carlos, I've always been serious, she said.

Robinson was out at his nice big house running the push mower over the grass the Sunday afternoon when the rocket went up in the air. The grass was growing a foot and a half overnight, and vines and cane took root and burst out of the soil if you went in to have a drink of water. The rocket made a magnificent yellow and purple wash over the entire western sky. Robinson barely looked at it, though he knew his wife was aboard. He whistled for Oliver, a very old and decrepit Dalmatian, the same dog who had lived in the dorm with him at Yale. Last night Robinson had forgotten to let him in, and the poor dog had slept on a patch of cane shoots. Robinson remembered his dog at five in the morning, and went out in the backyard looking for him. Robinson heard all quiet except for the cracking sounds of growth in the hedge, which was thirty feet high. He heard whimpering sounds above him. The cane had grown under the dog and lifted him up eight feet in the air. The dog was looking down at him. Robinson met the dog's look. We love each other, Robinson said. Don't be afraid. He got his ladder and lifted Oliver down from the cane tops.

Love slays fear, said Robinson.

She was surprised by all the maritime terms they used. Then Carlos took her to the center of it. She thought it was a museum in the center of the ship here. She couldn't figure why they'd put the thing in here, taking up so much room.

You little silly, said Carlos. Here's where we're all going to live.

Everybody on board was naked by then.

Say, he said, could you get a lick job in before vespers?

My ears hurt, she said. When do we get to outer space?

What outer space? Nobody has that much fuel left, Carlos said.

They hit down on a swamp near Newark.

It was a short ride, like all the last ones.

153

PETE RESISTS THE
MAN OF HIS OLD ROOM

'WHO IS *THAT*?' hissed the woman at the corner. Pete and Tardy were necking. They could never quit. They hardly ever heard. The porch where their bench was was purple and smelly with creeping pot plants. Their child, who was thirty, rode a giant trike specially made, he being, you know, simple, back and forth on the walk, singing: Awwwww. Ernnnnnn. Oobbbbbbb.

The man, remarked only by the hissing woman at the corner, who was Tardy's mother, walked, or rather verged, here and there, undecided, froth running down his chin and a dagger in his hand. He had an address printed on some length of cardboard. His fingernails were black.

'Out! Out of here, you mange!' shouted Tardy's mother.

'In, in, in!' the hairy man in the street shouted back.

Pete looked up. 'It's my old college roommate. Lay off, Mama,' Peter expressed, rising.

The fellow in the street straightaway made for Pete but got caught in the immense rose hedge. 'I knew I'd find you! Peace! Joy! Communion at last!' the filthy fellow shouted as he writhed, disabled.

'Son of a gun!' roared Pete. 'Look here, Tardy. It's old Room Man!'

'Jumping Jesus, do these thorns hurt!' shouted the filthy hairy fellow. He'd lost his dagger in the leaf mold. That hedge really had him.

'What say?' shouted Pete.

'I got no more discretion, Pete boy! I'm just a walking reminiscence! Here I am! I remember you when you were skinny and cried about a Longfellow poem! Your rash! Everything! Edna, Nannie, Fran! Puking at the drive-in!'

'I thought so,' said Pete to Tardy, low, his smile dropped aside. 'Would you get me my piece, my charm?'

'Your spiritual phase!' the filthy hairy fellow was screaming. 'Your Albert Schweitzer dreams! Signing on the dorm wall with your own blood!' shouted the awful man who was clogged in the hedge.

'Yes,' Pete said, lifting the weary corners of his lips.

Tardy lugged out the heavy piece.

Pete took it and jammed home the two big ones.

'Remember Juanita and her neat one? Played the cornet with her thing and you did the fingering?' screamed the wretched fellow all fouled in the hedge.

Yes.

He cut half his hedge away when he fired the double through it. The dagger blew out in the street along with the creep that held it. All the while Tardy's mother stood with crossed arms.

The son stopped his giant trike. He said, 'Ernnnnn,' to his dad on the porch.

'Albert,' said Pete. 'Take care of the stuff in the street,' and within minutes the son was back with the wagon attached and the scoop.

'It makes me not hardly want to kiss anymore,' Tardy said.

BEHOLD THE HUSBAND
IN HIS PERFECT AGONY

IN THE ALLEYS there were sighs and derisions and the slide of dice in the brick dust. His vision was impaired. One of his eyes had been destroyed in the field near Atlanta as he stood there with his binoculars.

Now he was in Richmond.

His remaining eye saw clearly but itched him incessantly, and his head turned, in necessity, this way and that. A clod of dirt struck him, thrown by scrambling children in the mouth of the alley he had just passed. False Corn turned around.

He thanked God it wasn't a bullet.

In the next street there was a group of shoulders in butternut and gray jabbering about the Richmond defenses. He strolled in and listened. A lieutenant in his cups told False Corn what he wanted to hear. He took a cup of acorn coffee from a vendor.

A lovely woman hurried into a house, clicking her heels as she took the steps. He thought of his wife and infant son. They lived in a house in Baltimore. His wife was lively and charming. His son was half Indian, because he, False Corn, was an Indian himself, of the old Huron tribe, though he looked mostly Caucasian.

Now he wore a maroon overcoat that hit him at mid-knee. In his right pocket were the notes that would have got him killed if discovered by the law or the soldiers.

156

He turned and went uptown, climbing the hill from the railroad.

False Corn's contact was a Negro who pretended, days, to be mad on the streets. At nights he poisoned the bourbon in the remaining officers' saloons, where colonels and majors drank from the few remaining barrels. Then he loped into a spastic dance – the black forgettable fool – while home-front leaders gasped and collapsed. Apparently the Negro never slept, unless sleep came to him in the day and was overlooked as a phase of his lunacy by passers-by, who would rather not have looked at all.

Isaacs False Corn, the Indian, the spy, saw Edison, the Negro, the contact, on the column of an inn. His coat was made of stitched newspapers. Near his bare feet, two dogs failed earnestly at mating. Pigeons snatched at the pieces of things in the rushing gutter. The rains had been hard.

False Corn leaned on the column. He lifted from his pocket, from amongst the notes, a half-smoked and frayed cheroot. He began chewing on the butt. He did not care for a match at this time. His cheroot was a small joy, cool and tasteless.

'Can you read?' False Corn asked Edison.

'Naw,' said Edison.

'Can you remember?'

'Not too good, Captain.'

'I'm going to have to give you the notes, then. God damn it.'

'I can run fast. I can hide. I can get through.'

'Why didn't you run out of Virginia a long time ago?'

'I seen I could do more good at home.'

'I want you to stop using the arsenic. That's unmanly and entirely heinous. That's not what we want at all.'

'I thought what you did in war was kill, Captain.'

'Not during a man's pleasure. These crimes will land you in a place beyond hell.'

'Where's that? Ain't I already been there?'

157

'The disapproval of President Lincoln. He freed you. Quit acting like an Italian.'

'I do anything for Abe,' Edison said.

'All you have to do is filter the lines. I mean, get through.'

'That ain't no trouble. I been getting through long time. Get through to who?'

'General Phil Sheridan, or Custer. Here's the news: *Jeb Stuart is dead.* If you can't remember anything else, just tell them Stuart is dead. In the grave. Finished. Can you remember?'

'Who Jeb Stuart be?' asked Edison, who slobbered, pretending or real.

'Their best horse general. If you never get the notes to them, just remember: Stuart is dead.'

False Corn stared into the purpled white eyes of Edison. One of the dogs, ashamed, licked Edison's toes. It began raining feebly. False Corn removed his overcoat.

'All my notes are in the right pocket. Can you remember the thing I told you, even if you lose the notes?'

'Stuart is dead. He down,' said Edison.

Passers-by thought it an act of charity. False Corn placed the coat on Edison's shoulders. What an incident of *noblesse oblige*, they thought. These hard times and look at this.

False Corn shivered as the mist came in under the gables. He chewed the cigar. Edison rushed away from him up the street, scattering the dogs and pigeons. Do get there, fool, the Indian thought.

False Corn's shirt was light yellow and soiled at the cuffs. On his wrist he wore a light sterling bracelet. It was his wife's and it brought her close to him when he shook it on his arm and felt its tender weight. He plunged into the sweet gloom of his absence from her, and her knees appeared to his mind as precious, his palms on them.

In the front room of the hotel a number of soldiers were sitting on the floor, saying nothing. Some of them were cracking pecans and eating them quickly. There was no heat in the building, but it was warmer and out of the mist.

His eye itched. He asked where there might be water. A corporal pointed. He found a bucket in the kitchen. The water was sour. When he finished the cup, he found a man standing on his blind side. The man held a folded paper in his game hand. His other arm was missing. The brim of his hat was drawn down.

'Mister False Corn?' the man said.

He shouldn't have known the name. No one else in Richmond was supposed to know his true name. False Corn was swept by a chill. He wished for his pistol, but it was in the chest in his garret, back in the boardinghouse. He took the note.

It read: 'Not only is Gen. Stuart dead. The nigger is dead too.' It was in a feminine script and it was signed 'Mrs. O'Neal.'

When he looked up, the one-armed man was gone. False Corn pondered whether to leave the kitchen. Since there was nothing else to do, he did. Nobody was looking at him as he made his way out of the lobby. He had determined on the idea of a woman between two mean male faces, the trio advancing before he opened the door.

But he was on the street now.

Nothing is happening to me, he thought. There's no shot, no harsh shout.

It will be in my room, decided False Corn, opening the door of the garret. Yes, there. There it sits. Where's the woman?

A bearded man was sitting on the narrow bed, holding a stiff brown hat between his legs. False Corn's pistol was lying on the blanket beside the man's thigh. The man was thin. His clothes were sizes large on him. But his voice was soft and mellow, reminiscent.

'Shut the door. I've known you since Baltimore, my friend.'

'Who are you?' False Corn said.

'An observer. Mrs. O'Neal. Your career is over.'

This *voice*, thought False Corn. He stood carefully, a weary statue with severely combed black hair to his nape, center-

159

parted. This man is little, he thought. I can murder him with my hands if he drops his guard, thought False Corn.

'You have a funny name, a big pistol, and you've been quite a spy. We know all the women you've been with.'

'Then you know nothing. I've been with no women.'

'Why not? A man gets lonely.'

'I've been more hungry than lustful in these parts. I have a wife, a child.'

I can kill him if he gets too easy, thought False Corn.

'I think I'll end you with your own pistol. Close your eyes and dream, Isaacs. I'll finish it off for you.'

'All right,' False Corn said. 'The rain has made me sleepy. Allow me to get my robe.'

He picked his robe off the hook without being shot. The robe was rotten at the elbows and smelled of wet dog. But it was familiar to him.

'What a wretched robe,' said the man in that reminiscent voice.

False Corn took a match off his dresser. Isn't this just to light my cigar? There was a flat piece of dynamite in the collar of the robe. He bent to the side, cupping his hands, and lit the fuse. The fuse was only an inch long. He removed the robe.

'You've caught your shoulder on fire, you pig,' cried the man. But it wasn't a man's voice now.

False Corn threw the robe toward the voice and fell to the door. No shot rang out. He fumbled at the latch. He saw the robe covering the man's face. The man was tearing the robe away. His beard dropped, burning, to the floor. False Corn shut the door and lay on the planks of the upper hallway.

There was a shudder and an utterance of rolling light that half split the door. False Corn's face was pierced by splinters. His good eye hardly worked for the blood rushing out of his eyebrow.

The thing was still alive. It was staggering in the doorway. Its limbs were naked and blackened. Its breasts were scorched black. It was a woman, hair burned away. False Corn kicked the thing in the thigh. It collapsed, face to the floor.

It was Tess, his wife. She looked at him, her mouth and eyes alive.

'I was your wife, Isaacs, but I was Southern,' she said.

By that time a crowd of the sorrowful and the inept had gathered.

CONSTANT PAIN
IN TUSCALOOSA

I WENT BY this Chrysler on my Honda the other day. It was a sort of cold green car, in front of the bank. This nigger was eating a banana, hanging his leg out the front seat on the curb. He didn't have socks. He was truly eating that banana. Eating it was giving him such pleasure, I rounded the block and came by again to see him finish it off. By that time he was throwing the peel in the gutter.

I shut off the bike.

'Hey, man! You can't foul up the streets like that!' I said.

He looked at me awhile and then got out and picked up the peel.

'Who's that car belong to?' I said.

I'm a very slight guy and about that time something embarrassing happened. The motorbike fell over on me and I couldn't squirm out from under it before the muffler pipe had burned the dook out of my leg through my jeans. I pulled my leg out of the bike and jumped around on the walk. One of my old girl friends walked by and I was humiliated.

'My sister,' said the nigger.

'You just sitting out here eating a banana waiting for her?'

'Correct.'

'Oh ho. You been educated.'

'Junior college.'

I was still hopping around somewhat.

'It hurt, don't it?' he said.

162

'Somewhat.' My leg was about to go over the border into some kind of new state of pain.

He had him another banana by then.

'You wearing a nowhere helmet, baby,' he said.

'What's wrong with my goddamn helmet?'

'Look like some other person ought to be in it. That's some kind of airplane orange, ain't it?'

'Lets 'em see you at night, brother.'

'What you come here criticizing my bananas for?'

'There was a way you were doing it, eating. Your eyes were big and your jaw humped out. You were really having fun. It's not the same with the one you have now. You're doing it more casual-like now, little bitty bites, more civilized.'

'I never came in your house watch you eat,' he said. 'Tomorrow I'm coming over your house watch you eat. I'm gone drive my sister's Chrysler into your house and hang out the window watch you eat. Where you live?'

'Wait. No offense. I didn't mean anything by it,' I said.

'Where you live?'

'I don't have to tell you that.'

'This Chrysler is my home. It's me and my sister's home. Where you live?'

'Three oh four Earnest Lane.'

If I hadn't been in such pain, I'd never have told him.

'This car's the only home we got,' he said. 'We be by your place tomorrow.'

His sister came out of the bank. She had on stilt shoes and this African jewelry all over her. She got in the Chrysler. I heard her talking to him.

'They turned us down for the loan,' she said.

He never even looked my way when they backed out and drove off. I was trembly. My stomach was upset, and my leg had never quit hurting. Another thing. I'd been driving my bike around town thinking things over about reality and eternity and went by the Baptist church several times reading

163

the marquee. It said: *Pay Now, Fly Later*. I'd decided I was going to quit fucking around and be a Christian.

So right in front of the church there's Dr. Campbell, the minister of that church, a big guy with not much hair left and old acne marks and a look in his eye like he'd never thought about nooky one way or the other and had had his children by a holy accident. We all have our flaws. I walked over to him.

'Say, Doctor Campbell, I'm surrendering my heart to Jesus.'

He laid scrutiny on me. The few hairs he had left were oily and carefully set in a dramatic way.

'Tell you what, my son.' He laid hand on my shoulder. He whispered. 'I'm not the person to talk to. I hate your guts, after what you did to that poor disk jockey.'

'He was a queer and it was an even fight,' I said. 'He had a baseball bat and I had a TV antenna. On the roof there wasn't anything else.'

'He's still lying out in Druid Hospital.'

'I know where he is. I take beer to him under my coat. What about Jesus? I was surrendering my heart.'

'I've got to this position, Ellsworth. I don't think Jesus wants you. He's too dead to want. He was a hell of a sweet genius guy, but he's dead. The only thing left is humanism. Are you humanistic?'

'Right on.'

'Precious are the hours we touch one another,' the son of a bitch said.

The Honda had hurt me so bad I was sort of timid about getting on it again, but it took me home. I sat in my house and listened to the two records I own on my Sears stereo. Three years ago my wife left this place. All the pictures she hung and the decorations she did are still around. Sometimes late at night on the phone she says she might come back. She says her condition is one of constant pain. She's been in constant pain in St. Louis, Fayetteville, Arkansas, and

Mobile. A guy in Fayetteville called me one night at one o'clock. He said, 'Who's this, is this the authentic *Ellsworth*?' Lots of people were in the room he was in and I could hear they thought my name was funny. 'You know what I just did with your wife, Ellsworth?' said the guy. 'What I did was get in an Ellsworth costume and have sex with her – har har har,' said the guy.

'Why're you calling me?' I said. 'I loathe her and don't give a spit for her career. She was something I screwed and nagged me into marriage. I'll tell you what I'll do for you, however. My name is Ellsworth and I don't know what yours is, but I don't like this laughter about my name. You and me, phone person. Just give me your name and I'll be in Fayetteville to take care of your number.'

'Wonderful, wonderful,' said the guy. 'We knew you'd be like that.'

You could hear my wife among the tittering.

Actually it tore the last shred out of my bosom. I don't love her, but she was mine, and I don't want anybody else to, either. She knows that, that's why she called. She wants me to join her in constant pain.

I set three places on my table and swept up the house. I was sweeping the front steps when my leg, the one that was burned, went through the top step and I was up to my hop in my porch. I wish my landlord could've seen that. Maybe eighty-five per shouldn't get you a palace on the moon, but goddamn, it ought to get you *something*. It sprained the hell out of my crotch muscle, plus tore my boot.

The rest of the day I just lay around and swore. I didn't even get a beer out of the fridge. After you've drunk a hundred fifty thousand Falstaffs, the taste goes on you.

I made sure the house stayed clean. About midnight I went out and looked over at Mrs. Earnest's flower tree. All her lights were out. I stole about fifteen blooms off her tree. Then I got this pussy-looking green dish my wife bought and put the flowers on the table. I bought some steaks in the morning.

I didn't have a barbecue, so I got a hub cap and pulled the grill out of the oven to go over it.

About three in the afternoon, they showed up in the Chrysler. I looked out and they were looking at the house, engine running. The spade had another banana he was chewing on. His sister was driving. I went out on the porch as if to check out the carb on my Honda.

'Oh, hi!' I called. 'Come in the house now you're here!'

They came in the front room. His sister shook hands with me. She had blue fingernails, long ones, and that African jewelry all over and some new elevated nigger scandals and her toenails were blue too. When she walked, she rattled like a walking chandelier. The guy had on a plain shirt and just looked like an ordinary nigger. He went straight for the fridge.

'You got any soda or yogurt around?' he said.

'Hold on. This ain't a delicatessen,' I said.

'It for straight sure ain't,' his sister said. 'You got a hole in your porch. Hey, look at the flowers!' she said. She went over and picked up one of the flowers out of the water. 'I get off on flowers,' she said.

I was so pleased, I guess I blushed.

She called her brother Rip or Reap, I couldn't quite make it out. He never called her name.

'Man, look at the number of these beers! Are you some kind of beer salesman?'

'I keep it for friends who drop by,' I said.

'Ain't nobody drop by here,' he said. 'You got some handsome steaks in there.' he made a motion for me to move aside so his sister could get a view of the fridge. 'Look at them steaks,' he said.

'I get off on big old steaks,' she said.

'We're gonna get those on the grill in a couple of hours. Let me put on some music and you people sit down and relax.' I put the two records on. 'I got some dope if you . . .'

'You *what*? We don't use no dope! We don't like no rock-and-roll music, either,' he said.

166

'I get off on Ralph Vaughan Williams,' said the sister. 'You got any Ralph Vaughan Williams?'

'Come out here, look at his barbecue,' the dude said to his sister. He was looking out the back door of the kitchen at my unit. 'That a space-age model, ain't it?'

After a while they said they were going out and sit in the Chrysler for the air-conditioning. I thought it was a ruse to leave for good. When they shut the door, I had to call back this yell that was coming out my throat. It was a yell that if it had come out would've been the weirdest sound I ever made.

I knew I'd hear the motor start. They were out there fifteen minutes. I couldn't stand it. I went and got a beer in each fist and killed them in four minutes. I pushed the curtain to the side.

The nigger was working on another banana and talking to his sister. She sat in the driver's seat looking like she was really grossed away by his eating etiquette. They got out and opened my door again.

'Get cooled off?' I said.

'We're out of gas,' said the nigger.

'It's cooling down some now. We can get those steaks on in half a sec. The other side of that record isn't so much of a roar. I turned it down. It's got some nice soft licks in it.'

'I'm a vegetarian,' said Rip or Reap.

'He's lying through his face, Ellsworth,' said the girl. 'This family man in Baltimore, he came out on the parking lot with two buckets of Kentucky Fried Chicken on his arms. He' – she pointed at the nigger – 'cruised by and robbed them right off the man. He put his face in the bucket and eat that chicken out just like a hog.'

'Beauty ain't gone keep you well forever,' said the nigger to her.

'He had slaw on his nose,' she said.

The nigger made a move at her.

'Freeze, buster,' I said.

'What you got can stop me?' He looked around.

167

I ducked in the back room and got that UHF antenna I messed up Oliver Darling with. By that time he was half-nelsoning his sister.

'Leave off, Rip, Reap!' I shouted.

He sprung off her and came out with something yellow from his hip. It was a banana. He was a larger-looking nigger now and he raced over and beat the damn light out of me. When I woke up, he was still laying on my burned leg with what was left of the banana, these peel fibers. They stung in a vicious way.

'Stop it, stop it!' his sister was saying. 'You woke him up, for Jesus's sake!'

I washed up and after we'd eaten the steaks, with light bread and ketchup, we were all lying around pretty sleepy. The girl drank half a beer. I'd drunk five or six for pain. The girl stood up and went to use the bathroom.

'Say,' I said to the nigger while she was out. 'I'm kind of in love with her. I know that's not the right thing to say now. It's just my feeling talking.'

'You *what*?' He got wall-eyed like a joke nigger.

'Got a crush on your sis. Don't come at me again. You don't need to get tough on me. Thought we could talk this out. You think I'd have a chance with your sister?'

'Yeah. Cause you're white and she's terrible tired. You weren't too bad-looking till I blued you all up in the face.'

She came back and sat down on the floor. Pretty soon she was fast away asleep.

'I'll tell you,' he said softly, 'you can't get away from people bothering you anymore. People coming by laughing at even what you eating. Don't move,' he whispered, and eased out of the room.

168

Deaf and Dumb

SHE HAD A certain smile that would have bought her the world had the avenue of regard been wide enough for her. They loved it at the Bargain Barn. But the town was one where beauty walked the walks as a matter of course, and her smile was soon forgotten by clerk and hurried lecher on the oily parking lot. She never had any talent for gay chatter. She could only talk in brief phrases close on the truth. How much is this? Is this washable? This won't do, it's ugly.

It hit ninety-eight degrees and the parking lot of the A & P was the worst, with heat rays thick over the black pavement. There were four Cadillacs out there with the rabble of other cars. She got in the Chevy Nova, no air-conditioning and failing muffler. Her husband was an intellectual in real estate. He was such an intellectual he never sold anything. He had a huge habit of honesty and viewed everything being built or traded as pure overpriced dung. Forty-eight thousand got you a phony shack with no trees and tennis privileges. Don't buy this turkey, he told the couples who were new in town, let's look for something good. But he never could come up with anything good. All the good stuff was held down by old people with oaks and magnolias in their yard. He sold a few grimy houses to hip people who didn't mind nigger-town.

So Minny and her husband and their four children squeezed by on nine thousand a year. They were in hock up to their hips. They owed everybody from Sears to Saks in Atlanta.

The letters from Saks were so gentle and decent. She loved Saks. The requests for payment approached the condition of love letters to her, which nobody else since she was in college had written her.

She remembered the one from Harold, who had taken her virginity.

'Gosh. Thank you, thank you. If you aren't heaven, I don't want to go there. You didn't have to but you did. I love you so much it hurts my chest bones. Thank you, thank you.' Just as if his voice were speaking it to her now.

She drove her Nova around town, delaying her arrival at home, though she was suffering from the heat. The children were out in the garage with a hammer, sharing it. They were using the hammer to smash the pictures she'd hung in the garage. It had been her idea to dress up the garage. To her mind, there was no reason the garage need be an ugly slot to park your car. The garage could be beautiful. She was a major in art in college, and though she was no great shakes as an artist, she loved beauty and fitting colors. Minny painted the telephones in the house yellow.

But at night, when the kids were asleep, her husband took pictures of her naked with a Polaroid camera ordered from Sears on the easy-pay plan. One of his rare big cash-on-the-barrelhead buys was a six-foot mirror. He took pictures in the mirror of her with him. He couldn't believe she was submitting to these things and wanted to capture it for immortality. The pictures showed a middle-aged man in all sorts of postures with a shy zestful woman, the man joined to her and aiming the camera. The pictures he kept high on a shelf and called his 'studies.'

When Minny got home, she scolded the children for destroying her pictures in the garage. This took the last of her energy. She was all done in, hauling the bags, finding the old places for the cans and hauling them to their spots. She went to the room where the air-conditioner worked, shut the doors and lay down.

She had an hour before everybody would be hungry and Daryl, the husband, would be in. In the bag leaning on her bed was four yards of orange cloth she would sew into a dress. Her youngest child opened the door and crawled into the bed beside her. This was her and their only girl. She was a small pulchritudinous thing, with strange heavy-lidded eyes. While Minny lay there, the child kicked her in the course of falling to sleep.

I can't sleep, said Minny to herself. Why isn't Charlotte watching them? Why has Charlotte gone home? She's paid to stay. They're my responsibility. The teen-agers come by our street so fast in their cars and on motorcycles. They found out there are no police on our street and they use it as a blasting alley. One boy I met with before college liked to speed that way.

We raced everywhere. He was always early for everything, the basketball games, the prom. We never even held hands. One time when we went swimming together he looked down at my feet and tackled me. He put my big toe in his mouth. I told him to cut it out. He got big in his swimming trunks and was humiliated. He said: Listen, I got to teach you how to swim. It bothers me thinking a person like you might drown just for simple lack of swimming. So he taught me how to swim. He had a nice body and cut out through the water like a motor. No reason to go that fast, as usual, no point in getting there to the floating dock early except just to get there fifteen seconds before the others. He always kept a comb, even in his swimming trunks. Had hairy knees that disgusted me. Said I don't want anything but would you at least look at what does want to. Pulled down his trunks. First one I really ever saw, miracle, although a little bit ugly. No wonder he was proud. All men ought to be proud. All I and the rest of us have is hair and a crease. What's so emotional about titties? Mine are fine, but I never understood the excitement. Guy in a convention in New Orleans said he'd cut off his arm to savor my chest. The easiest place to have wit is in the presence of another's need. Deaf and dumb

171

guy selling ballpoint pens comes up with a card saying I am deaf and mute, raising two children, help me out. I pretended I was deaf and dumb too. He was giving signs like mad and I was giving signs back at him that weren't real. I was looking in his face. Who let you have children in her? I thought. What's deaf and dumb intercourse like? Then I became ashamed and bought all his pens with the grocery money. Daryl was drunk and therefore understood everything when I came home. We ate rice with ketchup on it. My hobby is Daryl now that my other interests have had no chance to grow. Maybe I was never an artist, but I could be an interior decorator. Lucky for me Daryl is good-looking. I couldn't stand phonying-up to one with hair on his knees. They once tried to hire me as an interior decorator at the furniture place on Sixth Street. They offered me a salary of $5700 a year. Daryl got on the phone to the head-man. 'Who do you think you're trying to hire, some Goddamned darkie? My wife has an art background and all sort of cleverness. You got to raise the ante or she doesn't come at all. Let us know if you can get it up over nigger wages. I don't want to be ashamed of what my girl is bringing home every month.' They didn't up it and I lost the job. But I loved Daryl and his pride, I guess I have pride. I guess I'm lucky how much I love Daryl, who's a silly ass by any judgment. Some hot nights I dream about the beaches in Pensacola. But Daryl is my hobby. You can tell how good it is by the temperature of a man's come. Harold's was lukewarm ... I suppose I shouldn't think of it, being raised in the church. But with Daryl – once the kids are asleep – there's nothing like that hot blowing out in you when you are coming yourself. I, good Lord, thank You for that. It keeps a body going through the trash in daylight. Good intercourse is a work of art.

Minny was asleep.

The boys had found a king snake in the garage. The oldest boy hit it over the head with a hammer. Then he wrapped it round the hammer handle. The youngest boy brought it into the house.

Daryl hitched a ride with his partner at the realty and drank a hot beer in the car to calm his nerves, but when he opened the door he sensed that everything was not all right. He knew that he was two bourbons away from peace, and in his desperation he opened the wrong door, not the cabinet under the sink but the basement door, and tumbled down the rotten stairs.

The youngest boy heard the air-conditioner running in his parents' bedroom. He opened the door and saw Minny asleep beside the baby girl. He knew it was a sin for his mother to be asleep in the daytime, the baby-sitter gone.

He looked at her awhile. Then he hit her in the mouth with the hammer.

It woke her up. It also woke up the snake, who had been only stunned by the blow in the garage. The snake unwound itself from the hammer handle and fell on the bed. It rose and twisted since half its nerves were gone. It almost stood up. The boy was horrified and fled the room.

When this woman saw it, she thought she was still in a dream and she felt very guilty for her sleep.

MOTHER ROONEY
UNSCROLLS THE HURT

MOTHER ROONEY OF Titpea Street, that little fifty yards of dead-end crimped macadam east off North State, crept home from the Jitney Jungle in the falling afternoon of October 1965. She had on her high-laced leather sneakers and her dress of blue teacup roses; she had a brooch the size of an Easter egg pinned on at her booby crease; she clutched a wrapped-up lemon fish filet, fresh from Biloxi, under her armpit.

Mother Rooney had been served at the Jitney by Mimsie Grogan, an ancient girl who had converted back in the thirties to Baptist. Mimsie would hiss at her about this silly disgusting ritual of Fridays as she wrapped the fish. Mother Rooney was Catholic. She was old, she had been being Mother Rooney so long. In the little first-story bathroom of her great weird house no spray she bought could defeat the odor of reptile corpses stewed in mud. Her boarder boys, all gone now for a month, would sometimes come in late and use her bathroom to vomit in, not being able to climb the stairs and use their own. And sometimes they were not able to use even hers well. There would be whiskey and beer gravy waiting for her on the linoleum. Just unspeakable. Yet the natural smell of her toilet would be overcoming the other vileness, she could not deny it. A couple of the young men smarties would openly confess, in the way of complaining about the unbearably reeking conditions among which they were forced to puke last night, that they were the ones. One

174

of them even arranged his own horrid bountiful vomit into a face with a smile, such as a child might draw, and *this* she had to confront one morning at six o'clock as she came to the chilly tiles to relieve herself. Nobody confessed to that. But she caught on when she heard all the giggling up in the wings, at this hour in the morning. She wasn't deaf, and she wasn't so slow. The boys were sick and tired of her flushing the toilet and waking them all up every morning. Her toilet sounded like a volcano. Yes, Mr. Monroe had voiced that complaint before. He said it sounded as if this old house's back was breaking at last, it couldn't stand the tilt anymore. It woke them all up, it made them all goggle-eyed, everybody stayed stiff for two hours in their beds. Nobody wanted to be the one to make the move that finally broke it in two and sent them all collapsing down the hill into the Mississippi State Fairgrounds. What a way to wake up, Mr. Monroe complained. The situation here is uninhabitable. I don't know a man upstairs who isn't planning to move out of here as soon as he sees an equal rent in the paper.

She promptly brought down the rent to fifteen a month, and the boys all showed up downstairs Saturday night to celebrate, spilling wine and whiskey, which were illegal in this state, everywhere, and grabbing her ruggedly around her weary little rib cage and huffing smoke and rotten berries into her face, calling her the perfect landlady; but profanity began to be used in the dining room, and she was eager to remind them that hard liquor such as three or four of them were drinking was against the law in the state of Mississippi. The party got quiet. They all took their hands off her. They left like mice, not a backward look. She was so sorry to have ruined this party. It was too loud, it was drunken, but one thing had been agreeable to her. Their hugging on her had been good. The hugging. So many big boys had put their arms around her ribs and had not hurt her. She didn't feel a thing there, nary a lingering of pain, but a warm circle of her body Mother Rooney rubbed against. Oh oh, it was like old flannel cloth that had fingers. Give me that, honeys, she thought. Keep me. Watch me. Watch me, witness me make my old way till one day I've got my eyes closed and you'll . . . I'll keep you here at twenty-five cents a month, but you'll have to discover me dead, feel me with those large hands, you will circle me, wrap me, you boys made of flannel cloth. Some mornings Mother Rooney would pretend to lie toes-up in her bed past six-thirty, having to tee-tee agonizingly, but not going to the toilet and flushing it on time, and getting all she could out of her own old flannel gown. By seven the pain in her bladder would take her almost to true death.

Mother Rooney of Titpea Street came on.

Her boys had all left her now. Like mice. Not a whisper since. Some of them had said they'd write her every day. But not a line. Not a hint even as to whose facilities they were throwing up in nowadays. Her boys were lost in unknown low-rent holes of Jackson, the big midstate town of Mississippi. They had broken up their tribe. They . . .

She was deafened by thought; she'd kept it inside so long, there was a rumble. First thing she knew, she was at the doorknob leaning too hard; she broke the glass doorknob and the door gave. Still, she was a deaf-mute. If sound would come back to her, she could maybe hold on with her sneakers at the top of the hall. That retrograde dance at the top of her perilously drooping lobby, it couldn't come. She saw ahead of her the boards that were smooth as glass; she saw the slick boards beckoning her like a well down past the gloom of the stairs. The fish bundle jumped out of her arms and broke out of its paper and lit on the boards, scooting downward like a pound of grease. No sound would come to her. She flopped in her skirts; her face turned around for a second. She got a look at the wasted orange trees and a look at the sky. It was so chilly and smoky, but quiet. Then her sound came back to her. She was falling.

She put her arms out for flight. She kept her knees together. She knew she was gone. She knew she would snap. She forecast for herself a lonely lingering coughing up of spinal fluid – she could hear all her sounds now – when *fock*,

176

landing on the fish binding, she hit face-down on the boards as if entering water in a shallow dive.

The back of the house was black, such a black of hell's own pit. Something was trying to stop her from going down there. Her breasts burned. The brooch had caught the wood and stopped her.

How wonderful of the brooch to act like a brake, Mother Rooney thought. She had slid only to the edge of the stairwell.

She might have butted through the kitchen door, clear out the back of the house and down the kudzu hill, where there was death by snakes at most, terror by entwinement and suffocation at least.

The house stood, slanting backward but not seriously dismantled yet, over a kudzu-covered cliff that dwindled into red clods upon the grounds of the Mississippi State Fair and Livestock Exhibition. Mother Rooney lived in only the bottom story of the brown middle box between two three-story tubular wings with yellow shingles. The brown box was frosted gingerbread-style in white wooden agates and scrolls, and had a sharp roof to it. In the yellow towers, upstairs, was nobody. She had her stove, pot, couch, bed and dining room, where the boarders ate.

But they were gone.

Her husband Hoover was dead since 1947.

Meager breezes of human odor fell and rose on the stairs. Once last week she took herself up the stairs of the left wing and opened a room and buried her face in a curtain saturated still with cigarette smoke. She got *in* the curtain. This time she did not weep. She just held on, getting what she could.

Her rugs moved backward against the baseboards. You dropped a ball of yarn and it took off downhill; you spilled some tea and it streaked away from the dining room, over the threshold hump, and vaporized in the kitchen. The boards were really slick. But she would not nail things down or put gripper mats around everywhere. She wouldn't surrender. The only concession she made to the house was the acceptance of the sneakers from Harry Monroe, the medical student, who told her they were strictly the newest development from the university, already tested and broken in for her. What they were, were wrestling shoes Monroe and his partner, Bobby Dove Fleece, had stolen off a dead woman in the emergency room, a lady wrestler who had been killed down at City Auditorium. Mother Rooney could make it, with these sneakers, even though her feet didn't breathe well in them.

She lay hurt more than she then knew beside the stairs, and felt only as usual, surrounded by the towering vacant wings of her house. Now this horror that she had not personally cultivated at all, this queer renewal of sights and sounds in the air – ghosts – was with her.

Mr. Silas was whispering to her in the dining room. 'You are living in the cocked twat of the house. This house has its legs in the air. Not only is it ugly, it's an outrage, Mother. It's a woman's thing cocked beggingly between big old thighs. My shocked friends ask why I live here. I answer that it's what I can afford. I was homeless driving my motorbike and saw the "Rooms" sign. I chose at night. All I wanted was a pillow. Once on the porch, I fell in.'

'She snatched our money and gave us lard to eat,' said Bobby Dove Fleece.

This young man thought he was a genius. All of them were naughty, her boys.

The house tilted all of six inches. A black gap of air stood between the bottom of the porch and the top of the ferny foundation. A sweet waft of ruining potatoes hung in the gap. Hoover had buried the pile for winter-keeping in 1945. Was he ruining so sweetly in his grave? Mother Rooney wondered. Or did his soul lie like a dead putrescent snake in the plumbing under her commode? as she often thought.

But Jerry Silas, leaping from his motorcycle toward the cocked porch, smelled *sperm*, blowing him over from under the house: haphazard nature had approximated the smell with a rotting compost of yams.

178

Nature will always scandalize, Silas had told her. And since he was bare-chested, as usual in the house, Mr. Silas had flexed all his upper body, a girl-murdering suavity in his eyes, and made the muscles of his chest, stomach and arms stand out most vulgarly in front of her.

Oh, Mother Rooney wished Mr. Silas and all the young men back now, filling the wings and the upstairs with cigar and cigarette smoke, music, whoops, nonsense, coming down and arranging themselves noisily around her table to eat what they called her Texas pie – because it was so ugly, they said. And she, scooping out the brown stringy beef and dumplings and setting it on their plates with insulted vigor, *flak!* Oh, they kept her at the edge of weeping or of praying; she was hurt in her cook's heart.

Some juice spattered on Mr. Delph, the young pharmacist, and he announced, wiping it away: 'Fellows, Mother Rooney is not being a Christian again.'

They made her uncertain of even her best dishes, her squash casserole, her oyster patties. When they first had begun this business, she lingered in the kitchen while tears ran off her cheeks into her milky desserts.

But for them just to be here she wished, calling her anything they wanted to. Let them mimic Father Putee behind his back as he advised my poor carnal body, the two of us seated on the couch in the dining room.

Mother Rooney regained the picture of that rascal Mr. Worley, the student at Millsaps College. He was loitering up the stairway listening to Father Putee, and she saw him, dressed only in underwear for her benefit. When Father Putee would finish a sentence, Mr. Worley would snap the waist of his underwear and look upward to heaven. Finally, Father Putee, an old person himself, heard the underwear snap, and turned. But by then Worley was gone, and Harry Monroe was in his place, sitting fully dressed, waving his hand. 'Hi, padre. I'm just chaperoning you two.'

Let them, let them, she wished.

Let them take me to another movie at the Royal Theater,

179

telling me it is an epic of the Catholic faith, and then we sit down and see all of that Bulgarian wòman in her nightgown prissing about until that sordid beast eats her neck, the moon in the window. Let them ride me by St. Thomas's Church, as Mr. Worley says in the back seat to Mr. Hammack, the young man who tunes organs, and asking it again to Mr. Delph: 'Don't you hate a fish-eater? Hammack, Delph, don't you?' They go on and on, pretending to be rural hardshells, then stop the car under the shadowy cross in the street. 'Let's kill a fish-eater.' They ask me to find them one, describing how they will torture one like they did in the Middle Ages, only nastier, and especially an old woman fish-eater. Maybe let her live for a few weeks until she has to beat on the door with her own leg bone to be heard from the street.

Then let them all come down to the table in their under-wear, all except Mr. Monroe, who is in on the joke so far as to have his shirt off. I'm in the kitchen and see Mr. Silas stand up and say this: 'Pre-dinner game tonight! Here it is! If any old, creeping, venerealized, moss-covered turtle of a Catholic scab-eating bimbo discarded from Pope Gregory's lap and rejected by the leprous wino in back of the Twentieth Century Pool Hall comes in here serving up any scum-sucking plate of oysters of a fish-eating Friday night, we all pull off our jockey shorts and wave them over our heads, okay?' 'Yahhhhh!' the rest of them agree, and I peep around and see Mr. Silas putting the written-up piece of paper in his elastic underwear. I wait, wait, not sure of anything except I am getting the treatment from them for asking each one if he was a Catholic by any chance when they first boarded with me. Then: 'But where *is* our sweet Mother Rooney?' I hear Mr. Silas chiming, lilting. 'With her charming glad old heart, the beam in her eye of a reconciled old age? Her mushrooms and asparagus, blessed by the Lord? Her twink-ling calluses, proud to tote the ponderous barge of house-holdery? Benedictions and proverbs during the neat repast, and an Irish air or two over the piano afterwards, to bed at nine?' says Harry Monroe. 'To flush at six,' says Bobby Dove Fleece.

I sneak in, for I did want music in the house, and had bought the secondhand piano for the corner over there. I know well that Mr. Hammack can play. I did hope in my heart that someone could play and young men would sing around it. At least they are not doing what Mr. Silas threatened they would. And I ask, 'Are you really going to sing some Irish songs afterwards?' – passing the fried oysters. Blind drooping of the eyes as if they'd never seen me before. Mr. Silas, who works at Wright's Music Store and is a college graduate, asks, 'Do the Irish have a music, Harry?' Mr. Monroe took a lot of courses in music at his college. 'They have a uniform national fart,' Mr. Monroe replies.

I'm already crying, steaming red in the face over the hot oysters. I don't care about Irish; I'm not Irish, for mercy's sake, nor originally Roman Catholic. I just wanted music, any kind of music. I just wanted music, and I tell them that. 'Sorry,' Mr. Monroe ventures to say. And they all eat quickly in silence, running back to the wings and upstairs without a word. Next day they all come back from work and school and don't give me a word. Only Mr. Monroe comes down at evening to eat some soup left from lunch.

But then, of course, the call from the police the next night, saying they know, they have been following, the crude public display of nudity I allow in my boardinghouse, and that there have been complaints about vulgarism. Then I know it must be Mr. Silas, whose light is on. I see as I put down the phone and look up at the left wing. Just to check, just to be sure, still scared from perhaps hanging up on the real police, I walk up there, though it takes a lot of breath.

But knocking, there is no answer, and I open the door and right in the way is Mr. Silas naked, stiff and surprised, but he seems to be proud at the same time. But how did he do it?

I ease the door to. There's only one phone in the house, mine. Mr. Silas cries out vulgarly behind the door; he's lifting his weights, his barbells – and what sounds, what agony or pleasure of his body.

Yes, let my boys come back to me with all that. Even Harriman Monroe, who drove them all from the house, who told my boys to leave. Let slim Harry, who turned just a wee bit prig on us all, come back. Dearheart, though, he was hurt by the loss of a musical career. And Bobby Fleece mentioned to me privately that Harry Monroe was not making it as a medical student, either. Harry does not take care of his health in the meantime. He breaks out with red spots on the face. I tried to feed him, diet him on good vegetables at night. I asked him what he ate in the day, and he answered me. Women, he said. Whereas Mr. Silas used to sneak down to eat everything I have left. It was a secret between us, how much Mr. Silas ate. It went to six pounds a day.

The brooch was standing up like the handle of a dagger. It had unclasped. It had not behaved. The pin of it was sunk three inches in her bosom. Where it went into her was purple and mouth-looking. An unlucky bargain – the biggest bauble ever offered on the counters of the Emporium, uptown. It had been designed for a crazy czarina who could yank it off her chest and fend back lechers in the alley.

Mother Rooney surged up on her haunch bones. She worked her lips together to make them twinkle with spittle. She shucked off her ugly shoes by rubbing each ankle against the other, folded in her legs under the moon in blue roses of her hip, pushed herself against the stairwell. In general, she arranged the corpse so that upon discovery it would not look dry, so that it would not look murdered or surprised in ugliness.

At least, she thought, no bag of fluid inside her has ruptured. No unspeakable emission like that. She wondered about the brooch. Do you pull it out? The body would be prettier without it. But her boys had made her conscious of her body. She was a sack whose seams were breaking, full of organs, of bitter and sour fermenting fluids. Her body threatened to break forth into public every second.

Concerning the brooch, she feared blood, a hissing of air, perhaps a rowdy blood bubble so big it would lift her out of the hall, through the doorway, into the street.

Oh, such alarm, such wild notoriety!

Oh, Mother Rooney hurt like a soldier.

She remembered from the movies at the Royal: Don't talk. Each word a drop of blood into the lungs. And what about thinking? Mother Rooney had always conceived of mental activity as a whirlpool of ideas spinning one's core. Wouldn't that action send blood-falls to her lungs and elsewhere? She imagined her body filling up with blood because she was really thinking.

The deep itch of the pin came now.

She saw the pin running, shish-kebabing, through her heart, lungs, spleen, pancreas, liver, esophagus, thorax, crop, gizzard, gullet – remembering all that apparatus, wet, hot and furcated, she had pulled out of chickens in the 1930s. Then she thought of the breast, drumstick, pulley bone, and oh! – that hurt thinking that, because the pulley bone snapped and often punched into the hand.

So thinking it could be either way – a lung wound or shish kebab – she guessed she had better stop this whirlpool mental activity, for safety. It could be that shish kebab wasn't definitely fatal because, once the pin was pulled out, all the organs might flap back to their places and heal. But she dreaded feeling them do this inside her, and so she left the pin alone.

It came to her then that she might make her brain like a scroll, and that by just the tiniest bit of mental activity she might pull it down in tiny snatches at a time and dwell on the inch that was offered by the smallest little tug of the will, like the scrolled maps in schoolrooms. Perhaps she could survive then, tensing her body in a petite, just a petty, hope.

First was Hoover, the son of a sewage-parts dealer who fled Ireland in 1915; Roman Catholic Hoover Rooney, bewildered by snot and asthma. Then there was Hoover Second, his working son in overalls. Wasn't there something holy about the unsanitariness of their brick and board cottage on Road of Remembrance Street? How the yard grass was shaggy, and the old creamed tea from breakfast time was found in chipped cups with five or six cigarettes floating on top like bleached creatures from a cow pond's bottom; their black Ford with plumbing manuals in the back seat which smelled like a gymnasium with a melting-butter smell over that. Sometimes Hoover stopped at stop signs – I remember once in front of the King Edward Hotel – and a wine bottle rolled under my bare foot. I was tired, and when Hoover drove up to the lumberyard where I was a secretary, I would hop in and pull my shoes and stockings right off. Then one day Hoover grabbed my foot, and holding it in his lap, he took what he told me was his dead mama's ring and put it on my little toe and said, 'Baaaa!' I told him it degraded her memory. And he eased my foot out of his lap, started the car, and I had to hold my foot in the air to keep the ring from falling on the dirty floorboard, because Hoover grabbed my body and held me really hurtfully, so I couldn't get my hands free. How he laughed, making his face orange. With those desperado sideburns and slit eyes, he looked like something from Halloween. He had a hot metal body odor that came up close to the degree of unpleasantness. He smeared my mouth with his hairy lips and chin. I felt like I was eating down steel filings, and forgot I was thirty and he just a boy of early twenties. I laughed.

For being Annie Broome of Brandon, Mississippi, supposed to be at my Aunt Lily's promptly after work every day to eat our supper together, supposed to attend Wednesday-night church with her this evening. I saw my daddy drilling Hoover with a glare like at a snake doctor or a vegetarian. But I never told Mother or Daddy much at all, just sent them one of Hoover's postcards with an airplane picture of the shores of Ireland on it, and told them I'd been converted and that

Hoover was the one. Then, back in the car with Hoover, I quiver in that red moan against his marvelous hard tongue.

Plus all the other strange hours I felt like the robber queen. I called in sick to the lumberyard. Hoover picked me up at eight. He and his papa didn't start off the day till ten.

She lay cold in the hall of the old house. She waved her ring finger at the whirlpool. Stop. Blood, she thought, fell out of her mind into her lungs. If she could just shape her mind with a timid effort requiring no breath, she could beckon the scroll, easing it down in millimetres. Flies had found her. She fought them, thinking.

That malt cereal that the old man ate every morning, it got on his cuffs and his newspapers from Dublin, and he wore his napkins like a bib, tucked under his neck, which glucked with the tea and cereal. His yellow cheeks and red beard, they should've sent him home to shave at one o'clock, but he was not American yet; more like a Mongolian with his thin eye slits; then his brogue so thick you imagined he carried heavy cereal always in his throat, had to choke back a slug of it to talk. He did not care and tinkled loudly with the door of the bathroom open while he talked to Hoover and me about religions, the mediocre number of them. It shocked him. There were only a hundred-odd Catholics in all Jackson then, 1916. Hoover courted me on the settee. I waited for the old man to flush, but he never did. I thought about that yellow water still lying there and saw green Ireland floating in it. The hairy lawn of the house, and Hoover's body odor, and the whole milky stink of the house, they cut on me very sharp. And Hoover's breath was of some iron pipeline.

I was happy, sucked right into the Church, because I got its feeling. In St. Thomas's it was clean, dark, cooling and beautiful, with wood rafters of cedar, gloomy green pictures of Jesus, St. Thomas and the Jordan River in glass. Also, it was tiny and humiliating. It was a thrill to cover your head with a scarf because you were such a low unclean sex, going back to Eve, I guess, making man slaver in lust for you and not be the steward he was meant to be. You were so deadly, you might loop in the poor man kneeling next to you with your hair. I saw Hoover bending on the velvet rail. I felt peculiarly trickful, that this foreign cluck would moo and prance for a look at my garters, that his slick hair would dry and stand up in heat for me. In St. Thomas's I was thrown on that heap of navels, hair and rouge that makes the flesh-pile Woman, which even the monks have to trudge through waist-deep, I thought, before they finally ascend to sacredness. God told me this, and I blushed, knowing my power.

So I thought, that day when Hoover and I sat on his couch at one o'clock, thirty years old and smoking my first cigarette and drinking *tea*, that when he began playing sneaky-devious at my parts, with a whipped look on his face, this wasn't Catholic or Irish from what I knew of them, and that it was more Mississippi Methodist in Brandon, Mississippi, with the retreat at Lake Pelahatchie and Grady Rankin working at me with his pitiful finger, and I told Hoover my opinion, leaving out Grady and so on. We both jumped through our eyes at each other then. We were soggy and rumpled as when you are led to things, and I let him, I did, let him do the full act, hurting on his bed beyond what God allows a woman to hurt. God pinched off all but a thimbleworth of pleasure in that act for me, I mean, as long as I had Hoover my husband. But I let out oaths of pleasure and Hoover in that silly position . . . sometimes I take my mind up to the moon and see Hoover in that position, moving, with nothing under him. I laugh. The hunching doodlebug, ha ha ha! I was in this filthy house doing this, with an Irish Catholic. He said America was an experiment. He said I was safe in the oldest religion of historical mankind. On his bed I believed him: my hurt and fear turned to comfort.

Oh, but Papa Rooney wasn't proud of his boy for getting his wings on me. The old man was really there at the door watching us. He'd become more an American. He'd come in

186

to shave, and was here on us viewing Hoover in that silly position and me too. He called me names I'll never forgive, and Hoover too. He cried, and threw cups on the floor, and lay down on the couch, talking about what he'd seen and on and on. I was numb awhile, but then I started moving, low-pedaling around the house, while Hoover sat on the bed looking at his bare feet. I found the broom and swept up the teacups and then swept the rug right beside Papa Rooney, put all the dirty lost glassware in the sink, filled it with hot water. I mopped the tiles in the kitchen and flew into the bathroom at the bowl and sink. I scraped them all with only a towel and water, then found the soap and started using that everywhere. I went back in the halls, I fingered the dust out of the space heater. I found a bowl of cereal under the bed with socks and collars lying in it. I made the old man's room spanking-clean. I made a pile for his stained underwear in the back closet. Then it was four o'clock in the afternoon. I sat down by Papa Rooney, who was still on the couch. He looked tearfully at me. 'Annie, my boibee!' he said, and smothered me into his arms, asking forgiveness for what he had said. We went and sat by Hoover, while the old fellow told us about our marriage. I was scared. There seemed no other way, with Papa Rooney and his arms over our shoulders.

Except for Papa Rooney watching us all the way up the aisle, I doubt we would've married; we did. Through the ceremony we were both scared of – with Father Remus talking words of comfort over our heads to Mother and Daddy, who hung back and were shocked – we tied the knot.

Mother Rooney's head stood wide open in the twirl of remembrance. Blood, eye juice and brain fluid roared down to her lungs, she thought. Too hard, too hard, her thoughts. There were noises in the house as the wind blew on the windows, which were loose in their putty. The hallway was dark. It was her box. No light, now; her coffin space.

Mother Rooney shrieked, 'Be loud on the organ! Pull my old

corpse by a team of dogs with a rope to my toe down Capitol Street, and let Governor White peep out of his mansion and tell them to drag that old sourpuss Annie to the Pearl River Swamp. Oh, be heavy on the organ!' She shocked herself, and she remembered that Papa Rooney had died insane too, thinking that Jackson was Dublin.

The hell with the scroll! 'Everything!' she howled.

The old man went crazy in a geographic way at the last, at St. Dominic's Hospital. He shouted out the names of Dublin and Chicago and Jackson streets as if he was recalling one town he knew well. He injured his son Hoover, behaving this way. Hoover became lost; he saw the blind eyes of his daddy and heard the names of the streets. His daddy didn't know where they were. But Annie also recalled the sane old fellow at his last, how he'd fallen in love with her; loved her cleanliness and order; loved America, because he was getting rich easily and enlarged the sewage-parts house so that now Hoover was a plumbing contractor too. Papa Rooney told her he was in love with peace and money and her – Annie.

Annie made Hoover build her a house, a house that would really be a place, so Hoover would know where he was. He seemed to, when the house was up. There was actually no reason for Hoover to go insane, because, unlike his father, he loved the aspects of his job. He loved clear water running through a clot-free pipe. He loved the wonder of nastiness rinsed and heaved forever out of sight; he loved the dribbling water replacing it in the bowl, loved the fact that water ran hot and cold; he loved thermostats. He adored digging down to a pipe, breaking it and dragging the mineral crud and roots from it, and watching the water flush through, spangling. He got high and witty watching that one day at twilight, and the slogan came to him, like a smash to Hoover's mind: 'The Plumber's Friend.' That was how he advertised his firm in the *Clarion Ledger* for twenty years.

Hoover went jumping hard and erect to the gingerbread house with yellow towers, driving home with his first ad in his pocket. On Titpea, he saw the house lit up in all quarters;

knew his gentle Annie waited in one room. He knew he must have the wings full of baby sons, soon. Annie opened the door for him. He took her body. He was almost gagged by the odor of flowers and her supper of spaghetti, which was very new then, but he blasted her; bucked her upstairs, and perished hunching her to the point he didn't know when his orgasm was, but kept on hunching in a trance. He knew she was frail as a peaflower. He liked to snap her and squeeze her.

Oh! Certainly, how much, how so, so much Hoover wanted to be both a plumber's friend and a father, every evening. And Hoover Second came, finally, hurting more than any of those books told, because those books were written by men in some far-off tower, and they couldn't know. The intern leaned on her stomach. Great Lord! The nuns held her. They giggled. 'He's looking for another baby, dear.'

There could be no doubt that Hoover was. Again and again, and something was wrong. Not just that Mother Rooney couldn't have any more babies, as she couldn't, but Hoover's desire to be both a plumber's friend and a father was destroying her. The dearie loved plumbing, but he got to see less of it every year. The company was big and he had to employ many men in the expansion. He could do nothing but sit at his desk and inventory and buy and and sell, in his business suit, and he didn't have the old man's love for pure money. How many times, she asked, how many times did I see him leaning over the toilet bowl smiling at the water? How many times did he deliberately break some rod or other in the tanks at home, or rip something out that wasn't brand new, so he could drive down to the place in the night for a part? How many times did he look at me as if I was brand new too, and had worked once, then fagged off?

Bless his heart, he had to remember the night of what we both thought was Hoover Second's right vigorous making, the night he came home with his first ad in his pocket. Oh, I knew in my heart without doubt that was when, because

189

the pains of the entrance and the exit almost matched up. Pity his name, poor Hoover had to remember that he had had a little dirt from the pipeline on his breeches that night, and that he stunk some from heaving away and watching the men work. Lovely, wronged, one-son Hoover Rooney, heaving away and mating me, he had smeared my legs with mending compound off his ankles. Charming Hoover, who began showing up late in twilight absolutely negrified with pitch spots and sweat beads and his business suit done in forever with gunk. I knew what the dear was doing, that he was leaving the office at noon to parade out on one of his jobs among his plumbers, who probably didn't want him out there. He peered into the deepest and filthiest work going, careful to lift a pipe for some Negro, stumble against the roofing tar, for luck and because he desired so to be a plumber's friend. He came in manly and proud of his day's work's grime, looking like he wanted to break my back. Through the years he tried different combinations of filth and ruined bundles of suits, for luck, but he had no more with me. I had shoved out the boy that I had, for mercy's sake, and I tried to tell him so with my hurting eyes. It would not take – get in that silly position till Christ came!

Then Hoover went insane, yes, long before Hoover Second was killed and the house began tilting. In the middle thirties, when he was losing money every day, he almost gave me up and turned on the house. He sat on the dainty loveseat in the lobby when he came in, and soiled that, then lay back in the studio upstairs on my Persian divan with cornets and red iris on it, rolling the suet off his breeches until the pretty pattern was blurred; slept silently away in both wings with his rusty cheeks hard on the linen, for I could see the half a face Hoover left behind in the mornings, the big fans of palm grease where his hands had known my guest towels, and the wallpaper of clover flowers, but especially on my lovely fat pillows, everywhere. Oh, Hoover you were late for supper *again*, hung down so heavy with dirt. You were private and sulky and unhungry. You were so ugly and angry when I opened one of the doors on you, as if you'd been found out in your love's rendezvous. Pretty soon you had the house back like the cottage on Road of Remembrance, where you could've grown agricultural products on the floor.

You had a place again, dearest, and I had none, but only Hoover Second that you almost forgot, wanting Third through Four Thousandth. I loved, loved. What could I do, though? Little Hoover. I see him most of all for his feet and little toes, hot and dimpling from the bath water, and his steamy curling hair, his tiny wet marks on my rug. It was always him just coming from the water that I . . . like a fish you pull up, wondering what? And there the marvelous slippery rascal is, breathing something else than you breathe. Christ, the horror as he grew up and I saw he did, he did breathe something else. Oh, in the earlier days when Big Hoover attacked me in gangs, every one of them more mind-less and slaughtering, hurting, ahhhhh; when he draped on me afterward, nicking his dirty fingernails together, and he was heavy as the island of Ireland and had just tried to mash the whole country into me, and he would smoke then, roughhousing his cigarettes and letting them fall in pieces all over the bed. Well, I see too Hoover Second nestling by me after his bath, and think that my little baby, who didn't even know he had his man's business between his legs, was left to me when I was almost too tired to look at him and love. But I did, and I cupped his infant's peabud in my hand and held the softest most harmless unhurting thing in the world, and fell asleep in beauty.

I watched it stalk and grow too, and shiver — that funny time when he was open and proud with it and had just found it out. We called it Billy. Nuzzling against my side, he would want to know which neighbors had Billy. He asked if the air, clowns, toy soldiers and Cream of Wheat had Billy. I told him no, and we divided the world like that, with Billy and no Billy. He would kid me then, and ask about rocks, mud, the Jitney Jungle, underwear, as he hiccupped with the jollies. I guess he was telling his first racy jokes.

Sure enough, the days came so very soon when he hid his boyhood sprout from me, and it brought on a sweet pinch in my heart to see him finger away and snap up his pants with a rude look when I burst in on him unawares in the bathroom. There were two hurting worlds for me to endure. Big Hoover, coming at me with his never-faulty club with the head of an apple as he stands red and greasy as an Indian of naked insanity; his world, so slow and grinding. Little Hoover, slipping away just out of hand-reach in all the rooms of my big house, so I seem to see only his heels in the cruel scuffed leather of his shoes. And he was gone, a teen-ager and suspicious.

I was snagged, and only my unwanted hands to look at.

Came that afternoon quiet as a bird's breath when the world itself blew up, and all through the house there lay newspapers with inch-high letters on them about the war. Hoover dropped them on the floors and they filled up our Plymouth, so you made a dusty crackling sound climbing in upon the seats. We drove to St. Joseph's School. There he stood under that oak near the storm fence and the basketball court, in a ring of friends, talking quietly. All of Jackson was so quiet and breezeless. We couldn't hear the boys, but I know it was about the military situation. You thought they should be in the classrooms, that they were hatching something illegal and were hoodlums. Hoover Second was tall and not so pretty now, and in his large wool pants he looked skinny and just a little stupid. He noticed us; his eyes were black and hard. He felt called on to spit, and he did. He waved to his friends. Then, now, he was up in the left wing packing, and didn't want me near him, I knew, because the war idea made him even more a man. Oh, I thought he was through, though, and I was innocent and walked up to kiss him, crying already, and hung on his small bones for half a minute because I knew I had it coming to me.

It was mine too, that three-second vision of Hoover Second partially blind without his steel glasses and naked on his feet, when I bumped the door to his room open. He held his underwear in one hand and his other hand rested in the groove below the belly where it joins to the legs; he was pink from his bath. And yes, he was tenderly awful with his coiling wet hair, his dim eyes that felt toward me at the door. Who are you, Mother? he seemed to say. He stepped quickly into his underwear and abided my weeping weight, rushing upon him. 'What is it?' he says. I wanted to say, 'This is it: That you, something like you, should have been the one, that I was made for somebody like you; that what I see of your muscles and hair and your crumpled stalk tells me somebody like you would have been kind and right, that I'm crying now for how safe the world is with your skinny tenderness in it, how delicate its girls must be to deserve you, how lucky they'll be, how Europe seems like a rough metal planet to eat you on its cold soil or in its foggy air. Please, please, don't you meet any of Hoover's nieces in Ireland, who would eat you just as quick as the Nazis, and you watch out for, you step around Ireland and Irish like the plague. Oh, Hoover baby, you hide in the tiny dark unfindable corners and ditches and clouds and cupboards of Europe, and do come back to your mama and she will find you a girl.'

I do not believe all the terror Hoover Second was supposed to be in his airplane, because I know he couldn't see to do it; that he unloaded a record amount of bombs on German cities and set them afire; that he flew unofficial missions to 'grind them to powder.' He was so happy in the photograph with his crew. I believe that he was shot at unmercifully, and that he came back a hero with his legs full of brutal powdered lead, dug up in Europe's cold earth. Big Hoover told me once, trying to twist the knife over my not being pregnant – we were out of church and behind Mrs. Pitcaithly with her brood of boys and saw them wait in the cold weather for a taxi – 'A mother is the sum of her children.' Very cute and salty, Hoover, but you will wish to explain to me how this charming saying applies to me all the way through. You tell me Hoover Second has gone off as a soldier, and I would say, all right, that's me, I would've gone off too. Then you tell me Hoover Second was a war hero, risking himself, going beyond orders in an airplane called the Ugly Fierce Sparrow, to put the bombs in Hitler's lap, and I say again, all right, this might be an undiscovered hero fool part of his mama. But tell me, Hoover, if you were pushing on, what part of me was it that came back to Jackson wounded but out of the crisis, and tinkered together a wreck the Civil Air Patrol gave him for twenty dollars, that Piper thing which pooted and fluttered over Jackson and swooped over the towers of this very house, then proceeded to drop here and there, on the grounds of the capitol building, on the governor's mansion, on St. Thomas's, on Millsaps' campus, on main-street Jackson, on the football game in Clinton, white unspooling rolls of toilet paper that he had stolen out of the basement of St. Joseph's High School; and enjoyed the scandal and the protest that the *Clarion* wrote up about it, until they found out who it was: *a veteran* with a rich sense of humor! Then the schoolchildren ran out on the playgrounds at lunch period, hoping hoping hoping that he would drop a roll of rump-wiperage down their throats; and the whole town, running out to caress the paper, to find the real spool dropped from Jackson's man of the air. What part of me ran to the airport every morning couldn't even finish his cup of coffee, like he was still on some schedule? What act have I done at my wildest is there that would remind you of Hoover Second's crash and irresponsible burn on the tennis courts of Mississippi College, when there were miles of flat unpopulated fields all over the county for him to choose from? Find me somewhere in the sum of the parts of that burned airplane, dearest, and think again on that charming saying 'the sum of her children.' The little coeds, with their rackets, were telling the police how Hoover Second had come down on them repeatedly, how they had to scamper, and the preacher students were still pronouncing on the wreck when we arrived, two hours later. I sat down on the courts and I was never in a more foreign land than on the scorched tennis courts at the scene.

We die, Mother Rooney thought. Even me, in this cold hall, by accident. But God – God damn it, yes! for you, Hoover, to hike off with a broken heart and die of self-inflicted plumber's pneumonia when the house did tilt, it seems, a week after Hoover Second's crash. But I know it wasn't. I got three more mooning years from you, who never looked at the boy in his life except as the first number of numbers that didn't come. For you to die, God damn it, for *you* to be the one, with everybody saying: 'Sure. Completely understandable. He's borne that grief.' All your dirt started piling up in the back of the house, didn't it? Your heart was broken, it had been stretched so much when the men with the jacks couldn't do anything about the tilt. Godarooney, Goddamn. Thanks for not omitting to fill the bathroom with colorful phlegm when you went. Thank God we didn't live on together and dredge up memories of false romance from our past. Don't think, dear, that I missed those scrubby melancholy kisses of old age.

Mother Rooney had never taken even an aspirin, and now she was harsh and proud.

She heard Harry Monroe's English Ford outside, with its drizzling ruptured halt at the curb. It was a ghost again, she thought. But she thought of how Harry Monroe had cured her of being afraid every October when the fair came and when she thought she heard something down the hill in back calling her – Mother! Mother! Mother! Harry took her out in the backyard and proved to her that what she was hearing was the men getting the cattle out of the trucks, and when they didn't move right, the men would lay on with sticks and shout, 'Motherfucker!'

'It's just the Four-H boys saying *motherfucker*,' Harry explained. Mr. Harry Monroe thought he was being such a clever learned adviser to her. But from Bobby Dove Fleece she knew Mr. Harriman Monroe wasn't making it as a medical student.

Harry Monroe was really there in the doorway.

He called, 'Mother Rooney?' He wore his sophomore lab coat as a cape on his shoulders; he had a fat little book in one hand and a bottle of wine in the other. He was handsome in an old public way. His face was not smooth. He had wanted to play the horn more than know all he was forced to know at the med center of Ole Miss.

He found her. He saw Mother Rooney regarding him. He hit the light switch, and he saw her cartoon yellow hair in its old bun, her bunions shining through her stockings, and the white, blue-rosed dress.

Mother Rooney crooned, 'I'm gone, Harriman. You pull off your clothes and let me get a look at you, baby. You were the one, but you always just hurt me. I deserve this. Don't you be shy. I walked in on Jerry Silas completely naked one night. He was so muscular. He was a wonder. I have seen young men. You aren't the first. Don't you be ashamed, Mister Monroe.'

Harry Monroe said, 'I know you saw Silas. He's on the porch. I'm going to take his ass tonight. Don't you lose control now.'

'You ran my boys away. You ruined this house.'

Mother Looney, he thought. He shut the door and locked it to keep Silas and the other fellow out. 'I'm the only one that did care a little,' he said to her. He knelt by her and saw the brooch buried in her and the blood dripping down the old ravine of her breasts. He didn't want her to see him blanch. He thought she was in shock. 'I brought you this bottle of wine. I saw Silas at the Dutch Bar and we thought we'd surprise you tonight. You must take up drinking.' He peered at the wound some more. 'I brought this book, the *Merck Manual*. You can read in it and tell your own disease by the symptoms. You can advise the doctors.'

Aw hell, Monroe thought. The bottle of wine was a third drunk, and the *Merck Manual* was an old one he'd got out of the pharmacology trash basket.

'You were always ugly to me. Is Jerry Silas out there? I want to see him. I have a crush on him,' she said.

196

She's with it. She's not in shock, Monroe thought.

'I'm not going to let them in,' he said.

Two men were outside the door, falling on the porch and yelling to him.

'You don't like Silas, Mother. We all knew he was . . . he lifted weights. Didn't just lift them. The weights possessed him. He sent off for special underwear and for red oil to rub on his body. He bought a camera that he could activate from across the room while he lay on his bed, flexing. He'll kill himself when his stomach muscles start sagging.'

Oh, but they didn't sag. Mother Rooney thought, when I walked in on him and he was naked and stiff, but twinkling in his eyes so joyously that it was clear he couldn't hurt a woman in all his health, either. He would have been tender, friendly, out-of-doors with you. Oh, he maketh me to lie down in green pastures, but where was he and where was his pasture? And, yes, he restoreth my soul, but all I got was used up. And, yes, his rod and staff, they comfort me – and they would have, but where was he, and where was the comfort I was entitled to? My cup runneth over with hurt-juice.

'Mr. Silas wanted me to be thirty again,' Mother Rooney said.

Monroe leaned on the stairwell with his head in his hands. He yelled out to the porch for them to shut up. He opened the *Merck Manual* and began turning pages.

'You cannot like him. You cannot like any of us. We were the ugliest people as a group. Didn't you see how marked out for losing we all were? Hammack, Worley, Delph. I sometimes wondered how all we shits got ganged up in this – this beautiful house. But especially you can't like Silas. Silas breathes out a smell of broiler shanties and rotten pine, and he is always sweating. He's lost his job at the music store, but he flourishes on, trying in different ways to prove that he is not from Fig Newton, Mississippi, that a certain type of mass-produceable chicken wasn't named after his father.'

197

'You are very sharp toward others,' Mother Rooney said.

'Oh, I know me,' Harry Monroe said. 'A man who was so bad in music he was booted out of the Jackson symphony, and now almost failing med school.'

'But you keep on being so cruel to me. You won't open the door and let me see those boys. There are *two* boys out there, aren't there?'

'One of them isn't a boy,' Monroe said.

It was strange to him to hear the two on the porch, still savagely drunk, and to realize that he himself, who had put down more than any of them, was now sober as Mother Rooney was.

He said, 'The fellow with Silas is seventy years old. He was at the Dutch Bar and we thought we'd bring him over as a – a gift, a present to you. The old guy is ready to be your companion from now on out; he already has a crush on you, Mother. Listen!'

She had begun to rise, hissing at him.

'I know it's horrible now. But I and Silas wanted to make amends to you, really. We are so sorry for what happened in this house. You know, it started with the little joking insults, and then it grew to where hurting you was a cult. You really occupied us. Especially those of us who were taking a lot of bad traffic in the shit of the outer world and were originally endowed with a great amount of rottenness in our personal selves. The next thing would've been murdering you. I always felt the police were ready to break in any minute.'

'You prissy little scholar. I could've taken it,' Mother Rooney said. 'You don't know the hurt that's come to me. It tells me I'm alive, hurting.'

Monroe looked at her forlornly. 'Do you think you can take that pin wound in your chest now?'

'I don't know.' Mother Rooney sank, remembering the pin. What to do? Monroe wondered. He drew away into the dining room and sat on the couch. 'Puncture' was all he remembered. He was very busy with the *Merck*, after making

198

the phone call. She heard the pages ruffling and Harry mumbling.

'. . . do not bleed freely and the point of entry seals quickly, making the depths of the wound ideal for the propagation of infective agents. Tract should be laid open and excised and *débridement* carried out in the manner described under Contaminated Incised Wounds.'

Mother Rooney also heard a loud mauling at the door.

Silas and the old guy were making a ram attack on it. Monroe yelled unspeakably filthy words at them. His pages were still rippling. Then he threw the book out through the front bay window and there was a horrendous collapsing of glass. Then the ambulances came squalling up Titpea. By mistake, two of them came to the same house. Monroe ran on. There were steps and voices and the red lights outside.

Mother Rooney bellowed, 'Is it the police, Harriman? I always thought they'd come in and stop Hoover's cruelty to me. I thought they should have been at the tennis courts at Hoover Second's crash, declaring it illegal and unfair, and restoring him to me. But they never came. They're worthless. Tell them that if they try to get in the door.'

Harry Monroe studied the standing brooch on her chest. Do you pull it out? And because the brooch looked silly sticking in the old lady, he walked to her quickly and snapped it out, then flung it down the hall at the back of the house.

He unlocked the door, and there was big Mr. Silas, asking, 'What is occurring? I've got the lover here.' The old man was riding piggyback on Silas's huge shoulders; he had combed his white hair back with his own drunkardly, lonely spit, using his fingers, and he was scared to death. The two men waddled in, looking at Mother Rooney.

Monroe ran at Silas and slugged him in the eyes and Silas abandoned the old guy and fell into the dining room upon Monroe. A brawl could be heard by Mother Rooney. The table went over. Silas was reaching for Monroe, who kicked away and whimpered, and that was what the brawl amounted to.

The old boy lay dazed in the lobby, fallen where he was

shucked off Silas. He had landed hard and didn't move. Then his body, with its ruined hairdo, started sliding on the slick boards, face up, down toward Mother Rooney. He moved on down and she saw he was really a red old drunk.

The first ambulance crew thought he was the one and rolled him out expertly. The second crew noticed the woman bleeding. But she was standing now, and went out to the ambulance walking. One of the ambulance men had to go in and break off Silas from Monroe, and now Monroe was another case, and Mother Rooney sat beside him and petted him, all the way to the hospital.

RAY

FOR GORDON, BILL, ELIZABETH

I

RAY IS THIRTY-THREE and he was born of decent religious parents, I say.

Ray, I didn't ever think it would get to this. The woman I love and that I used to meet in the old condemned theater and we would wander around looking at the posters and worshiping the past, I just called her Sister like her parents, the Hooches, did. Her mother lives in that house with that man. Her grandmother was a Presbyterian missionary killed by the gooks.

Ray, you are a doctor and you are in a hospital in Mobile, except now you are a patient but you're still me. Say what? You say you want to know who I am?

I have a boat on the water. I have magnificent children. I have a wife who turns her beauty on and off like a light switch.

But I can think myself out of this. My mind can do it. It did it before, can do it again, as when I was pilot of the jet when I was taking the obnoxious rich people in their Lear from Montreal to New York to Charlotte to Pensacola to New Orleans to Mexico City to the Yucatán to Tuscaloosa, Alabama, because they had an old friend there.

You can do it, mind and heart. You can give it the throttle and pick up your tail and ease it on. You can do it, Ray.

For instance, look at this male nurse. He weighs three hundred pounds. He's got flab in his eyes, but he used to weigh four hundred. Now he's divorced his second wife and

205

has no remorse and is moving to Key West for a higher-paying job. He has no care for other people because his own elephantine system keeps him employed. You would fire him, Ray. Except you can't fire anyone now.

Nether. That's a good one. Hang on to a word like *nether*.

Her nether hoot. No, I don't, nether. This is the netherlands and it will nether get worse. That is the awfulest netherest laughter.

I just threw up my netherest soul. There's nothing left, nether. My eyes are full of yellow bricks. There are dry tiny horses running in my veins.

That was three weeks ago, Ray. Now I am clean. My head is full of light. I am a practicing doctor again and it is necessary I go over to the Hooches.

My heart, my desire. Sister!

The stacked tires, the station wagon half-captured by kudzu and ivy, the fishing boat on wheels, the tops of an ash and a pine rising from the falling ravine behind the backyard, and in front, the house, a peeling eyesore, the complaint of the neighborhood. The Hooches!

The Hooch children are afraid. The car seems to have plunged up from the ravine. The smaller Hooches are fearful.

The roof of the garage has fallen in and around it clay pots are scattered through the lustrous ragged fronds.

The Hooch family is large and poor.

I have seen the moon make an opaque ghost of the backyard, and I have seen the Hooch animals roam out into it, smelling the life of themselves. They enter the border of visibility and pass through it into the uncanny.

Time and time again it comes back. Where the Hooches buried Oscar in the backyard near the fallen garage. Where the broken flowerpots were pulled away to make a place for Oscar. Where a single white wild blossom occurred under the forever stunted fig tree, making no sense at all, certainly not to dead Oscar.

The others of the street are not of their homes as much as the Hooches. The loud and untidy failures of the Hooches

206

pour from the exits. Their broken car is on the curb in front, pasted over with police citations. Around the base of a ragged bush near the front door is wrapped an old rotten brassiere. In the small front yard parts of toys and soaked food lie. A rope hangs from a second-story window. The drainpipe has been beaten out of place by the children.

The Hooch family has a familiar, I am saying, a certain familiar joyful lust and ignorance. They are mine. They're Ray's.

I say they are mine.

'Hi, Doctor Ray. You got that morphine for me?' says Mr. Hooch.

'Sure.'

'I do like that fog.'

Mr. Hooch climbs up on his crutch.

'I guess I'm a fairly worthless bastard, aren't I?' he asks.

'You are. You've perfected it,' I say.

The old man is tickled.

'Are you horny, Doctor Ray? You want me to call Sister?'

'No, thanks.'

'There's nothing to drink. I've drunk everything there is to drink.' Mr. Hooch throws out a cough, very nearly pukes. Revives. 'Didn't you say you used to be a drunkard, Doctor Ray?'

'I did,' I say. 'Almost got kicked out of the trade for it.'

I can see it makes the old man feel better to hear it. 'Ray,' he says. 'Ray, boy, that old morphine is sudden, hey? I'm fogging away.'

'Your leg already better?'

'Already. Listen to this, Doctor Ray. I know life all round, up and down. I have become my dreams. I have entered the rear of Mother Nature and come out her mouth, and I am the sin that is not ugly.'

'That's fine,' I say.

'It hurts my leg to talk like that,' the old man says.

From the back of the house, looking over the fishing boat and past it to the wide, brittle leaves at the crown of the

207

unhealthy magnolia, there comes Mrs. Hooch with her Pall
Malls, a blotched woman in a bravely colored wrap, her legs
lean and veiny. She arrives out of breath. She sits in the
flaking chair.

'What are you looking at, Doc?' she says.

'Everything in your backyard looks hungry,' says I.
'There's a bird that looks like he doesn't know what to do.'

'It's all we got.'

Looking out at the unhappy foliage.

'Ever since I wasn't a virgin no more, things have slid
down,' she says.

'There must have been love or something,' I say.

'Sure, but it was all downward.'

I say, 'Are you hopeless?'

'Close,' she says.

'Well,' I say, 'I brought another bottle of Valium.'

'The preacher was here,' she says. 'He couldn't do anything. I told him every time you came you left us happier.'

'God bless the pharmacy,' I say.

Outside, there are two small heads wobbling in the fishing
boat. The Hooch twins, the young set. They have older twins
too, and three children between these pairs.

'You want to talk today, Doc?' Mrs. Hooch wants to
know.

I say, 'I get tired of people. All of them driving around in
their cars, eating, having to be. All of them insisting on
existing.'

'But you help people,' Mr. Hooch says.

'I'm one of them,' I say.

'If you're sad, do you want to see Sister?' Mrs. Hooch
says. 'I think she's still in bed.'

'Maybe I will,' I say.

Sister is always in love with somebody, sometimes me. There
is a capricious wisdom she has about attaching herself to
anybody for very long, although her loyalties are fast. She
plays the guitar well and has a nice voice that she keeps to

herself. Life has been such for her that she has no attitude at all. She expects no sympathy. Two of her teenage lovers died in an accident at the railroad tracks. That's when I met Sister. I rode down to the tracks, and she was standing there in a long sleeping gown, two weeks after the accident.

'What's wrong, girl?'

'I growed up.'

'You want to go home? I'm a doctor. The preacher called me. They're worried about you.'

'Ain't nobody should worry. I'll be here.'

'I can give you a pill.'

But she said to leave her be.

So I drove back to the fancy rich thing of my home in my Corvette. In back of my house is the swamp, where all the creatures are either singing or angry or sexed up. My three well-fed and luxuriously moving furred Persian cats roam around with their big eyes. The back door was open and in front of one of their feed dishes there sits a mother raccoon. She's got two little raccoons with her, who are having a really good time. One of the cats tried for them, but I kicked it back through the kitchen. 'Listen,' I said, 'I am the emperor here. I reign.'

Ralph and Robert, my rich brothers, approve. But because of them, I can't even say my name.

But then I had to go back, to see Sister, to see if she's still there at the railroad tracks.

She was. Her gown was wet with tears and she was shivering bad.

'Nothing'll help,' she said.

Henceforward we were together.

'Sister, do you have a real name?' I said.

'Sister's enough,' said she, 'but my real name is Betty, and my age is eighteen. My grandmother was a Presbyterian missionary, but the Chinese Communists killed her. My pappy's from Mississippi. He ain't worth nothing, but there he is. He never worried about too much and his words is always kind. It was hateful for him to get shot in the kneecap in World War Two. But there he is. I don't want to talk about my momma too much because I don't like her. Her name's Agnes and she acts like that name.'

'Well,' said I, 'I did my part in hurting the gooks back for you, Sister. I flew support missions for B–52 bombers in Vietnam.'

'You flew what?'

'An F–4, called the Phantom. It's a jet airplane.'

'I've seen them jets pass over me and thought about them,' Sister said.

Her figure and face were lively and charming. Her legs were open, dark-skinned, negligent, as in the posture of lust. She had Cajun blood from her mother. Her hair was thick and black, and I suppose her beauty was astounding, even in the dirty gown and her eyes red with nervous grief.

I don't feel that good about women anyway, nor gooks, nor sand-niggers, nor doctors, nor anything human that moves, with its zealous raving habits. Then I met Sister and my trust came back, my body was flooded with hope.

'You hear about Uncle Sweat?' she asked me once while we were making love. 'He tried to take off in a plane and crashed it into the state pen, Parchman, over in Mississippi. They didn't even have a judge or nothing. He was already there.'

'Never heard about him.'

'Last week Aunt Viola was in a rage about Uncle Tom's carelessness and she dropped a chain saw on her foot.'

'Terrible.'

The thing I like about Sister is that every hurt she mentions, every hurt she has, she gives it back twice in love. She beats the hell out of my wife, who looks like somebody on television.

My town now is Tuscaloosa. I want you to know about some of the people here. My friend Charlie DeSoto, for example. He and his sweetheart Eileen came in, both of them wanting the drug that would help them stay in love without the grinding nervousness they had, because they *were* in love and they wanted to make it stick. Yet they induced tension in each other. Charlie was going for the booze, Eileen for the Compazines and coffee.

The name DeSoto was important, Charlie thought. He's a manager of the soap factory to the south of town and has made happen important steps toward antipollution of the Black Warrior River, into which his factory used to dump all the chemical wastes it had. It killed fish, and generally screwed up the water vegetation for fifteen miles downriver.

One night Charlie was waked up by a noise in his backyard. He caught hold of his hatchet, hoping it was a criminal, for his life had been dull lately. But when he went outdoors in the cold air, DeSoto – who was of course the namesake of Hernando de Soto, the discoverer of the Mississippi River who perished in 1542, probably of greed and arrogance – saw there was no criminal. The man in the backyard was not running. He was crawling, almost wallowing, toiling on the brown rye grass of Charlie's yard. The man lifted his face and said 'Listen, friend, I can't take it anymore.'

DeSoto considered that for a while, a whole day, actually. Charlie liked considering things. Best of all, Charlie DeSoto liked considering Mr. Wently. Now this Wently was a man who came by DeSoto's house every morning, *every* morning at exactly 7:45. This Wently was a man somewhere in his seventies, and he was regular. But so was the dog, Albert. Albert belonged to two gentle lesbians, Marjorie and Jane. And the minute Wently showed himself on the block, Albert came out viciously and barked. But the old man was never appalled, for he knew Albert was just a loud coward.

DeSoto wanted to kill Mr. Wently, was the problem. He could murder Mr. Wently for the regularity of his habits. Wently had a three-piece suit and sunglasses and a cane. DeSoto owned no gun, but if he had one, he would have killed Wently first thing.

One day it was a glorious day, and the red and yellow

leaves were falling all around the street, since it was fall, the dying beautiful season of the year.

DeSoto was reading about the original de Soto according to Rangel, his diarist on the expedition from Florida.

Sunday. October tenth, the Governor de Soto entered the village of Tuscaloosa, which is called Athlacia, a recent village. And the chief was on a kind of balcony on a mound at one end of the square, his head covered with a kind of coif like the almaizal, so that his headdress was like a Moor's, which gave him an aspect of authority. He also wore a mantle of feathers down to his feet, very imposing. He was as tall as that Tony of the Emperor, our lord's guard. A fine and comely emperor of a man.

Hernando remained seated with him a short time, and after a little he arose and said that they should come to eat, and he took him with him and the Indians came to dance. And they danced very well in the fashion of rustics in Spain. At night Tuscaloosa desired to go, and our Commander de Soto told him that he must sleep there. He slept there notwithstanding his reluctance.

The next day de Soto our Governor asked him for carriers and the rest of them he said he would give at Mobile, the province of one of his principal vassals.

Monday. October eighteen, St. Luke's day, the Governor de Soto came to Mobile, having passed that day by several villages and mountains with two Christians slain by Indians who did not take our passing through their village peaceably. The soldiers stayed behind to forage and scatter themselves, for the region appeared populous. And there came with the Governor only forty horsemen as an advance guard, and after they tarried a little, that the Governor might not show weakness, he entered into the village with his chief, Tuscaloosa, and all his guard went in with him. The Indians danced an *areyto*. While this was going on, some soldiers saw them putting bows and arrows slyly among some palm leaves and other Christians saw that below the cabins were full of people concealed.

The Governor put his helmet on his head. He warned

the soldiers. Luis de Moscoso and Baltasar de Gallegos, and Espindola, the captain of the guard, and only seven or eight soldiers were present. Gallegos went for Tuscaloosa, but the chief was hidden in a cabin and Gallegos with his knife slashed off the arm of an attacking Indian. Some got to their horses and killed the savages with lances. I was hit thrice by arrows. Women and even boys of four years fought with the Christians. Twenty-two of us died until the other Christians rescued us with the firearms.

At the last, we had twenty-two dead and their fortification was empty. We had killed four thousand of them.

Many pearls and a great store of corn were found.

Tuscaloosa and all his family were dead. We turned the great tall Indian over. A soldier named Stellus had fired the buss straight through his chest from five lengths.

Sometimes Charlie DeSoto read that passage to renew himself with his old perhaps ancestor. He got neither any special horror or delight from it, but it reminded him of the adventurous perversity in himself that he cherished.

Then he thought: What was the *it* that fellow was talking about he said he couldn't take any more of?

This was a friendly city, Tuscaloosa, though there were sirens to be heard most parts of the day and the state asylum across the way was full. On the streets you might see such as this: a small man wearing a football helmet, walking in front of a man in a black suit and white Panama hat, the larger man in black frequently striking the smaller one over the helmet with a broom handle. They were inseparable companions, and the man in black always tipped the clerk five dollars for a Coca-Cola at the Jiffy Mart.

But we were talking about this time in the morning, 7:45. And here comes Mr. Wently by DeSoto's house. This time DeSoto more than ever wanted to slay Mr. Wently. Wasn't there an old bow and arrow in the house somewhere? The hatchet – where was it? Quick!

The dog, Albert, from the lesbians' house attacked. But Wently's routine allowed him nothing but routine, and

DeSoto's rage allowed him nothing but passion. It is terribly, excruciatingly difficult to be at peace, thought DeSoto, when all our history is war. Look at that whining half-poodle, half-schnauzer Albert. Half-bred to sit at home, look elegant, and eat and fart. Half-bred to throw its vicious teeth into the unknown villain. Wently is killing everything.

DeSoto called in to the soap factory to say he was sick, which was true. He was sick with thought. He lingered awhile, watching a few joggers pass his house – healthy, harmless, in love with the thought that health promised the whole thing – bigger breasts, penis, chest. *Endurance*. That's it. If you can cut through it with peace and joy. If you can give health to those around you. But DeSoto didn't feel like it just now.

I want Wently, thought DeSoto. I want to purchase his death.

Maybe there are worse guys than me, he said to himself. For example, the guy from Minnesota who hummed all the time. He seemed to be furnishing the score for every puny adventure of his life. Always the hum, tunes various, dense, thin, *largo, allegro*. A trip to the café would take him through a sonata. There was a tune for feeding his cat, another for his goldfish, another for watering the plants in his crummy color-clashing apartment. He had no radio or phonograph. His time with women was limited – by them. But on he hummed incessantly, arrogantly, until somebody broke his mouth at a graveside ceremony one afternoon. DeSoto played Ping-Pong with him once. The hum was infuriating. They were odd tunes, nothing familiar. This man's game was mediocre, but it must be sung about. Every gesture must be styled by the hum, every blazing inconsequential adjustment had a song. Maybe he had been to too many movies, watched too much television. But the hum incensed Charlie DeSoto even more than Wently incensed him.

He got out his French horn and played a few quick scales, then an inventive cadenza, to impress himself with his culture.

The next morning there was Wently and there went Albert

pretending to be at him again. DeSoto was sitting on his front steps reading the paper and Wently passed within three feet of him.

'Hello, damn it,' said DeSoto.

The old guy neither replied nor missed a stride. The cane clicked, the shoes, which were rubber-soled, flapped through the leaves on the sidewalk.

DeSoto went to the soap factory, but he was in a state. The workers under him wondered what had happened. He drank on the job, cursed, was loud and impatient, lit and stomped out many cigars. A handsome young man of thirty-four, Charlie was beheld a despot of years. Usually a well-groomed and soft-spoken fellow, today he wore slovenly pants and shouted.

His girlfriend, who was Eileen and was his secretary, almost called the doctor, who was me. But instead she locked the door to the office and faced Charlie.

'I've got something temporarily that not even love will cure,' he said.

The next afternoon he walked around the block to see where Wently lived. He had never known exactly. It was a tall green house with a splendid porch. Wently was rocking in a rocking chair, pushing himself with weak jolts of his cane. He was wearing the three-piece suit. He must have been a man of some means. Big oaks and an enormous magnolia comforted his yard. In a chair next to him rocked a younger man who held his face in his hands, as if in anguish. Wently, decided DeSoto, was also driving this fellow crackers. The two were not speaking. Wently was staring ahead serenely, fascinated only, it seemed, by himself and the system of his rocking – not even by the weather, which was medium blue and fine.

DeSoto observed the grief of the younger man – Wently's grandson? his nephew? Then he walked back home and inquired among the neighbors. It was Wently's grandnephew. DeSoto had been in there right on it.

At 7:40 the next morning DeSoto began his own walk

around the block. He was wearing a headdress, cheap, from the K-Mart, and he carried his French horn with him. From thirty feet away, he saw Wently coming toward him on the walk. Should he? Yes. DeSoto played a chain of blats in the high register. Maybe Wently was deaf, but he was not blind.

Anyhow, the old man just passed him.

'Jesus!' cried DeSoto.

A woman professor he knew was just leaving for work in her car, and she saw and heard it all. I'm making a donkey out of myself, thought DeSoto. For the rest of the day he could not eat, and he practiced self-abuse in all possible ways, sort of living in the toilet at the soap factory, moving from stall to stall so as not to invite the looks of the curious and their hellos and how-are-yous.

In the night DeSoto studied gentle thoughts. He attempted to dream of his sweetheart and her delicate parts; of light pleasures he had known, such as reversing the clock an hour when daylight saving time was over; of healthy food; of morning light on the small green ears of corn in his patch last summer. He hummed the placid tune 'Home on the Range' several times through. But sleep would not come. He poured himself a tomato juice and took five B-complex vitamin pills, which were supposed to be settlers. But eventually he found himself sitting furious and awake in a chair that faced the window to his backyard.

He was there an hour, through some ten stale Lucky Strikes he had found in a drawer, when he saw the figure slough across the fence in the light of the moon. There was no doubting it was a man, a whole man. DeSoto watched him roll onto the earth and begin squirming on down the lawn. DeSoto was transfixed by the man's progress. When he saw him reach the driveway, DeSoto stood up from his chair. He hurried out before the man could reach the next yard.

'What's with you, fellow?' demanded DeSoto.

The man rolled toward him. DeSoto recognized his body, perhaps his face from their first encounter, the set of hair and forehead from their second. It was old Wently's grand-nephew. The neighbors said his name was Ned, a namesake of Wently, who was Edward. Ned was around thirty, but his face was haggard, his eyes heavy with bags and his mustache scraggly and askew, as if false and pasted on at a wrong angle. DeSoto had brought his flashlight.

'I say, what's going on?' he asked again, as Ned Wently blinked his eyes in the light.

'I'm *trespassing*, señor. Better let me have it.'

'What's this *señor*?'

'Aren't you Spanish?'

'It's a lie,' DeSoto said. 'Now answer my question.'

'I finally let him have it,' the Wently fellow said. 'He never knew what hit him. They took away my liquor, my dope and my piano, and they sent me to live with him. I'm interviewing for one dumb job after another. Got one tomorrow at the fucking *soap* factory. That hideous, fucking soap factory that's screwing up the river?'

DeSoto switched off the flashlight.

'Let him have it, did you? Never knew what hit him? Come see me. I'm a foreman at the factory.'

The younger Wently did not respond. He crawled off the driveway and through a hole in the fence of the neighbor's yard.

'Why are you *crawling*?' Charlie called after him, to no use at all.

DeSoto was early on the job, at 6:30. He had to open a lot of the doors himself and his only company for a while was the maintenance and sweeping crew. The fumes of the place were violently sweet and sour. He was hungry, horny, happy, and handsome, and he made up a chant to life and himself. I am Charlie, he sang. Hai hai, hai, hai hai, hai!

Charlie DeSoto had had no sleep, but he was elated. He sat behind his aluminum desk, speculating on the gross points of the homicide. *Let him have it* would indicate a gun, or maybe poison. Truly, it could be anything when you put it together with *Never knew what hit him*. Ned would cover it. DeSoto would help him if he had to.

Eileen arrived earlier than usual, and she was all worn out. The old DeSoto car, which she had bought just as a flirting joke to please Charlie – though the orange leather interior was nice – was smoking and stalled at traffic lights. And the driver's door would not open because of some fault in the lock.

She was confounded and thrown into a perilous dither by Charlie's alterations. Moreover, she had cheated on DeSoto the previous night. The man was not nearly as handsome as DeSoto, but his desire for her was constant, soft, a genial tribute to the shrine of her body, and she recalled even the Bible said that was okay. She had allowed the man everything. Now nothing assuaged her guilt. Poor Charlie, poor Charlie, she muttered, sleepless and insane with contrition.

She had to arrive early and make his appearance at the office comfortable. Also she was very erotic, and her satisfaction was not close. She had driven by Charlie's house earlier in the morning. He was not there. The mystery was compelling a storm of expectation. Here was his car in his parking slot at the factory. She hurried in, her body showered but slick again with a new sweat of the day.

She looked pretty and clean by the time the plant air conditioning had cooled her down. DeSoto responded to her chic wool skirt and satin blouse, and, as always, her dark trim ankles and sandals. She was about a quarter Lebanese and it seemed that all the best traits of that race had sprung up in Eileen suddenly.

They were alone in the office.

What happened behind the locked door was sacred to them both. It was a drunkenness of the bodies. DeSoto was charming and expert at his job, as was Eileen, and DeSoto could bear the fact that, minute after minute, Ned Wently did not appear for an interview with him. It wasn't a make-work job. Ned would have a small, quiet office near the truck docks, a supervisory position. Something higher than he should be hired at, really, but DeSoto would bring in the muscle to make it possible.

As for DeSoto's early morning, it was exalted by the absence of old Mr. Wently on the sidewalk at 7:45. The day was clear and merry without him. DeSoto met the loud bark of Albert with an understanding smile. He also saw the pet monkey come out of Lester's house next door. DeSoto went over and took the morning paper out of its paws, speaking to the monkey, whose name was Amy, in monkey whispers, and taking the nice animal back to his own kitchen, where DeSoto made a huge breakfast. He peeled a banana and opened a can of sardines for Amy, put them on a plate with a napkin nearby.

There was nothing about a death on the block in the newspaper.

Now the office door was locked and DeSoto was near to entering Eileen, with her skirt around her blouse and the tops of her stockings close to her sex. Charlie adored this half-clothed demonstration of lust almost better than anything. There was a call in, however, that a Mr. Ned Wently was waiting outside to see him.

Eileen stood off to the side. She shivered when Wently came in.

He was garbed in a rough tweed suit. His hair and mustache were combed a little, but he still looked disoriented, worse in daylight. The bags under his eyes were dark. His shoulders were wide, but his legs were bowed and thin. The stain of some red sauce was on his neck.

Wently looked at Eileen. His eyes lit up with the normal sex-crazy look of a man. But then he threw his weak gaze at DeSoto, and Eileen left the room.

They sat down, DeSoto and Wently, the desk between them, and were quiet for a spell.

'I've got something for you,' said DeSoto at last.

'And I've got something for you,' said the younger Wently.

He pulled out a small silverish .22 automatic pistol. DeSoto regarded it. It looked like the foetus of firearms.

'You let him have it with this?'

'I didn't even have to after you scared the fuck out of him with the headdress and that horn. He already had a big cancer and heart disease. You took him to the edge, man. With peace and routine, he would've lived forever. So I never had to fire a shot. Just pointed it seriously.'

There was a long silence.

'Then all we needed was the ambulance.' Wently's eyes were welling with tears. 'Thing is, he loved me. He willed everything to me. I broke his heart when I pulled this thing on him.'

Wently began openly weeping.

'But he owed us one, my daddy and me. My daddy was swamped with debt and in precarious health when he was supporting us and my grand-uncle Edward. Edward didn't always live in that big green house, you know. He's sucked off the family with his goddamn routine and righteousness for years. Until he had his own stack of green and a place. Tell you what, man. These people, these peaceful people leave as many bodies behind as those big war copters in Nam, where I also had to go.'

'Then you feel justified?' said DeSoto.

'No!' Wently stared at DeSoto. Then he bent and put his face in his hands, as DeSoto had seen him doing in the porch of the Wently house. 'I feel awful guilty. I put him in the ground.'

'Come on. Get out of it,' DeSoto said.

'*You* get out of it, DeSoto! Have you seen the crap spilling out of those pipes from this puking factory into the river? Where I used to fish when I was a little boy, there ain't nothing but nasty white soap twenty feet down.'

'Shoot me in the thigh,' DeSoto said. 'If you shoot me in the thigh, I'll get you a job,' said DeSoto.

'I don't need it. I got his will money.'

'Then just shoot me in the thigh. I need some of the pain.'

DeSoto put his foot on the desk. Wently shot off one low in his thigh.

*

220

Wently went away with a new perspective.

That was all by way of showing you how I come to know Charlie DeSoto and some others. Because I met DeSoto and Eileen in the emergency room. Nowadays, DeSoto fakes a limp, happily. The bullet is in there so deep and harmless and near the bone, cutting for it would be a shame.

Eileen came by to see me by herself later. She was really something to grab, after you got through the usuals. But I liked Charlie and I had rules.

This was all when I was thirty-three and divorced.

2

LAST YEAR I won some awards for my papers at the conventions: 'The Nervous Woman and Valium,' 'Three Seraxes a Day for the Alcoholic,' 'Satyriasis and Acute Depression.' But I quit flying the jets for anybody. Too many pilots around today, especially in the rich class. Some little eleven-year-old will crawl up in the cockpit with you and describe not only the whole panel but continue about your life and your girl-friends, know your astrology sign like the back of his hand, and scold you for lighting up a Kool at the point you'd like to light him up, open his door, and let him deal with the suck at twenty thousand feet.

Ray even teaches a popular night class at the university now. It's open to just about anybody except people I don't like or think I won't. People who work on foreign cars are good. I like botanists and geologists also. These men and women who run from five to twenty miles a day are pretty good sorts. And wrestlers, tennis players. But a category of worst is doctors' children in revolt. Give me an honest nigger any time of day. I'll even read his essays.

I got a little tight and flew right in the sun one afternoon for thirty minutes, and now old Ray has a little eye damage and is very selective about what he reads, which is very little. A man of medicine forgot to wear his sunglasses.

The Hooches are healthier. They've even spruced up their place a bit, but nothing very severe. There's not so much trash around the doors, and their yard looks better, maybe from the fact that their animals have multiplied and the stratum of dung over the grass is near solid. Mr. Hooch has a job and needs very little of the morphine now. I think he's proud of himself as a gimpy tugboat first mate, and he can let his language go wild without worry because everybody else on the boat is bent in the mind too.

'I was saying the other day, Doc, I was telling Poot Laird, "The large bird flies and roars because it has the span. The small bird creeps and misses because it hasn't." That's what I told Poot.'

'That doesn't sound half-bad,' I said. 'What was Poot's reaction?'

'Nothing. He can't talk. A cottonmouth bit him in the tongue when he was little. Only expression he's got, is after a big supper and beer, he lifts a leg and – '

'Poots,' I guessed.

'But strange, like somebody mumbling.'

Mrs. Hooch, Agnes, is happier to see less of Mr. Hooch and have more income. And what she has done with some of it is buy a cassette tape recorder that she uses to record her smaller children, unbeknownst to them, and play it back at supper time to prove to them how much of a dreadful curse they are. She makes them listen to it while they eat. She quit cigarettes, but she's worse than ever. She buys twenty pulp magazines a month and answers all the happiness and sexual quizzes in them. She won a Sony TV by coming in third on a mass-murderer quiz in *Oui* magazine. On the TV she watches Home Box Office movies, which cause her untold anguish for not being slim, twenty-three, in a black dress and pearls, with a submachine gun in her hands, in an old fort on the Mediterranean. She bought clothes and combed her hair so she looks sort of like three decades away from something like that, and I could see Sister's lovely genes in the woman somewhat. In fact, with three ten-milligram Valiums in her, Agnes Hooch is beguiling. Until she opens her mouth, and there are the missing teeth.

I paid for Sister to go to the University of South Alabama in Mobile. She thought she'd like Mobile. But there was no way she could cut college, not even a semester of it. She fell in love with two different boys and they both dropped out too. Now she's a waitress in Atlanta, making a lot on tips and using marijuana by the wagonload. I received a scrawled letter and five one-hundred-dollar bills – her college fee – and a lurid photograph of her in skimpy waitress costume, receiving between her lips the huge member of a fat conventioneer, name badge on his coat, drink in his hand, eyes shut with pleasure and mouth open like a murdered boar. It was made up with the club's name on the bottom. It was clear she was involved in a filthy, lucrative industry. In the letter she wrote:

'Ray, I'm rich, but this ain't me. There's nobody to talk to and I'm turning into hate. Please come and marry me. This ain't me.'

I took the next plane out and got a taxi down to the club. I'd always liked Atlanta, and it was grievous to have to despise every building and every bus stop, every mansion and its trees, every club with jazz music and rock and roll pouring out.

But I was Ray, ex-Navy pilot, who used to even have a pistol on me. Old valiant Ray from 1967 to 1969. Gas up, load up, get ready for the worst and give it worser back.

Sister was in Heloise's with two men around her. It wasn't long before she was in the cab with me. The thing was she looked even younger, fresher, long legs in black hose. She cried and we did a lot of kissing. Because of the photograph, I was cooled down toward much gesture of lust for her, though. Besides, I had already met my next wife over in Jackson, Mississippi.

'You ain't going to marry me, are you?' Sister said. 'I guess that picture was too much for you,' said she.

'Yeah, it went over the line. I can take it in the abstract, but it's not the same photographed. You don't want any marriage thing or you wouldn't have sent it to me.'

'You're right, Ray. I just want this.'

We hugged in the cab and in the airport and in the plane back to Tuscaloosa.

It was football season and my girlfriend's son was a quarterback for Murrah High in Jackson. Early on, I knew I was in for another marriage, and this one full of love and a slight goddamned bit of wisdom. We went to all the games together all over the state of Mississippi, and her handsome jock son was the star everywhere. He was a very cool, light-voiced lad who kept fish, had read a few books, and took off his cleats when he came in the condominium on the parquet floors. The house was gorgeous, snug in shades of blue and melon, lots of okay furniture around. The ex-husband was a doctor – Christ! – who was very busy and very important. Westy, my girl, was from Iowa, the daughter of a dentist and a corn farmer who is one hell of a feisty wonderful gentleman. He gets me in a corner and tells these old-fashioned clean filthy jokes to me. His wife shrieks and he laughs. He laughs so much he weeps for sixteen minutes. Westy's brother is an orthopedic surgeon in Omaha.

There is no escape from doctors. They surround me as I surround myself.

Westy has an uncommon adventurous warmth to her, a crazy hope in her blue eyes, and a body that will keep a lover occupied. I was gone for her about first sight.

She was forty, had another son off at the University of Wisconsin, and a thirteen-year-old daughter who received her entire sustenance, by what I could tell, from her private telephone. There was also Tina, the live-in maid, an illegal immigrant from Chihuahua, who cooked Mexican holistically and, with other Mexican immigrants in the community, read the Holy Bible every night. They had converted to

224

Assembly of God and had nothing for Catholicism and the priests. But the FBI knocked on the door one night when Westy and I were into a little wine and quiet, and the whole flock of Mexicans had to go underground with their Assembly of God friends.

It was a great storm and a great shame. Tina was worth, with her cumin and bay leaf, any ten doctors you can name.

It was a rebirth for old Ray. I hadn't seen high school football since I played it at one hundred and fifteen pounds and one cold night in Crystal Springs, Mississippi, got knocked over a fence and on to a cinder track in the middle of the cheerleaders by some hulking freak who later found his way to the Chicago Bears. That was my last punt return, and I went seriously into Fine Arts after that, where you could play with yourself and get applauded for it. Murrah High was full of blacks now, and you didn't go in the restrooms at the stadiums, where they stayed by the hundreds for the entire game, talked mean, and got themselves numbed out on controlled substances. That is, those who weren't in the band or on the team. The band had an amazing queer black boy named Dean Riverside out in front of them who did more boogie and stretch than the law allowed, the band into 'Play That Funky Music, White Boy,' and the synchronized Chargettes throwing their legs around the whole affair. They actually made you enamored of the asinine, by God. Such style and earnesty!

One night, when I was in Saigon, a chicken colonel's wife walked past my Yamaha motorbike on the street. My eyes got wide and my heart was molasses. She walked by me, clicking her heels, tanned legs so lean, a fine joyful sense of her sex uplifted at the juncture of her thighs. Her face was serene, her eyes were blue, and she was, as they say, music. I recall the Rolling Stones' 'Lady Jane' was pouring from the door of the nearest bar. But she was not mine. I could never have her, and my heart was broken. The image of her kept me pure for years. I resisted the whores in Saigon, mainly out of a horror of VD, and never cheated on my first wife, mainly because there was nothing I ever saw like the chicken colonel's wife again. Until I met Westy.

Westy does not talk much about the act of love. She just does it with all her heart. Her children are beautiful and polite, and she has never threatened suicide, which my first wife was good for at least once a month, maybe thinking her period entitled her to it. We're all God's creatures, but some of us can be especially ugly. I had from this union three beautiful children to present to Westy. She liked them, and the second night we were together, with my two youngest heavenly blessings running around, Westy said, 'I want you and all of it.'

'Hey, Doc, I hear you're getting married,' says Mr. Hooch.
'That's right.'
'You look happy and good, Doc. Me and Agnes wanted to invite you to have the wedding right here at the house. We'll clean it up and the preacher will be free.'
'Thanks. I got a lot of sentiment for the place, John, but this lady is really fancy and I'm afraid it's going to have to be at the old Episcopal Church.'
'Well, could we get invited?'
'You didn't get the engraved invitation yet?'
'I don't know. I don't read much mail.'
We went out to a heap of circulars, letters from the police, utility bills, pamphlets from the Cancer Fund, and unread newspapers in the front hall. I picked through it awhile, but I couldn't find the envelope from Westy. Then there was a shriek from the top of the stairs. It was Sister.
'I've got the cocksucking invitation up here!'
Mr. Hooch looked very sad.
'She ain't right, Ray. She sings at night and smokes that marijuana all day and don't eat much. Go see to her, if you would.'
Her room was well set up. She had an expensive stereo system with Devon speakers, a microphone stand, a Martin guitar on the bed, which was brass and costly, a thick oyster-

shell carpet on the floor, a tape deck, rugged white thick curtains on the window, and the walls were solid acoustic tile as well as the ceiling. It was a studio. It smelled like she'd lit ten joints about eight seconds ago. It had its own refrigerator. The door shut behind me as if in a vacuum unit.

Sister was wearing only panties and a red halter. I'd never seen her look better. Actually in good light, I'd never seen this much of her.

She had the invitation from Westy in her hand and sat on the bed.

'Ray, you told me once that you needed to make love twice a day or you got very tense and had headaches. But I need it four times a day and I'm getting to be a better singer every day.'

I didn't say anything. I was still taking in her and the room.

'There's a man with a glorious voice I sing with named Marcel Smith. We do duets and we are making a lot of money around town and we might get an album contract with some people up at Muscle Shoals.'

'That's wonderful,' I said.

'Just like your marriage,' Sister said.

'I've got this woman. You'd like her,' I said.

'I probably would. What do you want to do?'

'Find it and live it,' I said.

'Don't you want me too?'

'If it wouldn't be too much trouble,' said I.

3

AFTER A RAY kind of honeymoon in Florida, where I composed myself as a father and husband, children from seven to twenty running around my mind and knees, I get a jet, the DC–8, a lovely bird that flies a lot of people, and sit back and dream until La Guardia in New York, queen of the Eastern shore.

227

At Columbia University there are fifteen doctors, three from the South I know, alcoholics themselves. I read them my paper. I get the applause and the check.

(I have another paper on women, unfinished. Like Freud, I threw up my hands.)

Columbia University got me a companion for dinner at the Russian Tea Room. She was Laurie Chalmers, a Jewess with large bosoms, very visible in a velvet dress. She was a tall, frank girl. After the meal we went back to the room they gave me at the Cornell Club, where Laurie Chalmers disrobed and lay on her back on the bed and described herself as constantly starved – for food and liquor and Southerners. Her family was in Charleston, South Carolina, and she said she missed the South despite her job, that was high-paying. She was an anesthetist.

She was a gorgeous and restless lady, with an amazing amount of beard around her sex. While she talked to me, she chewed a corner of her pillow. Her feet were perfect and unlined and unknobbed in any way. She ate me, just like another delicious thing on her menu. I felt rotten, cool, and unfaithful, yet I came with an enormous lashing of sperm, which made her writhe and lick. Then Laurie Chalmers fell sound asleep.

Ray, listen, I said on the plane back. You don't have the spiritual resources to cheat on your wife. You feel wretched and sinful and hung over, without having had any liquor. Adventures in sex are just not in your person anymore. You know too many people already. Your conscience is banging your head off and you can't even eat your eggs.

So I ordered a double vodka to hose down my conscience.

The idea to keep at it came on, but I beat it back with thoughts of Westy.

Westy fixing up our house in Tuscaloosa.

Westy with her big blue eyes.

But this lousy barnacle of unfaithfulness would not leave my mind. It is enough to be married to a good woman. It is plenty.

228

Ray, the filthy call of random sex is a killer. It kills all you know of the benevolent order of your new life.

Then the plane is in trouble. The bad things in my head have passed through the air and gone into the engines of the DC-8. Starboard engine is gone, finished, and the plane begins rolling. The stewardess loses everything. Her poise is all gone.

So I go up to the cockpit. One of the pilots has fainted. They're young boys, about twenty-eight.

'Want me to take it?' says I. 'There's no big disaster,' I say. 'Keep the nose up, asshole. Keep the nose up. Yes. Pull back all the way. What's wrong with him?'

'We've never had any trouble before.'

I get the fainted pilot out of his seat, and while the other boy is leveling it, I try to get some action on the bad engine, meanwhile putting in my order for a second double vodka.

We're headed the wrong way, but that's okay. We set it down in Birmingham. Suits me. I didn't have to get another plane to Tuscaloosa. I called Westy and she came over to pick me up.

'Ray, are you all right?' asks she.

I asked her to pull over so I could get out and vomit.

'Darling. Did you drink liquor in New York, darling?' she says.

'Yes. I violated my rules,' I say. 'Darling, let me have a piece of your Big Red gum.'

'I missed you, Ray,' she says.

Says I, 'I missed you, Westy, in the worst way.'

She is such a clean German. The car is clean. I invent cheerfulness from my heart, the biggest engine.

'Ray, there's something else wrong. Not just the liquor,' Westy says.

'There's nothing wrong,' I say.

'There's something you should tell me. Something's with you. Something's lying heavy on you.'

'Basically, Westy, I would like, after we say goodnight to

229

the children, that you sit on my face and let me lick your thing. Like on the honeymoon.'

'Oh, boy,' she says.

Westy is so happy. Her feet are moving this way and that way over the car pedals.

Sweet God, there is nothing like being married to the right woman.

4

WE HAVE COME up in a meadow, all five hundred horses. We are in the Maryland hills and three hundred yards in front of us are the Federals, about fifty of them in skirmish line. What they can't see are the five Napoleon howitzers behind us.

Jeb Stuart is as weary as the rest of us, but he calls for sabers out. Our uniforms are rotting off us. It's so hot and this gray cloth is so hot. There is a creek behind us. I dismount and we send the orderlies back to the creek. It is delightful to see them bring water back to the horses and me. The water is thunderously refreshing, though you can't drink too much if we have to fight. I would prefer not to fight them, but I can see they've rolled in a cannon and mean business.

Thing is, all the blue boys are going to die. And we have to do something quickly or they'll tell General McClellan where we are.

Stuart says to me, 'Hold two hundred horses with you, Captain. Let us start the cannons and I will go forward.'

Then we kissed each other, as men who are about to die.

Our horses covered the howitzers.

They let off theirs. It hits in the trees. These are fresh boys. They don't even really know how to shoot. Yet all of them must die.

I say, 'General Stuart, I can kill them all from here. I suggest we don't charge.'

He made the order to hold the sabers up.

'What do you mean?'

'Observe us, General.'

We had captured an ammunition wagon and it had the twenty-pound shells in it. You could hit a chicken in the middle of the head from this range.

'Do it rapidly, Captain.'

I make the order. The cavalry feints to its left. The Federals are confused. Pellham fires the howitzers.

Ooooof Oooof Oooooof Oooooof Ooooooooof.

Then again. Five of them are left, and all wounded. One older man is standing up, living but bewildered, with all his friends dead around him.

'Hello, friend,' I say.

'Are you Jeb Stuart?'

'No. I am his captain,' I say.

'It was too quick for us, Captain,' the man says.

Then the banjo player came up and we drank their coffee and ate the steaks on the fires. We threw earth over the dead. Stuart went out in the forest and wept.

Then all of us slept. Too many dead.

Let us hie to Virginia, let us flee.

I fell asleep with the banjo music in my head and I dreamed of two whores sucking me.

5

I LIVE IN so many centuries. Everybody is still alive.

6

WHAT I LIKED was the tea and bridge club. There were a lot of people around, beautiful young women and handsome men, young and old. It was a large living room in a mansion, and they threw the curtain back after the bridge was over.

Husbands and wives were naked in different positions. It was like a dream. A soft-spoken woman asked us to go up on stage and remove our clothes. We were a little bit ashamed. But once Westy and I were into the act of love, we could not help it. There was a woman in real estate. She was wearing a violet gown, high-heeled silver sandals. She had a lecture stick. She did a lot of pointing with it at Westy and me. She said Westy and me were the newest thing.

When I had given my sperm to Westy, the audience stood up and applauded.

Good old Tuscaloosa.

7

THERE IS RAY'S son Barry, a boy with a sweet brain and only fifteen.

There is Ray's sister, Dorothy.

There are Ray's parents, Elizabeth and Bill.

There are his nephews, Ken and Taylor, and his brother-in-law, John, another doctor and a good one.

8

HOW ABOUT WE have us a nature walk? The trees, the mountains. Or let us dance at Lee's Tomb, the cavernous saloon near the river and the docking port for trucks.

Sister was there, as were Charlie DeSoto and his girl, Eileen. They are married now. And they look very sad. There is something about marriage that brings on a certain sadness, as if burying the glad part.

Sister is prosperous now that she and Marcel Smith have an album out that is selling big. She has a marvelous suntan and she is wearing jewelry all over her. She looks very self-assured and gives me a self-assured kiss. The Locust Fork

Band is playing. That's Asa, Dwight, Bill. God bless you, niggers, for the music.

Besides the small friendly vagina and the blue eyes, Westy has sympathy. We shall be married forever.

Westy, my wife, my darling.

I hate to depend on another human being this much. But nobody is his own boy. Her breasts, her lovely feet, her cheerfulness, her care.

But I still want to fight. I still want to put it to somebody, duke a big guy out. Like the asshole who came in who had shot two of his children and broken the arm of his wife. He was an alcoholic red-neck and had a lot of Beechnut chewing tobacco on him. He really smelled lousy. Before I could ask him anything, he found a razor blade and came at *me*, his doctor! Lucky that Ray still has his quickness. The bastard missed me with the razor, and I kicked him in the gonads.

Certain people are this way. They kill everybody around, for one reason or another. He went to the pen, but I would like to see him tortured in a dungeon to get back the suffering he has caused.

The waving grass of the prairies, the moon settling over Minnesota over the lake. Me and my son Barry are having a good time. It is sunset and there are no loud noises. There are only us, and we've caught some bass and pickerel. My daughter Lee is paddling the canoe for us. Utter fucking peace.

Debbie, psychotherapist, is another person I'd like to see buried. She thinks you get the best out of people when you get them all in a room and ask them humiliating questions. She's about six feet tall and drives her Fiat convertible around town, being queen of the world. She's from Ohio, which is the worst state in the union.

Ohio is silly.

Ken, my nephew, once asked me as we were going to sleep after some snapper fishing in Destin, Florida: 'Promise me something, Uncle Ray?'

'What?'

'That when I die I won't be from Ohio.'

9

HERE IS SOMETHING about my class at the university. The pretty faces, the yearning to learn. Deborah, Sammy, Lenora, David, Edward Jurgielewcz, Ondocsin, Triola, Slubowski, Scordino, Edric Kirkman – they are all trying to learn.

The land is full of crashing jets, carbon monoxide, violent wives, and murderous men. There is a great deal of metal and hardness.

The subject of today is breast cancer. Why is there so much of it? Why the mastectomies, why the cancers of the uterus? Why in the hell is there so much cancer today, anyway?

Ray's humble opinion is that it serves us fucking right.

10

OH, HELP ME! I am losing myself in two centuries and two wars.

The SAM missile came up, the heat-seeker. It stood up in front of me like a dick at twenty thousand feet, and the squadron captain told me what the hell was going on. He was a nigger from Louisiana. I think that was the first time a nigger saved my life. Flight Captain Louis Diamond saved my life and I shot the SAM missile out of the air.

Fuck you, heat-seeker! Take some cold steel!

Then when Quisenberry was down on the beach and the gooks were running out to capture my friend from Mississippi, I slowed it down and turned the nose of that Phantom almost perpendicular to the ground. I used the cannons and missiles to clean them away. I saw their heads fly off and their chests.

Tough shit, gooks! You ain't going to get Quisenberry.

He lives now, handsome and a credit to his race, a lawyer in Los Angeles.

I am very proud of the things I did for my country. I fought for the trees, the women, who, when they quit talking, will let you, etc.

Westy, Westy. It's a miracle.

When we get rid of the carbon monoxide, this will be a hell of a country again. Start with Ohio.

Drop the big one on Ohio.

11

WHOEVER CREATED RAY gave him a big sex engine.

I live near the Black Warrior River and have respect for things.

12

I'M FALLING IN love with Sister again, who is not my wife. After my breakfast, which I hate to eat but is necessary for the tummy, after the multivitamin tab in case I miss something (one of those fuckers might just connect and root me up again), the house is uninteresting and I get out a *Penthouse* magazine. There Sister was, almost exactly. Not her, of course, but right on the button as to looks and smile, nipples, feet. I really find good-looking feet irresistible in a woman. I came near to losing a patient while I was looking at her feet. She wasn't anything for looks besides her feet. Hubba hubba. I almost fell face-down in her thing while I was doing her appendectomy.

Sister. Listen. I want you. My beloved wife does not seem awfully inspired in the bedroom lately. She's more interested in the house, the yard, wood, and soil.

'I knew you'd be back, Doctor Ray,' said Sister.

We were where she sang. The lights on the stage were

235

going full blast. Why the young idiots of today like multiple lights running around and two hundred decibels of guitars and organ, I can't tell. They want to make war out of peacetime. You can't even play Ping-Pong without some young asshole lighting up a pinball machine next to you that sounds like a serious invasion.

Sister quit the set right in the middle and we went to the Hooches and up to her room. She put her feet up for a while and then got naked. Her eyes looked tired a bit. Her toes were chafed by the high sandals she wore. But she was a violent delight. For about an hour we went into the beautiful nowhere together. When she came, she screamed like a man getting stabbed. Lucky that the room was fixed for sound.

'It's not enough,' she said after she was relaxed some. 'I want it all the way up my ass. Every inch of you, Ray.'

She went and got the Vaseline.

None of this should happen, but it does.

'What have we proved?' I ask Sister.

'That it can be done,' she said. 'I love you, Doctor Ray.'

'Sister, I have serious doubts and a filthy conscience.'

'Not near filthy enough for me.'

There was a knock on the door. Sister began scrambling around for her clothes, as did I. It was Maynard Castro, the preacher. He was a studied man of good will, as far as I knew. There are some good Baptists, and Maynard was one of them. He bade me hello. Then he sat on the bed next to Sister. Maynard had a trimmed beard and gold-framed spectacles.

'I came by to say how much I liked your album. My wife adores it too. We play it constantly. I was going to ask a special favor. You are so admired by the young people in town, I wonder if you'd sing for us at the church during the Youth Impact next month.'

Sister lit a cigarette.

'You'd give them peace,' said Maynard. 'You have given me peace.'

'Which song? I thought they were all pretty nervous.'

' "High on the Range". There is an eerie joy in that tune.'

'There ain't any hope in that song. That's about high misery because she's loved too many people. She's about done in, 'cause she spread it too thin.'

'I see it as Christlike. It is full of sharing.'

'All right, I'll do it.'

'I appreciate it, Sister.'

When Maynard left, Sister laid out on her back and began weeping.

'I've done it, Ray. I've loved too many people, and now it hurts to love.'

Said I, 'I've got the same disease, sweetest.'

'I need to make love too much.'

'Ditto,' said I.

'And pretty soon, I want it again.'

'There's not much that's truer,' I said.

On the way out, I heard Mr. Hooch whistling on the back porch. He must've just come home from work. Agnes was sitting by him in resigned melancholy. Mr. Hooch was swinging his bare feet, sitting on the porch railing, swarthy from his work on the tugboat. Agnes was back on her Pall Malls. I borrowed one from her.

I couldn't tell there was anything wrong with his leg. After the skimpy backyard, you looked into the foliage of the ravine, the car with the wooden Indian at the steering wheel now rotting off the fierce colors of its face. The smaller Hooches, who aren't so small anymore, aren't afraid of that thing anymore either. The grave of Oscar is plentitudinous with heavy white blossoms. It is like a memorial back here, nature doing the main work, going at it in random dereliction with spouts of large beauty here and there.

There has not been time to say that little Constance Hooch had her legs backed over by a school bus and lost one of them. She is out in the yard near the ravine, walking peacefully on her artificial leg. She's a ravishing little thing of eleven. The other twin, Ethel, stays close by, very considerate. They are running down some of the early lightning bugs with a Mason jar. The older twins are out front fixing up a broken motorcycle. You can almost smell the wreck coming on when they get it going.

Mr. Hooch says, 'Guess what I told the foreman stevedore today when we were docking. He's been long on my list of shits in the world. He's always nagging about tiny things. He's a big man with the makeup of a warhorse and the mind of a shrieking little woman. I told him little certificates come out his mouth and he ain't got the wings of a bee.'

'That's fine,' say I. 'That's the way to tell them,' say I.

Some of the white ducks come up in the yard from the ravine. The twins pick them up and pet them hard.

This here's the day Dr. Cullen in the History department has asked me to address the American Civilization class, because we talked the other night about Franklin and Jefferson, who were inventors and public helpers, and I have a little knowledge of them.

So now, class, I say:

'Americans have never been consistent. They represent gentleness and rage together. Franklin was the inventor of the stove, bifocals, and so on. Yet he abused his neglected family. Jefferson, with his great theories, could not actually release the slaves even though he regularly fornicated with one of them. One lesson we as Americans must learn is to get used to the contrarieties in our hearts and learn to live with them.' Etc.

I am infected with every disease I ever tried to cure. I am a vicious nightmare of illnesses. God cursed me with a memory that holds everything in my brain. There is no forgetting with me. Every name, every foot, every disease, every piece of jewelry hanging from an ear. Nothing is hazy.

Westy is back. She is developing her entrance into the real-estate profession. She has a dream of being her own person, making her own money. I've never seen her prettier. Yet she's tired. The Westy of the encouraging eyes is tired. At forty-two, she looks as if she's throwing in the towel. Me, I've been visiting Lee's Tomb a lot and taking in too much sound and bourbon. I get up choking. Some mornings I don't even know I get up.

Sabers up! Get your horses in line! They have as many as we do and it will be a stiff one. Hit them, hit them! Give them such a sting as they will never forget. Ready? *Avant!* Avant, avant, avant! Kill them!

Horses gleaming with sweat everywhere, Miniés flying by you in the wind.

Sometimes there is no answer from your wife, even when you're sweet as pie. Sometimes there is no answer from the world. The trees are furry with green, the beach is rolling, the old houses stand straight and thick in the shade of the oaks. And Sister and I are in love.

I read the paper as I was waiting in the emergency room. Sister is dead, and they have Maynard Castro as probable cause. Three times through her precious brain. Maynard just could not take the beauty. Not a sign of sexual molestation. No sign of nothing except an outright shooting in the night-club where she sings.

He couldn't even wait for her to sing at the Youth Impact.

Lewd stories came out about him, as told by his wife and others. Repressed sexuality that finally pitched him over into total craziness.

Sit on that, Ray. Your left arm is gone.

13

THE GULLS ARE coming in to the dock and fighting over the can of sardines I left out for them. I couldn't finish it. I should eat. Sweetest Sister is gone and Westy is gone, and it is hard to swallow a cracker. Out in the gulf you see the edge of your world, many boats, and people falling off, silhouetted by the sun. Arms up, screams, goodbye. The moon is coming in red. Small-craft warnings are out. Over the crumpled horizon the moon seems to roll away the clouds and be a great ruby marble.

Barry and I are here. We aim to catch some fish.

Lee and Barry are also back here in Tuscaloosa with me. Hold old Ray close, everybody, for he is estranged from the clear home that he once knew.

I almost forgot. My dogs are here too. We're all in here now and we are having fun pitching pennies in a minnow bucket. We are about to eat the delicious ribs from Archibald's — happy nigger that smokes them the best — and my daughter Lee and I have had a good time at the university pool. She comes down the slide hollering with glee. She's a water lady of nine years. We go off the diving board together in a backflip. Through the water and swimming forward.

This is me at the trial.

'Doctor, did you ever hear Doctor Castro threaten the woman?'

'No.'

'Did you yourself ever have sexual relations with the deceased?'

'No.'

'You are under oath.'

'The answer is no.'

'Semen was found in her vagina.'

'Not mine.'

'But Doctor Castro has alleged that he saw . . .'

'I'm not on trial here.'

Maynard stood up, crying, and confessed. You couldn't understand too much of what he said through the weeping. But there it was. He rushed over to me and hugged me. I came up with a quick stroke from the old Navy practice and sent him sprawling back to his lawyer.

In their secret hearts, such perversities as Maynard know there are things they can never have, things they have wanted with all their hearts. So they kill them. Most preachers are

240

this way. Their messages seem benevolent, but they are more evil than the rest of us walking pavement.

When I fly again, it will be against the preachers.

14

AFTER THE TRIAL, this man comes up to me. I'm so full of trouble I don't even recognize him. Holy God, it's one of those students I taught in that American Civ class. He wants me to read his poem.

CERTAIN FEELINGS

I have certain feelings about this room
I have certain feelings about doom
I have certain feelings about trees and gnats
I have certain feelings about this and that

I have certain feelings about firearms
I have certain feelings about the girls and the guests
I have certain feelings about firearms
I have certain burglar alarms

I have certain strains of Mozart in my soul
Certain helplessness I cannot control
Though I guess when all is said and done
I have certain feelings

They always say Southerners can write. So I slugged this skinny lad. I laid him down the steps. They took this on the local TV, and I watched it with Westy. I was in my white suit and I duked away this harmless poet. He tumbled down a lot of steps and his family is saying they'll sue.

No matter. I'm in Westy again. The thing seemed to have turned her on. Not the violence, but the lonely trouble. Cornelia Wallace called me up about publishing her novel. Fame on the TV got me back to Westy.

She covers me with kisses. Tears running down. Ray heaving, wife receiving. Hear me, poets. I have certain feelings.

15

IN THE MOON that comes over Dauphin Island, over the bay, we see the gray-blue chariots of the gods move across its face. The wind is running from the south. The night is clear. The blinking lights of the airport tower are throwing out against the color.

The hurricane is over and many people are dissatisfied that it killed no one. Bob the hurricane came in and just sort of raised the water, blew a few phony cupolas off the houses.

Ray meets one of the detestable children of the modern day. I delivered her baby and now she's delivered her modern self onto the world. She was at the 7-Eleven when I was buying crab bait.

'Are you, I'd guess, a Taurus, Doctor Ray?'

'Yes. Nice to see you.'

'What are you doing here?'

'Fishing with my father and my son.'

'Oh, how macho. Just like a Taurus.'

'Yes, isn't it?'

'I'm divorced now.'

'Oh.'

16

WESTY AND I are hugging. The thrill goes all around the world. I seem to have made her pregnant. Westy is worried about having a retarded idiot at her age, and we have too many children already. But I want it, moron, imbecile, whatever's in the cards.

Come forth! Take flight! Son or daughter of Ray and Westy!

When the day is done, I have seen ten patients and the sun is setting out over the trees. Westy sits on the bed crying, face in her hands. She doesn't know what to do about the baby. She is scared of it. Another thing to fly and die.

Dr. Ray breaks into tears himself. He washes them away with cold water, but they flood again. The baby in Westy's womb looms up like the huge fetus at the end of *2001*. Our baby, our baby.

Two more days and it turns out she wasn't pregnant, after all. My brain was in squalor and torment. But now it's like another friend I lost in Nam.

'Edward, what you got?'

'I've got something, something on me!'

Then I saw it, the SAM missile go into his exhaust. It was a big white flower spraying in the night. There was Edward, lieutenant commander from St. Paul, Minnesota, a nigger who saved my life twice, falling to pieces. There he goes.

I should have delivered him. I should have been awaker.

Mr. Hooch was at the funeral, of course. Sister was lying all fixed up in the coffin. I couldn't go by to see the body or smell the bank of flowers. Mr. Hooch is a strong man. His wife trembles and smokes. The Hooches have lived in CM (Constant Misery), and now their first claim to fame is dead.

I was shivering. Westy was holding me with her slim arms.

'You really loved her, didn't you?' says Westy.

'Yeah. Westy, I'm sorry, but I did.'

'She was lovely. But don't you think I'm lovelier?'

'Yes.'

'Is everything just sex and music?'

'No.'

'You're awfully down.'

'I need more sex and music.'

Mr. Hooch shook my hand and said, 'We almost had a success with Sister. I told Agnes, "What the Hooches can't help, they can't help. People born on a bad wind just ride and take it." '

243

'That's the thing to tell Agnes.'

'We've seen Sister in one way, and now we're seeing her
another way. My daughter fell in with the wrong crowd. We
all make mistakes. We didn't know everything about the
preacher. He didn't know everything about himself.'

I said, 'My God, Mr. Hooch, that's the way to talk.'

He said, 'It's my only goddamn talent. When I quit talking,
I'll be as dead as my daughter. Hold my arm, Doctor Ray.
I'm about to fall down.'

We held each other, everything rushing around us from all
corners.

Agnes Hooch has said nothing during the funeral. The heat
in the cemetery is a hundred degrees and we go out to the
hole in our suits and dresses, hats, sunglasses. The little
Hooch twins have quiet, hallowed looks beyond grief. I see
the maimed one hobbling on her artificial leg with the hot
wind rumpling her dress. She is a vision of permanent agony.
Toward the end of the ceremony Mrs. Hooch raises a dreadful animal wail of fearful, unknown, soprano lamentation.
But the wooden Indian in the station wagon never batted an
eye.

17

LOOK HERE, YOU were involved in one murder, says the
voice over the phone, so here's another. I called you because
you've got experience. Maybe he was a bum, but he was a
good bum, and I know who did it.

I was not involved in any damned murder, I say.

Well, there's a corpse out in Capitol Park, name of Buster
Lewis. He's been around a long time. Friendliest, wisest
drunk in town. In fact, I'll say it, he was my uncle. I'll meet
you there. A teenager did it. If you don't come see me, I'm
going now to kill the kid with my thirty-eight. Then there'll
be two, and I'm on my way to Mexico.

Why me, fellow? There's the police, you know.

Yes, there's the police, but you're cute. Besides, I was a corpsman in the Marines. You get the picture?

Are you a nigger? I say.

Could be, the voice says.

I'll be there, I say.

My Corvette wouldn't start. So I jumped in Westy's Toyota. Edward, Edward, Edward, here I come in this here Jap econo-car! Just hang on.

18

BUT CAPITOL PARK can keep for a while. Let's talk about Judy – Judy and her apartment. She's a lady who ran for mayor on the strength of her large, loving personality. Judy's an honest port. She's not the malicious and bored ground crew. Sometimes there is a true person waiting to talk to you and comfort you, and Judy is it!

I'll tell you, God, you've brought some manure and beauty down on this doctor and aging pilot who saw you face to face over the Sea of China one night, but the blue honest port that he came down to is Judy, who's traveled a bit herself over the herd of crabs in politics. How sweet to be in her place and have her hold your hand.

God makes people like Judy. Poem.

19

THERE AIN'T NOBODY here and the fog is rolling around. For a moment I'm entering a zone of Edgar Allan Poe privacy. The border of vague in a semi-German or Greek swamp. Rising sins from my past are coming up and haunting my insides, and there's this miserable dew on my buckle loafers. Look here, I'm an important doctor on a mission, I don't have to wait here for creepy phantom business. Then I hear the hiss and the voice.

'Over here, Ray.'

'Give me a light.'

Out in the park I see Uncle Buster with a bloody face. He's breathing pretty well. But he's in shock. Healthy and large for a wino. I tell the man with the flashlight to raise the feet.

First dawn I have seen in fifteen years, twenty years, twenty-three years. I was a Boy Scout at Camp Kickapoo. I was smoking grapevine in the cabin and Mr. DeLard called me out: 'If I ever have to call you out again, Ray, even though you're a Life Scout, I'll have to dismiss you from the troop. You're supposed to be a leader, and here you are smoking.'

I have always needed a great exhaust system. DeLard had his Luckies on the top of his knapsack. He was a hairy, frantic man. I went back in the cabin and lit up another piece of grapevine, because I had information. This here was the only time ever I was mean – with *information*. Mr. DeLard ran into the cabin. He had a Scout suit on and was forty.

'Okay. I warned you.'

'Leave me alone.'

'You're out of the troop.'

'No, I'm not! We live next to you, Mr. DeLard. My dad bought a high-power telescope for my astronomy badge. I turned it around to your bathroom and me and my dad and mother saw you beating your meat!'

Many Scouts in the cabin heard this. It was the first time in my life I'd ever been mean. I was always gentle until people shot at me.

I was a Life Scout, very solid. I knew how to start a fire, eat raw minnows, mold, and worms when it got down to survival. Then I went into Explorer Scouts, which led to flying in the Civil Air Patrol, which led to training on the T-33s in Biloxi, which led to the F-4 Phantom, and I could speak a little French and I was a captain when Edward was gone in the gray-pearl over Hanoi, which is what Tom Wolfe called it, and he was right.

With the Rolling Stones on the tape on my right side and the whole U.S. hugging my back in this hot cockpit, I'm throwing off my mask as I see the MIG-21 come up after the gooks shot my commander Edward down.

Channel 16. 'Daya, menta, menta, casa, casa, casa, casa, casa!' International jet talk. Telling the gook pilot to get out of the air or I'll bury him.

He still rises.

'Vaya casa, vaya casa.' Go home or you're dead, son. I've got everything on me, and this plane and me will make you burn if you stay up here twenty more seconds.

But he comes up twirling like a T.

Well, hell. I want him! I turn the Rolling Stones all the way up, all the states of the U.S. shine behind me.

He's in the scope. I'm almost upside down and he's trying to get back home but it's too darned late.

'You speak English?' I say.

'Uh, yes.'

'Are you Catholic?'

'Used to be before Communist.'

'I want to know your name and how old before I kill you.'

'Lester Sims, twenty-three, lieutenant, Hanoi base.'

'Lester Sims?'

'Translating. Lu Gut. Trying to fly away.'

Then the buttons when he got into the middle of the scope. It's so easy to kill. Saw him make the bright, white flower. It's so fucking hard to live.

Big orange lights in rectangle on my carrier, the *Bonhomme Richard*. Lots of handshakes.

It was the start of what I've got, and no nooky, no poem, no medicine or nothing will make it go away. Jesus, my head!

Six years of medical training at Tulane. They said six to satisfy the med laws. I only had four. But four's all it takes to get the drunk breathing good.

'Shit, he's alive!' I said.

The fellow put down the flashlight.

By God, it was Charlie DeSoto. From the old days of Eileen and Charlie. He had a sad mustache and balding blond hair.

'I knew he was going to make it when I called you,' said

Charlie. 'I've got him and two more uncles in town. This one's a lush and a teenager hit him over the head with a two-by-four. The little punk is over at his grandmother's house and I've got the thirty-eight, like I told you. Eileen has left me, and I really don't care anymore.'

I walked over to the house with the light in the parlor. It was four in the morning. I knocked on the door and the grandmother opened it. I asked for the phone. While I was calling for the ambulance, the criminal walked up. He was a big innocent-faced frat boy in an Izod shirt.

'I'll tell you, these scummy winos come out there and scum up the view of the park. It's more than you can take.'

I said, 'Bring me the thing you hit him with.'

'Sure. Hey. Tomorrow you've got to come up to the Sigma Chi house and have some beers with us. Some of the brothers said you were a keen teacher in Am Civ.'

The service answered.

'It's just one of those things,' said the student when he got back with the thing.

I bashed the fuck out of his ribs with it and his grandmother screamed.

We put them both in the ambulance.

I healed everybody.

20

WE WEAR GRAY in the big meadow and there are three thousand enemy in blue, much cannon and machinery behind them. The shadow of the valley passes over our eyes, and in the ridge of the mountains we see the white clouds as Christ's open chest. Many of us start weeping and smiling because we will die and we know. Last week we thought we were immortal.

'Shall we charge, my commander, or shall we fall back? We have nothing but our sabers and our pistols, which are cowardly.'

'*Up!*' yells the commander.

You take the saber from your left thigh and hold it straight above. The pennants go higher. You put the cavalry hat down because the sun is against you. Around you there is nothing because the horses are in perfect line. The sun is coming over the raised sabers.

'Commander, we could fall back. Our horses can run away from this.'

There is no turning back. Hold sabers. We will walk to them until they shoot and then we will charge.

Everybody was killed. One Union private lived to tell the story.

If warriors had known this story, we would have taken the war to the gooks with more dignity.

21

ME AND THE machines saved Uncle Buster. He woke up wanting some wine. All ready to be a bum again. Go out there in the park, safe from vigilant idiots who get their haircuts at fifteen dollars.

22

'EILEEN LEFT YOU?' I hadn't been listening too good.

'For a month now. She didn't like my friends. She used to be nothing but love. Now she's just complaint and fury. What happens to women, Ray?'

My clinic is on a small offstreet. Through the window I can see the trees waving back and forth as the thunderstorm comes on. Linda Ronstadt is on my tape deck. I turn her down. I was listening more to 'Blue Bayou' than to Charlie DeSoto, honestly. One afternoon I saw a gorgeous stag raise his head out of the hedge of yellow flowers. Right here in the middle of the city. There is a creek that runs down to

249

the Black Warrior River and there is a thick swamp as it meets another creek, where there are deer and immense snapping turtles. It's a haunted place, full of tales. Sister may be there now.

'What?' I light up a Vantage.

'I don't understand what happened to her after we got married.'

Charlie had acute gastritis over a peptic ulcer. Lots of buttermilk, if you can stand it.

'Look, Charlie. I'm going to stick you with some morphine and I'll drive you home. Drink the buttermilk and sleep as long as you can. But this is the only time. Morphine is dangerous.'

'Don't tell me. They used it in Nam.'

'Okay. Let us not use the Demerol or any of the other shit after this. We're just going to have to wait and see if your belly comes back for you. It should. A belly does.'

'I got a raise. I'm the plant manager now. There's a girl at the office who's twice as good-looking as Eileen. She wants to lick my dick. I don't know what to do. I'm sick.'

'Your blood pressure is up. Knock off the salt. Buy yourself some garlic pills.'

'Garlic?'

'Trust me. We'll get them at the drug on the way home. You're the last patient today and I want out of this office. Catch "M*A*S*H" and make love.'

'Why do women change after you marry them? She hates all my friends and is always tired when I try to get it on.'

'You want to go fishing soon? My son and I have been catching some nice bass.'

'You haven't told me a damned thing about women.'

'I tried to write a paper on the subject once. Pick up a *Cosmopolitan* magazine at the drug. Women read it to find out who they ought to be and then that's who they are. A guy whips his pudding when he sees the new look in bathing suits. If Jackie Kennedy sucked you off, your ulcer would go away.'

'Can you get her to do it?'

'No,' I say. 'For doctors, they have Claire Bloom and Lee Remick, but simple street shits like you just have to buy *Penthouse*.'

Charlie smiled.

It is always a sign of health when the smile can rise. His eyes are brighter. This handsome bastard will outlive me, and I resent it.

The nurse comes in with the needle. She's trained in the great med center at Birmingham and she is a knockout. Her hair is blond and curled. She's about five-nine, a tall girl, twenty-six, and her legs are an amazing long event. Beyond that, she's just a straight honest slut. I never had her. It is a perversity, but I hired her just to tempt myself and resist, as a man who's quit smoking keeps a pack of Luckies on his desk just to see what he won't do anymore.

Rebecca puts the needle in him. When Charlie phases out, he lifts his hands in prayer. She looks at me quickly. She takes down the top of her uniform. The large dark-nippled breasts are there. Charlie is lying in the leather chair and she lowers herself to him.

Certain things are private and it is tacky to witness them.

In three weeks his ulcer was cured. He came by the office to tell me how delightful it was to be healthy. He told me he paid Rebecca for a week, but all the rest was free. Eileen was still in Georgia, waiting it out, knowing she was hurting Charlie. Women enjoy revenge more than the worst Apache.

Then sabers up and we knock the fuck out of everybody. With the cherished dream of Christ in our hearts. Basically, the message is: Leave me the hell alone or give me a beer.

Yes, I have seen the rain coming down on a sunny day. I have seen the moon hot and the sun cold. I have seen almost everything dependable go against its nature. I have seen needless death and I have seen needless life. One old mule of eighty came into the emergency room who had abused three wives, beaten his youngest son, twelve, with a tire tool, and had borrowed from everybody in Gordo. He had a heart attack and he was in intensive care, all hooked up to the machines and the monitors. He wanted to talk to me.

'When I get out of here, I'm going to kill all those sons of bitches, Doctor.'

I'd brought Rebecca with me. She can bring a man back. She can bring a woman back. A lesbian on Methadone came in wanting to die one afternoon. Rebecca put the bottle up and I straddled her, looked down her throat, opened it, and eventually got a pint of buttermilk down her. Then she was fighting and weird and we had to get the heavy stuff in her. After she was calm, Rebecca took her skirt off and sat on her face and the girl licked her wide hairy organ. I watched this one because I thought the girl might die.

But Ray confesses he deliberately lost the bastard who was eighty. I told everybody to get out of the room and I bent down my face and looked him straight in the eye.

'What are you going to do when I get you on your feet again?'

'Kill the sons of bitches!'

I yanked out the connections and shut down the monitors and let him pass over the light into hell. By the time the crew came in, I had all the stuff going again.

'I lost him!' I screamed.

Rebecca saw me in the hall. We lit cigarettes.

'You killed him,' she said.

'Well, hell,' I said.

'You want to get it on, Doctor Ray?'

'I can't. I have a wife. Westy.'

She said, 'I want you to screw me, darling.'

'Yeah. But I killed the old guy. Never did that before.'

'He deserved it. Let's go dance and fuck.'

'I forgot how to dance about twelve years ago.'

'Yeah. But we could just go to my place, and fuck. You ever hear Jimi Hendrix? You and I could've saved him, poor old genius nigger.'

23

'RAY?'
  'Yeah?'
  'They got me.'
  'Contact, Ed. I'm hearing you.'
  'Put your spirit with mine now, old lieutenant. I'm ashes.'
Then he was.

The last time Sister came to me at the clinic, I wrote this
record and this prescription.
  – Female, 23. She has made one album and her next one
is in process.
  – Her mother, almost nonexistent.
  – Her father, a philosopher.
  – Her family. Two sets of twins, one of them recently
backed over by a bus, plus two others.
  – Her situation. Singer. Uses marijuana heavily. High
blood pressure. 150/90. X-ray shows dark spot in the upper
left lung.
  Prescription:
  – Valium, 25 mg. Every four hours until appetite returns.
Prednisone, 200 mg. One every other day for two weeks.
Then a half-pill every other day. 60 days. No refill.

24

PAT AND I go out in my little MG. I don't have the Corvette
anymore because of the gas. But I like my little 73 Midget
and the sky. You get this low and you get to look at the sky.
  So me and Pat go out to the airport to look at the new
two-million-dollar Learjet, and we get in the cockpit, and I
show Pat the controls.
  Pat is a wonderful guitarist from Chicago, as well as a
medieval scholar and poet. Nobody's killed him yet.

25

EVERYBODY I LOVE is in the jet. We try New York, but it's no good. I've got the .32 machine pistol that I killed a gook in the head with. He was dead and he had a hand grenade in his hand. But he threw a knife into the neck of Larry. We were all fueling at Ton Sa Nut. Fifteen F-4s all in line. You couldn't ever kill enough of them. Vietnam was like fleas.

Never had a whore in Saigon. Never gambled my money. Quisenberry and I mainly just talked ourselves to sleep, then dropped Dexedrine when the horn sounded.

Harry King was flight control one night at the Tuscaloosa airport and brought Don in on auto-pilot from Chicago after he'd turned the plane in a storm and fainted.

Ray is out here with his beeper on his leg, just watching the planes come in over the blue lights, for no reason except to find my meditation again. Somehow the AM waves are getting into my beeper and I hear 'Eleanor Rigby' from the Beatles. Where *do* all the lonely people come from? Ray is starting to sound like a man who was once a disk jockey. Because he's run-down. I'm full of dopey tears and just as groping and lousy as the next citizen.

So I just wander into flight control. Harry's very lonely with all the Teletypes. What in the hell comes in but an F-4 from the National Guard in Birmingham. He touches down, then off, wheels it out, gone at five hundred miles per hour. Beautiful Phantom.

'How you been, Harry?'

'Ray! Goddamn, you're here!'

Here looking at the flat charts of the flight territory all over the world and Harry, still wearing his tie from WW II. He's driving his crummy Toyota since the gas crunch and we talk about that. We share one of those huge TV dinners made for two. Not much to do here now.

The beeper sounds and it's Rebecca.

'What?'

'Nothing, really,' she says. 'I handled it. I'd just sort of like you to run back here and dick me.'

'I don't have it in me,' I say.

'Okay. There's another message, from Westy.'

'Put her on,' I say.

'I just cured three creeps with a light assist from your buddy, Doctor Litchens. You can't imagine the swine I'm going to have to do a number with tonight.'

'Put Westy on.'

It was fifteen minutes. Harry and I were finishing up the chicken on the plate when she called. I hadn't heard a straight and clear message from her in three months.

'Ray? Raymond Forrest?' My first two names.

'I hear you, darling.'

'Ray. We can make lovesies again.'

'Holy Christ!'

'Yes,' she said. 'I want to be lovely all over you again.'

I was so entranced I forgot Harry King was right there beside me. You never get a whole conversation over the beeper like this unless you got somebody relaying it. Rebecca did it and was listening in.

26

I NEVER WOKE up feeling better. Made coffee, eggs, bacon for all my six children.

No complaints.

27

THE BEEPER GOES off when Westy and I are doing something. We have our tongues so deep into each other's and I am sucking her beautiful feet. It's Rebecca.

'Mr. Hooch and Agnes bought a propane lantern and it

255

exploded. He's almost dead from burns, Doctor. She has second-degrees.'

Hooch was burned to a crisp and he weighed about a hundred pounds. His system was so exasperated, it was a total moan. The protein and the platelets and the nerves were wrecked and closing. His kidneys were going out. His liver count was as high as a man's who hadn't eaten in three months. The calcium was not protecting his lungs. Yet on fruit juice and plasma, his mind stayed. Even brighter. What an organ. You got a third of it left and you can still be a genius. For a while we couldn't even get creamed field peas down him. He was burned down to the condition of the inside of a steak as Texans like them.

'You tried to kill yourself, didn't you?'

'No.'

'Yes, you did. You know better than to light up a leaking propane tube.'

'I get tired of my wife and me. There ain't much going on since Sister except my mouth.'

'Gimme a poem, Mr. Hooch. Let's hear the best.'

One of the humiliations of my life was that my own secret poems never touched the poems of this old fart. All his genes must have run a pretty direct route into Sister.

FIRE AT NIGHT

by J. Hooch

Fire at night and it's me. I've been born with pain
So this is sort of the same.
Agnes talks about forty years ago.
Her love is around, but I never got her mind's number.
Love is above and behind you,
But somewhere, honey, I've got to find you.
We bad luck together and it ain't ever going to get better.
We worse when we try to get better.
We got the jinx and the voodoo visited upon us.
But it's New Year, so I'll light myself up
With a cup of gas.

256

It'll be a hell of a feeling.
And this one will really, really be the last.

'Not bad,' I say.

I go back to the dinette and sit with Rebecca. I smoked about four Luckies in a row and looked into her face without saying anything for a while. Rebecca's face is a charm. She goes heavy on the blue eye makeup. Her neck is a longish classic from the old paintings of what's-his-name. Her nose is forward and long. She lights a Lucky and the exhaust is gray through the large sensitive nostrils. She's half-Jew, the rest Greek. Okay, now I've come back from the humiliation of never thinking up a better poem than Mr. Hooch. Then we go through two cups of coffee apiece. Modigliani.

'No, he's not, goddamn it.'

'There's not much here at the hospital.'

'There's the Freon tube.'

'They won't let us use it yet.'

'I have a key that's copper-colored in the far right drawer of the front desk in the office. There is a forty-five pistol right next to it. Put it, the key, in that little safe. If you can't open it, get a pillow from one of the chairs, push it over the muzzle of the gun, and shoot out the lock. I'll meet you at the hospital.'

'The FDA won't . . .'

'Do it, bitch. Move it quick.'

It worked. Then I sent him over to plastic surgery.

28

I BROUGHT A new Goliath harmonica made by Hohner into J. Hooch's room. By then he weighed a hundred and thirty and was looking fairly decent.

'Gimme that son of a bitch. Whose is that?'

'Yours.'

*

A month later he was back at the Hooch house. I would put
the MG on neutral to hear the strains coming from Sister's
studio. His bed was there. He's moved to it, all the guitars,
the stereo around him. The old boy was playing the hell out
of the harmonica. He was at a hundred and fifty and going
normal.

'I'll be what my daughter was trying to be!'

'What?'

'Already got myself recorded. All I need is a drum. I read
Sister's diary! Goddamn it, I'm a great old son of a bitch!'

The dirty dog was playing the harmonica every time I came
by the house. I'd just shut the car down and listen to the
tender sorrow coming through the forty-eight reeds.

Then with duty on my mind, I go by the emergency room.
Nothing. The usual hurt niggers, but all's in control.

I am late coming home and Westy is pissed off. Yes, I had
some bourbons, and I guess I just sort of threw her nightgown
up and tried to.

Women enjoy conversation.

Lube does not come in before talk.

I got up to brush my teeth and prove I'm not drunk.

All right.

Afterward, I ate her slowly. I hadn't eaten much all day.

29

ERD. #92. #Doe4. Utap. At 40–50. Range. In Clear. Solid.
Ventro.

30

THE OTHER NIGHT one of the deranged creeps got out of
his car at the emergency room, swinging a Magnum in his
hand. He had already swatted his granddaughter in the head
with it, plus shot his regular daughter in the tit.

I had been shooting the .30/30 with my boy Barry that day.

I asked him to ride into the back lot with me, because I was a doctor who understood him. Something about my stern eyes that calms even wild men down. He gave me the gun. We got way out there where nobody could hear. I played some country music for him while I pulled a towel over the barrel of the .30/30 and rested it into his ribs.

'What was you going to say?'

'Light up a cigarette for me,' I said.

While he did, I let one go through him.

'What'd you do?'

'Let out some of your spleen and piss,' I said.

He fainted, of course.

I took him back to the main entrance and kicked him out. Now he'll live but be warned. I've still got his Magnum.

31

NOW I GUESS I should give you swaying trees and the rare geometry of cows in the meadows or the like – to break it up. But, sorry, me and this one are over.

32

I GOT AUDITED by the IRS because I hadn't filed in four years.

So I went up there to the Federal house. They had called me over the phone and finally got rude. I tend to procrastinate on business like this because I feel I don't owe anything and already fought for the country. I'm for the straight ten percent. I'd file before anybody then.

She was not so stern when she met me. I had all my forms. She went off in the room and talked to her boyfriend for thirty minutes. I went down to the first floor and got some coffee. Saw a nigger in a Federal suit and asked him if I could try out his gun. There was nothing else to do. Then I got some Nabs. Those are fun. I ate two and spat out the third. Welfare niggers who don't work for a living are all over the place.

Finally she got back to the desk. She had to make another call or receive one.

This was enough. I went back in the other room, raised up her skirt, and stuck the meat in her. She was talking to her boyfriend and moaning.

Now I am clean with the IRS.

33

ELEMENTS OF PROTEIN float in. B-12 for sanity, vegetables, and Oscar, the mysterious warrior that sails in the bloodstream. Can be cancer or the warrior *against* cancer. I'm dreaming of this. I'm dreaming of the day when the Big C will be blown away. I'm dreaming of a world where men and women have stopped the war and where we will stroll as naked excellent couples under the eye of the sweet Lord again. I'm dreaming of the children whom I have hurt from being hurt and the hurt they learn, the cynicism, the precocious wit, the poo-poo, the slanted mouth, the supercilious eyebrow.

Then I wake up and I'm smiling. Westy asks me what's wrong.

'Christ, darling, I just had a good dream, is all.'

'I'll bet it was some patient you screwed. You rotten bastard.'

She hits me over the head with a pillow.

Violence.

Some days even a cup of coffee is violence.

When I can find my peace, I take a ladder to the hot attic and get out the whole plays of Shakespeare.

Okay, old boy. Let's hear it again. Sweat's popping out of my eyes, forehead.

Let's hear it again. Between the lines I'm looking for the cure for cancer.

34

LET'S GET HOT and cold, because, darling new thing, we're going through the weeds and the woods and just the sliver of the moon comes in through the dead branches, and the running rabbits and squirrels are underneath and above. Henry David Thoreau is out there thinking, loping around. Louis Pasteur is out there racing with the bacteria.

We went to the planetarium in Jackson, Mississippi, my hometown. Elizabeth, Ray, Lee, and Teddy. Elizabeth is on the couch with her crocheting. Lee is reading her new bible, Proverbs. It's raining out. We've cut the yard in the front, and the train whistle is hooting.

'A gentle answer quiets anger, but a harsh one stirs it up.'

'It is foolish to ignore what your father taught you. It is wise to accept correction.'

They say, 'Dad, take it easy. Quit going so fast.'

My daughter has a secret friend named Fred, and my son Teddy has a secret friend named Jim.

We all sleep together in the big wooden four-poster where I grew up, tiny innocent arms and legs and imaginary friends on top.

Ike, Ken, Carol, and Ginger are at my ex-brother-in-law's place, and I join them to fish at the wide kidney-shaped lake at the bottom of their rolling lawn. Dr. John and Dr. Ray trade a few compliments. John would give you the shirt off his back. It's a shame my sister, Dot, isn't with him anymore. There were differences. His wife, Mindy, is sweet and has Buffy and Moffit. I forgot to mention my beautiful nieces, Hannah Lynn and Maribeth. Everybody's around and we are flying kites over the tall oaks, the Black Angus cattle are roaming comfortably in the taller weeds, and the geese control their placid squadrons.

Ike is a playwright and Ginger has just come back from Europe with her Gitanes, one of the essential deeds of young females. Looking back at the house, it's a low wooden castle.

35

THEY ASKED ME where I wanted to go to graduate school and I said Tulane, for medicine. Finished in three years. Or maybe it was four.

36

ONE OF THE great bad strokes I did was marry the prettiest girl on campus. I was so horny and everything else was pretty nothing except red bricks and Baptists, a few queers in the drama and English departments. I got thrown out of my room by a senior who thought he could box. I knew nothing about boxing. This was supposed to be my roommate. He was a blond, acned guy, and he was punching me. So I said, 'Stop.'

He quit, though he was still shifting, bouncing.

'My name's Wild Man Thomas,' he said.

37

IT'S QUIET, UTTERLY quiet, except for the air conditioner going in my room. The companionship is with the air alone. I am asking forgiveness for all my sins, on my knees. I got to get my mind in a higher sphere.

38

I WAS TREATING a large old woman who spat in my face. I fell backward into the heater, face-forward. This is to prove that I'm not always the hero.

39

NURSES HAVE SAVED me. I wander through the day like a horde often. I can't hit the directional signal on my car. I trip over my unredeemable cockiness. I drop a can of 7-Up in the hall and fall down in front of Dr. Everything, the world surgeon I always wanted to meet and impress.

One evening, late, I was watching a nigger up in a tree picking his nose. The nigger worked for the electric company and was apparently new. He'd climbed up the tree next to the light pole.

'What you laughing at?' said another big nigger behind me, wearing a helmet.

40

FOR NO CLEAR reason Ray will have it out with the plants in his place. His anger comes up when he looks around at the expensive greenery and all the deathly care people give to plants when, if let alone, all plants are fine. Plants can talk, he's heard: 'Eat me. Eat me.' That's all Ray's ever heard. Anybody besides Ray see *Little Shop of Horrors*? A great plant in some creepy Jew's flower shop starts calling out, 'Feed me, feed me!' He eats people. So the Jew goes and accidentally kills a number of people and their faces appear in the blossoms of the plant.

Ray has lost it. He kicks over the plants and yells abuses. Mainly, it's because his poems are not going well and he still can't come anywhere close to old J. Hooch.

Westy comes in. She's disturbed.

'Are you drinking, Ray?'

'No. Get me a drink.'

She's wearing beige sandals and her toenails are maroon. She has a glass of milk with her, reaches back with it, pours it over the crease of her buttocks and fetches my tongue in.

I'm as earnest as an evangelist when I mount her.

41

BILL, MY DAD, came over to check on me again. He's been everywhere, from hard-crushing Depressionville to Russia. Got him the new Mercury that gets twenty-seven miles per gallon on unleaded, high visibility. He still looks handsome. Still the man who gave me life. Seventy-five years old. Afflicted only by deafness and arthritic feet. Always got money, maybe pull out a thousand of the five hundred of them he's worth now.

Bill roomed with Senator Eastland at Ole Miss. He and the great senator were going to be law partners. But Bill had to go back to Homewood, in Jefferson County, to support his family. Bill is a naturalist and is determined not to let Ray not listen to his advice now because he never had any advice for Ray when he was young.

Bill looks good.

He has the open, eager eyes of a man who has confessed and tried to put it back right. He always gave me the advantages.

42

COMING BACK FROM the convention in Omaha, I was thinking about my first wife. Because you have to be honest. You are packed with your past and there is no future.

We got married stupid and frantic, Millicent and me.

264

Things at one point were lovely. The children were lovely, and waiting for them was a miracle like the rainbow. And although you try to get shut of those gorgeous moments when we had nothing but good neighbors, the pines, and the sky to look at, it's true, we had a sublimity. Our children are ready for the world, and they are handsome enough and know enough science.

I have seen so many people not worth saving, not worth putting the tubes into.

God jokes with his best ones.

What release, to look into the past the way I just tried. A petrified log just rolled off my heart.

43

CHARLIE DESOTO IS in the office.

'Ray, I've discovered that my wife is a lesbian, or at least so far divorced from usual commerce between us that love words do no good. Love-making hurts. It seems to be an inconvenience. It's smelly, messy. She makes me feel like a raper. I can never satisfy her. This baffles this poor fool who married her and had so many, I can't tell you, uh, loves with her. She prefers to sleep with her old coloring books. Nothing sensual I can say to her touches her. I've been drinking too much. I've used cocaine, LSD, listened for the phone, waited for her letters, since we've been apart. What do I do?'

'Split. Get out of this CM.'

'But I still have wonderful love dreams of her.'

'You can have dreams of somebody else.'

'I envy you and Westy. You sit there very smug.'

'Get off of it. Westy's a hell of a woman, but I've had three months with no nooky. People are like weather where she grew up. I'm terribly sorry your wife's queer.'

I went to Hooch's house. The yard is cleaned up. The back-yard is raked and the grass is growing around it like a billiard table. They are clean and neat now that Sister is dead. He's working on the tugboat and looks two decades from his real age. He and Agnes don't sleep in the same room anymore. He lives in Sister's acoustic-tile room, and he plays those records and he writes his poems that beat the hell out of mine.

And the old man is sixty-seven. He's got himself an Olivetti automatic typewriter and plays Sister's album over and over.

He picks up her brassieres and her pictures and her underwear.

He handed me one:

> Grief is
> Looking at the wooden Indian where your
>   little ones should be.
> I bought a new color teevee.
> All the people you should be are on the screen.
> Everybody is pretty.

44

THERE WILL NEVER be, stepson, another person that I have respected and loved as much as you.

Your stepfather will not fall down. Your stepdad Ray has created abuse and horrors in the house because of him and drink. I wasn't born straight. God gave me a hundred-and-fifty IQ and perfect pitch on instruments. Sometimes I don't hear. I am having a constant burn-out on communications. Nobody means any harm. Everybody is swell. Just can't get through to anybody.

You, boy, will travel with beauty. Not just righteousness, which is easy, but beauty too. I saw you at Murrah move like a genius. You are a chieftain. You threw the ball, you scrambled, and the niggers dropped it.

Never be cruel, weird, or abusive.

I promise not to take a jet anymore.

266

I love your mother.

Amy, Bobby, too.

This boy is so full of loves the juice comes out his eyes.

Alt. 2000, 1000, 500, 120, flaps down, lights on? Yes.
Port. Pork and beans.

Pick the football up, travel rearward on your legs, the way
is clear, there is your receiver, arms up in the lights on the
green field. The football leaves your arm like a quail. He's
got it. Runs into the last green zone.

45

ARE WE HERE? Is everybody here? I have scored six points,
the lights are up, but the stadium is empty. Want to do it
again, Westy? Want to get married again? Want to be in the
day instead of just walking through it and paying the bills?
The deck has gone out from under my legs and we're on the
rocks and we're on fire. Handsome craft, pure white, with
sails up and now it's not going anymore. She was blue-eyed,
white. But now it's raining fire. Everywhere you lift your
eyes, a rain of cinders.

You get to the end, and you're still swimming.

The people sing. My heart is all over my front yard. I am
still reading Bill Shakespeare.

Bob Moony's here. Mr. Hooch is here. There's no other
reason to be in Tuscaloosa.

Mike White is here. For God's sake, where else *is* there?
That's why a lot of people are here.

All we have is together.

And sometimes I cure others.

Christ be with my friend Phil Beidler. He has a polyp on
his vocal cords. I thought he might have C. Called Ned
Graves in Jackson, Mississippi. Best one in the world with
the knife on the throat. Phil was knocking down two packs
of Marlboros a day. Like me, he loves his ciggies. Called Ned
up. He was drunk, but wanted to fly over and get the C out

of Phil. But good old Phil didn't have it. Ned's only twenty-eight, works in clear weather. No damned war memories. He just walks in with five knives, and can see cancer with his own eyes. Knifes them off. Only lost two patients in all his time. A nurse was the cause once. She overanesthetized the little boy. Ned went out in the parking lot, put the nurse in the front seat of his Mustang convertible, sat there saying nothing for fifteen minutes. She didn't have a driver's license and she was night-blind – big, thick glasses.

'You killed him,' said Ned.

'I wish you weren't so emotional.'

'You killed the boy.' Ned drew on his cigarette. 'Walk home.'

'I live in Pelahatchie. That's twenty miles.'

'Walk home.'

So Ned is there, and I think of Ned. Sometimes it is better to think of your friends.

46

IN DESPERATION, I got a little dog named Elizabeth, spotted, three-quarters bird dog, abandoned by some person and running around the parking lot of the apartment where my stepson Tommy lives. You know how dogs are faithful. But she chewed everything. She chewed the shoes, the Oriental rugs, and the windowsills, plus leaving diarrhea all over the house. But her eyes were deep, hopeful, and oozy with affection. Thing is, her existence broke up Westy and me almost. Elizabeth ate a couple of pairs of Westy's sexiest sandals.

Born to chew, apparently.

The feet of Westy are so beautiful.

I finally wanted to get rid of the dog.

The bare feet and the toes in the golden high heels will bring a man on when he's entering his lady. You look at those and hear your woman moaning with pleasure and there's something so deeply elegant to the erotic that you've got to look into *Penthouse* after you've finished making love to be sure it really happened.

So I took the little dog out and kissed her goodbye.

47

I HAVE TALKED of pornography and medicine and love of art – which is Mr. Hooch's poems.

Many friends around.

And I work here and crank up the bodies that are slow.

Westy has gotten so absorbed by inflation and her step-children that she does not raise her happy irises to me any-more. She cleans the clothes and makes suppers and if she is not a lesbian, then what is she?

I am drinking five bottles of wine a day just to stay cool. Looking forward to the football at Alabama. I'm not going crazy and am not violent. I could play better tennis if my habit on nicotine would give up. I roam in the past for my best mind.

48

I HAD A little hashish and some Jack Daniel's, so I went out to Tuscaloosa airport, broke in the hangar, and took up the Pfeiffer Wire Learjet. Wanted to go everywhere. Refueled in Atlanta. Then I was all out of chemicals and had to do it on guts to get near Toronto, over the border. No chance. I was out of fuel, lights were off. So I crashed it in a small lake by the woods. First time Ray ever had a crash. Had his son's new guitar so as to strum along and almost burned it up too.

I walked away from there and the Lear blew up and took away about an acre of pines. I could not believe I lost that much good equipment. But wait a minute. The explosion lifted my son's guitar out of the cockpit, and I saw the bright strings loft over the pines and I ran and caught it.

So I hitchhiked back to New York, where I had a friend.
I got a sailboat to outside of Philly. Then I rode a train back
to here.

I was black as an Indian when I arrived at the door of my
tranquil house. I'd lost weight. I was back to a hundred and
forty, as in high school. My lovely, caring brother Robert
was in the house. They all had huge eyes, worrying if I was
dead.

'Who are you?'

'Your relative,' I said.

49

WESTY GAVE ME a roll yesterday. A good one. Toes and all.

Also the phone came in from Mr. Hooch. He's beating the
shit out of Shakespeare with his new ones.

50

YOUR HAT'S ROTTING off. It's hot. You're not sure about
your horse. Or the cause. All you know is that you are
here – through the clover, through the low-hanging branch,
through the grapeshot.

All of it missed you.

Your saber is up, and there goes your head, Christian.

51

I SEE NO pressing reason to get out of bed. The lights are
off and it is raining and the covers are the cave I dreamed of
when I was a child. I am pretending to be sick – a faker like
some of my patients. I dream of monsters that cannot get
me. Ha ha. The covers touch me like mother hands. The
memories of war talk in the house when I was growing up

270

jabber around, and I close my eyes and bury my face in the pillow like little Ray of three. Bill and Elizabeth told me what an unexpected event I was, and that's how I feel to this day. Even I don't expect me. If I could happen, anything could.

Sister is knocking on the door, with a cry as dismal as when I first saw her in her funny gown on the railroad tracks.

Charlie DeSoto is knocking there too. He says he's got a new bow and arrow. My God, that interests me about as much as a traffic jam.

'You want to shoot some gar?' he says.

Westy was out of town. There was nothing else crazy to do. So we went. We went out Highway 82 to the swamps of the Sipsey River. And there the huge, rolling, scaly, comb-toothed, vicious-snouted gar were not waiting. We were over our shoes in mud, and it was drizzling dirty rain, getting chilly, and the water was as still as oil. There was one wood-pecker going at it in the high branches of a dead tree. It was the only sign of life, and we'd been there two hours.

Charlie looked up at the woodpecker. Then he loaded the bow.

'Aw, Charlie,' I said.

'If I don't kill something, I'm going to kill my wife,' he said.

Says I, 'Go ahead. You ain't going to hit it, anyway.'

But he did. The arrow rose from the bow as dead-sure as a heat-seeker and skewered the lovely redheaded thing, went on up into the air with the bird still on it.

52

TO LIVE AND delight in healing, flying, fucking. Here are the men and women.

53

HE WADED, THEN swam. Then he came back the same way, sand and tears in his eyes. I say, 'You must've been shooting that bow for a while.'

'I been having hate in me since my wife turned lesbian or narcissistic or whatever,' Charlie says. 'But look, I've killed this beautiful bird. Ray, you've got to do something for me.'

He looked like the creature of mud with a feather in his hand.

I have sympathy because a lot of the people I have loved and given to have never especially loved or given to me, and Westy is colding off like the planet, except I can't believe it in either case.

Nothing really to say except in some reaction like on the television.

Now I am looking at the bird with the arrow through it.

And all it does is make me very sleepy.

54

RAY MEETS WESTY at the fancy yellow restaurant. She's looking pretty tired and old now. In the deep sparkling blue of her eyes I see a certain dangerous blank. Is Ray to blame? The rings and the other jewelry twinkle on her. I am looking at the other side of the hill now, at the sunken eyes, at the grim desperation of the earlobes. On her forehead Westy wears the wide frown of surrender.

'I am an old woman,' says some voice.

'No no no no no no no,' says mine.

'Ray, you care more about the sorriest scum than you do me.'

'No, I don't,' I say.

'Among your friends there is not one decent straight solid person. They are entirely the mange, as far as I am concerned.'

I say, 'What about Charlie DeSoto? He wears a suit.'

She just looked at me hopelessly.

'There is something about you, Ray, that wants to set yourself deliberately in peril and in trash. One of these days you won't come back alive. You are drinking again. You've had three vodka tonics.'

I ordered a fourth. Some old hideous baby in me wanted to see Westy pissed.

'You lousy ignorant bitch,' says Ray.

Westy got up and left, leaving me to bum a ride back to the office.

At the office there were a number of people in line. I went over to the back window and looked out over the creek, then down to it and the slick granite rocks through which it rushed. Who was it said we were invented by water as a means of its getting itself from one place to the other?

55

I AM LOOKING at the swelling hordes. I know too many goddamned people, too many wretched Americans at this point. Between the hours of healing, I dream of dropping the ace on much home real estate in hopes that many citizens will get trapped inside in the wide handshake of phosphorus.

Nothing wrong with me. For example, somebody's wife comes to see me. She says, Doctor, what's wrong? She says, I seem to have given all I can to make everybody comfortable, yet they despise me. All of my food and laundry elicits nothing but contempt in their eyes.

Back over in Mississippi my friend Wyatt Newman and I invented this girl that you took to the drive-in. She was rather large and leggy with huge breasts. During the movie she would start, after putting one hand to her brow, humping and moving her sex back and forth in motions of her inner time. She would sigh and pant. The fool who had dated her, skinny and never had any, would move over to touch her tits and give himself ease as well as affection to this large woman who was about to have to come over the whole idea of herself. But when he touches her, she knocks him away.

'Animal!' she screams.

Women are fucking awful. Sister was the one exception.

56

RAY IS CRAWLING this afternoon. Many things have broken down in our nice house. The only glory I see is the glory I saw as a jet fighter. I went through the clouds and brought up the nose of the Phantom, lifting at twenty-one hundred land miles per hour. It was either them or me, by God. I loved those clean choices. And I loved my jet. I loved all those aerodynamics, the rising and diving.

Something's wrong.

Westy and I are not close in the old way. My dreams are big discouraging monsters, hellish. Had one that was a walking building, which was my high school. It was my old high school chasing me down the block.

I tell you, if not for his old records and his Shakespeare, Ray would be a casualty of the American confusion.

Like yesterday. Eileen, DeSoto's wife, wanted to talk with me at the office. She was pale and she had developed a dramatic deepness in her voice. It was huskier, more Northern. I think she comes from Selma, Alabama. I am not an expert on lesbianism, mind you.

'I want to describe what it is like, Ray,' she said.

I said, 'First let me say that I am not an expert on lesbianism.'

'That's okay,' she says, 'I was shocked myself. I had fever and the shakes. It was like a big dream where you can't help walking toward the place although it's scary. There were a lot of voices and mouths. Then I became one of the mouths. I became one of the soft naked girls, and an ecstasy ran through every part of my mind. And I was there at the place and it was familiar, like coming back to something you had as a child.'

'Why'd you come see me?'

'Because you're a friend of Charlie's and he's very hurt. Besides, you are a doctor, aren't you?'

'Let me fuck you,' I say. 'It will be good for you. Doctor's orders,' I say. 'Come on,' I say, 'you crazy lesbian bitch – ohh, uhh, uhnn, touch it!'

57

AND YET WITHOUT a healthy sense of confusion, Ray might grow smug. It's true, isn't it? I might join the gruesome tribe of the smug. I think it's better with me all messed up.

I looked at the Nembutals this morning and thought for about three minutes about going over to the other side. Westy is snoring per usual. I love to hear her snore. I love to hear her come too. The whisper: 'Aw, you made me come!' Puts it out there like a pratfall, footing lost. If I could only get her to wear the high heels when she's nude, as in *Penthouse*. Going over to the other side, I'm not sure I could fuck, shoes or no. So I ditched the whole idea.

58

TWO THUGS WERE looking for me when I got off work today.

Here's something.

'We got reason to believe you let our uncle die when he coulder been saved.'

That old case several months ago. I was guilty.

'One of them nurses that was close to our family told us,' said one guy.

'We going to make you a flat doctor,' said the other one.

They were bikers and wore leather and studs and wrist

RAY

guards. Two black-and-silver Harleys behind them. I felt very sleepy.

I said, 'Yes. I let the old man son of a bitch die.' I was too tired to lie. I said, 'Come on, boys. One of you will get hurt bad, but there are two of you.' I was staring them down. They were huge, grimy creatures. The huger one was wearing a tattoo on his arm – skull and crossed swords.

Death is everywhere. Why do these killers on motorbikes think they have the corner on it?

'Come on,' I said. 'I'm full of death,' I said. 'Come and get it.'

'Huh?' said the grimier thug. He was one of those hairy men who go out of their way to be ugly. His hair was to his shoulders and he had a bald spot on the top of his head.

'Yes!' I shrieked. 'I come from the Navy and I know how to kill in a fight! One of you is going to get it. I don't right now have the energy but to kill one.'

'Kill?'

'Come on!' I hollered. 'Give it to me!' I took off my jacket.

They were not moving. Then they both moved fast and they slugged me around, mainly half-jabs to the belly. I never got a lick in and I fainted.

I guess this was justice in a way. I was sore when I came to, but to be truthful, I felt good. I was bleeding a little, but I felt fresh as sweet sixteen.

Such was my relationship with Westy at the time that she withdrew in disgust when I came home with the damage to my cheeks and forehead. There is a streak in some women that beats the shit out of a response to pain if the wounds are really sloppy. Even the old joys we knew could not abide against Westy's sense of the sanitary.

59

The thrill the suspense the spontaneity are
all hanging suspended by one ankle.

276

> There is one pompous tall bully I know
> Who shall be served.
> He shall perish in the hot foam of his cruel
>   absurdity. He shall be boiled alive.
> His own power glide shall run him over.
> His snide poems shall be twisted screw-wise up
>   his organ's exit.
> Then we bring on the major stuff.
> Rumors, backbiting, the hissing intimations.

That was a poem scratched out by yours truly when he had had a long season of no nooky. But now my loneliness is not preying on me as in the old days.

'What are you doing, Doctor?' says the new nurse.

'Writing a poem,' says I. 'Getting myself my own medicine.'

'Oh,' she says. 'I always loved poetry absolutely to pieces!'

Here's some nooky, thinks I.

She was about twenty-three and the nurse's dress fit her okay. She was green-eyed, svelte, with ample bosom, etc. There wasn't the hard face of stupidity such as you see on most nurses. My eyes go to her feet and even there I see a bit of style. Some kind of trim-line whites showing a great deal of the fetching ankle and the blue veins Ray loves.

'I liked your lectures on nervous anxiety last year,' says she.

I'm just grooving on those veins in her feet.

Says she, 'Would you read me one of your poems? God, a doctor who writes poems.'

'Let's fuck instead,' says I. What do we have?'

'Nothing. A couple of grown babies with runny noses. One of them's a woman who demands to see you personally.'

'Who is it?'

'She's the suicidal Lebanese one that leases the Learjet through her law firm.'

'Okay,' I say, 'we'll fuck tomorrow.'

I pass by the mirror and see I'm still semihandsome. But you can never trust your own way of seeing.

OVER HANOI. HENDRIX coming in clear. Coming down
from high nowhere to blue somewhere to spy the water and
the *Bonhomme Richard* in the luminous China Sea. There
was a certain spirit that had the controls and guided me in
to make the deck. It was the last of the last if you didn't.
God bless America. At the last moment it is all spirit, because
five things could go wrong before the hooks catch you and
you are climbing out of the cockpit.

Oh, Captain, my Captain.

I saw the hospital in Hawaii. It turned my heart. I saw
and heard them interviewing the wounded. The doctor goes
in and asks a boy who's just lost a leg: 'Do you feel different
about life now?'

I need to hear Sister's voice.

Sister, Sister.

Ray is lucky. Ray can walk, think, and be a fool in his
poems. I am lucky and I feel like fornication. Fellow doctor
told me that there is some change and refreshment of hor-
mones when you are with a lady overnight. Never knew that,
but I will definitely study it for my long paper on the Nervous
Anxiety of the Age.

Oh, God, my shirt isn't ironed! Etc.

Let us meet again, we with our gray and forward hats on a
million horses. Pushing the attack toward Washington, D.C.
Our loves have evaporated. We run counter to them. Looking
at the vista, there are cavalrymen of every race and creed.
There is the beauty of the horses, with a steam like cumulus
rising from their nostrils. Are we in line?

'Raise sabers!' says the general.

Eventually every man's a sword. I'm riding down the lines
and see Commander Gordon looking downcast. On myself
I have the wool short jacket with every color of the rainbow
on the breast.

'You haven't your saber, Commander. Raise it and you will see your men raise theirs.'

'Sorry. I was thinking about my ex-wife. Brings you down. I know I'm going to die and that brings me down.'

'If you use the new pistol correctly, I don't think you'll die. We are about to launch the Air Force. Shoulders up, Commander! We've got every horse ready on its feet. We will race on water and then bring out the pistols. Every bullet is a heat-seeker. There's no use of my going through the book with you.'

'Sabers up!' Commander Gordon says.

Behind him five thousand silver sabers rise.

'What do they have? What do their hired soldiers have?'

'We caught them short. All they have is the old lead. The machine guns. The air will bring down the potency of our jackets.'

Christ, here we go. Not a chance, but what a territory to gain!

Their cannon just missed me as my horse started running on the water. We are high on our horses and laughing and I can hear the shrill Rebel yell behind me. They are throwing out phosphorus bombs, and I see some of the men go down. My men just laugh and the horses climb the banks. What an open field. We are laughing and screaming the yell.

It is an open field.

61

IT WAS NOON. I could not eat.

I went over to the Hooches because I knew the old man was off for a break from the tugboats.

Mr. Hooch was there and I caught him in the very act of writing. It was about Sister, his dead daughter and my dead lover.

In the ground my daughter is but should not be
My mind and face is coming strong toward
    victory
In the ground but better her singing for the
    worms
Than the town and all of its terms
Below what happened, she lies, in no disguise
My daughter always loved the earth anyway
And when I put ear to live grass I can hear
    her
I can hear her, I can hear her, I can hear her.
And when I stand up I am dirty in my veins
I am soiled throughout. That's Sister
Mister.

He took a Kool off me. I was humiliated by his poetry and I had to go to the bathroom to cry loud. It was a storm of tears.

Sister was with me. 'Keep on, Doctor,' she said.

His wife came out and gave me a nod.

When I think I'm doing good, I have to come over and see that I'm not even in the contest. In fact I have put the old fart in contact with an English prof at the school, who's also a poet. It seems that the *Collected Poems* of J. Hooch are going to be a published fucking reality.

I was laboring on another one when that new nurse came in again. She was quite a choice and I was out of nooky going on four months. For some weird reason I began lying to her lavishly. They were not harmful lies. I invented a whole new biography and person. I get tired of being him, Ray, all the time.

'And so when I jumped out of the U-2 and saw all the Chinese around me, I knew there had been a misreckoning on someone's part. Instead of killing me, however, they were friendly, knew that I was a doctor in training, and introduced me to all the ins and outs of acupuncture. I guess I began to write poems about then.'

'Wow. Do you ever write about sex?'
'Often,' I replied.
'Does anyone ever get enough sex?' she asked.
'The spring in me is very tight. Nothing else will do except gigantic fucking and sucking.'
'Are you speaking poetry to me now?'

62

SOUNDED LIKE SOMETHING. It was in cold weather. From my heart I follow the ghost voice. It is leading me and leading me and leading me.

Oh, my! Oh fortunate fool! It is the voice of Westy and she wants to screw. I adore a woman who shouts for screwing. I adore! What with her legs in the air! What with her coming! What with her cheer and despair together!

Close your eyes, darling, and have the old original pleasure! Tongue in, tongue out. Big hard sexuals.

Ah, my God, you've made me come!

Everyone thinks it's a crisis at sunrise, but I do not. I think of rising in the Phantom at dawn and the dawn intense – orange, yellow, violet, blue-black – the day very present because it could be the day of your death.

Westy lifted her legs around me. She wanted to see the old miracle of my big thing going in.

What a paradise of delight marriage can be.

Nothing comes close to Westy in the pussy department.

And you can see how my poetry is improving.

> I'm climbing the high oak of learning.
> I'm feeling the old force of yearning.

Hoo! Ray! Fucking Ray! Ray in the fourth decade!

Ray, yes, Ray! Doctor Ray is okay!

Charlie DeSoto and Eileen are together again. The nurses are getting married. Westy is coming with the hot oils and the balm. The Alabama team is still whipping everybody in sight. My patients are calling. Bill is getting ready to fish. Elizabeth is looking in the Holy Bible. Mr. Hooch has his hands on a pencil.

Sister!

Christians!

Sabers, gentlemen, sabers!